The MOONHAWKER

D1253384

The **MOONHAWKER**

GEORGE A. FOX

iUniverse, Inc.
Bloomington

The Moonhawker

iUniverse books may be ordered through booksellers or by contacting:

iUniverse
1663 Liberty Drive
Bloomington, IN 47403
www.iuniverse.com
1-800-Authors (1-800-288-4677)

ISBN: 978-1-4620-4648-5 (sc)
ISBN: 978-1-4620-4649-2 (hc)
ISBN: 978-1-4620-4650-8 (ebk)

Library of Congress Control Number: 2011915113

Printed in the United States of America

iUniverse rev. date: 10/18/2011

Contents

To my grandchildren Anna, Fox, Emma, and Keaton;
they are the future.

Acknowledgments

To my wife, Rozalyn, whose patience and encouragement made it possible; to my daughters, Stacie and Inger, whose love and richness in those fresh young years gave me depth and feeling; to Washington Island, whose beauty and solitude gave substance to my writing; and to the people of Washington Island, who are truly the most rich in character I've ever had the good fortune to meet; I hold them all dearly in my memories.

Disclaimer

Although this novel was in part built around real places, people, and events, the story is fiction, and the characters in it were developed purely for the purpose of serving the plot. Any correlation of substance between any of the characters in this book, and that of real persons, alive or dead, is purely coincidental.

CHAPTER 1

The Adventure Begins

June 1976.

Burning its way through the morning haze, the sun was rising to what promised to be a beautiful day. A 1971 Chevy Malibu pulled in front of West High School and parked in one of the visitor parking spaces. The door opened and a tall, good-looking man in his midthirties got out. He had ash brown hair, green eyes, and a mustache, and in spite of the earliness of the season, he was already sporting the start of a healthy tan. He was dressed casually with a light brown sport jacket and a white shirt open at the collar. He slammed the car door shut, cut across the drive, and walked gingerly up the front steps and into the school.

Once inside, he went directly across the commons, through the glass doors, and into the main office. The secretary behind the counter looked up as he approached. "Good morning, Mr. Gunner," she said with a smile, "and congratulations."

"Thank you," he replied. "Is the big honcho in yet?"

"Oh yes, he's been waiting for you. Let me tell him you're here." With that, she pressed the button on her intercom. "Mr. Thrison," she said, still smiling, "Atticus Gunner is here."

"Send him in," came the response.

Principal Bob Thrison, a man in his early fifties, looked up from behind his desk as the door opened and Atticus poked his head in. "Hey there, outlaw," he said with a grin, "come in and close the door." He rose to his feet and extended his hand toward Atticus. "Welcome aboard, Mr. Assistant Principal," he said, beaming.

This wasn't their first meeting by any means. Not only had Bob Thrison been present at Atticus's interview for the assistant principal's job the night before, but their friendship went back to when Atticus started graduate school. Since then, Atticus had gotten to know Bob and his family well. He and Bob played handball at the gym on a regular basis, and both Bob and his wife, Grace, had been there for Atticus when he went through his recent divorce. Actually it was Bob who talked Atticus into applying for the new assistant principal position now that he was finished with his graduate degree.

"You did a beautiful job at the interview last night," Bob said as he shook hands with Atticus. "I was impressed."

Atticus smiled. "I'm sure you had an influence on their decision."

"Sure, the superintendent asked for my input, but it wasn't me that got you the job; you did that on your own, my friend."

"Well, thank you anyway," Atticus replied, suppressing the uncertainty he still held over applying for the position. Atticus loved teaching and had been selected as teacher of the year two years in a row before going back to graduate school; he still had some misgivings over his decision to move up the career ladder into education administration. But because of his restless nature and the ever present desire to move on to new challenges, he had made the decision to go for it.

"I have a budget meeting in an hour," Bob said, "but I've got a little time, so sit down and talk for a minute. I understand you start August first."

Atticus sat down. "Yes," he said, "McTagert is sending me a contract in the mail; I'm supposed to sign it and get it back as soon as possible."

"Does your ex know about the offer yet?"

"No, not yet."

"How about the girls?"

"No, they don't know either, but they'll be with me this weekend, so I'll tell them then."

"They already announced the appointment on the local news this morning," Bob replied. "So they may already know. Tell me, what are your plans until you start here? I imagine you have to find a summer job."

"Believe it or not, I've got a four-week job teaching sailing for the university athletic department."

"You and boats, Gunner; sometimes I think you got water on the brain."

Atticus smiled; that kind of comment was typical coming from Bob. Because of the age difference and Bob's desire to constantly prove he wasn't getting old, there was always that bit of a putdown with anyone younger than himself, but Atticus didn't mind; he just sloughed it off.

"You still race that C-15?" Bob went on.

"When I can."

"What about the girls? Do they still go sailing?"

"Yes, when they can."

"I understand your ex is doing very well at the university hospital."

Atticus's ex-wife was a bright, up-and-coming pediatrician, but he felt uncomfortable discussing his former wife. "Yes, she is," he replied matter-of-factly.

"Well, I just wanted to congratulate you and remind you to get that contract signed as soon as possible."

"Yes sir, Mr. Boss Man; I'll take care of it right away," Atticus replied jokingly in a poorly contrived southern drawl.

"Asshole," Bob replied, shaking his head. "I'm serious, Gunner."

Atticus smiled. "I know you are, and don't worry, I'll get it in as soon as I can."

"So what's up for the rest of the day? I know what you should do; get your fanny over to the gym and practice your handball skills so I don't keep mopping up the court with you."

"Thrison, that's exactly what I was going to do, but as luck would have it, I've got a three o'clock appointment with Jim Mortson, so I had to cancel."

"That's the attorney that represented you during your divorce, isn't it?"

"None other."

"What's that all about?"

"I don't know; he wouldn't say."

"That's a bit strange, isn't it?"

"Well, after you've been through a divorce, lots of things seem a bit strange, especially when they come from an attorney." Atticus got up. "I'll be checking with you in a few days," he continued as he started for the door. "Good luck with your budget meeting."

———•◆•———

It was three o'clock as Atticus walked up to the receptionist's window. "Can I help you?" the woman behind the window asked.

"I have an appointment with Attorney Mortson at three," Atticus said.

"Oh yes, Mr. Gunner; they're waiting for you in the conference room." She pointed toward the closed door on the other side of the lobby.

"They?" Atticus questioned.

"Another attorney," she replied. "Jim will explain; just knock on the door and go right in."

Atticus knocked on the door, opened it, and stepped inside. Jim Mortson introduced him to the other attorney, William Markup from New York. Atticus shook the New York attorney's hand but said nothing.

"Sit down," Jim said. "You're not going to believe this one, Gunner, but this may be your lucky day."

A little suspicious but most definitely curious, Atticus sat down.

Without hesitation, the stone-faced New York attorney opened his briefcase and spread some papers out on the table. He looked at Atticus. "I'm here to offer you a job," he said.

"I already have a job," Atticus replied.

"So I understand, but I think you'll want to hear what I have to say anyway."

Atticus shrugged. "It's your nickel."

The attorney smiled at Atticus. "If you don't mind," he continued, "I'd like to confirm that you're the right Atticus Gunner."

Again Atticus didn't respond.

"Mr. Gunner, how many people died worldwide as a result of the Second World War?"

"I used to tell my students, somewhere between sixty and seventy million people," Atticus replied.

"How many Jews died at the hands of the Nazis?"

Atticus frowned and glanced over at Mortson. "No one knows for sure," he replied with some reluctance, "but over a million at the Auschwitz camps alone; why?"

"Mr. Gunner, you served in a small special operations unit under the command of Major Gaperman in Germany; is that correct?"

"Yes, that's correct."

"Where is he now?"

"Dead."

"What happened to him?"

"He was assassinated three weeks after I returned stateside."

"You had a nickname for the major; what was it?"

"Guppy."

"The unit also had a nickname for you; what was that?"

"Excuse me?" Atticus replied with a frown.

"They called you the Hawkman; isn't that correct?"

"The whole unit was known as the Night Hawks," Atticus replied.

"Yes but you were the Hawkman."

"Mr. Markup, I don't know where you're going with this, but that was a long time ago; sixteen years, if my calculations are correct. Besides, the operation of that unit was classified top secret, and as far as I know still is. Because of that, the Night Hawk unit isn't open for discussion; at least not by me."

Unfazed, the New York attorney continued, "The unit's job was to identify and hunt down escaped Nazis suspected of war atrocities, and you were considered the best hunter in the unit; thus the nickname Hawkman; that is correct, isn't it, Mr. Gunner?"

Atticus didn't respond.

"Mr. Gunner, you're the man we are looking for. So now, if you'll allow me, I'll tell you where I'm coming from. Have you ever heard of the Morgan Group?"

"No, I can't say that I have."

"They are a small group of wealthy individuals who try to identify issues in the world that not only need special attention, but can be effectively addressed by a single individual with the right qualifications. We are the legal firm that represents that group in their quest, and you, sir, are the result of our latest search. So, as I said before, I'm here to offer you a job."

"Doing what?" Atticus asked.

"To take on the job of school administrator for the Washington Island school up off the tip of the Door County peninsula here in Wisconsin."

"That's a real island, isn't it?"

"Yes, it is."

"The school can't be very big."

"No, it's not; about a hundred kids."

"You're asking me to forgo an offer to be the assistant principal here at Madison West, and instead take on the job of running a school that has about one hundred kids in it, isolated on some island?"

"Yes, that's correct."

"I'm sorry, but there is no way I would consider that, or could even afford to, if I were so inclined; I'm not a martyr."

"We'll pay you $310,000 plus give you a brand-new thirty-two-foot sailing sloop in exchange for one year of your services, and that's above and beyond whatever you can negotiate as a salary from the island authorities."

"You're kidding me."

"No sir, we don't kid."

"Why me?"

"For one thing, you're certified to take the job. But more importantly, we think you have the background and skills necessary."

"Then there is more to this offer than simply operating a school," Atticus replied.

"Yes, we believe so; but I don't want to understate the challenges connected to managing the school either; there are challenges there too. The school and its problems may not be my employer's main concern, but there is little doubt they will become intermingled as you proceed, and that intermingling will likely test every skill in your repertoire."

"And what are the main concerns you folks have?"

"That, Mr. Gunner, is where your very special background comes into play."

"Are you trying to tell me there is some kind of a neo-Nazi connection here?"

"That will be up to you to determine."

"Where does Attorney Mortson fit into all this?"

"He will take over the management of the financial aspects of the contract we have with you."

"There are obviously other conditions connected to all this; what are they?" Atticus continued.

"There are three major conditions; first, you must stay on the job for one full contract year. And you need to understand the job is not ours to give; that means you must land it on your own. Second, no one outside this room is to know we have retained your services.

That condition is for the security of your employer. And third, you are to approach this situation via the back door—no one is to know your arrival on the island was intended for the purpose of seeking the position. That condition is for your security."

"That leads to more questions than answers," Atticus replied. "What if I don't get the job? I'd lose out on the opportunity here in Madison."

"That's true, Mr. Gunner; however, there is a consolation prize. If you actively seek the job, but do not get it, for whatever reason, or if you get fired prior to the completion of your contract year, you will be paid $25,000, and we will write off the use of the sailboat as a given for time served; the boat of course will return to our ownership."

"That could result in a substantial loss for me."

"Yes sir, it could; we're not paying you to lose, we're paying you to succeed."

"Why is the boat part of this offer?"

"Because sailing is your passion, and besides, what better way is there to approach an island than by sailboat?"

"What's the value of this boat?"

"$276,000."

"That's a lot of money in itself," Atticus replied. He looked at Attorney Mortson. "Jim, you haven't said a word since I sat down."

"Atticus, this could be a dream come true, or it could become a nightmare. I have no idea which; all I can say for certain is, it is for real. But whatever you decide, it has to be based on your willingness to accept the challenge."

Atticus breathed in deep and let it out slowly. "There's an awful lot to consider," he said. "My kids, to say nothing of all the other unknowns; I need time; how long do I have to make this decision?"

"You have now," Attorney Markup replied.

"Now?"

"Now!" Attorney Markup pushed a contract over to Atticus. "All I need is your signature to make it happen."

Atticus read the contract through carefully; he then looked up at Jim again.

Jim nodded.

Atticus studied the document one more time. Then after a long pause, he signed it and slid it back over to Markup.

Attorney Markup slid a $5,000 cashier's check over to Atticus. "You'll need some money up front," he said.

"Does the boat have a name?" Atticus asked.

"Yes," Attorney Markup said as he gathered up his papers. He closed his briefcase, placed his hands on top of the case, and looked at Atticus. "She's been christened the *Moonhawk*," he said, "and she's at the Green Bay Yacht Club waiting for you."

"The *Moonhawk*. You knew I was going to sign that contract before you talked to me."

"Yes sir, I did. We make a practice of knowing the people we seek, and we seldom make a mistake in our judgment."

———————◆———————

Atticus rolled over and buried his face in the pillow as bright sunlight flooded the bedroom. "Get up, Dad," came the voice of his older daughter, Stacie, as she pulled open the curtains.

Atticus opened one eye and looked at the clock. "It's only 6:30 in the morning," he mumbled. "What are you doing here?"

"I'm here too, Dad," came the gruff voice of his other daughter, Inger, only she punctuated her presence by jumping up on the foot of the bed.

Stacie, a pretty girl of fourteen, with brown hair and dark eyes, walked out of the bedroom and into the kitchen. "Get up; I'll start breakfast," she said over her shoulder. "You have to take us to the mall this morning."

"I don't have any food in the apartment," Atticus replied, still half asleep.

"Mom said you probably wouldn't, so she sent some with us. Now get up."

Atticus turned over only to see Inger still sitting on her knees at the foot of his bed, grinning at him. At just under nine years old and small for her age, she was a pretty little blonde with big blue eyes, a smart mouth, and more gumption than most kids her age. "What are you guys doing here this early in the morning?" Atticus asked.

"We're here to bug you," she replied, still grinning at him.

"Yeah, well, you've managed that. What else are you doing here?"

"Mom got called to the hospital," she replied.

"Inger, come on so Dad can get up!" Stacie barked.

Reluctantly, Inger slid off the bed and started for the kitchen. "I need new tennis shoes," she remarked as she walked out of the room.

"Yeah, and I need about six more hours of sleep, but I'm not going to get that either."

"You promised, Dad," she replied from the kitchen.

"Well, that just goes to show you," he said as he slid out of bed, "you can't believe everything you hear, and only about half of what you see."

It's always difficult to compare one sibling to another, but most people who knew the Gunner girls agreed. Physically, Stacie looked like her father, while Inger had many of her mother's features. Personality-wise, however, it was a different story. Stacie, being older, was undoubtedly more aware of what had gone on during the divorce and was likely more impacted by it than was Inger; how much, was hard for Atticus to determine; actually, it was hard for him to even think about. Stacie was more cautious, more introverted, more organized, more deliberate, and more industrious.

Inger, on the other hand, was spontaneous, very assertive, vocal, inquisitive, and far more inclined to step out of her comfort zone. Atticus had a tendency to banter back and forth with both girls, but because of the differences in their personalities, it seemed to take place a bit more with Inger than it did with Stacie. But setting all that aside, there was no doubt that they were both the two most important people in his life, a fact that didn't really hit home for Atticus until after the separation and divorce set in.

It was still before eight o'clock when Atticus came out of the bathroom, dressed for the day. The smell of fresh coffee and toast filled the kitchen. "I didn't think I was supposed to see you guys until Friday," he said as he sat down at the table.

"Well, you know how it is with the hospital," Stacie replied as she put the toast on the table.

"Yes, I'm afraid I do," Atticus said. "So did I hear right? Do I have to take you guys to the mall this morning?"

"Yes, I have to pick up an outfit, and Inger needs a new pair of shoes. If you don't have the money, Mom said she would help."

As Inger poured a cup of coffee for her father, he intentionally bumped her slightly on the arm, causing her to spill a little. "Dad," Stacie remarked, "you're supposed to be the adult here, remember?"

"I just wanted to see if she was on the ball," he replied.

Inger made a goofy face at him and then sat down at her place at the table.

"Yes, I've got the money," Atticus continued. "As a matter of fact, I've got more than that."

The girls looked at him.

"I've got a job—two jobs actually; well, one part-time for the summer, and a full-time one after that." This, of course, wasn't exactly an accurate statement given the new circumstances, but he wasn't about to delve into the truth yet.

"You got the assistant principal job at West?" Stacie exclaimed.

Atticus nodded.

"What's the summer job?" Inger asked. "Scraping boogers off the city sidewalks?"

"Now that is sick," Atticus replied. "That sounds more like your kind of work."

Stacie just shook her head with a disgusted look on her face.

"But regardless of that degrading remark," Atticus went on, "I'll tell you both what my summer job is anyway. I have a job testing out a new thirty-two-foot sailing yacht on Lake Michigan for the summer." Another half truth, but it was too late to change directions now. "And," he went on, "if you treat me right, maybe you guys can come along for part of the time."

Both of the girls' eyes got as big as saucers.

"Really?" Inger asked.

"Yes, really."

"And someone is going to pay you to do that?" Stacie asked.

"What kind of a question is that?" Atticus replied jokingly.

"How much?" Inger asked.

"More than you can count."

"When do you start?" Inger went on.

"As soon as I can make arrangements to pick up the boat."

"Can I come?" Inger asked.

"You can both come."

"Today?"

"Well, not today," Atticus replied, "but maybe tomorrow."

Inger looked at Stacie. "What are you going to do about summer cheerleading camp?"

Stacie shook her head. "I can't back out now; no way. Besides, my whole future depends on qualifying for the freshman team. Maybe I can go later on," she said, looking at her father.

"Yes, I'm sure that can be arranged," Atticus replied. "We'll talk it over with your mother and see what we can work out."

———◆———

It was a little after eight o'clock on Thursday morning, the second day after the meeting at Mortson's office, when Atticus turned off the highway and continued down Harbor Road toward the yacht club. He and Inger were on their way to take possession of the new boat. They were going to load supplies on board, check it out, and head up along Door County in the direction of Washington Island, just to put the new boat through some preliminary sea trials, or so Atticus had declared.

Inger could only come for one day; arrangements had been made to meet her mother tomorrow at noon in Ephraim. Her mother wasn't at all excited about the prospect of open lake sailing, and she only agreed after Atticus assured her he would stay within the confines of Green Bay. Atticus knew the whole yacht testing thing seemed illogical to her; after all, she was anything but stupid, but she had long since given in to his crazy adventures and seemed to write it off as just another Gunnerism.

Inger was curled up in the back seat amongst sleeping bags, boxes of dry goods, coolers, and a myriad of incidental items Atticus had brought along. She had been there sleeping for most of the ride up to Green Bay. He felt a little bad that Stacie wasn't there too, but he understood why she stayed behind.

No doubt about it, Atticus was on a high. He was so pumped over the whole idea of acquiring a thirty-two-foot sloop that he hadn't really thought beyond it. Even thoughts about what kind of a strategy he was going to use to approach his first objective, Washington Island, hadn't jelled yet.

As they drove through the open gate of the yacht club and up to the clubhouse, Inger sat up. "Dad, I'm hungry," she said, rubbing the sleep from her eyes.

—◆—

Inger was still sipping on her orange drink as they entered the Club Shop after breakfast. They walked directly over to the counter. The man behind the counter looked up. "Good morning," Atticus said as

15

they approached. "My name is Atticus Gunner, and we're here to pick up the *Moonhawk*."

"Oh yes, Mr. Gunner," he replied, "we've been expecting you. I'll get the paperwork so you can sign for its release, and then the harbormaster will take you out to your new boat."

Atticus thanked him, waited for his return, and signed the release forms. After about five minutes, a short, stocky young man in his midtwenties came out of the shop and walked over to Atticus. "Good morning, Mr. Gunner," he said, "so you're here to pick up the *Moonhawk*."

Atticus smiled and gave him a confirming nod.

The young man turned and started walking toward the doors that led out to the boat docks. Atticus followed with Inger taking up the rear. "She's located in slip L6," he said over his shoulder. "We'll brief you on her electronics and everything, and then she's all yours. You do know how to sail, correct?"

"Oh, I think I can manage."

"Have you seen her before now?"

"No, I'm afraid not," Atticus replied.

"She's one beautiful boat, I can tell you that," he said.

"She?" Inger interjected. "Why do you refer to the boat as a she?"

The young man smiled back at Atticus. "Your daughter?"

Atticus nodded. "Don't pursue it," he said.

Ignoring her father's comment, Inger continued. "Just kidding," she said. "I already know why men refer to all boats as women; they're beautiful and serve an honorable purpose."

The young man just smiled and continued to walk.

They followed the catwalk out to the last gangway and continued down past the six or seven large yachts tethered to their slips. As they approached L6, Atticus stopped; there she was, backed into the slip stern first, resting at her moorings. She was indeed beautiful; she had a glistening snow-white hull with all teak decking, iodized mast and boom with bronze-colored sail covers, and across her stern in gold embossed letters was the name, *Moonhawk*; everything about her was first rate. Inger went on board immediately and looked below deck.

"I told you she was a thing of beauty," the harbormaster said, "but I have to ask; I read where you are a teacher, and that the boat is completely paid for. I know it's none of my business, but that boat is worth close to $300,000. How in the world can you afford something like that? Did you win the lottery or something? Or are you selling drugs?"

Still struck with awe, Atticus stepped on board. "Yes," he replied paying no attention to the young man's comments, "something like that."

——◆——

It was a beautiful afternoon with no clouds in sight as they sailed past the big navigation marker and out into the open waters of Green Bay. With a gentle breeze out of the southwest and a rolling two-foot swell running to the east, they headed north up along the cliff-laden shores of Door County, a place often referred to by the Chicago summer visitors as the Cape Cod of the Midwest. With her mast tipped to the east and her port beam raised slightly to the wind, the *Moonhawk* was making an easy six knots under full sail.

Although this was Inger's first time on a boat of this size, she was no stranger to sailing; she had often sailed with her father on Lake Mendota, and for her size and age, she was an excellent and hardy hand. As a matter of fact, it probably wouldn't be many years before she would give her father a run for his money. Wearing a life vest and safety harness, and with the agility of a gazelle, she went about the deck, helping her father to raise and adjust the sails while the boat slid with grace through the rolling seas. After Atticus ran the boat through various maneuvers to test her handling, and confirming that the boat was beautifully balanced with absolutely no weather helm, he turned the tiller over to Inger.

Sitting in the cockpit with his back to the weather, listening to the wind hum through the rigging and the waves hiss as they slid beneath the hull, Atticus watched his young daughter handle the boat with absolute authority; he was in a state of total bliss. The boat itself was overwhelming; he loved sailing, and the *Moonhawk* was indeed an elegant and beautiful piece of engineering. She was wide at the beam, but sleek and well balanced. Her hull was of a new fiberglass composite reinforced with balsa core and carbon fiber. She was teak throughout with all stainless steel fittings. Her mast, boom, and sails were custom made from the finest materials; she had a ten horse Volvo Penta diesel auxiliary engine, ship-to-shore radio, plus all the electronics necessary for a first-rate yacht of her caliber. The boat even included all the extras, from mooring lines to foul-weather gear, even an auxiliary hand-operated bilge pump.

———◆———

After a full afternoon of sailing with the last glow of day hanging low on the horizon, sails down and running lights aglow, the *Moonhawk* finally slid into Egg Harbor under auxiliary power. As they came in along the face of South Bluff, they passed a big trawler already moored for the night. Atticus maneuvered the boat past the trawler, turned in a little closer to shore, and finally gave a reverse thrust to the engine to bring the sloop to a standstill in the calm water. The harbor was already encircled by the onset of evening fog as Inger went forward and dropped the anchor. Only the tops of the cedars could be seen through the drifting haze, and once the engine went silent, the sounds of civilization seemed to disappear completely; all that could be heard were the gentle whispers of the restless water against the hull and the occasional hoot of an owl off in the distant woods. By the time they had raised their mooring light and secured the boat for the night, the fog had become so thick that even the neighboring trawler had disappeared from sight.

Tired from the rigors of the day, both Atticus and Inger went straight below and lit the lantern. Then with the hatches all closed to keep out the dampness, they sat down at the galley table to a warm but simple supper of stew and hard rolls. Afterward, with little else to do, Inger sat up on the portside berth with her knees tucked up under her chin and watched her father finish putting things away. "Dad, I see you brought your club along," she said, looking down at the cardboard box sitting in the middle of the companionway.

"Yep," Atticus replied, glancing down at the tethered ax handle sticking up out of the box.

"How come?"

Atticus shrugged. "I don't know; just for luck, I guess. You know how I am about the stick."

"Stacie and I used to sit on the steps and watch you practice with it. Mom said you were trained to use it while you were in the army. Is that true?"

"Yes, I guess you could say that, but that was a long time ago," he replied. "Now it helps me stay in shape."

"Mom told Stacie you used to wake up in the middle of the night and think you were still in the army; is that true?"

Atticus kept unloading dry goods into the cabinets and didn't respond.

"The army was an important time in your life, wasn't it?"

"Yes, I guess you could say that," Atticus replied.

"Did you fight in a war, Dad?"

"No, not exactly."

"Mom said you did secret stuff."

"Enough about the army," Atticus said.

"When we were little and asked you about the army, sometimes you would sing us some of the songs. You used to sing us a really sad one; how did that go?"

"I don't know which one you're talking about."

"Oh yeah, I remember," Inger said, and she began to sing it:

Oh say, did you know that a long time ago, there were two little children whose names I don't know. They were carried away on a bright summer's day, and were left in the woods so I heard some folks say. They sobbed and they sighed and they bitterly cried, until at last they grew weary and laid down and died. Now the robins were sorry when they saw they were dead, so they picked strawberry leaves and over them spread. And all day long they sang their sad song for babes in the woods, until God came along.

"Yes, I remember now," he said. "I also remember that your mother didn't like me singing that song; she thought it was too sad for your little ears."

"It was sad. Stacie and I used to talk about it; who wrote that song anyway?"

"I honestly don't know, honey. I just know where I came across it."

"Was it while you were in the army?"

"Yes."

"Where?"

"I was going through a file of documents gathered from a concentration camp in Germany. It was scratched out in pencil on a scrap of paper. It was written in Polish, but a translation in English was attached to it. The attachment also said it was given to a guard by a little Jewish girl just before she and her little brother were herded off into the gas chamber."

"A gas chamber?"

"Yes; a place where thousands of people were murdered by the Nazis during the Second World War."

"Even children?"

"Yes, even children."

"Why?"

"Because war makes people crazy, and sometimes they end up doing horrible things."

"When you were in Germany, did you ever see any Nazis?"

"Yes, but enough about that. Tomorrow is going to be a big day. I'd suggest you go forward and get into your PJs, brush your teeth, and climb into the sack. We're going to have to get an early start in order to make Ephraim by noon."

—•◆•—

After Atticus finished putting things in their proper place, he went forward to check on Inger. She was already fast asleep. He returned to the galley, grabbed his sweatshirt, turned off the lantern, and went up the steps into the cockpit, closing the hatch behind him.

The night air was cool and damp. Atticus reached down and flipped over a seat cushion to avoid the dampness and sat down. Staring up at the fog-filtered moon, his thoughts finally drifted to the big picture; the whole barrage of contract expectations he signed on for were beginning to flood into his mind. It played like some overused TV plot, but as unbelievable as it was, there was no doubt in his mind now that it was all for real. He thought first about the unexplained implications of what he'd been hired to do; he tried thinking, not of substance, but in terms of strategy. He would approach the most obvious first and then take on the other as it presented itself.

First and foremost was the job. Playing it by ear, he would come in through the back door, just as was required by his contract. That is, he would not approach the job directly as though he was seriously interested, but instead he'd make known his qualifications and see if he couldn't spark some sort of interest. If he could do that, then he would try to manipulate his way into an interview. Throughout the entire ordeal, of course, he would begin the process of gathering pertinent information. The whole thing would be tricky, but if he played it smart, he just might be able to pull it off.

As to the second part, the undefined but implied evil, he had always been a champion for the downtrodden. In Atticus's mind, there was no

22

question that absolute power in any form was evil. It didn't matter whether it smacked of religious, political, or cooperative motivation, absolute authority was always evil. During his time in the military, when he was involved in tracking down those responsible for Nazi war crimes, that reality came up close and personal for Atticus. He had been exposed through documents, testimony, and pictures of what happened to the victims of the Third Reich through the exercise of absolute power, and as a result, he had developed a deep hatred for fascist thinking in any form. The implication that something like that was connected to Washington Island, ridiculous as it seemed, sparked more than a little interest. But if there was something there, Atticus was sure it would raise its ugly head in due time.

————◆◆◆————

Just as Atticus was about to call it a night and head for bed himself, he heard the sound of voices drifting across the water. At first it was quite faint, but as he listened, it became obvious they were coming closer. Atticus searched the foggy darkness but could see no one. Judging from the swearing, it was also obvious they'd had a little too much to drink. He continued to scan the darkness; he could hear the splashing of oars but could see nothing. Then, just as he was about to give up, he spotted two small rowboats about twenty feet apart coming out of the mist.

"Hey," a man in the nearest boat hollered, "there's a God damned sailboat!"

"Hey, you there on the sailboat!" a man in the second boat hollered up at Atticus. "We need some help; we can't find our boat! It's a big trawler anchored along the cliff somewhere; have you seen it?"

"Yes," Atticus answered as he looked at the *Moonhawk's* compass to get his relative bearings. "I saw it earlier; it's about a hundred yards off to the east!" He pointed in the direction of the trawler. "You guys know you shouldn't be out here in a small boat on a foggy night like this!"

"Shit," one of them replied. "What do you know, we found ourselves a God damned genius!"

"Do you have a compass?" Atticus asked.

"Do we look like we got a compass, genius?"

Atticus didn't respond.

"I think we'd better come on board and call our boat so they can honk the horn or something!" With that, the first man started rowing toward the *Moonhawk*.

Atticus stepped down into the cockpit, slid open the hatch cover, and reached inside the cabin to retrieve his club, just in case there was trouble. The rowboat clunked into the starboard side of the *Moonhawk*, and one of the men immediately pulled himself up under the safety rail and onto the deck.

Atticus stepped up on the cockpit coaming again. "I'm sorry, but no one is allowed on this boat without my permission," he said bluntly, "and I want you off now!"

A knife blade flashed as it snapped open in the intruder's hand. Then without warning, the man stepped forward and lashed out at Atticus, trying to cut him, but Atticus stepped aside and deflected his attempt harmlessly with his club. The simple maneuver caught the intruder off guard and spun him partially around, exposing his back to Atticus. Immediately, Atticus rammed the butt end of his club deep into the intruder's kidney. The man's mouth fell open as he dropped to his knees. With the knife still in his hand, he turned partially toward Atticus in an attempt to get up. The move was pointless, however, as

Atticus, holding the club parallel in both hands, immediately swung the left butt end across the intruder's face, smashing him in the cheek and sending his head twisting violently to the left. For the intruder, it was a devastating blow; he fell to the deck, dropping his knife. Then with his foot, Atticus shoved the man under the railing and off the boat; he hit the water with a loud splash.

Atticus then turned toward a second man as he came on board over the bow. He too was coming toward Atticus with a knife, but stopped abruptly. As Atticus rose and started toward him, the man jumped over the side. Atticus went back over to the rail and looked down. A third man was busy pulling his injured companion back into the rowboat. The man who had jumped overboard was dog-paddling as fast as he could toward the second boat. "Let's get the hell out of here," he sputtered. "That son of a bitch is crazy!"

As the two boats slipped away into the fog, Atticus stepped up onto the cabin roof. He watched as they disappeared into the mist. After a short time, a voice came drifting back out of the darkness. "Hey Mr. Moonhawker, or whatever the hell they call you; my friend is hurt bad; you better hope we never meet again!"

Atticus stepped down off the cabin roof without responding. As he entered the cockpit he spotted Inger standing in the companionway, watching. "How long have you been there, young lady?" Atticus asked.

"Long enough," she answered.

Atticus shook his head. "Well, it's over now, so you can get back in bed where you belong."

"Dad, you need something more than that stick," she said, still excited. "You need a gun!"

"The stick will do just fine," he replied, tousling her hair. "Now come on, it's past your sack time."

25

"What if they come back with a gun?"

"Honey, they won't be back. They were looking for easy pickings and didn't find it; I don't think they could even find us again if they had to."

"But what if they do? What good would that stick be then?"

"Hey, I'm going to use this club to beat off all the sharks."

"Dad, it may come as news to you, but there aren't any sharks in the Great Lakes."

"Maybe you're thinking of the wrong kind of sharks."

She rolled her eyes.

Atticus reached over and hung the ax handle back on the hook. Even in the faint light, he could see the beautiful dark grain running through the solid hickory handle, the handle he had so meticulously sanded and polished. It truly was a joke with everyone who saw it, especially his daughters, but tonight Inger may have seen it in another light. Although the ax handle wasn't exactly the same as the half shaft, it did represent a defensive skill taught to Atticus during his time in the military. He thought back to his training instructor. He could still hear him screaming, "There are only three rules governing the effectiveness of this weapon: one: be preemptive, two: know where to strike, and three: have every intention of putting your opponent completely out of commission as fast as possible." It all seemed so very much in the past now, but for Atticus, who didn't like having guns around, the hand-polished ax handle did give him a certain sense of security.

——————•◦•◦•——————

The reflection of the sun off the water was dancing on the ceiling of the cabin when Atticus opened his eyes. Leaning back against the bulkhead, he slowly turned his head back and forth to get the kinks out. The sweet aroma of bacon frying filled the cabin. He sat up and stretched. "Good morning there, Dink," he said, "you're really on the ball this morning."

Inger was standing in front of the stove, cracking eggs into a skillet. She was wearing tennis shoes, bleached-out Levis, and a sweatshirt with the sleeves cut off. Her pretty blonde hair was combed back neatly on the sides and held in place with a barrette. "You better hurry, or your breakfast is going to get cold," she replied without taking her eyes off what she was doing.

"Your wish is my command," he said as he slid off the bunk and slipped into his pants.

Atticus headed into the water closet to shave and clean up. When he returned to the galley, the table was set and Inger was pouring hot coffee into his mug. Atticus sat down. "Well, this is a real treat," he said. "You continue to amaze me; what's the occasion?"

"Well, I figured it would probably be the last good meal you'd have until you came home. I mean—you know, back to the city."

Atticus always seemed to brush off serious matters with both his daughters. It wasn't that he didn't care; in many cases, it was simply that he didn't know how to handle it. Deep inside, he felt like a failure as a father. He had bailed out of a situation at the cost of the two most important people in his life and never really came to grips with the impact of that. "Don't worry about me," he said, once again evading the issue. "I've got plenty of food to last through the week. Besides, you've been looking forward to going with your mother to visit your cousins this coming week."

"I know," she replied.

"We'll plan another trip as soon as we can. Who knows—maybe next time Stacie will come too."

"Doubt that; she's not much into sailing anymore."

"Well, partner, not everyone likes the same things. You and I like sailing; Stacie, right now, likes her social life."

"You mean boys!" Inger interjected with a disgusted look on her face.

"Well, it won't be too long and you'll be just like her." Atticus got up and took his dishes over to the sink. "Come on," he said, "I'll help you with these dishes so we can get underway. The water is dead calm this morning; that means we'll probably have to motor all the way to Ephraim."

"Why don't you go get things ready? I'll do the dishes."

"Yes ma'am," he replied as he gave her a quick kiss on the forehead. "This is a real treat." He grabbed his sweatshirt off the bunk and went up on deck.

The bay looked a lot different in the morning. He scanned the area for signs of his friends, and sure enough, the trawler was still resting silently at anchor. One rowboat was tied off the stern rail, but there was no sign of the second boat. A couple of towels were hanging over the railing, but other than that, there was absolutely no movement on board; Atticus surmised they were probably sleeping off a very bad hangover. The seagulls were already floating on the air currents above the white limestone cliffs, and true to the forecast, there wasn't a breath of air moving in the morning sun; the water was as smooth as glass and as green as an emerald.

Atticus climbed back down into the cockpit and looked at the location where the ruckus had taken place. There was a big smudge of blood on the cockpit coaming, and down along the gunnel was a piece of a broken tooth. He retrieved the deck pail, filled it with water, sponged off the bloodstain, and sloshed the remaining water along the deck to whisk the rest of the debris off into the bay. After that, he looked over at the trawler once more for signs of life; seeing none, he continued to make ready to get underway.

———————◆·◆·◆———————

With Inger at the helm, the *Moonhawk* chugged out past the trawler toward the open lake. Atticus looked once more over at the big old boat; there were still no signs of life on board.

Turning his attention to the open water, he sheltered his eyes and studied the horizon. After a few moments, he pointed. "There," he said, "off the starboard bow—a buoy. Do you see it?"

"Yes, I see it," Inger replied.

"Head her straight out past that buoy, then turn to starboard and head up the coast."

Ahead, with their limestone cliffs still in the shadows from the morning sun, three bluff heads jutted out from the mainland. Inger rounded the buoy and headed north as instructed. A group of small islands were about two hundred yards off the point of the nearest bluff. "Those are the Strawberry Islands," Atticus said, pointing toward them. "And behind that nearest bluff is Ephraim. To get there, we have to go through the Horseshoe Channel; that's the narrow passage between the nearest island and that bluff. Do you think you can handle that?" he said jokingly.

Inger gave him a goofy look; Atticus laughed. Then, glancing off the stern, he noticed the trawler had left her anchorage and was headed their way. He had hoped this wouldn't happen, but he wasn't surprised. "Inger, I'm afraid we're going to be a little late if we don't increase our speed," he said, trying not to alarm her. "Open that throttle as far as she'll go."

"But I thought you said all that did was waste fuel."

"I know, but this time we'll make an exception—so push it."

Atticus knew Inger sensed something was wrong. She looked back and saw the trawler. "That's the men from last night, isn't it, Dad?" she said.

At first Atticus didn't respond. Finally, he nodded yes. "And I think I better take the helm until they get by us, if you don't mind."

Inger turned the tiller over to her father and slid over on the seat to give him plenty of room.

As the *Moonhawk* made way toward the channel, the trawler grew in size until they could see every detail. As they neared the cut, Atticus steered the sloop as far into the shallows as possible in order to give the big boat plenty of room to pass. But instead of veering off, the trawler continued directly toward them. The nose of the big boat plowed a huge wake as she closed in. Then just as it seemed inevitable that she was going to run right up over the stern rail of the *Moonhawk*, Atticus threw the tiller hard to the left. The sloop wheeled to starboard. Inger held tight. The bow of the trawler plunged on past, barely missing the stern rail. The sloop yawed deep to port as the trawler's huge wake swept beneath her hull. The stench of diesel fumes hung heavy in the air as the trawler's big gray side slid on past. The man standing at the railing smiled at them.

Suddenly, there was a flash of light from the trawler, followed by a loud crack and a zing; a bullet had just ricocheted off the base of the mast. Atticus dove forward, pulling Inger down to the floor of the cockpit. Then there was a second flash, followed by a loud thud as a bullet slammed into the cockpit coaming. Finally, the trawler turned and headed out past Horseshoe Island under full power.

After making sure Inger was okay, Atticus reached up to the tiller and corrected their course. He then cut the engine back to cruising speed as he watched the trawler move off. The name *"Kamora Moo"* was printed across her stern in big black letters; beneath it read, "Port of Chicago."

As the boat disappeared around Horseshoe Island and headed off for places unknown, a cold chill ran down his back. Atticus made a mental note of the name. Last night was certainly an unexpected and dramatic experience to say the least, but today it went way beyond that; no matter how he tried, Atticus couldn't shake the feeling that this was just the beginning of something. All became very quiet on board the *Moonhawk*.

———◆———

After they rounded the big bluff going into Ephraim, the breakwater came into view. At the end of the breakwater was a flagpole flying the flag of the Ephraim Yacht Club. Behind the breakwater lay the harbor, the clubhouse, and a restaurant. The big beautiful maples standing along the shore were just beginning to display their summer greenery, and still further back, one could make out the storefronts and a road that ran through the heart of the small resort community. A church steeple stood above it all; its white horizontal siding shone brightly in the late morning sun.

Inger went over to the open hatch, leaned on the cabin roof, and looked out toward the town; nothing had been said since the incident.

Finally, Atticus spoke. "You know—I don't think we should tell your mother what happened last night or today," he said calmly. "Maybe we should just keep that between us."

"Okay," she replied without looking back.

"I'll contact the Coast Guard and let them know about it," he went on.

"When?" she asked.

"As soon as I get a chance," he said, but before the words even came out of his mouth, Atticus knew he wouldn't, at least not yet. He surmised Inger knew it too.

Atticus cut the power to an idle as they rounded the end of the breakwater and proceeded into the harbor. With the exception of four big yachts, the docking spaces were empty. He picked a slip with easy access to the parking lot and slowly swung the *Moonhawk* into position for mooring. The parking lot was vacant. The dining room portion of the clubhouse had a big sign hanging in the window, "Closed for the Season."

After securing the boat, they hauled Inger's suitcase, sleeping bag, and pillow to the parking lot and put everything down on the sidewalk. Inger sat on her suitcase; Atticus sat on the curb next to her.

Not knowing what to say, Atticus picked up a few pieces of gravel laying in the gutter next to his feet and started to throw them away one by one. After a few long moments, he finally looked over at her. "With the exception of last night and this morning, we had a good time," he said.

Inger nodded.

"We'll go again, only longer."

Again she nodded.

"I'll call when I get home next Friday. Maybe we can do something. Okay?"

"Like what?" Inger asked.

"Like clean my apartment," he said with a grin.

"Oh boy; what a thrill. I suppose you left a bunch of dirty dishes in the sink."

"Just a few."

"They must really be ripe by now, unless Stacie went over and cleaned the place like she was supposed to."

"That's right. I forgot she said she was going to do that," Atticus replied.

"I bet she didn't forget," Inger went on, "and I also bet she didn't go over there either."

Just then a station wagon pulled into the parking lot and swung over toward them.

Atticus stood up.

The car pulled into the parking space next to them. A small, slender woman wearing a gray pantsuit stepped out. She greeted Inger warmly and asked how her day of sailing went.

Awkwardly, Atticus stood by unnoticed as Inger and her mother chatted. Finally, he asked, "Where's Stacie?"

Without responding, the woman moved to the back of the car and opened the tailgate. "Come on, honey," she said to Inger, "we better get your stuff loaded; we've got a long ride ahead of us."

As Inger started to load her things, the woman looked at Atticus. "It's four hours up here and four hours back," she said. "Stacie decided she didn't want to spend that much time in the car just to see you for a few minutes."

"Oh," Atticus replied as he handed Inger her bag.

"Ya know," she continued as she closed the tailgate, "when you're finished with your so-called job up here in the middle of nowhere, you might want to have a little talk with Stacie."

Atticus ignored the jab. "About what?" he asked.

"I got the kids' report cards, and Stacie ended up with a C minus in biology."

"Well, I didn't do so great in biology either," Atticus said, stuffing his hands in his pockets. "How were the rest of her grades?"

"They were good, but she is going to need a good science background when she gets into college."

"College is still a ways off."

"Once again, you completely miss the point, Atticus. Boy, for an educator, you sure are lackadaisical about your own daughters! I wish, just once, you'd be the one to set some standards with them."

"I'll talk with her when I get home," he replied, looking at Inger. "How was Inger's report card?"

"Well, her grades were good, but some of the teacher comments weren't so hot. Her biggest problem is she talks way too much."

"We'll have to have a little talk about that too," he said, winking at Inger.

"I don't think you're funny at all, Atticus Gunner!" she said while opening her car door. "Come on, Inger, we have to go."

Inger opened her door. Then remembering, she went back and kissed her father good-bye. She returned to the car, paused, turned, and looked at him once again. "Be careful Dad—okay?"

Atticus, still standing on the curb with his hands in his pockets, gave a nod and smiled.

Inger got in the car, slammed the door shut, and rolled down the window. "I'll see you Friday!" she said, waving, as the car pulled away from the curb.

"Right; Friday!" Atticus said, returning her wave.

The car rolled out of the parking lot and disappeared down the road. Atticus stood there for a few moments and then started walking slowly back toward the boat. There was already an emptiness deep in the pit of his stomach, and for the moment anyway, he wondered just what he was doing to let himself get into a situation like this.

CHAPTER 2

A Place Called Washington Island

Atticus crawled up on the cabin top and looked at the base of the mast. There was a gouge in the rooftop mast guide plate where the bullet had hit and ricocheted off. And down in the cockpit coaming, there was a perfect bullet hole where a slug had slammed through the fiberglass and wedged in the inner balsa core. If he dug out the slug, he could probably determine the caliber, but in the process he would make a mess out of the fiberglass, so he decided to leave well enough alone and simply settle for patching the hole when he got the chance. Thank God Inger wasn't hurt in any way, but if he ever had another encounter with the *Kamora Moo*, he vowed there would be a far different outcome than there was this go-round.

Turning on the ship-to-shore, Atticus dialed the weather channel and turned up the volume. A monotone voice came forth from the speaker: "A major storm front will be approaching the western shore of Lake Michigan and the bay of Green Bay by Sunday. Gale force winds out of the west are expected to accompany this front as it moves across the open waters of Green Bay and Lake Michigan Sunday evening. Small-craft advisories are already being posted along the shores of Green Bay, with full gale warnings up for the open waters of Lake

Michigan. These storms will bring with them heavy rain and wind, and may contain hail. All mariners are advised to take appropriate precautions."

Atticus turned off the radio as he opened the icebox. He grabbed a jar of mayonnaise, opened a can of tuna, and started to mix some sandwich spread.

"Anyone on board?" a voice came from out on the dock.

With a table knife in one hand and a half-empty can of tuna in the other, Atticus poked his head out of the open hatch. A boy who looked to be about seventeen was standing on the dock with a small suitcase in one hand and a jacket in the other.

"What can I do for you, lad?" Atticus asked, looking at the teen.

"Are you sailing out of here pretty soon?" the boy asked, holding his arm up over his eyes to shelter them from the bright sun.

"Just as soon as I grab a bite to eat."

"Which way you headed, north or south?" the boy asked, still shading his eyes.

"North—why?"

"Do you suppose I could catch a lift with you to Washington Island?"

"Why do you want to go there?" Atticus asked.

"I live there."

Atticus paused for a moment, looking at the boy, and then spoke again. "I'll tell you what," he said, motioning him to come on board. "Come down here and we'll talk about it while I eat."

Atticus went back to making his sandwich. The boy climbed on board, came down the ladder, plunked his suitcase and jacket on the starboard bunk, and sat down next to them. "This is really a nice boat," he said, looking around. "How big is it?"

"Thirty-two feet," Atticus replied, glancing at the boy out of the corner of his eye. "So you live on Washington Island?"

"That's right," the boy said, still looking around.

"Your folks have a cottage up there?"

"No, I live there year round."

"Then you go to school up there?"

"Yes."

"How many people live on that island, year round, I mean?"

"About five hundred I guess."

"How long have you lived there?"

"Three years now; I'm originally from Chicago; my dad's retired. He used to work for WBM. When he retired, we bought a place on the island and moved up there. Are you a teacher?" the boy asked, looking up at Atticus.

"I used to be, why?"

"I thought so."

"Why is that?"

"No reason; I just knew you were. I can tell by the way you're always asking questions."

Atticus smiled as he finished making his sandwich. "Are you hungry?" he asked, looking over at the boy.

"No—that's okay. I just ate a little while ago."

"Well, all I've got is tuna fish, but there's plenty of it. There's the bread; dishes are in the cupboard if you're interested."

Atticus picked up his plate and put it on the galley table.

"Well, if you don't mind, maybe I'll just have a little sandwich," the boy said, eyeing the sandwich Atticus had just made.

"I kind of figured you might," Atticus replied with a smile. "Help yourself."

The boy got up to make himself a sandwich. Atticus walked over to the icebox. "What do you want to drink?" he asked, opening the lid.

"I'll have a beer," the teen replied without hesitation.

Atticus pulled out two cans of root beer and went back to the table. He sat down, placed one in front of himself, and slid the other over in front of the boy.

"That's root beer," the boy said. "I'll have a real beer if you don't mind."

"I don't think so," Atticus replied, "at least not today."

"I'm not a minor, you know; what makes you think I'm a minor?"

"Oh, I can tell by the way you're always asking questions."

The boy grinned at Atticus and then started to eat his sandwich.

"Tell me," Atticus said, "if you live on Washington Island, what are you doing here?"

"I've got a brother that lives down in Sturgeon Bay. I caught a ride down to see him for a couple days."

"How did you get off the island?"

"Oh, we got a ferry that runs back and forth," the boy said as he opened his root beer.

Atticus finished his sandwich, put his dish in the galley sink, and then went over to the chart rack and grabbed the chart. Opening it, he sat back down at the table. "Well—let's see," he said, looking at his watch, "the breeze has freshened, so if we leave now we could probably make Washington Island by about six o'clock. Have you ever done any sailing?"

"I've got a little Sunfish," the boy replied as he put his dish in the sink.

"I'm not much for picking up minors without parental permission, but I'm going to take the risk today. By the way, my name is Atticus Gunner, what's yours?"

"Ken Shernie," he said with a big grin.

Atticus extended him his hand. "Well, Mr. Shernie, you got yourself a ride home."

Shaking hands with Atticus, the boy's grin got even bigger.

———◆———

The ship's clock struck eight bells; it was four o'clock. Off the starboard bow at a distance of seven miles lay Washington Island. Off the stern, six miles to the rear, lay North Point Bluff, marking the northernmost point of the peninsula. The clear blue sky was now cluttered with clouds. Every once in a while, a cloud drifted in front of the sun, turning things cold and gray until it passed. The wind had also increased throughout the afternoon, and the seas were now running at about four feet out of the west with an occasional whitecap.

The *Moonhawk* was heeling well to port and driving hard under full sail. Atticus was sitting with his back to the wind, wearing his down-filled jacket and wool skullcap. His legs were stretched across the walkway, bracing himself against the starboard seat. "We should make the island in less than an hour at this rate," he said, looking over at Ken, who was sitting in the opposite seat with his hands stuffed deep in his coat pockets.

"How fast are we going?" Ken asked.

"A little over nine knots," Atticus said, looking down at the speed indicator. "If you're getting cold, there's a foul-weather coat down below in one of the lockers."

"No, I'm okay; I'm glad we're not just starting out; it looks to me as though the weather could get downright nasty by tonight."

"Not according to the Weather Channel," Atticus replied, looking up at the sky, "at least not until Sunday."

Ken laughed as he pulled up his collar. "I wouldn't put too much in what they say if I were you. Up here they have a reputation for being wrong more than they're right."

Atticus looked out over the water. The swells rolled endlessly off to the east. The late afternoon sun just broke out from behind a cloud, turning everything from gray to an emerald green. As the sun spread across Plum Island, its foliage turned a deep green and the low limestone cliffs along the shore glistened in a golden hue.

"Is that the island ferry?" Atticus said, pointing at a big black and white boat lumbering along toward Washington Island about two miles off the port bow.

"Yep; looks like the *Andrea*," Ken replied as he turned to get a better look.

"The *Andrea*? Do they have more than one ferry?"

"We got three."

"What do they do in the winter? This must all freeze over."

"They got an ice-breaking boat."

Atticus looked up at the taut sails. "It must get pretty lonely up here in the winter," he said as he switched his position in order to give his right arm a break from the tiller.

"Well, the only thing I really miss are the foxes."

"Foxes?"

"Yeah, girls! Man, there's a lot of them up here in the summer, but not many in the winter; other than the islanders, that is."

Atticus laughed. "What are islanders?"

"People who live on the island. Are you married, Mr. Gunner?"

"Used to be, but not anymore."

"You said you used to teach, what do you do now?"

"Well, I just got a job as an assistant principal for a high school in Madison."

"Why don't you come up here and work? Then you could go sailing every day."

Atticus chuckled. "That would indeed be an interesting experience, but I'm afraid that would be a whole lot easier said than done."

"They're looking for a new administrator."

"What happened to the one they had?"

"He just quit; I don't know if he retired or got fired. I know people didn't much like him, myself included; he was old and kind of out of touch."

Atticus felt the cold wind bite at his hands and face. He zipped his coat up tight around his neck and pulled his cap down over his ears as they closed in on the island.

———·◆·———

As they approached the main harbor on Washington Island, Atticus had the boy drop the sails while he started the engine. The water calmed down as they transitioned from the open lake into the security of the natural harbor at the south end of Washington Island. Easing back on the throttle, Atticus looked up at Ken as he secured the main sail to the boom. Off the starboard beam, the muffled roar of the surf rumbled as it spent its momentum against the outer banks of Detroit Island. Ken climbed back into the cockpit. "How did I do?" he asked.

"Excellent!" Atticus replied smiling at him. "We'll make a sailor out of you yet."

The young man grinned. "I really enjoyed this afternoon, Mr. Gunner, and I want to thank you for bringing me home."

"You're welcome, but now that you've dragged me all the way up to your island, where's a good place for me to dock for the night?"

"See that long concrete dock off to the left?" Ken said, pointing. "You can tie up anyplace along there."

Atticus eased the boat in along the walkway, and Ken jumped off and held the *Moonhawk* while Atticus went below to get the fenders and the mooring lines. After the boat was secure, Ken went below, picked up his suitcase, and came back up on deck. Atticus was kneeling at the base of the mast, securing the main halyard as Ken jumped off the boat.

Ken looked back up at Atticus, "Is there anything else I can do to help, Mr. Gunner?"

"No, I think that's it, Ken," Atticus replied as he stood up.

"Well, I guess I'll be leaving then—thanks again."

"You're welcome, lad—take care."

"How long are you going to stay?"

"I don't know, but as long as I'm here, I'd like to see what your island is like."

"Listen, I'm going to call my dad to come and get me; can we give you a lift someplace?"

"No thanks, I think I'd like to get straightened away here before I venture out."

"There's a wedding dance downtown tomorrow tonight," Ken went on, "why don't you come to the dance; I'll introduce you to a few people."

Atticus shook his head. "No thanks," he said. "I'm really not much into wedding dances anymore."

"Suit yourself," Ken responded as he proceeded to walk away. "Thanks again."

Atticus started below and then paused. "You can tell me where the nearest restaurant is though!" he hollered out to Ken.

"About two miles that way," Ken replied, pointing down the road. "You want a ride?"

"No thanks, I'll walk later!"

━━━━•◆•━━━━

After Atticus finished cleaning up, he grabbed his down jacket and headed up on deck and off the boat. Dusk was settling in. The air was cold but it felt good to stretch his legs. There was absolutely no one in sight. The *Moonhawk* tugged gently at her ropes, and her mast stood cold and dark against the stormy sky. He put his hands into his coat pockets and proceeded toward the road.

He walked past a gray shed behind the ferry office. To the left was a refreshment stand with a "Closed" sign hanging in the window; to the right, two gift shops and a gravel road that led down past two big storage tanks and ended along a wooden dock. The main road continued off into the woods. Tall birch and maple trees flanked both sides of the road, and their branches formed a natural canopy overhead.

By the time he reached the first indications of life, his thoughts had turned to food. As he neared a crossroad, a small filling station stood off to the right; there were two old gas pumps in front with a peaked roof that extended out over the pumps; an old Model A Ford sat up on blocks just to the right of the station. The place was dark, and Atticus wondered if it was still in use. Across the intersection was a small stone building labeled "US Post Office." Next to it was a small grocery store, closed of course, but a brightly lit Coke machine stood in front. Down the road to the left, he could see four or five street lights about a mile away. He turned the corner and started to walk toward the lights. Tall grass, partially matted from the winter's snow, bowed low as the wind scurried across the open field to his right. It began to mist.

Suddenly, the darkness scurried off as the road lit up from behind; an old pickup pulled up alongside and stopped; the passenger door flung open and a woman's voice called out, "Want a ride?"

Atticus stepped up on the running board and swung himself inside without saying a word. A heavyset, middle-aged woman who could barely see over the steering wheel glanced over at him. "I don't think I've seen you on the island before; you must be a stranger," she said as Atticus slammed the door shut. "Are you looking for a job?"

Before he could respond, she ground the shift lever into first gear, roared the engine, and took off with a couple of good jerks. "What in the world are you doing out walking on a night like this?" she continued, slamming the shift lever into second gear.

"Well, I'm looking for . . ."

"You look like an educator," she interrupted before he could finish. "I used to be a teacher; I taught fourth grade at the school here, now I run the island newspaper—oh, I'm sorry, my name is Jody Kerfam; what's yours?"

Atticus smiled. "Yes, I am a stranger to the island," he replied. "I got here by boat, so I don't have a car, and I'm not looking for a job, but what I am looking for is a place to get something to eat. And finally, my name is Atticus Gunner."

Jody smiled, "Touché," she said glancing at Atticus again. "You know about the job then."

Atticus smiled. "Yes, ma'am."

"The only place to eat on the island this early in the season is the Dawn Restaurant. You'll be able to get something there; I'll drop you off. If you don't mind my asking, what do you do for a living?"

"Ironically, I am a school administrator."

"Well, how about that—you wouldn't happen to be a cop too, would you?"

"No, I'm afraid not; I know nothing about law enforcement."

"Ever been in the military?"

"Yes."

"Well then, you're as qualified as Bert Federman was. He didn't know anything about being a cop either, but he did serve in the military."

"Ma'am, I'm afraid you lost me. What has being a cop got to do with being a school administrator?"

"Actually nothing—you do know, however, they are looking for both a constable and an administrator, only in the form of one person."

"No, I didn't know that. You mean they intend to hire one person to be a full-time administrator and a full-time cop?"

"That's right."

Again Atticus chuckled. "Good luck on that one."

The truck approached several buildings on both sides of the road. Jody pulled over across from the restaurant and stopped. "Well, tell me," she said, "what's your first impression of Washington Island?"

"It seems like a very beautiful place," he replied as he opened the door.

"Well, Mr. Gunner, you either love this place or hate it, but either way, it gets into your blood; most people can't seem to simply walk away from it."

"I'll keep that in mind," Atticus said as he stepped out of the truck into the misty night. He slammed the door shut, and Jody roared the engine and took off again.

Atticus hurried across the street and into the restaurant. Once inside, he walked over to an empty table along the wall, took off his coat, and hung it on the coat tree next to the table. The place was empty except for five teenagers sitting at a table across the room. One of the two girls got up and walked over to Atticus. "Can I help you?" she said, looking down at him.

"Yes, do you have a menu?"

"No sir, I'm sorry, we don't, not tonight anyway."

"You mean you're not serving food tonight?"

"Yeah, we're serving food but you have to order from the blackboard up there." She pointed up at the blackboard on the wall behind the counter.

"Okay—I'll have an order of pea soup and a glass of milk."

"Sorry, we don't have any pea soup left."

"Oh—okay, do you have any of the bean soup left?"

"Yeah, we still have some of that."

"Okay, I'll have some bean soup and a glass of milk then."

The young lady turned and started toward the kitchen. Halfway there, she stopped and looked back at Atticus. "Do you want that soup in a bowl?" she asked.

The boys at the table all began to laugh. "No, Joni, he wants it in a paper bag!" one of them blurted out.

"Oh drop dead!" she said, looking over at the table. "It also comes in a cup," she continued, looking back at Atticus.

A station wagon pulled up in front of the restaurant and honked the horn.

"There's Peter," one of the boys said. "Come on, let's get out of here!" The three of them hurried out the door and hopped into the car, and sped away. The girl left sitting at the table got up and disappeared into the kitchen with Joni.

Alone in the dining room, Atticus stood up and started walking around. It was a pleasant place; there were lacy white curtains hanging in the windows, and the walls were covered with enlarged reproductions of old photographs. There were pictures of old wooden schooners and shipwrecks, old buildings and docks, and some people standing in front of an old hotel next to a horse and buggy. There was a picture of an old logging crew, and another of several old sailing ships frozen in the ice, but the one that Atticus found most intriguing was a photograph taken on a dark stormy day off a pier. A huge wave was breaking over the pier, and the two men in the picture were leaning hard into the wind. The label under the picture said, "North Point, south of the Boils, during the Storm of 1913."

"Your food is ready, Mister."

"Thank you," Atticus said as he sat down at his table again.

"Are you a teacher?" the girl asked.

"I used to be."

"What do you do now?" she replied.

"Well, I guess right now I'm a sailor."

"So is my dad; he works on an ore boat."

"I imagine he's gone quite a bit then?"

"Yeah, he lives in Sturgeon Bay, so I don't see much of him anyway."

"I take it you live on the island here with your mom then."

"And my brother." She smiled at Atticus and then walked back over to the table where her girlfriend was seated.

Another car pulled up in front, and a man wearing a yellow raincoat got out and ran into the restaurant. "Hi there Joni, Kris," he said, giving the girls a nod while at the same time unsnapping his raincoat.

"Hi, Mr. Gorpon," they replied in unison.

"You want something to eat?" Joni asked.

"No, I just want to talk to this gentleman for a minute," he said, walking toward Atticus with a smile. "I'm assuming you're Mr. Gunner," he went on.

"Yes, my name is Gunner."

"My name is Butch Gorpon; mind if I sit down for a minute?"

"No, not at all," Atticus replied.

The man was short and stocky, in his early thirties, with broad shoulders and the beginning of a beer gut. His shirt was unbuttoned three buttons from the neck, exposing the dark thick hair on his chest. He had a round face, with a thin mustache, and his dark hair was cropped short. His eyes were dark and piercing, and when he spoke, they sparkled with enthusiasm. He looked as though he could have just stepped out of any one of the pictures on the wall.

Butch sat down facing Atticus, straddling the back of a chair between his legs. "I understand you're a principal for a big high school in Madison," he said.

"Assistant principal."

"I'm the president of the school board and the police committee here on the island, and we're looking for both. Dick Shernie called me and said you gave his boy a lift from the mainland. He also told me that from what the boy said, you just might be the kind of person we're looking for. I'd like to make you a proposition."

"What kind of proposition?" Atticus asked.

"Are you planning on staying here through tomorrow?"

"Yes."

"Well, Mr. Gunner, I know you have another job, and that you may not be interested in what we have to offer, but then again we may not be interested in you either, so here is my proposition: if you'll spend tomorrow with me, I'll give you a complete unabridged tour of the island. After that, if we are mutually interested in one another, I'll explain the job and set up an interview. If there is no interest by either of us, at the very least you'll have firsthand knowledge of the island and, as a result, may want to consider a new, permanent, and beautiful docking location for your boat at a much cheaper cost than what you're paying now; that is, unless you really enjoy the concrete confines of the Green Bay Yacht Club."

"How did you know I was at the Green Bay Yacht Club?"

"I checked."

Atticus was surprised at how fast this man had done some checking and wondered what else he knew, but for now he dropped it and continued on. "Well, Mr. Gorpon, I don't really plan on changing jobs, and I'm not a big fan of tours, but I might be interested in different docking arrangements, so I'll take you up on your offer. When do we start?"

He smiled and extended his hand to Atticus. "I answer by the name of Butch," he said, "and I'll pick you up in the morning."

Atticus smiled back as he shook Butch's hand. "I answer to just about anything," he replied, "but my friends call me Atticus."

Atticus got up from the table and walked over to the cash register. He paid his bill, left a tip, grabbed his coat, and started for the door. Butch was standing at the door, waiting. Butch said good-bye to the girls, and then the two men walked out together. "Can I give you a lift back to your boat?" Butch asked. It wasn't raining at the time, but with the frequent flash of lightning off to the west, Atticus decided to accept the offer.

———•◆•———

Atticus was awakened by the loud blast of a boat horn. Startled at first, it took him a few seconds to get his bearings. Finally, he crawled out of bed and looked out the cabin window. The morning fog was tinted gold by the sun as it attempted to burn its way through the mist. A ferry boat was backing away from the fog-shrouded dock.

Grabbing some clean socks and underwear out of his duffle bag, Atticus went into the water closet to clean up and get dressed. He just finished when he heard Butch's voice outside. "Hey in there, are you going to sleep all day?"

Atticus slid open the hatch and stuck his head out. "I was trying, but the blast from that ferry woke me up."

Butch laughed.

"Come on board, we'll have a cup of coffee."

"Now you're talking," Butch replied. "Besides, I always wanted to see how the other half lives. Hey," he continued as he came down the ladder, "beautiful boat."

"Coffee's on the stove," Atticus said with a smile as he handed Butch an empty cup.

The two men spent the next few minutes exchanging small talk. Finally, they went up on deck. "You ready to hit the trail?" Butch asked.

"As ready as I'll ever be," Atticus replied as he motioned for Butch to lead the way. There was already something about this man that Atticus liked.

As they walked toward the parking lot, another ferry boat was just pulling into the dock with a full load of cars and people. "Looks like your first load of tourists is arriving," Atticus remarked.

"The weekend boats are always loaded this time of year," Butch replied, looking out toward the ferry. "It's mostly summer people coming up for the weekend, but as the season progresses, it'll get like that on every boat, every day; then it's tourist season."

"You don't seem overly enthusiastic about that."

"Let's not get into the whole tourist thing," Butch responded. "To me they're more a necessity than a welcomed commodity."

As they got into Butch's car, Atticus glanced over at the ferry office. "You know," he said, "I better go over to the ferry office and make sure it's okay to leave my boat at their dock for the day."

"It's all taken care of," Butch replied as he started the car. "I talked with Adrian this morning. He said you can leave it there all weekend if you like."

Atticus smiled. "Well, what do you know? The man's got clout."

Butch smiled without looking at Atticus, turned the car around, and drove out of the parking lot.

"Who's Adrian anyway?" Atticus asked.

"Adrian Fruger," Butch said, "the man who owns those ferry boats, the dock you're tied to, the parking lot, and two thirds of all those buildings, along with a good hunk of the island; even some of Michigan's Upper Peninsula."

"Sounds rich."

"He's got a few bucks."

"Does he live on the island?"

"Oh yes, except in the winter, when they do a little traveling."

"Sounds like one of the fortunate few."

"Yeah, I guess—but I don't really begrudge Adrian his money. He started with nothing."

"Self-made man?"

"Yep."

"Well, where to first, cabbie?" Atticus asked as he tried to roll down the window, only to find that it didn't work.

"We'll take the three-dollar overland tour of the island first. There's about forty-seven square miles of land, and over a hundred miles of road, so there's no way you're going to see it all today. I'll just take you to a few various spots to give you a flavor of the place."

"And when does the job pitch come?"

"We'll talk about the job before lunch," Butch went on. "Unfortunately, I have to work this afternoon, but you can use my car to go out and see old Spencer about docking your boat; I'll give you directions on how to get there. I've also taken the liberty to schedule an interview with the board at 6:30 this evening, but it can be canceled at any time if we so choose. If you decide to go through with the interview, you can pick me up at 6:15. If you're not interested, I get home a little after five—you can pick me up anytime after that, and I'll give you a ride back to your boat so you can sail off into the sunset. Does that sound fair enough?"

"Butch, you're up against some pretty strong odds. I have a very good job waiting for me in Madison. Not only does it pay well, but it provides me with a real career opportunity for future advancement. And that doesn't even take into consideration that Madison has the university plus innumerable culture exposures."

"First of all, I know what you're being paid; it's public information—I called. Believe it or not, we can match your salary. Second, it may come as a surprise but the University of Wisconsin is not beyond reach of this island. We also have people here who have actually received a degree from there. Third, yes, Madison does have culture and other things we don't have, but that argument is just as powerful in reverse; they don't even come close to having what we have here. And if, by the end of the day, you don't pick up on that, then maybe this island, or the job, isn't for you anyway. But I have to say, Atticus, I might not know you very well yet, but if I'm any judge of character at all, I see you as a risk taker."

"I also have two daughters who live with their mother in Madison, and that's a very powerful consideration for me."

"Yes, I know about that too. What you can offer them here doesn't have to take away from what they have in Madison; it could even result in a more meaningful relationship with them than you have now. You might want to think about that as you look around today."

"You're quite a salesman."

"I've been around the block a few times myself, Atticus. I left the island once to pursue greener pastures and ended up coming back."

Butch turned left off the main road and down a narrow blacktop lane that led into the woods; the arrow said "To Sunset Harbor." "Most of the exterior of the island is covered with woods like this," Butch said. "The southwest side has low-lying shores, stone-strewn beaches, and some marshland."

Coming around a bend in the road, they came to a beautiful little cove. The open lake, still restless from yesterday's wind, sent its endless procession of swells across the shoal at the mouth of the inlet. On the far side of the cove, set back from the shore, was a big old building. It was painted white with an open porch extending across the front and down one side. The grounds were covered with well-trimmed shrubs and cedars. A blacktop drive curved in past the building and down to a wooden dock.

"This place dates back to the 1800s," Butch said. "It started out as a boarding house, became a hotel and speakeasy during Prohibition; now it's a resort. It's not exactly a Holiday Inn," he continued as he turned into the drive, "but then the owner doesn't want that kind of clientele anyway. The people who come here are looking for a place to get away from it all."

Atticus looked up at the big porch as they drove past the front of the building. "Does he get a lot of business?" he asked, noticing its somewhat rundown condition.

"Mostly people from Chicago," Butch replied as they continued toward the dock.

There were two men standing at the bottom of a boat ramp. A big man wearing hip boots was knee deep in the water. The other man was in a wetsuit, bent over and trying to bolt a cable onto a large flat object lying half on the ramp and half in the water. A pickup was parked at the top of the ramp.

Butch stopped the car and got out; Atticus followed. "Hey Butch, come to help?" the man in the wetsuit hollered.

"Hell no!" Butch replied, walking down toward them.

"Did you bring any beer?" the big man hollered.

"Nope!"

"Then what the hell did you come for?" the big man replied; he and his partner laughed out loud.

Butch stopped next to the man in the wetsuit, who was still bent over trying to hook up a cable. "We just came to see what the hell you two were up to."

Walking about six paces behind, Atticus stepped over the cable and walked to the other side of the big object the men were working on.

"How you doing, Hepper?" Butch asked, looking down at the man in the wetsuit. "Are you going to get her the rest of the way out today?"

"That's the plan," he said, glancing up at Butch.

The other man walked out of the water and up next to Butch. "The frickin' surf put her over the shoal last night, so we dragged her the rest of the way this morning," he said as he wiped his big hands on his pants.

"Well, that does it," the man in the wetsuit said as he stood up. "Now we'll see if we can pull it the rest of the way out. By the way, Butch," he continued, looking over at Atticus, "who's your friend?"

"This is Atticus Gunner," Butch replied, "and this, Atticus, is Hepper Greshion; owner of this resort, and master scuba diver."

"I'd shake your hand," Hepper said, looking at Atticus, "but they're all greasy."

"That's okay," Atticus replied with a smile.

"And this is Tom Cline," Butch said, turning toward the big man.

Tom looked at Atticus with a blank expression but didn't offer him a hand. "Another frickin' city boy looking for a job?" he asked. "He doesn't look to me like he could handle a waitress job." The big man chuckled as he turned and walked away.

"You'll have to forgive Tom," Hepper said, "he's not big on outsiders."

"So what is this you're pulling in?" Atticus asked, changing the topic. "Looks like the rudder off an old sailing ship."

"That's exactly what it is," Butch replied.

The rudder was about twenty feet long and made of heavy wood beams pieced together with long rusty bolts. The wood had deep round gouges worn down along the grain of the timbers, caused by long exposure to sand and water.

"She washed into the shallows during a storm early this spring," Hepper said.

"The rest of the boat must be out there someplace then," Atticus continued. "Are you going to try and find it?"

"Nope," Hepper replied shaking his head. "All the hardware has been removed I'm sure, and other than that, there isn't much worth salvaging off the old tub this came from; she was probably a Chicago lumber hauler."

"What about its historical value?"

Hepper looked at Atticus like he was talking a foreign language.

"So what are you going to do with this?" Atticus asked.

"I'm going to stand it up here on a concrete slab next to my dock for people to see."

"Well, we got to go," Butch interjected. "We'll see you later, Hepper." Without further hesitation, Butch started walking back toward his car; Atticus followed. As they walked, Atticus glanced over at Tom Cline, who was sitting in the front of Hepper's pickup, smoking a cigarette.

Butch looked over at Atticus as he started his car. "I'm sorry about what happened there, Atticus. Tom is a little weak upstairs, but I wanted you to see that there are people up here who don't adjust well to strangers, and some of them are well above the likes of Tom Cline."

Atticus made no comment.

Leaving the old hotel, Butch turned left. After a quarter mile, Atticus noticed a bleached-out wooden sign alongside the road that read, "The Hersoff Place, Astrology Readings by Cynthia." A wagon trail in front of the sign led through the tall grass and down into the woods. "Well, if the islanders need to know the future, they can always get a reading by Cynthia," Atticus said jokingly.

"No, she's not here anymore; the old Hersoff place is deserted. As a matter of fact, most islanders consider the old house haunted."

"Really?"

"There's quite a story behind that place."

"What's a tour without a story?" Atticus replied. "I'm all ears."

Butch smiled over at Atticus. "To start with," he said, "Old Man Hersoff knew Hepper's grandfather; they used to communicate back and forth after Grandpa Greshion migrated to this country from England. Anyway, Captain Hersoff decided to come over to this country too. He bought thirty acres from Grandpa Greshion and built a big place down next to the lake at the end of that old road you saw back there."

"Six or seven years after Captain Hersoff moved to the island, his wife drowned in front of the place," Butch continued. "But when his second wife hung herself in the stable down by the house, people began to talk. That, however, isn't the end of the story; Old Man Hersoff also had a daughter whose name was Cynthia. After she grew up, she married a man from Chicago, and he died mysteriously a short time after they were married. Cynthia married twice after that, and both of them died in mysterious ways also. After the death of her third husband, she moved back to the island to live with her father. Less than six months after her arrival, the old man up and died; by then, most island folks were convinced she not only killed the old man but did away with all her husbands, and maybe her mother and stepmother too."

"Cynthia was very young when her mothers died," Butch went on, "and as far as the father goes, I simply think he drank himself to death. If you were to ask most islanders, however, they wouldn't agree with that. Convinced she was evil, the islanders labeled her a witch. She did always claim to be a mystic, and not long after the old man died, she set up shop in the house as an astrologist and medium for talking with the dead. Eventually, she pulled up stakes and went back to Chicago. Since then, she's had lots of offers to sell the place but won't. She claims she doesn't want to betray the family's ghosts. She still comes up for short visits once in a while, but the only person on the island who has any contact with her at all is Hepper Greshion. He kind of looks after the place for her; puts flowers on the family graves, stuff like that."

"You ever go down there?"

"Yeah, I've got a deer stand just off the edge of the yard, and it's never struck me as anything more than an old rundown house. In its day, it was quite the place though."

Butch took a right turn and headed east up out of the woods and across the interior of the island. There were open fields covered with tall prairie grass. Here and there were patches of wild spring flowers spread out in a blanket of blue and purple. The road was narrow with no center line, and the flowers grew wild right up to the edge of the blacktop. Remnants of a stone fence ran diagonally up over a hill, with a stand of freshly leafed birch trees running along its forgotten edge. The scene was almost like stepping into the past. "This used to all be farmland," Butch said, breaking the silence.

"So I see," Atticus replied as he noticed a partially collapsed barn along the roadside. "What happened?"

"Oh, it's hard to say," Butch replied with a shrug. "Once upon a time, there were about three thousand people that lived on this island year round. A lot of them were wiped out when the Depression hit, the rest by isolation and time."

"Any farmers left?"

"Yeah, there are still a few hanging on."

"What about the rest of the people who live here year round? What do they do for a living?"

"Oh, a little of everything, mostly service-type jobs, keep up the roads, maintain the power lines; that's what I do. We've still got a few that fish commercially. Others work for the ferry line, teach at the school, a few bars and stores, and a couple of building contractors. Then there are the summer people, of course."

"Sounds like a tragedy."

"Well, yes and no. You have to learn to accept the island on her terms. If you fight her, you'll lose. If you go with the flow, she's like a beautiful woman; intriguing, sometimes unpredictable, but always beautiful."

"She's too beautiful to stay fallow," Atticus interjected. "One day a big developer is going to come along and turn your island into a commercial nightmare."

"It's been tried a couple times but has always failed for one reason or another. There's a lot more substance here than meets the eye. If you come up here, you'll soon find out what I mean."

"You mean money and influence in the form of summer residents?"

"You catch on fast."

The car rolled up another hill and over a camelback ridge. As they came over the summit, the entire southeastern portion of the island came into view. The coastline was low and rocky, with huge sections of weatherworn limestone jutting out over the blue-green water. A cedar forest along the shore stood rich and green in the bright sunlight. The big lake extended out as far as the eye could see. Offshore, an ore boat was churning her way north past the island.

As they approached the east shore and drove into the cedars, Butch swung a right off the main road and onto a blacktop drive. The car rolled under a big wrought-iron arch supported by two masonry stone pillars. "I'll show you a nice little summer pad," he said, stepping on the accelerator again. The road weaved through the trees, up over a little mogul, and then circled in front of a very large and unusual home.

The main part of the building was shaped like a barn. The roof was covered with cedar shakes, and solid copper flashings adorned the eaves. One end of the structure was solid glass from roof to foundation. A large patio deck ran from the side of the house around to the front. A two-story carriage house and combination woodshed stood off to the left of the main building. Butch stopped the car. "Come on, I'll show you the inside," he said as he got out.

Atticus got out and followed. "Isn't it locked?"

"Yes, but I've got a key—come on."

"You've got a key?"

"Yeah, I look after the place when the owners are gone. They're supposed to be back today, so I've got to turn the heat up."

"Turn the heat up? You mean they heat this place all winter?"

"That's right, most of the summer people do."

Hanging next to the front doors under the overhang was a series of brass bells of varying sizes. Each bell was connected to a series of brass gears. "What's that?" Atticus asked.

Butch smiled as he pushed the key into one of the massive, hand-carved wooden doors and pressed the latch. "Ring the doorbell," he said.

Atticus pressed it; the gears began to turn and the bells started playing "Edelweiss." The clear, crisp tones echoed through the house as they stepped inside. "That thing has got to be worth a fortune, Butch."

"Fifty-five thousand bucks—or so I've been told."

The two men stepped through the foyer and into a huge open room. The ceiling was open clear to the rafters, with massive wooden support beams strung across the room. Six wooden posts of equal magnitude were located throughout the room. In the center was a large open fire pit with a black steel hood hanging over it. The entire floor was covered with deep-pile white carpeting. A long dining table with wrought-iron legs and a solid plate glass top stood at one end of the room. The rest of the room was filled with groupings of plush furniture, antique tables, and lamps. There was pottery, sculpture, and paintings from all over the world on the tables and walls. A polar bear rug was stretched out on the floor next to the fire pit, and the head of a rhinoceros was mounted on one of the walls.

Atticus stepped in front of Butch. "What do you suppose this place is worth?" he asked.

"Who knows?" Butch said as he walked up next to Atticus with his hands in his rear pockets.

"What does this guy do?" Atticus asked as he walked around the room, looking at things.

"His name is Doebuck, he owns the Z&B International Shipping conglomerate out of Chicago."

"If this is their summer place, where do they spend their winters?"

Butch shrugged his shoulders. "I don't really know," he said. "I don't think anyone on the island does; maybe Adrian Fruger. Actually old man Doebuck comes here from time to time during the off season, so you can't really call it their summer place."

"I've been in Florida, California, Europe," Atticus said as he looked up at a painting on the wall. "I've seen beautiful estates before, but I would never have expected something like this up here in the middle of nowhere. Are there others?"

"Oh yes, maybe not quite as elaborate, but close."

"What surprises me is that they're not vandalized or robbed."

"Not up here; the place is too isolated, and strangers are too conspicuous. Besides, it's a well-known rumor that a lot of the property up here is tied to the underworld."

"Really," Atticus replied. "Is it?"

"Who knows—frankly, I think it's a bunch of shit. I think it's just a rumor that no one tries to discourage because it makes people think twice. It's cheap insurance, if you know what I mean. Well, I've got a few things to do; go ahead and look around if you like. It won't take me long."

Butch proceeded to open the house and make it ready for its owner's return. The two men then hauled wood from the wood shed and put it in the wood box next to the fire pit. As Atticus dumped his second armload into the wood box, he looked over at Butch, who had just finished cleaning the ashes from the fire pit. "Butch," he said, "what are these people like, anyway?"

"From what I know about them, they're okay; Mr. Doebuck is kind of quiet, but there's no question he wears the pants. He's got a personal butler that goes everywhere with him. He doesn't say much; I think he's a bodyguard of some sort; carries a concealed handgun with him at all times. The missus, on the other hand, is something else. She's got a real elitist attitude, and some strong opinions that go along with it. When she gets on something, there's no stopping her, but she's just here in the summer; like I said, he's here off and on pretty much year round. They're definitely in the upper crust of the self-appointed island aristocracy though; not the kind of people one wants to get on the wrong side of."

For the first time, Atticus thought of some of the comments made by Attorney Markup. "Have you ever heard of the Morgan Group?" he asked.

Butch shook his head. "Can't say that I have; what is it?"

"It's not important," Atticus replied.

The two men walked out of the house, locking the door behind them. Instead of heading for the car, Atticus started around the house. "Do you mind if we walk down by the shore and have a look-see?" he asked over his shoulder.

"Not at all," Butch replied as he changed direction. "The shore along this side of the island is rocky—not so good for boats, but very beautiful."

They walked through a stand of mature birch and maple trees past the front of the house, and then they went through the cedars and out onto the rocky shoreline. The rocks lay flat in a horizontal shelf. Some sections had broken off and dropped down into the water. Pieces of driftwood were strewn along the shore where the winter's gales had dropped them. Moss was growing on the rocks wherever the cedars were thick enough to shelter them from the sun's warm rays. Atticus walked over to the edge. The emerald green swells surged between the rocks and crevices, occasionally belching spray straight into the air; it rumbled like a muffled shot from a cannon.

"You got anything like this in Madison?" Butch said, walking up next to Atticus.

"It is beautiful, isn't it?" Atticus replied, looking out over the open expanse.

To the south about three miles, an open, rocky, treeless point of land jutted out into the lake. On its rounded crown stood a huge, seven gabled, stone building; its dark silhouette looked austere against the bright blue sky. "That's Bondin's Rock," Butch said, "and that's the old Bondin place on its crown. Or I should say, used to be."

"What do you mean?" Atticus asked.

"Well, the Bondins used to be a big name on the island back in the early nineteen hundreds. At one time, they owned two thirds of this place, but he went under when the Depression hit; bad investments I guess. The place stood empty for a long time; all the while I was a kid. No one wanted it, standing all alone out there on that cold rocky point. That old manor was like an icon for the island, a source of many stories and mysteries. We used to love to hate that place. Then last fall, the leader of some separatist group bought it. Now it's a real place of mystery. If you want weird for real, there's one for the book."

"You mean an antigovernment group?"

"Exactly; they got 'No Trespassing' signs all over the grounds; the place is patrolled with dogs and armed storm trooper–type guards; no one is allowed out on the rock anymore. The owner is commando trained or something, and seldom leaves the property except to go off island for periods of time, but the guards remain; they are always present. I was on the property once to work on a big old trawler that comes in there once in a while, but other than that, I give the place a wide berth now; too bad, as kids we used to play out there a lot."

"You said you worked on an old trawler?" Atticus asked.

"Yeah; I guess I didn't tell you, I'm also the island's marine diesel mechanic."

"What was the name of the boat?"

"I couldn't tell you. They didn't give me a whole lot of opportunity to look around much. It was a beat-up old thing though, I can tell you that—why?"

"Just curious, that's all. I had a little run-in with a trawler on the way up here."

"Well, it wouldn't surprise me if it was them, they're not nice people. He spouts a lot of hate rhetoric, but he hasn't really done anything, so there isn't much we can do about it, and believe me, people have tried. That character and his friends aren't really welcome here, but unfortunately he has also made friends with the Doebucks, and that makes him untouchable."

Butch looked at his watch. "It's about noon, so we'll head over to my place for lunch. We didn't get nearly as much done as I'd hoped for, but this afternoon when you go down to see my friend Spencer, you'll see Jackson Harbor and the whole north shore. I had hopes of taking you to the sand dunes swimming area, the mountain, the airport, Schoolhouse Beach, and downtown, but that will all have to wait for another day. By the time you're done with old Spence, you'll have a good flavor of this place. Our deal still stands for the return of my car, but for now let's talk a bit about the job." Butch turned and started back up through the yard toward his car.

"To start with," Butch said as they approached the car, "the administrator's job and the constable's job were both separate full-time jobs with separate full-time pay. Mr. Ploder, our administrator, has been here for three years and is retiring, but if he hadn't, we would have fired him because we're not happy with his performance. Our constable, Bert Federman, was the island cop for years. We were very happy with him, but he managed to kill himself in a car accident here on the east side of the island last winter. Unfortunately, the island can't afford to put up the money needed to fund both of these jobs separately and still be competitive with the outside world. So what we did was take the money that the island paid to both of them, restructured the jobs, and consolidated them into what we feel is one workable position—then we applied both salaries to that position."

Opening the car door, Butch slid in behind the wheel, while Atticus crawled into the passenger side. "Tell me," Atticus interjected, "how can you possibly take two jobs, both with full-time responsibilities, and consolidate them into one position? Do you honestly think that's workable? That just doesn't compute in my book."

"We did it by taking a number of the administrator's responsibilities and redistributing those that didn't have to be done by the administrator personally. Second, when we looked at the constable's job, we not only found some things we could drop, such as checking for locked doors at businesses and homes, but we also found that it really wasn't a full-time job. After those adjustments, we built into the new consolidated position the right for this individual to target his or her attention according to need, rather than time on the job. Realizing that even with these adjustments there will still be areas of conflict from time to time, we decided to leave it up to this individual's discretion, as long as it's posted with the dispatcher. That may not always be the most palatable with islanders, but unless they want to raise the money to pay for two positions again, they're going to have to learn to live with it."

"Tell me, exactly what will the administrator be responsible for?"

"Our current administrative assistant will put out meeting notices, make the payroll, pay the bills, keep the books, handle the cash flow, send out the tax levy notifications, and file the state and federal financial reports as required. The administrator will hire, fire, and supervise all personnel, build the budget with the board, conduct the annual meeting, see that an annual external audit of the books is done each year, attend all school board meetings, develop an acceptable working relationship with the state and federal governments, maintain the appropriate curriculum and school organization, and assist and advise the board in the negotiations with school personnel."

"What about student discipline?"

"Teachers do their own, except in extreme cases."

"Sounds like you're talking about a full-time job right there."

"But you have to keep the job in proper perspective, Atticus. Remember, we have less than a hundred students, K through twelve, only seven full-time plus two part-time teachers, a janitor/bus driver, and one administrative assistant. That's hardly a big operation, and it is very much self-running when all things are in place."

"And what about the constable?"

"That's far more flexible. You'll operate out of the school administrator's office. We'll provide you with a car. It'll be your responsibility to wear a badge and keep the peace. There is very little to do in the off-season, which is generally the time when school is the busiest. You may have an occasional death. You may have an occasional excessive drinking issue at a bar or on the road; maybe a domestic issue or two, but nothing that a good country cop couldn't handle. If you do need additional backup for something special, there's always the county sheriff. You would be expected to be seen at the island's special events, such as the summer carnival, but here again, how you use your time is at your discretion."

Atticus sat quietly as they drove back across the island. As they arrived at Butch's place, Atticus looked over at him. "Ya know," he said, "I'm not making any promises, or a commitment, but I would like to go through with that interview tonight. Is that still on the table?"

"You got it," Butch replied as he cranked hard on the wheel and drove up past the white picket fence and into his yard.

"One last thought," Atticus said as Butch came to a stop. "You do know, Butch, I have absolutely no law enforcement training or experience."

Butch got out of the car; Atticus followed. "Neither did old Bert, and he did just fine," Butch said.

Atticus made no further comment.

————◆◆◆————

That afternoon, Atticus had Butch's car. He turned left out of Butch's driveway and headed north through town (or at least what the islanders called town). It consisted of three bars, a real estate office, the Legion hall, the mercantile store, the power cooperative where Butch worked, and the Dawn Restaurant, where Atticus ate last night. As he approached the north end of the island, he pulled over to the side of the road and studied the map Butch had given him. After a few moments, he turned right and headed east. After five miles of moguls and hills, he came to a small village called Jackson Harbor. The main road divided into two, the left ran down the shoreline, the other went directly out onto a concrete pier. Atticus followed the road out to the pier.

There were several commercial fishing boats tied along both sides of the pier, with an icehouse out at the far end. Beyond was the narrow opening of the harbor. Beyond that was a small island with high limestone cliffs, about two miles off the north shore of Washington Island. Still farther out lay a string of small islands whose silhouettes faded as they fell off into the distance and over the horizon. To the immediate left along the shore were three net barns, a small but well-kept cottage, and a couple of old fishing boats resting on skegs down close to the water. Further back, in amongst the trees, were a number of cottages with boat sheds of varying sizes.

Atticus parked the car. A man unloading boxes from a fishing boat out toward the far end of the pier looked up for a moment and then went back to work. Hundreds of seagulls were soaring around the boat; their screeching filled the otherwise quiet afternoon with mayhem. Atticus walked out toward the commotion.

The rough-looking man, in his late fifties with a four-day growth of stubble, looked up again from the boat as a gull swooped down past Atticus. "Say there, sonny!" he barked at Atticus. "You better look out for those God damned birds; they'll pick your eyes out!" Then he laughed as he threw another box full of fish off the boat onto the dock.

Atticus smiled but made no response.

A pickup backed up to the boat. A young man about Ken's age climbed out and started loading boxes into the back of the truck. When he finished, he jumped back into the truck and drove off. The old man stepped off the boat, walked right past Atticus without acknowledging him again, and went into the icehouse. When he returned, he was pulling one end of a hose. He proceeded to hose down the interior of the boat until the bilge pump kicked in and started to pump the brackish water out over the side. When he finished, he threw the hose back on the dock, took off his rubber boots, and set them neatly next to the helm station. Finally, he stepped off the boat, glanced over at

Atticus, and started coiling up the hose. "What can I do for you?" he asked as he continued his work.

"Just watching," Atticus replied.

"You a state man?"

"No."

"You up here for the wedding?"

"No."

"Isn't that Butch Gorpon's car I saw you drive up in?"

"Yes, it is."

"You're not up here looking for that school job, are you?"

"No, not exactly."

"You related to Butch?"

"No."

"What the hell are you doing with his car then?"

"He let me use it to look for docking for my boat," Atticus replied.

"You got a boat, huh?"

Atticus nodded.

"How big is it?"

"Thirty-two feet."

"How much water does she draw?"

"Five feet."

"Well, these are the city docks. You can dock here but they charge by the day. If you're looking for more permanent docking, old Spence is the man to see." He pointed toward the west side of the harbor. "It's pretty shallow going over there, but you can get through if you know anything about handling a boat."

"Spencer is the man Butch told me to talk to," Atticus interjected.

The old man shook his head. "Why in the hell didn't you say that in the first place, for Christ's sake?"

"Sorry," Atticus replied, "I didn't want to interrupt what you were doing. How do I get over to Spencer's place by land?"

"Well, you see that old red barn and shed with the wooden dock and old fish boat in front?"

"Yes, I see it," Atticus replied, looking over at the area where the man was pointing.

"Just go back out to the road, turn right, and you'll come to a sign that says 'Spencer's Dock'; that's it."

"Thanks." Atticus turned and started to walk away.

"By the way," the old man said, "my name is Quint Jebson, what's yours?"

"Atticus Gunner."

"Well, Atticus Gunner, have you ever been shit on by a cow?"

"No, can't say that I have," Atticus replied, turning to walk off again.

"Well, keep your hands up over your head," Quint said with a big grin on his face; "the shit from those gulls is about the same as that from a cow."

"I'll keep that in mind," Atticus replied.

———————————

When Atticus came to the sign that read "Spencer's Dock," he turned right and drove up into a well-shaded yard. He parked next to the red barn, got out of the car, and walked around the building. The big door at the end of the barn was open, so he stepped inside.

"Anyone home?" he called.

No one answered, but he could see a handsome old wooden power launch sitting up on some heavy sawhorses inside. Next to it was a short stepladder with a caulking chisel and hammer lying on the top rung.

Atticus walked back outside and looked around. A wooden dock went out over the water from between two smaller sheds. An old gray commercial fishing boat that looked to be about forty feet long lay quietly at dock side. He walked out to the old boat. Leaning over, he poked his head inside the open starboard storm gate.

"Hello there! Anyone on board?" he asked in a loud voice.

"Howdy," came a voice from behind.

Atticus turned to see a short stout man in his early sixties standing there. The man had short gray hair, a round face, bib overalls, and glasses; he was wearing a baseball cap. "Are you Mr. Spencer?" Atticus asked.

"Well, I'm Spencer; I don't know about the mister," he said. "And you must be Mr. Gunner."

"That's right," Atticus replied. "How'd you know that?"

"I saw Butch a little bit ago; he said you'd be dropping by. I understand you're thinking about becoming our new school administrator."

"Well, just thinking about it," Atticus replied. "This is a handsome old fishing boat," he went on, changing the subject.

"The *Jane*? Yep, she's been around for as long as you have. Butch tells me you got a thirty-two-foot sailboat."

"That's right."

"Wood or plastic?"

"Fiberglass."

"Plastic; what's her make?"

"She's an Erickson."

"That's a good boat," the old man said. "Come on, I'll show you another old boat."

Atticus followed him back into the barn.

"There she is," he said. "A 1949 Thompson. She belongs to a fellow here on the island. I just replaced the keel and a couple boards that were rotted out."

"Yes, I was looking at it before."

"Ya know, Mr. Gunner," the old man said, walking around to the other side of the boat, "you're going to have your hands full if you take that job."

"Why is that?"

"There was a lot of trouble at the school last year."

"What kind of trouble?"

"You name it; trouble with the teachers, the administrator, the community, even the state. It's going to take some doing to straighten it out."

"Is that why the administrator retired?"

"It was either that or get fired."

"What was the trouble with the teachers?"

"One was fired; five others quit."

"You mean six out of the seven teachers have to be replaced?" Atticus asked.

"That's right, everybody except my wife and Mrs. Boomer."

"Your wife is a teacher?" Atticus asked.

"Yep. Fourth, fifth, and sixth grade; has been for the last forty years."

"That's a long time. That's also a very high percentage of turnover. Who's Mrs. Boomer?"

"The administrative assistant."

"She's staying?"

"Oh yeah."

"Where does your wife stand in all of this?"

"The island is our home, Mr. Gunner."

"I understand," Atticus said as he turned to walk out.

"I hope I didn't scare you off—that wasn't my intention," Spencer said, calling out after Atticus. "I just thought someone ought to tell you."

"I appreciate that," Atticus replied. "Oh, and I forgot the real reason for coming here. Job or no job, I might be interested in a place to dock my boat."

"I'm a pretty good judge of character," Spencer replied with a smile. "You can lay your boat right there behind the *Jane* as long as you want. All you have to do is pay for the electricity you use."

Atticus smiled. "That's very generous, Mr. Spencer, but I wouldn't expect you to moor my boat for nothing. If it comes to that, we'll work something out." Atticus started to walk away again and then paused. "Is there anything I ought to know about the constable's job?" he asked.

Spencer shrugged. "Just that some people have raised questions about how he died. The autopsy report said he was drunk as a skunk, but as far as I know, and I knew old Bert for a long time, he never drank a drop in his entire life; he was a teetotaler."

"That's interesting," Atticus replied. "What do you think happened?"

Spencer shrugged. "I don't know," he said, "but I guess I'd be a little suspicious if I were the new constable."

"Thanks again," Atticus said as he walked away.

CHAPTER 3

The Interview

It was 6:25 p.m. when Atticus pulled into Butch's yard. He got out of the car, walked up to the front porch, and knocked on the door.

"Come on in!" Butch hollered.

Atticus opened the screen and stepped in, letting the door slam behind. "I'm sorry I'm late," he said.

"That's okay," Butch replied, coming out of the bedroom in his bare feet and buttoning up a clean shirt. "With my wife down in Sturgeon Bay and me not getting home until 5:15, I'm running a little late too. So how did your afternoon go?"

"Well, I met Spencer."

"Did he tell you his wife teaches at the school?"

"Yes, he did," Atticus replied.

"I suppose he also told you about the troubles we had."

"Yes, a little bit."

"Well, I'm ready to go," Butch said after he finished tying his shoes.

Atticus pushed his hands down into his pockets. "Are you going to fill me in on the rest of it?"

"Not much to fill in," Butch said, walking toward the door. "Basically we had an administrator who was out to lunch and a couple of teachers, especially one, who got too damn big for their britches, so we ended up cleaning house."

"I thought you only fired one teacher."

"We did, but by the time it was all over, all five of the off-islanders resigned."

"Should I interpret from all this that every time the administrator or a teacher does something that may not be in keeping with the island's mood, you simply tell them to hit the road?"

Butch stopped by the car and looked over at Atticus. "It wasn't anything like that," he said. "As a matter of fact, part of the static I've received over this whole damn thing was because I supported Mr. Ploder clear to the end, even though I thought he was as much at fault as the teachers."

In a short while, Butch pulled into the parking lot at the school. The main part of the building was an old, two-story, four-room country school with a bell tower. Around two sides of the older section was a flat-roofed one-story addition. Several majestic shade trees dotted the school grounds, with two big maples bordering the parking lot.

Atticus got out of the car and followed Butch up to the front door. They went inside, down a few steps to the left and into a small office. As they walked in, a woman sitting at one of the two desks looked up and smiled.

"Hello, Mrs. Boomer," Butch said as he approached. "What are you doing here this time of day, and on a Saturday to boot?"

"Oh, I had to come and post a few bills," she said, still smiling at Butch.

"Well, perhaps you can do that some other time; we have an interview here this evening."

"Oh, that's all right," she said, looking back down at her work. "I'll be quiet. You just go ahead with whatever you're going to do."

"We appreciate your conscientiousness, but I'm still going to ask you to leave," Butch reiterated, this time with a very distinct tone of assertiveness.

The woman continued to work for a couple of minutes, and then she slowly started to put her things away. Atticus judged her to be about forty-five years of age; she had a narrow face with thin lips and high cheekbones powdered pink with rouge, and she carried an air of haughtiness that even Atticus could feel.

Butch walked over to the window in the adjoining room and looked out at the parking lot. Lagging a bit behind, Atticus followed him into the room.

After the woman finished putting her things away, she walked over to Atticus. "Well, it looks like I'm going to have to introduce myself," she said. "My name is Vivian Boomer; I'm the administrative aide."

"How do you do?" Atticus replied as he sat down on the corner of a heavy table next to the office door.

"I take it you're the one they're interviewing," she went on.

"Yes, ma'am."

"I hope you don't sit on tables like that when students are around," she snipped.

"No, ma'am," Atticus replied without getting up. "When students are around, I generally stand at attention—parade rest, if I'm in a jovial mood."

Atticus could hear Butch chuckle. Mrs. Boomer gave Atticus a nasty look, and then without saying a word, she turned and walked back over to her desk, gathered her things, and strutted out of the office like a peacock.

"That was beautiful!" Butch said, still chuckling after she was gone.

"I take it you don't much care for her."

"I think she's a horse's ass," Butch said, sitting down at one of the student's desks.

"Why did you hire her then?"

"I didn't want to, but it's a government-funded job and she was the only applicant that had any bookkeeping experience. The thing I don't like about her is she's one of the island's biggest gossips, and the only reason she was here tonight was to find out what was going on."

Butch turned and looked out the window again as a blue Chevrolet pulled into the parking lot. Two women got out. "Here they come now," he said as they walked toward the school.

"How many people are on the board?" Atticus asked.

"You're looking at 'em."

Atticus was a little surprised but said nothing.

The two women came walking into the room; both Butch and Atticus stood to greet them.

The older of the two, a large woman in her midfifties, smiled at Atticus and extended her hand. "How do you do?" she said. "I'm Greta Bergason."

"Atticus Gunner," Atticus replied, shaking her hand gently.

"And this is Mrs. Trempson," Greta continued as she looked at the other woman, who was sitting at the table in the front of the room.

"How do you do?" Atticus said, smiling at her.

Mrs. Trempson was a small-boned woman in her midthirties, very attractive, with short-cropped hair and big eyes. She looked up at Atticus and smiled but said nothing.

Butch directed Atticus to pull up a chair and sit across from Mrs. Trempson. Then Butch sat down at one end of the table with Mrs. Bergason sitting at the other. "Well, I talked to both of you about Atticus here," he said, looking at the women. "You both know the circumstances that brought us to this interview, so as president of both the school board and the police committee, I would suggest we dispense with normal proceedings and simply talk about the job. We'll take the school administrator part first, then the constable's responsibilities. Is that okay with everyone?"

Both of the women nodded their approval.

"And you, Atticus?"

"That's fine," Atticus replied.

"I've explained to Atticus the responsibilities of both aspects of the job, and how we came to combine them. Greta," Butch continued, looking at Mrs. Bergason, "you've remained the most objective throughout all of this, so why don't you try to summarize for Mr. Gunner just what happened?"

"Well, I'll try," she said, folding her hands in front of her. "To start with, keeping teachers and administrators on the island has never been a problem up until a few years ago. We had the same administrator for over twenty years before Mr. Ploder, but he died in the middle of the school year three years ago. We couldn't find a replacement for the rest of that entire year, so when Mr. Ploder came along, we were most happy to get him. Unfortunately, since his arrival, our problems began to multiply. Not just because of Mr. Ploder, although he certainly contributed to the problems, but mostly because times are changing. Through attrition we've been forced to hire more off-island teachers, and they of course come here with different values and different expectations. On top of that, we are having more and more demands placed on us by the state. Not just in terms of what we should be teaching, but financial red tape and restrictions. The state would like to get rid of us as a district because we don't fit the mold. The only reason they haven't is because they can't figure out how to serve our geographic location."

"You mean attach you to another public school district?" Atticus asked.

"Yes," she replied. "And now their latest plan is to tax us for far more than we need, and to send the extra money down to Madison so they can give it to some big city school district who they say is far less wealthy than we are."

"You're talking about the negative aids plan?" Atticus interjected.

"Yes—and to go on with our dilemma, the islanders are changing too. They're becoming more hostile toward the school because they see this trend being supported by the teachers. The teachers are pushing for a more expanded curriculum and improved salary and benefits. The island is beginning to see the school as an agent of the state, rather than something loyal to the island and our ways. To add insult to injury, poor Mr. Ploder just couldn't cope. He didn't have the financial expertise to understand what was happening. He was unable or unwilling to articulate our concerns to the state or the teachers. Instead, he ended up fighting with both; needless to say, that didn't help the situation. In the end, we asked Mr. Ploder for his resignation and fired one particularly militant teacher. Four other teachers took his side and resigned."

"Butch, you told me what my responsibilities would be, but what else would the board expect of me?"

"We know there has to be a balance of all things," Butch said. "What we need is, not only a person smart enough to understand and articulate the issues, but someone who has got the guts and skill to manage it all."

"Yes," Mrs. Bergason said, "we need someone who understands the state and how it works, and who understands school finance. We need someone who can straighten out our whole financial situation."

Mrs. Trempson, who had been silent up to this point, finally spoke up. "I think, Mr. Gunner, what's most important is that we need somebody who understands the island; a person the community respects; someone the children can look up to for moral leadership. Do you go to church, Mr. Gunner?"

The question took Atticus by surprise. He paused for a few moments and then spoke. "Ma'am, I'm not really sure exactly what your implications are, but let me try to answer your question like this. To some degree, I am an agent of the state; that is, my license to practice my profession is granted by the state. Now that doesn't mean that I wouldn't fight for the rights and interest of the island people, but it does mean that I am sworn to uphold the Constitution of the United States. The right to practice one's religious beliefs without persecution or external infringement is one of those rights. In education, that means to uphold the separation of church and state, and that is what I will do. I consider that question an affront to my personal religious freedom."

"You mean you're not a Christian?"

"With all due respect, ma'am, that's none of your business."

"Nordien, for Christ's sake," Butch interrupted. "We're here to hire an administrator and policeman, not a reverend for your church."

"All right, Butch," she barked back, "but if you would have listened to me before, we wouldn't be in this mess!"

Mrs. Bergason calmly interceded into the conversation by continuing her inquiry about Atticus's knowledge of school finance and his philosophy of running a school.

By the time they got to the discussion of the constable's job, everyone was tired, and the topic just seemed to go flat. The responsibilities laid out by Butch prior to the interview were revisited but only superficially. That job was obviously considered insignificant in comparison to the administrator's job. The only new information presented to Atticus was that Mrs. Boomer would act as the dispatcher for him, and everyone agreed Atticus should wear a badge of some sort. Just before the close of the meeting, Atticus was asked if he would accept the position if offered.

He said he would give it serious consideration, but only after some concerns he still had were discussed and resolved to his satisfaction. Butch suggested they meet again next Tuesday evening, discuss them, and make a final decision at that time. Everyone agreed, and the meeting was adjourned.

The women left, and Atticus walked outside and stood in the parking lot while Butch turned off the lights and locked up the building. It was dark, and the air was turning cool.

"Well, what do you think?" Butch asked as he walked out of the darkness and up to Atticus.

"Mrs. Bergason seems to be a very intelligent woman and asked a lot of important questions; however, Mrs. Trempson bothers me a little; her simplistic black-and-white view of reality doesn't quite match what I see as the real world."

"Nordien's a good person—she just gets a little wrapped up in her religion once in a while," Butch commented as he opened up his car door. "All in all, I thought Greta was impressed; I know I was, and that's a majority. Now what do you say we go over to the Island Pub?

They're having a wedding dance—let's catch a brew before I take you back to your boat."

Atticus was tired and had a lot of things to mull over, but not wanting to throw a monkey wrench in Butch's plans, he agreed to tag along for just a short one.

———————

Butch pulled off onto the grass behind a long line of cars parked on the side of the road. As they left the car, the muffled sound of a band playing a polka drifted through the night air from the bar down the road. About thirty people standing outside the front entrance were drinking beer, talking loudly, and laughing. Atticus followed Butch as they made their way through the crowd and up to the door.

"Hey Mr. Gunner!" came a voice from behind.

Atticus turned to see a group of teenage boys standing in front of a car. Up on the hood of the car sat Ken. He was holding a can of beer. Raising his can, he smiled at Atticus. "What's happening?" he said with a bit of a slur.

Atticus didn't return his smile. "You better lay off that stuff, Ken, or your folks will be peeling you off the bathroom floor come tomorrow morning."

"Never happen," the boy replied. "I hear you interviewed for the job; how'd it go?"

Atticus didn't respond; instead, he simply turned and went inside. He spotted Butch at the bar and made his way through the smoky crowd.

"There you are," Butch said, looking around at Atticus. "I was just about to send the Coast Guard out after you."

"I just saw the Shernie boy outside, totally inebriated," Atticus said, climbing up on an empty bar stool.

Ignoring Atticus's comment, Butch leaned back on his stool. "I got someone here I want you to meet," he said. "Quint, this is Atticus Gunner; Atticus, this is Quint Jebson, a good friend of mine."

Recognizing Butch's friend to be the rough old duffer he had met that afternoon, Atticus smiled. "How do you do?" he said.

"Hello there, Atticus," the old man responded with a big grin. "Did you manage to avoid those gulls this afternoon?"

"What the hell, have you two met before?" Butch asked, looking back and forth at the both of them.

Atticus smiled again. "I guess you could say that."

The old man laughed.

"What'll you have?" Butch asked Atticus.

"I'll have a 7UP," Atticus replied.

Butch laughed. "How about you, Quint?"

"Sure, so long as you're buying."

Suddenly, Tom Cline stumbled up to the bar between Butch and Quint. With a shove, he knocked both men sideways off their stools; Butch fell into Atticus, and Quint caught himself but came close to knocking the woman next to him off her stool.

"Hey barkeep, gimme a beer!" Tom bellowed, paying absolutely no attention to the incident.

"You stupid son of a bitch, Cline!" Quint barked as he fought to regain his composure. "What the hell do you think you're doing?"

The big man turned his attention toward Quint and, without saying a word, took a swing at him. His fist caught Quint right square in the middle of his face, sending him over the back of his stool and sprawling across the floor. Then Tom grabbed Butch by the shoulder and arm and threw him clear across the room, plowing into about six people as he went.

The room became quiet; people stepped back out of the way.

Butch rolled over and got up on his hands and knees, shaking his head.

Atticus watched in dismay.

Butch looked up at Tom for a second and then, like an enraged bull, came up off the floor and charged head first into the big man's gut. Both men went careening down the bar past Atticus and fell to the floor. Butch rolled away and jumped to his feet. As Tom started to get up, Butch caught him with both a right and a left hook to the face. Unfazed, the big man stood up, grabbed a bar stool, and swung it. Butch tried to duck, but the stool caught him squarely in the upper arm and shoulder; it broke into pieces and sent Butch sprawling back to the floor wincing in pain.

Quint, shaking off his tumble, got up, ran back across the room, and jumped up on the big man from behind. Like an octopus, Quint wrapped his arms and legs completely around Tom. The giant staggered for a bit and then managed to peel Quint off like a tight sweater and threw him hard against a post in the center of the room. Quint fell to the floor, gasping for air. As he lay there, Tom walked over and kicked him hard in the gut. Quint curled up.

Atticus slid off his stool, picked up a broken bar stool leg from the floor, and walked over to Tom. Tom picked up a beer bottle from a table, broke off the bottom, and smiled at Atticus as he approached. "Come on, city boy," he said, taunting Atticus.

Without saying a word, Atticus swung his club, catching the big man in the wrist; the bottle went skidding across the floor. In the same motion, holding the stool leg in both hands like a firearm, Atticus swung the end of his club like the butt end of a rifle and smashed Tom in the face with all his might. The impact spun Tom around, but before he could turn to face his opponent again, Atticus swung the club a second time, this time like a baseball bat, smashing Tom across the back of his head; the impact made a loud thud. Tom went down like a rock and didn't move.

"Look out for the brothers!" Butch barked, still trying to get back on his feet.

Atticus looked up just in time to see another man coming from the dance hall, hell-bent for leather. He plowed his way through the crowd and headed straight for Atticus. The man swung wildly at Atticus. Atticus ducked under the blow and caught him hard in the right kidney with the butt end of his club. The man went to his knees, and again Atticus swung his club like a bat, hitting him across the back with another loud thud. He fell forward, face down, and smashed his head into the bar. After he hit the floor, he didn't move either.

A third man coming out of the crowd stopped dead in his tracks as Atticus took up a stance to meet his charge. "You'll pay for this, you asshole," he said without proceeding any further.

Atticus nonchalantly lowered his guard and walked over to the man. Without saying a word, he rammed the barrel end of his club hard into the man's midsection. As he doubled over, Atticus dropped his club, grabbed him by the back of his collar, and threw him forward as hard as he could; half running, half falling, the man flew across the room and crashed into the jamb of the front door. Stumbling, he made his way back to his feet and out the door. Atticus picked up his club and followed. The boys who had been watching stepped aside in order to give Atticus plenty of room to pass.

Atticus caught up with the man just as he started to open the door of his pickup. Grabbing him by the shoulder, Atticus spun the man around and jammed his club up under his chin. Lifting the man to his tiptoes, Atticus looked him straight in the eye. "What did you say?" he asked. "Did you just call me an asshole?"

"I didn't say nothing," the man mumbled through his teeth.

"Your last name Cline?"

"Yes."

"If anything like this ever happens again, and I'm around, they'll be picking all three of you up in a pine box! Do I make myself clear Mr. Cline?"

"Yes," the man mumbled.

"Get your ass back in there and gather up the rest of your sorry clan and get the hell out of here."

Atticus lowered his club. Without further comment, the man stepped sheepishly around Atticus and went back inside. Atticus tossed his club off into the ditch and followed him back inside.

Butch was just making his way to the door as Atticus came in. "I take it you sent old Billy Bob here back in to pick up his brothers," Butch said, still rubbing his shoulder.

"How's Quint?" Atticus asked, not responding directly to Butch's question.

"Oh shit, he's fine," Butch replied. "Hell, he's already saddled back up to the bar." Butch motioned over to where Quint had reseated himself. "Come on, I think you deserve a real drink now."

"Well Butch, I've had all the excitement I can handle for one day, but I will have that 7UP."

The two men went up to the bar alongside Quint. The bar noise slowly rekindled itself as though nothing had ever happened.

"Well, here we are again," Quint said, looking over at both of them. "Ya know, Butch, if this old boy can run a school as well as he can handle himself in a bar fight, you got yourself a real administrator."

"Yes, you earned yourself some respect here tonight, Atticus," Butch said. "The only problem is, the Cline boys don't take to losing very well, and at the very least, you'll be on their shit list for some time to come—oh, I doubt they'll ever confront you straight on again, but it's best you watch your back for a while. But I don't think I'm scaring you a whole lot, am I?" Butch went on with a grin.

Atticus looked down at the bar and shook his head again. "Butch, to be totally honest, I don't know what the hell I'm doing. I don't like bars, and I don't like barroom brawls."

"So what are you saying? You backing out of the meeting next Tuesday?"

Atticus paused for a moment. "No," he said. "Tomorrow I want you to call Spencer and tell him I'm coming around the island with my boat; I want docking for at least the summer. Then I'll hang around the island until Tuesday when we have our meeting; I'll ask my questions and raise my concerns. Then on Wednesday, if I can catch a ride to Green Bay with someone, I'll pick up my car. If all goes well at our meeting on Tuesday, I'll talk with some of my colleagues, my kids, the state—think things over, and let you know my decision concerning the job by no later than the following Monday. That's the best I can offer."

"I can live with that," Butch replied. "I'll call Spencer in the morning, and I'll see if I can arrange a ride to Green Bay on Wednesday, then I'll drive out to Spencer's dock tomorrow afternoon to let you know what I've worked out."

"Now take me back to my boat," Atticus said. "And Quint," Atticus continued as he stepped off the stool and looked over at the old man, "you take care."

Quint smiled. "I'll do that, young feller. And by the way, don't dilly-dally going around the island tomorrow, we're supposed to get some weather by tomorrow night."

Atticus smiled at Quint and gave him a thumbs-up as he followed Butch out the door.

CHAPTER 4

The Storm

The air hung heavy and still as the *Moonhawk* slid out of the harbor on the way to Spencer's dock. Her hull glistened bright in the morning sun as her small diesel engine chugged quietly along. Passing the horn buoy, she turned to port, heading north up the east side of Washington Island. The sloop would have to travel out into the open waters of Lake Michigan and clear around Rock Island, but it was a beautiful morning, and Atticus had plenty of time to make the trip, even if he had to motor the entire way. It would have been easier to go up the west side, but he wanted to see Bondin's Rock again from a different perspective, and also the rocky shoal that ran from the north end of Washington Island out to Rock Island; it was supposed to be a beautiful sight on a bright sunny day.

Atticus sat back, stretching his arms out on the cockpit coaming and steering with his foot on the tiller. The bleached sand along the outer shore of Detroit Island looked warm and inviting against the dark green curtain of cedar trees and the crystal clear water. A small boy stood on the beach, skipping rocks across the smooth water. He waved as Atticus went by; Atticus waved back.

In less than a half hour, Atticus was startled to hear a break in the rhythmic drone of the engine. Reaching over the tiller, he opened and closed the throttle a couple of times, but the engine just sputtered and died. He pressed the starter button; nothing. Something was wrong; he noticed the boat was setting lower than normal in the water. Atticus got up and hurried over to the open hatch. When he looked below, he felt a sudden sense of panic; there was knee-deep water in the boat. He stepped quickly down the ladder. *The bilge pump—why didn't it kick in?* he thought. Splashing over to the main switch panel, he flicked the master switch back and forth a couple of times; nothing. He threw the override switch for the bilge pump back and forth; again nothing. Everything was dead including the radio.

With his mind racing in confusion, he looked around. "Where am I taking on water?" he said out loud. "I haven't hit anything, so how can I be taking on water? It's got to be through a hull fitting or the drive shaft. Maybe it's a hull fitting, one that's below the water line; the electronic speed indicator."

Quickly he made his way back to the companionway ladder. Looking down under the cockpit liner, between the bunk and the engine compartment bulkhead, he could see water boiling up. Kneeling down in the cold water, he reached out with his arm, being careful to keep his chin above water. The fitting was too far back for him to reach. Sitting back on his heels, he took a couple of deep breaths and then plunged head first into the water. It was cold and dark as he felt his way along the inner surface of the hull. There it was; he felt the two-inch pipe fitting with water rushing in through it. Feeling around, he tried to find the electric cable with the attached mechanism. He found it, but the seal and the snubber nut were gone. Frantically, he felt around, trying to find them; nothing. Unable to hold his breath any longer, he pushed himself back out from under the water.

Taking another couple of deep breaths, he tried to calm down. Then he thought of the brass screw-on cap that came with the hull fitting; where had they put it? Atticus stood up and waded over to the sink. Opening the bottom door, he reached down into the water-filled cabinet and pulled out the canvas bag where all the odds and ends that came with the boat had been put. Quickly, he dumped its contents into the sink and started rummaging through it. His fingers trembled. The water had now risen almost to his thighs. He knew that in a few minutes, it would be too late. There it was; he spotted it lying amongst a couple of swivel pulleys.

Atticus grabbed it and made his way back to the companionway ladder. He took another deep breath and plunged down under the water again. He made it back to the open fitting and pressed the brass cap down over the open hole with both hands and started screwing it clockwise. His hand slipped; the water pressure blew the cap off, forcing him to drop it. He could hear it clunk against the hull as it slid down toward the bilge. Frantically, he groped in the liquid darkness to find it. After what seemed an eternity, his fingers touched it. With his lungs ready to explode, he pressed the cap down over the hole again. This time it caught and screwed smoothly. He tightened it down until it sealed, and then pushed himself back out. By the time he reached the surface, his lungs were clawing for air.

Atticus staggered back to his feet and crawled up the companionway ladder into the cockpit. Dripping wet, he threw open the starboard seat locker and reached in for the hand-operated bilge pump. Climbing back into the water, he placed the base of the pump on the bottom rung of the ladder, directed the hose up into the cockpit, and began to work the pump handle. The water belched from the hose and streamed out the scuppers at the back of the boat. Now for the long, laborious job of pumping the boat dry, but at least he was still afloat.

————•◦•————

Atticus looked over at the ship's clock. It was 6:45. His arms and back were aching, and he had a nasty blister that had rubbed raw at the base of his right thumb. Flexing his shoulders, he tried to work out the kinks. He looked around the cabin; everything was a mess; the bunk cushions, his sleeping bag, his clothes, even his pillow was sopping wet. But the water was less than ankle deep now. In another twenty to thirty minutes of pumping, the boat would be completely drained.

Totally exhausted, he climbed up the companionway ladder and out into the cockpit. He sat down and leaned back slowly, easing himself against the cockpit coaming; it felt good to sit down. Atticus looked around; he'd been drifting for over seven hours now. Off the port beam about three-fourths of a mile was Bondin's Rock, casting a long, dark shadow across the water from the late afternoon sun. To the north lay Rock Island, and still further to the north, Atticus could see the distant outline of two more islands. To the southwest, dark billowing clouds had begun piling up on the horizon.

Resting his head against one of the stern rails, he closed his eyes. Still obsessed with the near disaster, he tried to sort things out. Not only would he have to take everything out of the boat in order to dry, but he would have to do considerable work on the engine and electrical components before they would work again. Exhausted, and too drained of energy to be angry, the only emotion he could muster was relief; at least the worst was over.

Atticus lay there for a few minutes with his eyes closed. It was only after the cry from a gull winging overhead that he opened his eyes again. He raised his head and looked back again at the cloud-covered horizon. It was then it dawned on him that his troubles were anything but over. He sat up and looked back at the island. Even though he was only about three-quarters of a mile out, he knew that in a storm, Bondin's Rock would not be a welcomed sight. The nearest safety now was Jackson Harbor, but with the engine out of commission and no wind, he had absolutely no way to get there.

The more Atticus thought about his situation, the more daunting the prospect became. It would be dark in three hours; what would he do then? To try and sail into any harbor in total darkness, especially without power, would be suicide. To turn the boat and try running with the storm would be just as bad; he wouldn't be able to see twenty feet beyond the bow, and with all those islands out there, surely he'd end up on the rocky shores of one of them.

Maybe I should drop anchor, he thought as he headed below to check the water depth on one of the charts. Stepping off the last rung of the companionway ladder, he splashed his way over to the chart rack. Then remembering it was still up in the cockpit, he ran up to get it. He brought it back down and opened it on the galley table. After studying it for a few seconds, he shook his head in disappointment. "What a stupid idea," he said out loud, "I'm in at least a hundred and fifty feet of water."

Still standing at the galley table, staring out the cabin window, Atticus knew the only possible alternative was the one he dreaded the most. Lake Michigan was a bad place to be in a storm, especially in a thirty-two-foot boat, but he had no choice now but to sail the *Moonhawk* into the storm in a blind attempt to hold his own until the storm passed and daylight returned. He tried thinking of every angle possible; he even considered the possibility of swimming to shore, retrieving someone with a boat, and towing the *Moonhawk* in, but he soon gave up on that idea as another stupid thought.

"I'd better start getting things organized while I've still got time," he commented to himself. "The first thing I have to do is get the rest of this damned water out of the boat."

Sloshing his way back over to the bilge pump, he bent down and began to pump again. Once more the water began to belch from the hose. Atticus thought about the coming storm as he worked. The whole idea gave him an anxious feeling deep in the pit of his stomach. It wasn't as though he had never sailed through a storm before; he had—twice, as a matter of fact. Both times were on the ocean, and one of the storms was no doubt worse than anything he would experience tonight. But that was different; in both cases, he had been a crewman on board a considerably larger boat. In both cases, the captains were experienced and sea-hardened; they knew what to do. In both cases, there was a competent crew to handle the sails and take turns at the helm.

Atticus changed hands on the pump in order to give his left arm a rest. The handle dug into the raw blister on his right hand, but he knew he had to keep going; he gritted his teeth and continued. He thought about the island, the job, and the experiences he'd had, but somehow all that seemed very distant now. He remembered the picture of the great storm of 1913 at the restaurant. Then he thought of an article he once read in one of his sailing magazines about heavy weather sailing on the Great Lakes. The author wrote about how the treachery of the Great Lakes should never be underestimated, and although the waves seldom reach a height of over thirty feet, they are generally extremely steep and close together, making them a real threat to the most experienced yachtsman and the sturdiest of boats. "Christ, this is insane," Atticus said to himself as he stopped to switch hands again. "You'd think I was facing a hurricane instead of a thunderstorm."

The minutes passed like hours, but in spite of his aching muscles and sore hands, the last of the water was finally pumped out of the boat. Taking the pump, Atticus made his way forward, stepping over the wet cushions and sleeping bag that lay in the companionway. He threw the pump into one of the forward storage lockers and then stepped into the head. He opened the medicine cabinet and withdrew the first aid kit. Trying hard not to aggravate his raw hands any more than necessary, he managed to smear first aid cream on the worst of his wounds and cover them with Band-Aids.

After checking the forward hatch to make sure it was closed and secure, he grabbed a set of foul-weather gear from the hanging locker and went up on deck. Throwing the gear in the seat next to the tiller, he looked off to the southwest again. Long rays of sunlight streamed up into the heavens from behind the boiling cloud wall that stretched clear across the horizon. Although the storm was still too far away to hear the thunder, flashes of lightning were clearly visible. The smooth surface of the water still reflected what was left of the blue sky, but as his eyes scanned off into the distance toward the storm, its reflection turned cold and gray. Bondin's Rock still stood off the port side, but its brightness was also gone; instead, it looked barren and cold.

Atticus turned his attention back to the boat. Deciding he would use only the main sail reefed down, he removed the sail cover. He then cranked up the sail until the first reefing points were parallel to the boom. The sail hung limp in the still air. Carefully, he lapped the excess sail back and forth over the boom, tying each reefing point securely around the boom. He then climbed back up onto the cabin roof and finished cranking the sail up until it was taut. This sail arrangement greatly reduced sail exposure to the wind. Atticus reasoned that such an arrangement should give him enough forward momentum to allow him to negotiate the waves and maintain steerage, but not so much that he would lose control and be knocked down. Finally, he released the main sheet block so the sail could temporarily swing free. Taking a deep breath, he stood quietly in the cockpit and visually checked everything to make sure all was ready.

Satisfied with his preparations thus far, he went below, grabbed a life jacket, flashlight, matches, his safety harness, and the anchor light. Placing everything on the helm seat next to his rain gear, he went forward to the bow. After making sure the bow light had plenty of kerosene, he lit it and snapped the jib halyard to the top of the light and the jib sheet to the base. Back at the mast, he raised the lamp up the forestay until it was about three-quarters of the way to the top. In the cockpit, using the jib sheet as a downhaul, he pulled both ends tight and secured them so the lamp could not swing free.

Atticus knew Spencer and Butch would be wondering where he was by now; maybe they'd find Quint and come looking for him, but he also knew this was just wishful thinking; his success or failure now was between him and the elements.

Realizing he hadn't eaten anything since this morning, and not wanting to face the night on an empty stomach, Atticus decided to go below and rummage up some food. Once below, he found that most everything had been ruined by the water, but he managed to find a can of beans and some dry coffee. In spite of the complete disarray and cold dampness below deck, the aroma of brewing coffee soon filled the cabin with warmth.

Atticus sat down at the galley table and ate in complete silence. When he finished, he put his dishes in the sink, poured himself the last of the coffee, and put the empty pot in the sink with the dishes. Taking his coffee, he went back up on deck, closing and securing the cabin door behind him. He sat down and cradled the warm cup in both hands. The evening air was damp, and the thought of spending the entire night cold and wet was most definitely not an enticing one.

After taking a long sip of hot coffee, Atticus put the cup down on the seat next to him. He reached over and grabbed the bottom half of his foul weather suit and slipped it on over his pants. He stood up and snapped the suspenders. Next he slipped into the heavy yellow raincoat, and finally put on his life jacket.

Stepping back by the tiller, he stuffed the flashlight down between the seat cushion and the cockpit coaming, where he would be able to find it if needed. Finally, he laid the safety harness and rain hat on the seat next to him. Satisfied he had done everything he could to make ready for the storm, he leaned back to wait.

Saturated with sleep, Atticus opened his eyes. He could feel the soft movement of the boat and hear the creaking of the boom as it swung gently back and forth. It seemed as though he'd only been asleep for a few minutes, but the fact that it was dark did register as he began drifting off again. About two miles away, a bolt of lightning flashed and burned a jagged trail down from the heavy clouds above. Atticus opened his eyes again only to be greeted by the boom of thunder as it rumbled across the heavens. Startled, he sat up and looked around. The *Moonhawk* took on a ghostly whiteness with each flash of lightning.

The constant rumble of thunder seemed to be coming from everywhere now. Ready or not, this was it; his wait for the storm was about to come to an end.

With sore, trembling fingers, he snapped on his safety harness and attached its umbilical cord to one of the stern rail stanchions. It was only after he readied himself completely with the main sheet in one hand and the tiller in the other that he managed to slow his anxiety down enough to look around. A gentle swell was running out of the southwest, rocking the boat ever so smoothly, but there was still no movement of air. He could see Bondin's Rock with each flash of lightning, but instead of lying three-quarters of a mile off, she was now only about five hundred yards away, and off the port bow. To the right, at a distance of three miles, he could make out the low cliffs of Rock Island. Atticus knew that when the wind did come, he would have to bring the *Moonhawk* around quickly or he'd be driven into Bondin's Rock in a very short time.

The minutes ticked by slowly as he watched the storm close in. Then without warning, the tattletales tied to the mast stays began to flutter. The sail swung to the right and tightened, and the boat began to move as a light breeze freshened out of the southwest. Atticus swung the tiller to the left and turned the boat away from Bondin's Rock and headed to the east. As the *Moonhawk* crossed the breeze in its turn and picked up the breeze from the opposite side, the boom swung back across the stern. Although it was reassuring to have steerage again, it did little to relieve his mounting anxiety. Releasing the sail as much as he could, Atticus allowed the boat to fall off the wind and head in a more northeasterly direction.

Then just as silently as the breeze had come, it disappeared. The sail went slack and the boat slowed to a gentle drift. Atticus watched and listened in silence; all he could hear was the rumble of thunder and the creek of the boom as it swung in unison with the gentle roll of the boat. Then, very faint at first, but growing in intensity, a new sound came out of the night. It was hard to determine what it was at first, but then Atticus remembered racing in the Bermuda Cup off the coast of Florida; it was the growing sound of a heavy wind plowing its way across the open water.

Atticus yanked the rope loose from the cam cleat, releasing the tension on the main sheet. A flash of lightning lit the night just in time for him to see a careening wall of rain racing across the water toward him. Grabbing the tiller tight, he braced himself. Coming from just off the starboard beam, a wall of wind and rain hit the *Moonhawk* like a freight train. The initial shock lifted the sloop's stern slightly, driving her bow down. Lying on her port side, the *Moonhawk* turned to the right, exposing her broadside to the raging gale. Frantically, Atticus released the sail to keep from broaching. The boat heeled hard to port, burying her lee rail deep in the water. The end of the boom slapped down into the water as it swung hard out over the left side of the boat. Thinking for sure that this was it, Atticus grabbed for a stanchion and held tight, but instead of going all the way over, the boat paused; coming back to a twenty-degree list, she stiffened and held her own against the wind.

Regaining control of the helm, Atticus slid down into the cockpit in order to protect himself from the sting of the driving rain. Lightning flashed, striking the water so close that the crack of thunder practically broke his eardrums. Throwing his arm over the tiller and tucking it into his armpit, he started pulling in the main sheet with both hands. As the boom moved in, the sail bit into the wind. The boat heeled hard, but with a solid stance, it started moving forward across the wind. Visibility was almost zero. Even in the intense brightness of the flashing lightning, Atticus could barely see beyond the bow. Unable to look up for more than brief moments at a time, he had to navigate by the feel on the tiller and the heel of the boat. By turning his back toward the storm and putting his legs up on the downwind seat to brace himself, Atticus managed to get himself into a position that was at least tolerable. Tugging the main sheet down into its cam cleat, he locked the sail into position. Holding the tiller steady with his right hand, he reached over and retrieved his flashlight. Shining it on the compass, he managed to get a fix on his direction. Satisfied he was heading diagonally away from Rock Island and Bondin's Rock, his confidence began to improve.

———•◆•———

It was after one o'clock when Atticus decided it was time to bring the boat about and make his first tack back toward the southwest. Although the wind seemed to have eased up considerably and the worst of the storm had moved off to the northeast, there was still an occasional flash of lightning and rumble of thunder. His misery now was confined to the steady downpour of rain and the cold spray that came whipping up over the cabin roof at regular intervals.

Pulling himself back up into the cockpit seat, Atticus began to watch for the right moment. The seven-foot seas were steep and close together, and every once in a while, he would encounter a wave considerably higher than the rest. He wanted to make sure he didn't get hit by one of those in the middle of negotiating a turn. He didn't have to wait long before a strong fifteen-footer came rolling up out of the darkness. Holding his course steady, the *Moonhawk* took the wave off the starboard bow. Throwing spray back over the windward side of the cabin as the bow sliced through the crest, the sloop raised her stern and slid down the backside into the trough on her way up the next wave.

Atticus decided he would make his move in two more waves. The boat negotiated the second wave and dropped down again on her way to the third. As the next wave rose up, Atticus swung the tiller to the left, turning the boat into the wind. The *Moonhawk* took the wave head on, throwing spray out to both sides as she burst on through. With her nose in the air, she climbed up over the wave and then fell off as the crest swept beneath her hull. With the sail slack and the boat's forward momentum all but gone, the next wave rose up as though it had come out of nowhere. It was a rogue, far bigger than the rest. Unable to raise her bow fast enough, the sloop drove deep into the crest, sending a deluge of green water back over the entire boat. Careening up over the top of the cabin, the icy cold wall of water swept Atticus off his feet, crashing him hard against the stern rail. The wave then passed on and disappeared into the empty darkness from which it had come.

Stunned and totally drenched, it took a second for Atticus to reseat himself and get his bearings. When he finally did, he was amazed to see that the boat had finished her turn and was just beginning to run to the southwest. After readjusting the sail with trembling hands, he sat motionless, watching the last of the water drain from the scuppers. The endless procession of waves continued, each giving a loud hiss as they rolled beneath the hull and off into the darkness. Looking down at his safety line, Atticus yanked it to make sure it was still secure. A cold shiver went down his spine as he thought about how close he had just come to being swept overboard.

———— ◆◦◆ ————

As the night bore on, specifics began to fade. By the first hint of dawn, all Atticus could remember was that this was his third tack and he was once more headed in a northeasterly direction. The waves had dropped to three-foot swells, but the air was cold and heavy. The wind was light and only moved the sloop along at two knots. Pillars of fog moved relentlessly across the water. Sleep had all but overcome Atticus, and occasionally he would catch himself dozing. Even the drizzling rain that fell constantly seemed to be of little significance. With cold, sore hands and shriveled fingers from long exposure to the rain and wet, Atticus tucked them deep into the pockets of his raincoat in an attempt to ward off the numbness. The night's exposure had long since penetrated his rain gear; the cold now seemed to chill him clear to the bone. Steering with his leg, he huddled at the helm, shoulders forward and head down.

The sloop's bow rose and fell gently as it walked its way through the slow-moving swells. Like moving clouds, the fog would drift in, engulfing the boat, then as silently as it came, it would drift off until the next patch closed in.

Atticus decided the only way he would be able to stay awake was to get up and move around. He knew that leaving the helm of a moving boat in the fog was not smart, but if he didn't do something soon, it wouldn't much matter. Rigging a rope to the tiller, he tied it off securely amidship. His arrangement was totally inadequate as a self-steering mechanism, but for now it would have to suffice. Besides, it really wouldn't much matter if the boat drifted off course; he didn't have the slightest idea where he was anyway.

Stretching the kinks from his back, he took off his safety harness and threw it down on the seat next to the tiller. He picked up his water-filled coffee mug from the corner of the cockpit, emptied it, and then opened the storm gate and went below, closing it behind him.

The air below was damp and brackish. Stepping carefully over the wet items still strewn about on the floor, he made his way back to the galley and lit the lantern. Next he pulled the pot out of the sink, cleaned it out, and filled it with fresh water and coffee. He lit the stove, placed the pot over the burner, and then went over and plopped himself down at the galley table. After taking his rain cap off and throwing it on the table in front of him, he leaned his head back against the bulkhead and closed his eyes. Except for the soft swish of the water against the outer hull and the squeak of the stove as it swung back and forth on its gimbals, all was quiet. A gentle rain pattered softly on the cabin roof. Soon the air was filled once again with the sweet aroma of brewing coffee.

Pouring himself a cup, Atticus sat back down and sipped it in silence. Looking out the cabin window, he wondered what full daylight would bring. If the fog and rain continued, making port would still be a difficult task; just finding Washington Island in the fog would be a real challenge. In spite of his dilemma, Atticus was beginning to feel much better about everything. This whole ordeal had been a real challenge for both him and the *Moonhawk*, but considering everything, they had survived. What bothered him most right now was wondering what his new friends on Washington Island were thinking. By now they would know he was missing. The Coast Guard had undoubtedly been notified.

After finishing his coffee, Atticus put the cup in the sink. Making sure the stove was off, he grabbed his rain hat and went back up on deck. Sitting down at the helm again, he looked around. It was considerably lighter now, but the fog was still thick. It wasn't raining, so he reached down under the cockpit cushion and pulled out his navigation chart. After carefully reconstructing the various courses he had taken throughout the night, he estimated his position to be ten or fifteen miles northeast of Washington Island. He wasn't sure what to do; for all he knew, those calculations might be extremely inaccurate. Nonetheless, he was going to have to make a decision soon. If he was anywhere near right, it would take at least three hours to get within shooting distance of the island. By then he felt sure the fog would be dissipating. Then, of course, there was always the chance that he was much closer to the island than he had calculated, or that he might even miss the island completely.

Atticus brought the boat about. The dense fog surrounding the boat drifted slowly off, like a gray cloud hanging low over the water. As it drifted off, visibility opened up. Looking around, it was as though he were sailing in a large open room with gray pillared walls and a misty white ceiling, but there was no land in sight.

It was 9:30 the next time Atticus looked at his watch. Once again, the chill of the damp air began to make him shiver. It was raining lightly again, but the heavy fog was beginning to dissipate. With visibility at about a mile, Atticus would look up from time to time, scanning the empty horizon for some hint of landfall. Seeing nothing, he would lower his head again in order to keep the rain from running down his face.

Then, sensing a presence, he looked up. Wiping the water from his face, he searched the misty horizon. "It's a boat!" he said out loud, reaffirming his discovery. "A fish boat—and it's headed my way!"

Totally elated, he jumped up to get a better look. Sure enough, he could see her black-and-white bow cutting through the water and the black diesel smoke belching from her stack. "I never thought an old fishing tub could look so good," he said with a smile as he watched her close in.

When the boat came within fifty yards, she swung in a wide circle until she was running the same direction as the *Moonhawk*. The engine throttled down as she moved in to about thirty feet off the *Moonhawk's* starboard beam.

Looking over at her, Atticus could see a young man's smiling face as he stood just inside the open portside gate. As the boat moved a little closer, the wheelhouse door opened and an old man stuck his head out. "Gunner, just what in the hell do you think you're doing?" he hollered.

Recognizing Quint, Atticus smiled shouting back, "What does it look like I'm doing?"

"Do you realize that every frickin' boat for a hundred miles around is out looking for you? Christ, they've even got the Coast Guard out!"

"I couldn't help it; I couldn't get in last night!"

"What do you mean, you couldn't get in?"

"I sprung a leak and flooded out my engine!"

"You sprung a leak? What in the hell were you doing out in the storm anyway?"

"Not during the storm, yesterday morning!"

Drifting away a little bit, Quint rolled the wheel and brought the boat back in close again. "You mean you've been dead in the water since yesterday morning?"

Atticus nodded.

"Why didn't you call for help?"

"My radio was dead too!"

Quint just shook his head.

"How did you find me?" Atticus shouted.

"A ship spotted you on their radar early this morning! Since then a Coast Guard cutter and I have been looking for you; we were just lucky, or unlucky, depending how you look at it!"

Atticus smiled. "Where are we anyhow?"

"You're about nine miles northeast of Rock Island! Another two hours north and you would have run smack-dab into the Boils! That would have been a real trip for you!"

Atticus didn't know what the Boils were, but from the tone of Quint's voice, he figured it was probably not a good place to be. "I'm glad you came along when you did then!" he replied.

Quint gave a big spit of tobacco juice out over the side of his boat and smiled once more. "Drop that crippled wing you got stickin' up in the air there," he hollered, "and we'll hook a line to ya!"

Atticus climbed up on the cabin roof and dropped the sail. By the time he finished securing the boom, Quint had maneuvered his boat to within twenty feet off the sloop's bow. With the stern gate open, Quint's young helper was standing at the transom, ready to throw Atticus a rope. Atticus leaned out over the bow pulpit and made ready to catch it. The boy cast the line toward Atticus, but it fell short and landed in the water. As the boy coiled it back for another try, Atticus glanced up and saw Quint looking back at them out of the rear window of the wheelhouse. He smiled to himself, knowing Quint was probably swearing at their incompetence. The boy flung the rope again, and this time Atticus caught it. Bringing it down under the bow rail, he looped it over both of the bow cleats and secured it. He then cupped his hands around his mouth and shouted, "I'm ready on this end! Tell Quint to take it easy; I don't want to pull the bow cleats off my boat!"

The boy nodded.

Atticus heard the clutch in Quint's boat engage and hurried back to the cockpit as fast as he could. He'd no more than reached the helm when the rope tightened and the sloop started moving forward. With his foot resting on top of the tiller, he leaned back and stretched his arms out on the cockpit coaming. He was still wet and cold, tired, and extremely hungry. He didn't know how or where he would manage to dry things out, or where he would even sleep, but for now he didn't care; his ordeal was over.

It was just past noon, still cloudy with a haze hanging in the air, when the two boats crawled into Jackson Harbor. Spencer was standing on his dock when they arrived. Quint's helper untied the tow line and threw his end over to Spencer. Quint backed away from the dock. "I'll see you in a few minutes!" he hollered as he slid past the *Moonhawk*.

Spencer pulled the bow of the *Moonhawk* in and tied it off. Atticus went below to retrieve his fenders and mooring lines. When he returned, he secured one of the mooring lines to the stern cleat and threw the other end to Spencer.

"Well, young fella, I was afraid we might not see you again after last night," Spencer said, looking up at Atticus as he pulled the stern in.

Atticus was tying off the fenders and looked up. "That thought crossed my mind once or twice too."

"It must have gotten pretty rough out there."

"Yes, it got real nasty for a while."

"That it did." Spencer grunted as he bent down to tie off a line. "Blew down about fifteen trees and knocked out power for half the island. Even blew down Fingerson's old barn over on Townline Road."

"Well then, being a lineman, I don't imagine Butch had a very good night either," Atticus said as he took off his rain gear and threw it into the cockpit.

Finally, Atticus stepped off the boat onto the wet dock. "Well, Spence," he said, holding out his hand, "I'm a little late, but I want to thank you for letting me dock here."

Spencer finished shaking Atticus's hand just as Quint and his young friend came walking around the corner of Spencer's barn. "Well, Gunner, what's it like being back on dry land?" Quint blurted out as he and the boy came walking out on the dock toward them.

"Very good," Atticus replied.

"Oh, by the way," Quint went on, putting his rough hand on Atticus's shoulder and looking over at his young companion, "this is Bill Sorenson, my helper. Bill, this is Atticus Gunner, your new schoolmaster."

"How do you do?" the boy replied. "I saw you the other night at the dance. I don't think anyone is going to give you much static at school."

"Well, let's not jump to conclusions," Atticus said. "I'm not the new administrator or island cop yet. I do want to thank you for your help this morning though."

"You gonna let him dock here, Spence?" Quint asked.

"As long as he wants," Spencer replied.

"Shit, I don't know, he might let the damn thing sink and plug up your channel."

Spencer and the boy laughed. Too tired to smile, Atticus just shook his head.

"I'll say one thing," Quint went on, "you sure as hell have had your share of events for the short amount of time you've been here."

"That, my friend, is the understatement of the year," Atticus said as he sat down on one of the pilings.

"I suppose every God damned thing down there is soaking wet," Quint remarked, looking into one of the cabin windows.

"That's right," Atticus replied, "including the engine."

"Well, Butch can fix that. I suppose all your clothes are wet too."
Atticus nodded.

"You need some shut-eye," Quint said, looking back at Atticus again. "Come on, I'll take you over to my place."

"Your place?"

"That's right, my place!" he said as he started to walk down the dock toward the barn, with Bill tight on his heels. "You got something against that?"

Without any kind of a comeback, Atticus got up and followed. "Spencer?" he said, stopping momentarily. "Thanks for everything. I'll get things straight with you tomorrow."

"Don't worry about a thing," Spencer replied. "Your boat will be safe here, and we'll have plenty of time to make arrangements."

Atticus smiled, and then without another word, he turned to follow Quint.

Once up on the small porch, Quint kicked off his boots and opened the door. "Take off your shoes, boys," he remarked, stepping inside. "I don't like cleaning more than I have to."

Atticus peeled off his wet tennis shoes and stepped inside. Following Quint and Bill, he walked across the small kitchen and into the living room. There was a big stone fireplace across one end of the room, two high-back easy chairs, and a big leather couch. A grandfather clock stood in the corner. Atticus was surprised; he hadn't pictured Quint's abode to be quite so domestic.

"I'll get you some dry clothes," Quint said as he walked down the hall just off the living room. When he returned, he was carrying a pair of bib overalls and an old sweatshirt. "These may not be your style," he said, throwing them over to Atticus, "but they're clean and dry."

"Thanks," Atticus replied as he caught them. "I could use a shower too, if that's possible."

"Help yourself. There's towels and stuff in the cabinet. Bill and I are going out to lift our nets. I'll be back sometime this afternoon." With that, Quint turned and was on his way to the door.

"See you later, Mr. Gunner," Bill said, following Quint.

"Oh!" Quint barked, stopping just short of the kitchen door. "Help yourself to whatever you need. There's food in the icebox and two bedrooms upstairs; take your pick."

The kitchen door slammed shut. In a few seconds, Atticus heard the truck start up and pull away.

When Atticus finished his shower, he got dressed and went back out into the living room. Too tired to even think about food, he went straight upstairs. He walked into the first room on his left. The outer wall was gabled with big double windows. White lacy curtains hung on the window, and a brass bed, neatly made, stood in the middle of the room. Atticus walked over to the windows and opened them wide. He went back over to the bed and flopped down; it felt good to lie down and stretch out. Closing his eyes, he listened to the raindrops fall from the eaves. Within seconds, he drifted off into a deep sleep.

CHAPTER 5

Pretty Woman

The *Moonhawk* sat quietly at dockside with her hatches wide open. Her entire deck was covered with items laid out to dry. Climbing on board, Butch stepped over a garbage bag half full of wet groceries. With both hands straddling the open hatch, he stuck his head inside. "Anybody home?" he asked.

Atticus, who was buried halfway inside one of the cabinets under the sink, backed out. "Good morning," he said, looking up at Butch.

Spencer, carrying a wet cardboard box, came out of the forward cabin. He stepped over Atticus and handed the box up to Butch. "Here," he said, "make yourself useful."

Butch took the box and set it down on one of the cockpit seats. "How you guys doing?" he said, coming back to the companionway.

"Pretty good, thanks to Spence here," Atticus grunted as he stood up. "We're darn near done with everything except the engine compartment." Butch climbed down into the boat. "Well, how have you been?" Atticus continued with a smile. "I haven't seen you since Saturday night."

"To be honest, I've been busier than the devil since that storm," Butch replied.

"Did you and Troy get everything straightened away?" Spencer asked, leaning back on the edge of the galley table.

"Yes we did; we finished last night."

"That makes for a short weekend," Atticus replied.

Butch shrugged. "Well, at least I've got a couple of days off now, but from what I hear, you went from the frying pan into the fire Sunday night."

"I guess you could say that," Atticus said, dropping back down to his knees. "The worst part will be getting the electronics and engine back up and running."

"Well," Spencer said, cocking his hat back on his head, "Butch here is the man for that; he's the best marine mechanic on the island."

"I knew there was a reason I shouldn't have come down here," Butch replied with a grin. "I'll go get my tools out of the car."

When Butch returned, Atticus and Spencer were wiping out the inside of two more lockers. "I understand you stayed at Quint's place last night," Butch said as he put his toolbox on the table.

"Yes, he even gave me these clothes to wear."

"I was going to ask who your tailor was."

"Very funny!"

"Where's Quint today?" Butch went on.

"He's out fishing; said he'd be back by noon."

"Did he lose any nets in the storm?"

"Yes, last night at supper he said he lost two sets."

"I bet he was fuming and swearing over that."

"He wasn't too happy about it, that's for sure." Atticus sat back on his heels, ringing the water out of his rag into a pail. "You know—that Quint is something else. In spite of working all day, and being absolutely irate over losing those nets, he still insisted on making a huge supper. He prepared a feast that would put my grandmother to shame."

"Yeah, well, that's Quint," Butch replied. "He swears like a trooper but he'd give you the shirt off his back."

"Tell me something," Atticus continued. "Quint's got three bedrooms in that house of his, and he keeps all three made up perfect, all the time. How come? He lives there all by himself, doesn't he?"

"Yes, he lives alone," Butch said as he loosened the bulkhead cover on the engine compartment." Then he paused. "Spence, why don't you tell Atticus about Quint; you've known him a whole lot longer than I have."

"That I have, just about my whole life I guess; what do you want to know?"

"Start with the bedrooms," Butch replied.

Spencer grunted as he got up off his knees. "It might surprise you, but Quint used to have a wife and two daughters. All three were lost at sea about twenty years ago."

Atticus looked up at Spencer. "Lost?"

"Yep, it was a cold November day when Perry Dillin set out for Sturgeon Bay. Perry and his missus were going down to pick up a new stove. Quint's wife and his two daughters went along for the two-day outing. Quint was supposed to go with, but he'd been sick with the grippe, so he stayed home in bed. The missus wasn't going to go, but Quint insisted. His two girls had never been off the island, and a chance to go to Sturgeon Bay just didn't come along that often in those days. So she and the girls went." Spencer paused for a moment and then went on. "They made it to Sturgeon Bay. Spent the night in the big hotel, and then the next morning they loaded up Perry's new stove and headed for home. That's the last anybody ever saw of them."

"Was there a storm?" Atticus asked, still looking at Spencer.

"Yes, they had a real blow that day!"

"What happened?"

Spencer shrugged and said, "Nobody knows."

"My God," Atticus said softly. "How old were they? The daughters, I mean."

"Seven and eight—since then, Quint has kept those bedrooms made up as though they were coming back any day now."

"Does he ever talk about it?" Atticus asked.

"Nope, he's never said a word to anybody from the moment they came up missing to this very day, and if you say anything to him about it, he'll either change the subject or walk away."

Atticus shook his head, and then he opened the next cupboard and started to wipe it out. Spencer went back to work in his locker, and Butch finished taking the cover off the engine compartment. No one made any further comment.

"Gunner, where did you lose that fitting?" Butch asked, breaking the silence.

"It's around in back of the engine compartment."

"I've got to take a look at that," he said as he crawled down under the portside quarter berth to find it. "I can't imagine what the hell would make a connector fail, unless someone did a piss-poor job of putting it in."

Atticus finished the last floor locker on his side of the boat. As he rung the water from his rag, he glanced over and saw Butch kneeling in front of the engine compartment looking at something in his hand. "What did you find?" he asked.

Butch didn't reply.

"What did you find?" Atticus asked again.

Without saying a word, Butch tossed the object in his hand over to Atticus. Catching it, Atticus looked it over carefully. "This is part of the snubber nut from the speed indicator; it looks like it's been cut in half with a pincher or something."

"That's right," Butch said "and I bet your automatic bilge pump didn't work either."

"No, it didn't—why?"

"Because the wires have been cut."

Atticus looked back down at the object in his hand and then back at Butch. "You mean someone tried to sink my boat intentionally?"

Spence backed out of his locker and looked at Butch. "The Cline boys," he said. "They're certainly dumb enough, and there's no doubt they've got it in for Atticus after Saturday night."

"I don't think so," Atticus said after thinking for a moment. "This took somebody with brains and a plan; the Cline boys don't strike me as having much of either. They would have had to make some very quick decisions, and take fast action, to have done this before we arrived at the boat after the bar incident. No, I don't think this was done by the Cline boys."

"Well then, there must be someone else out there who really doesn't like you," Butch said softly.

"Yes," Atticus replied, "and I think I've got an idea who."

"What are you saying?" Butch asked.

"I'm not sure what I'm saying, but this boat was completely checked out before it was put in the water by the Green Bay Yacht Club. And since then, the one and only time the boat has been left unattended was while it was at the ferry dock."

"Then that points right back at the Cline boys," Spencer interjected.

"No," Atticus said. "I think it points to an incident I had before I arrived on the island—some drunks trying to board my boat one night down by Egg Harbor last week. The next day, they tried to run me down and took a couple shots at the boat near Horseshoe Island; they had a big gray trawler. Butch, that's why I asked you if you knew the name of that trawler you worked on for that gang over on Bondin's Rock."

"You must have really pissed them off," Butch replied.

"I beat one of them up and pushed him overboard."

Butch chuckled, shaking his head. "You seem to have a real skill for making friends."

"It must be my magnetic personality," Atticus replied as he picked up his pail and went up on deck to dump it.

When Butch and Atticus walked into the school Tuesday night, the other two board members were already there. With few formalities and even less conversation, they were soon seated around the meeting table once again. This time there was no sign of Mrs. Boomer. Butch tapped the gavel on the table and called the meeting to order. "Mr. Gunner," he said, "you said you had some concerns that needed to be addressed before we could conclude the issue of the administrative position. So why don't you proceed, and we'll address them as we go."

"Okay," Atticus replied, "I'll try to take them in logical order—the first question, of course, pertains to salary."

"We'll match the contract you've been offered in Madison in every regard," Butch replied, with Mrs. Bergason nodding her approval.

"With the understanding that the offer will include the responsibilities of both the school administrator and the constable position."

"And the length of the contract?"

"Two years."

"There are a number of teachers to be hired before next school year; who will hire them?"

"You do the hiring."

"The budget?"

"You do that in conjunction with the board."

Atticus paused for a few moments and then shifted his position slightly. "Okay," he said, "I apologize if this sounds a bit blunt, but I guess that's the way it has to be—I am willing to accept your challenges, and your goals, but only with what I consider essential conditions for me to meet them. First of all, I would prefer a one-year contract; that will give us a way out if we're not compatible. In my contract, I must also have just cause and due process; that will ensure that I won't be fired prematurely at the whim of some disgruntled individuals. Further, the same criteria must also be applied to the constable's position.

"As to the administrative aide," Atticus continued, "I suspect there will be confidential issues concerning school matters as well as police matters; I will need the authority to hold her accountable; that means the authority to maintain or fire Vivian Bloomer.

"Finally, because this dual position is both unique and demanding, I must have full flexibility of my time in order to make it work. I expect you to hold me accountable for the outcomes of my responsibilities, not some ill-defined expectations of how I should or should not be using my time. I also expect to work under the authority of the full board, not separate or independent board members." Atticus leaned back in his chair. "If we can agree to these terms, and you still want me to take the job, I will accept, pending there are no unforeseen complications on my side. If, on the other hand, you cannot, I understand, and I'd suggest you keep looking. I'm not interested in stepping into a situation where I would commit professional suicide by default, and without these safeguards, I feel that is exactly what I'd be doing. I don't know what to expect from this job, but I have a very strong suspicion there are going to be some real hot button issues."

Butch also shifted in his chair. "Mr. Gunner, there is no doubt in my mind that you are the one for this job, but I am only one of three. So if you'll excuse us and wait outside, the three of us will discuss it and try to come to a conclusion." He rapped the gavel and declared the meeting move into closed session. Atticus got up and walked out of the room.

———————◆———————

After about twenty minutes, the lights went off in the meeting room and Butch and the two women came walking out. The women said, "Good evening," and went past Atticus on the way to their car. There was absolutely no indication as to what had happened in the meeting by either of them. On the other hand, Butch came walking up with a big grin on his face. "Well, Mr. Gunner, you got yourself a job offer. Now the ball is in your court." He extended his hand out to Atticus.

"They agreed to all my conditions?" Atticus asked as he shook Butch's hand.

"Every one of them."

"Mind if I ask what the vote was?"

"Two to one," Butch replied.

"And the one?"

"I think you know who that was. It doesn't really matter though; Greta and I carried the night with a resounding approval. Come on; I'll take you back down to Spencer's dock. You need a good night's sleep, and then I'll pick you up in the morning at eleven o'clock so you can catch the noon boat."

"Did you manage to find a ride to Green Bay for me?"

"Not yet, but I will by the time I pick you up."

The two men got into Butch's car and headed for Spencer's dock.

———•◦•———

The next morning, Atticus sat drinking his coffee while sitting on Spencer's dock; a whole myriad of thoughts flooded through his mind. First, there was a sense of accomplishment. He had actually managed to get the job offered to him, and with safeguards built into the contract. Equally astounding, he not only matched his Madison offer, but was now fully eligible for the Morgan Group pay on top of it. As a result, he would be making close to three-quarters of a million dollars for one year of service, and that was no small matter. Second, the thought of living and working on an island really excited him; Washington Island was a beautiful place. Third, what had happened to him since starting this adventure was certainly bizarre, but it took him back to a prior time in his life, and even though it left him with a very uneasy feeling, it also sparked his sense of intrigue and adventure; he actually found himself looking forward to the challenges.

The one thing that still bothered Atticus was the unknown impact his move would have on his girls. He finally concluded that he would simply have to hope for the best.

At a little after eleven o'clock, Atticus grabbed his duffle bag and started to walk toward the road. Walking along the blacktop, Atticus looked up just as Butch's station wagon came around the corner and headed his way. After stopping, Butch reached over and opened the passenger door. "Did you think I'd forgotten you?" he asked with a big grin.

"No, it's such a beautiful day I just thought I'd start walking," Atticus replied as he got in the car.

Butch pulled into Spencer's drive to turn around and then took off again in the direction of the ferry dock. "I've got you a ride to Green Bay," he said, looking over at Atticus.

"Anyone I know?"

"The Doebucks."

"Those people with the fantastic summer home?"

"None other! You'll be riding in style."

"I suppose they have a limo."

"You hit it right on the head; a big black one."

"I hope they won't mind dirty Levis and an old duffel bag; I'm not exactly dressed to mingle with high society."

"Don't worry about it," Butch said as he wheeled around the corner again. "You'll probably be riding in front with the bodyguard anyway."

"How did you manage a ride with them?"

"I was over at their place this morning working on some electrical problems, and they mentioned they were leaving today, so I asked if they'd mind giving you a lift to Green Bay. After they learned who you were, they were more than happy to offer their services."

"Beggars can't be choosers," Atticus replied.

"Don't be quite so flippant. This is a perfect opportunity to get a little flavor of the power structure up here. Watch and learn, my friend, especially Mrs. Doebuck. The old man doesn't seem to have much to do with island issues, but she does, and as she goes, so goes the island in many ways."

When they arrived at the ferry dock, about fifteen cars were in line to board. The cars were moving forward slowly as they were loaded one by one. Butch eased his way through the congestion, out onto the dock and up to the ferry office, where he parked. "Come on," he said as he opened the car door, "I saw Doebuck's limo coming up the line."

Atticus grabbed his duffle bag and got out to follow. They walked down through the line of cars until they came to a black Cadillac limo driving forward slowly. As they approached, the car stopped and the driver's door opened; a husky man of medium stature stepped out.

"This is Atticus Gunner," Butch said to the driver, gesturing toward Atticus.

The man nodded and motioned for Atticus to get into the front passenger seat. As Atticus walked around the front of the car, the back window on the driver's side went down. "We'll see that he gets to Green Bay safe and sound, Butch," the man seated in the back said. Butch nodded and thanked Mr. Doebuck, waved at Atticus, and then headed back toward his car.

As Atticus crawled into the front seat, he placed his duffle bag between his legs and pulled the door shut. He glanced over at the driver and gave him a smile. The driver gave Atticus a stern but pleasant nod. It was obvious the man was wearing a sidearm under his sports jacket, and apparently he wasn't at all concerned that Atticus saw it.

The dark glass behind the front seat went down, exposing the rear passenger compartment. An elderly man in the back seat smiled and said, "Butch tells me you're in need of a ride to Green Bay."

"Yes sir, if it's not too much trouble," Atticus replied.

"No problem at all," he said, "any friend of Butch is a friend of ours." The man was dressed in a cardigan sweater and leisure pants. "My name is Munster Doebuck, and yours is Atticus Gunner. Is that correct?"

"Yes sir."

A heavy-set lady wearing a printed dress and a lot of gaudy jewelry came waddling up to the car from the direction of the ferry office. The driver stopped; she opened the rear passenger door behind Atticus and started to work her way in. "Well, I got through to the Claymores," she said to her husband as she slid awkwardly into the seat. "Oh," she remarked as though pleasantly surprised when she noticed Atticus, "and who do we have here?"

"This is Mr. Gunner," Mr. Doebuck replied, "and this is my wife, Edna."

"How do you do, ma'am?" Atticus replied.

"My goodness!" she said, still looking at Atticus. "You're not exactly what I expected."

"I'm sorry, ma'am, I came up here on a sailing trip—I'm afraid my clothes are . . ."

"Oh, that isn't what I meant," she interrupted, "you're a lot younger than I pictured. I expected to see a man with some gray hair."

"Oh, it's getting there," Atticus said with a smile.

"I suppose it is," she said graciously. "I guess when you get to be our age, everyone looks young." She rearranged herself into a more comfortable position and spoke again. "Well, Mr. Gunner, tell me, how do you like our island?"

"As you know, I'm still very much a newcomer, but so far I like it very much."

"I'm sure you do," she replied. "Munster and I have been coming up here for over twenty years now; the island has become our second love, so we know exactly how you feel. The island is a unique and lovely place. I hope as you settle in on your new job, you'll learn to appreciate the people as much as you do the island."

"I'm sure I will," Atticus replied.

"I know you're a well-educated young man, tuned into the rigors of our society, but I think you'll find it considerably different up here."

"Yes, I've pretty much accepted that fact already."

"By most people's standards, the island people are poor," she went on, as though Atticus hadn't responded. "They can't afford many of the luxuries that most Americans have become accustomed to. Many people would consider them uneducated and shallow, but as strange as it may sound, they like it that way. They're very happy just the way things are, and we've learned through the years that the best approach is to not change things too much. If you can do that, you'll learn what lovely chaps they really are."

To that comment, Atticus had no response.

———————•◦•———————

About an hour later, the ferry pulled into the Gills Rock Ferry Terminal, and after another twenty minutes, they were driving down the ramp and up the steep hill past the restaurant. In all this time, no one said a word except Mrs. Doebuck, who talked continuously. She reminisced about the years gone past and how the island had changed. She talked about the Great Depression; about Prohibition, and about the rum-running days. She talked about the ferry boat service in the early days and how, after Adrian Fruger took it over, he brought the island back to life. She talked about the museum she helped to develop and about the art festival she organized, which was now an annual event. She talked about the summer concert, about the summer theater, and about how all these things were of tremendous benefit for the islanders. The fact that all these events were held in the summer, when her rich summer friends were present, and at a time when the real islanders were far too busy trying to eke out a living by providing services for the likes of her and didn't have the time or money to participate in her kind of activities, never seemed to enter into her thinking.

By the time they were about twenty minutes down the peninsula, Atticus could take no more. He felt compelled to pursue her thinking, and as he did, it became increasingly apparent that she really knew very little about the island outside her elite summer social clique, that in all reality, social events such as wedding dances and island fairs—the kind of things that the islanders actually participated in—were not at all of her doing. They in fact were considered beneath her dignity. Further, she knew very little about the island children or the school, nor did she care.

Mr. Doebuck remained silent during the course of the conversation, but it was obvious he was listening and clearly picked up on the implications of Atticus's questions and comments. After a time he leaned forward, tapped the driver on the shoulder, and gave him a nod. The window went up and the conversation ended. Atticus was left sitting alone in the front seat with the driver.

When they arrived at Sturgeon Bay, the driver pulled over to the curb in front of the first gas station. "There you are, Mr. Gunner," he said, pointing to the passenger door. "This is where you get out."

"This is Sturgeon Bay," Atticus said. "Perhaps you didn't understand; I need to go all the way to Green Bay."

"This is where you get out," the driver repeated, and once again he pointed to the door.

Atticus paused for a moment, and then, getting the drift, he opened the door. "Thanks for the lift," he said as he grabbed his bag and stepped out of the car. "Maybe I can return the favor someday."

The driver gave him the finger. He then pulled the door shut, and drove off.

With his bag in hand Atticus walked toward the gas station. There was a county sheriff's car parked at the pumps; two police officers were coming out of the gas station as he came across the drive. "You seemed to have lost your ride there, cowboy," one of them said to Atticus as he approached.

"Yes sir, I'm afraid I have," Atticus replied.

"What's your name?"

"Atticus Gunner."

"Do you have identification?"

A bit taken back, Atticus took his wallet out and handed the officer his driver's license.

"Wait a minute," the other officer said, "did you say Atticus Gunner?"

"That's correct."

Both officers looked at his license. "That's the guy the chief was talking about this morning," the second officer said. "Did you just come from Washington Island?"

"Yes," Atticus answered, somewhat puzzled.

"Where are you headed?" the second officer asked.

"To Green Bay to pick up my car."

"Would you mind going down to the station with us? I'm sure Sheriff Dawson would like to talk to you. I'm also sure he'll find a ride for you down to Green Bay."

"No, I don't mind," Atticus replied, still very puzzled.

———————◆———————

The sign on the glass read "Door County Sheriff." The officer opened the door and stuck his head in. "Chief, Mr. Gunner is here."

"Have him come in!" boomed a voice from inside.

The officer opened the door and stepped aside for Atticus to pass.

"So you're going to be the new constable on Washington Island," the older man sitting behind the desk said as Atticus approached. He then stood up and offered a hand to Atticus. "I'm Sheriff Jeff Dawson; have a seat."

"Seems news travels fast up here," Atticus said as he sat down.

"Butch Gorpon called me Monday and said they were looking at you for the job; he wondered if I could run a background check on you."

"And did you?"

"Yes, as a matter of fact we did. Seems you'll be the most educated police officer we've ever had up in these parts. I didn't find a whole lot of law enforcement training in your background though."

"No, I'm afraid I know very little about being a cop, but I was led to believe that being an island constable isn't really that big of an issue."

"Being a keeper of the peace always becomes a big issue at some time or another."

Atticus didn't respond.

"I'm just saying," the sheriff went on, "make sure you go into this with your eyes open. Know your strengths, and know your limitations. And above all, don't be afraid to ask for help if you need it."

"Thank you; I'll certainly keep that in mind."

"I see you were in the military, Seventy-Ninth Signal Battalion, Cryptography, attached to Seventh Army Headquarters, Stuttgart, Germany, Intelligence Division. Obviously you're anything but stupid, but tell me, have you had any training in firearms?"

"Some."

"You can handle a weapon then."

"Yes."

"Do you intend to carry a sidearm?"

"To be honest with you, I haven't given it much thought. I'm really more oriented toward running the school."

"I knew Bert Federman. I went up there with the coroner to investigate his death. He was a good man. He didn't much care for firearms either."

"Just what were the circumstances of his death?" Atticus asked.

The sheriff shrugged his shoulders. "I don't know," he said. "I know a number of islanders have raised questions; I have myself, but we couldn't find any evidence of wrongdoing. I also know about the drinking questions; I didn't think he drank either, but maybe he was a closet drinker. Twenty years on Washington Island could drive just about anybody to drink; that's just my opinion, of course. Truth is, I just don't know what happened, and in reality, it's out of my jurisdiction."

"What are the connections between the county sheriff and Washington Island?"

"Well, they're part of the county, as I'm sure you already know, so we do have an obligation to provide police services—or did, I should say. However, they wanted a full-time deputy to be appointed by them, but at our expense of course, and we couldn't accept that. So, with the help of their summer friends, they managed to get special legislation through the state allowing them to go it on their own. We still have to provide a car and whatever support services they might need, but other than that, they're autonomous."

Atticus looked at the sheriff. "Interesting," he replied.

"Yes, isn't it? Oh, and by the way, I got you a ride to Green Bay with Matt Brown; he's the game warden for this neck of the woods. He's going down to Green Bay tonight. He said he would pick you up at six o'clock in front of the restaurant right across the street from the courthouse here. That should give you just about enough time to grab a bite to eat before he arrives."

Atticus rose to his feet, thanked the sheriff, and started for the door.

"Oh, and one more thing," the sheriff said as Atticus opened the door. "I still have Constable Federman's badge and sidearm here; as soon as it's confirmed that you have officially taken the job, I'll send them up to you. I'll also send up a car for you to use. Good luck, Mr. Gunner, I meant what I said about help if you need it."

"Thank you," Atticus replied again.

"One more thing," the sheriff continued, shaking his head. "I just have to ask—why? Why would a bright young man like you, a man who obviously had it made in Madison—why would you come up here in the middle of nowhere and accept a dead-end job on Washington Island? Is there something I don't see?"

Atticus paused for a moment; he wasn't about to divulge any of his reasons for being there. "I don't know," he replied. "What I do know is, the more I find out, the more determined I become." Atticus smiled at the sheriff and then closed the door as he left.

———◆◆◆———

It was late Saturday morning. The bright sun radiated from the hot concrete, and the smell of exhaust hung heavy in the air. Atticus turned off University Avenue onto the crowded parking ramp.

Bob Thrison had called this morning and invited Atticus to lunch at the Downtowner. Knowing Bob as well as he did, having lunch together was not all that unusual, but today it was different, and Atticus didn't quite know how he was going to handle it. Knowing how strongly Bob felt about Atticus pushing on for bigger and better things, Atticus was certain when he found out he was considering a job on some rinky-dink island out in the middle of nowhere, he would go berserk.

Finding an empty stall, Atticus parked the car and walked over to the stairwell that led down to the street below. He hurried down the steps and out onto the busy sidewalk. Walking briskly, he cut across the street. The Downtowner was on the corner—its large neon sign flashed off and on over the entranceway. Atticus went inside and walked past the bar into the dimly lit dining room. Standing by the receptionist's counter, he looked around. "Table for one, sir?" the hostess said, walking up to him.

"Ah—no thanks," Atticus replied. "I'm supposed to meet someone here."

"Does she have a reservation?" the hostess asked. "If she does perhaps I can . . ."

"It's a he, and there he is," Atticus interrupted, spotting Bob and another man in a booth toward the back of the room. "Thank you anyway," he said as he walked away.

"Hey Atticus," Bob said noticing him. "I was beginning to think you weren't going to show."

"I had a little trouble finding a parking place."

"I can understand that," Bob said. "Here, I want you to meet someone—this is Tom Kozuszek. He works for the Financial Aid Department at the State Department of Public Instruction."

"How do you do?" Atticus replied, extending his hand toward the man.

"This is Atticus Gunner," Bob said to Kozuszek. "He just accepted the new assistant principal position at West."

Kozuszek smiled at Atticus. "Congratulations."

"Come, sit down," Bob said, sliding over in the booth.

"No, sit here, Mr. Gunner," Kozuszek said as he stood up. "I've got to go anyway, Bob. It was nice to meet you, Atticus. Maybe we'll meet again sometime."

Atticus waited for Kozuszek to walk away and then slid into his spot. "Did you say he worked in Financial Aid at DPI?" he asked Bob quietly.

"Yes, why?"

"Just curious."

"Well, how is your sailing class going?" Bob asked. "Why haven't you called me? I tried to get ahold of you but you're never home."

"I really haven't had a chance; I had a lot of things I needed to get done."

"I've got two extra tickets to the concert at the Union Theater tonight," Bob went on. "I was hoping you'd get in touch with me soon enough so you could get a date and go with Grace and me."

"I'm sorry."

"Have you got plans for tonight?"

"No, not really."

"Well then, what do you say?"

"About what?" Atticus replied. "The concert? Or a date?"

"Both."

"Well, I'd enjoy going to the concert with you and Grace. I'll even drive so the two of you can make out in the back seat, but I'm afraid you're out of luck as far as a date goes."

"Very funny," Bob replied with a disgruntled look. "When in the hell are you going to start reaching out to make a new life for yourself? People are going to start thinking you're gay."

"Maybe they'll think we got something going."

Bob just shook his head. "Gunner, you're so full of shit."

"Bob, look, I know you're trying to help, and I appreciate it, but I'll be damned if I'm going to start hanging out in bars just so I can pick up some flaky broad."

"I hate to be the one to break it to you, Gunner, but there are other ways to meet people."

"I hope you didn't call me all the way down here just so you could lecture me about my love life."

"No, actually, I thought maybe you might want to play some racquetball at the club this afternoon. Grace and the girls are going shopping, so I have some time."

"Now that sounds good," Atticus replied with a grin. "I think I can squeeze that into my busy social schedule."

"Say, by the way," Bob interjected, "while I'm thinking about it, McTagert called me yesterday and wanted to know when you were going to sign your contract; you haven't turned it in yet?"

"Bob, I've been busy."

"Yes, I know. That's what I told him, but he wants it in this week, so sign the damned thing and put it in the mail today, okay?"

"Yes, I'll take care of it," Atticus replied, not wanting to raise the issue at that moment.

After the waitress took their order, Bob continued to talk about the upcoming evening. He was prone to rambling once in a while, and when he did, Atticus simply tuned him out. Glancing across the room toward the entrance, Atticus noticed three young women enter the dining room. As they sat down, something struck a chord. The tall, ash-blonde girl sitting in between the other two looked familiar, and yet he couldn't place her. She was a beautiful creature with a long slender neck and beautifully proportioned features. Her long hair was piled loosely on top of her head and bounced gently as she moved. Atticus didn't seem to have a great deal of luck meeting women in his present circumstances, and as a result didn't pursue it, but there was something strikingly different about this one; not only was she stunning, but he couldn't seem to take his eyes off her.

"So which do you want to do?" Bob's voice echoed, jolting Atticus back into the conversation.

"Want to do?" Atticus asked, trying to pick up the conversation again.

"Do you want to go out to eat with Grace and me, or do you want to meet us at the theater?"

"I think I'll meet you at the theater; I've got some errands to take care of after we finish playing."

"Well, suit yourself," Bob replied. "You're going to miss a good meal."

"I'm sure I will," Atticus said, glancing over at the girl again, "Perhaps some other time." This time her eyes met his.

"Sir?" came the waitress's voice. "You ordered the shrimp?"

"Ah, yes," Atticus replied, looking up at her.

She set the shrimp platter down in front of Atticus and a steak sandwich over in front of Bob. "Say," Bob said as he started to eat, "are you going home to get your shorts and stuff?"

"Yes. Why?"

"Well, while you're there, why don't you grab that contract, sign it, and bring it back to the club with you? Then I can take it to work with me on Monday and give it to McTagert personally."

Atticus was trapped; the job issue was front and center now. "I'm not going to be taking the job," he blurted out without any prelude.

"What?"

"I've been offered another job."

"Another job?" Bob repeated with a dumbfounded look. "Are you serious? Where?"

"Washington Island."

"Washington Island? Where in the hell is that?"

"It's out in Lake Michigan."

"Doing what?"

"Managing their school and being the island cop."

"Are you serious?"

"Yes, I am."

"You've got to be kidding!"

"The school has about a hundred kids—K through twelve. And the island has about five hundred year-round residents."

"And you're seriously considering this?"

Atticus nodded. "Yes, I am."

"And a cop? What are you going to do, give parking tickets to seagulls?"

"Something like that."

Bob sat there for a moment, looking at his plate as though he were searching for a solution. Finally, he looked back up at Atticus. "Do your kids know about this?"

"They've agreed to go up with me and look it over for a week or so."

"Do you have any idea how hard it is to break into the Madison school system?" Bob asked. "Atticus, you're bright; if you put your mind to it, you could really move up the ladder. In any career, you have to start where you can meet the right people. How many chances for promotion do you think you'll get on that island?"

"None—but I might find myself."

"Christ, man, you're thirty-six years old. You better find yourself pretty damn soon." Again Bob shook his head.

"Look, I . . ."

"Forget it," Bob interrupted. "Let's eat."

During the course of the conversation that followed, or lack of it, Atticus forgot about the young woman. It wasn't until he and Bob walked past her table to leave that he glanced at her again. Again she looked up at him and smiled, but this time she said hello. Atticus returned her greeting politely but continued to follow Bob.

"Who was that?" Bob asked after they got out of earshot.

"I don't know," Atticus replied. "I think she's a former student of mine."

"Now that's what you ought to be going after, instead of some dumbass job on Washingmachine Island, or whatever in the hell the place is called."

"Yeah, really; she looks almost young enough to be my daughter—that's really good, Bob."

"Come on," Bob said, digging in his pocket for money to pay his bill. "She looked to be twenty-two, maybe twenty-three. You're right; she is young enough to be your daughter if you had a kid at say, what—thirteen? Besides, I didn't say you had to marry her."

Atticus laughed as he threw his money on the bar. "Frankly, I think you've got hardening of the arteries."

"We'll see who's got hardening of the arteries on the court this afternoon." Bob headed for the door. "I'll see you at the club in an hour and a half; don't be late."

The bartender came back with Atticus's change and slapped it on the bar. Atticus picked it up and headed out the door into the hot afternoon sun.

It was dark and the rain was falling in big drops that splattered as they hit the windshield. The rhythmic drone of the wipers hummed softly as Atticus pulled up to the stoplight on University and Park. People and cars were scurrying every which way in the hustle and bustle of a typical Saturday night on campus.

When the light turned green, Atticus stepped on the accelerator, crossed University Avenue, and continued down Park Street. To the left was Bascom Hill and the heart of campus. Straight ahead, one block down on the right, was the Union Theater. As he approached, automobiles were stopping on both sides of the street to let people out. Women were scurrying through the rain with their long gowns sashaying at their ankles as they ran for the protection of the theater lobby.

Atticus worked his way through the traffic entanglement and then turned left into the restricted parking under the Helen White Building, directly across the street from the union. He didn't have a parking permit, but he knew there would be no one checking on a Saturday night.

Pulling his collar up as he hurried across the street, Atticus entered the brightly lit lobby. Looking around, he tried to spot either Bob or Grace. Glancing at his watch, he realized he was a bit early, so he walked over to the corner of the lobby away from the crowd. Stuffing his hands into his coat pockets, he stood silently, watching the people.

He thought about the kids and wondered how they were getting on with their cousins. He felt a little better about things now. Friday night had gone well. Stacie decided to go along with him and Inger, so they went out to eat and then to a movie. On the way home, they had walked through campus. As they did, the three of them talked a lot about the island. The kids asked lots of questions, and Atticus felt many of their fears had been eased. He even seemed to sense a bit of excitement about going, especially with Inger. Things had also gone well when he talked to their mother about the possibility of his moving up there, and how he wanted the kids to go up with him for a week or so to check the place out. There wasn't any doubt she thought he was crazy, but surprisingly, she seemed halfway civil toward the whole idea.

It was raining hard again when Atticus noticed a silver Corvette pull up to the curb. A young woman wearing a purple evening gown got out. Holding a light summer raincoat over her head, she ran toward the lobby entrance. The cling of her silky gown showed off enough of her lovely frame to turn any man's eye, and Atticus was no exception. When she got inside, she lowered the coat and shook out her long ash-blonde hair, which fell to her waist. Atticus was surprised; it was the same young woman he had seen in the restaurant.

Suddenly, her name came to him. "Laura Bock—of course, her name is Laura Bock," he said to himself. The last time he had seen her was when she was a senior in high school; that was three years ago. Her family used to live right down the road from him. Her two younger sisters used to babysit his girls regularly, and her mother was an aide at the high school where he taught. He never knew Laura very well; that is, he never had her in any of his classes, but once in a while when he was walking home from school, he would run into her and her mother. She was a tall, pretty girl then, but she was most certainly a beautiful young woman now.

Bob's station wagon pulled up in front of the theater. At the same time, Atticus noticed a young man, clean cut and wearing an expensive suit, run into the lobby. He approached the Bock girl, and together they walked off into the crowd. Grace came into the lobby, lowered her umbrella, and looked around.

"Grace! Over here!" Atticus barked, raising his arms so she would see him.

Spotting Atticus, Grace walked through the crowd toward him. "Bob was afraid you might not be here yet."

"Oh, I made it," he replied. "I've been here for about ten minutes."

"Well, Bob should be back shortly; he's parking the car under the Helen White Building."

"That beats driving all over town on a night like this," Atticus said smiling at her.

"Well, how have you been?" Grace asked as she shook the water off her umbrella. "I think it's been more than a month since you've been over to the house."

"Just fine," Atticus replied. "Things have been pretty busy."

"So I hear—Bob tells me you're taking a job on some island."

"I kind of figured he might mention that to you. I suppose he's pretty upset."

"Yes, he is, but he'll get over it."

"Do you think I'm crazy, Grace?"

"Atticus," she said, reaching up and patting him on the cheek, "you must do what your intuition tells you; you can't take a job just because a friend wants you to."

"Thanks," Atticus replied. "I was hoping you'd understand."

"Frankly," she said, smiling at Atticus, "I think Bob is more upset about losing his favorite handball partner than anything else."

Atticus smiled again.

"What do the girls think about the idea?" she asked.

"I don't know for sure—we're talking about it."

"That's the most important thing; you know that."

"Yes, I know," Atticus replied.

"Well, there's my partner in crime," Bob said, walking up to his wife and Atticus. "I thought you'd be on crutches tonight after the mauling I gave you this afternoon."

"Is he like that around home too?" Atticus said to Grace. "He not only beats me at his own silly game, but then he has to gloat over it."

"That's my old man," she said, smiling at her husband.

"Well, he deserves to be beaten after telling me to take our job offer and stick it."

"Bob, now leave Atticus be!" Grace said.

"That's all right," Atticus chimed in, "I'm used to his rambling; I just tune him out."

"That's for sure," Bob replied.

"Okay, you two," Grace said, taking each of them by the arm. "You can argue about this later. Right now, I want to go to a concert."

Leading them both, Grace moved into the crowd and toward the open auditorium doors. "Have you got the tickets?" she asked her husband.

"Yep, right here in my pocket."

"Have you ever heard the Minneapolis Symphony?" she asked Atticus.

"No, I haven't," he replied.

"They're very good," she said.

The light in the lobby dimmed, indicating that the performance was about to begin. An usher took Bob's tickets and handed them a program as they walked into the auditorium. The sounds of rustling feet and the tuning of instruments filled the air. Quietly, the three found their seats and sat down. In a few minutes, the lights went down and the curtain opened. Without fanfare, the conductor walked out onto the stage. He stepped briskly up onto the podium. Immediately, a hush fell over the entire auditorium. When he raised his arms, it was as though the independence of each individual musician suddenly froze into one single unit. The baton moved, and the prelude to Tchaikovsky's *1812 Overture* began to flow through the air with the depth and feeling that only a live performance can create.

The time moved so quickly over the next hour that Atticus was caught off guard when the lights came on for intermission. He asked Grace and Bob if they would like to get up and stretch. They didn't, so Atticus excused himself and made his way out to the lobby. He no more than worked through fifteen or twenty people when he almost walked directly into the Bock girl. "Well, hello," he said, smiling at her.

"My gosh," she replied, "I certainly didn't expect to run into you again. How are you, Mr. Gunner?"

"I'm fine—it's Laura, isn't it?"

145

"Yes, it is; you seemed so preoccupied at lunch this noon, I wasn't sure you recognized me."

"To be perfectly honest, I didn't. You've grown up a little since I saw you last."

She smiled up at him. "Why, thank you. I'm assuming you meant that as a compliment."

Atticus smiled. "Yes, ma'am, I sure did—tell me," he continued, "how's your mom and the rest of the family?"

"Oh, they're fine. What are you doing now? Mom said she heard you were divorced, and Robin mentioned once that you went back to school. We all sort of lost track after you moved away."

"Well, I guess they're both correct; I am divorced, and I just received my graduate degree."

"That's really great—I mean about the degree—oh, I'm sorry," she said. "That didn't come out very well, did it?"

Atticus smiled again. "You needn't be sorry, it came out just fine."

"Where are you working now?"

"Well, I'm sort of in between jobs; I'll be starting a job on Washington Island."

"Really?" she said. "That's very interesting. I'm assuming it's for the school up there."

"Yes—you mean you've heard of Washington Island?"

"Oh yes; we're working on a project for the island."

"What kind of project?" Atticus asked.

"I work for the State Director of Vocational Education, and we've been working on a federally funded project for Washington Island for about a year now."

"You mean a project for the school?"

"Yes; as a matter of fact, it's ready to go. Do you know Mr. Gorpon, the president of the school board up there?"

"Yes, I do; that's the person who talked me into considering the job."

"Well, he's the person we've been working with."

"I'll be darned," Atticus replied.

"So you see, I know quite a bit about Washington Island."

"Have you ever been up there?"

"The director has a couple times, and Mr. Gorpon has been down here. I went to Rock Island camping with my sisters once, but we didn't spend much time on Washington Island. It does, however, seem like a beautiful place, and a couple of us girls have talked about going up there sometime this summer."

Atticus shook his head in disbelief. "I'm sure you'll enjoy it."

"When do you start?" she asked.

"I guess that's pretty much up to me."

"Now, are you going to teach or be an administrator?"

"I'm going to be the administrator; among other things, I guess."

"Really?" she said. "I can't tell you how envious I am. What a unique and interesting opportunity."

Atticus smiled. "You know," he said, "you're the first person I've talked to that doesn't think I'm insane."

Just then Laura's date came up from behind and interrupted their conversation. "There you are," he said, putting his arm around her shoulders in an attempt to direct her away. "Come on, I've got some people I want you to meet."

"Just a minute," she replied, taking his hand off her shoulder. "I've got someone I want you to meet first; this is Atticus Gunner—Atticus, this is Paul Becker; he's with CBM."

Atticus extended his hand toward the young man.

"Data systems consultant," he said, taking Atticus by the hand and shaking it briefly.

"Atticus is going to work for the school on Washington Island," Laura said.

"Where in the world is that?" Paul replied as he continued to look across the room at his friends.

"That's the island I told you about, where we are starting that project."

"Oh good God!" he said, looking back at Atticus. "My condolences, friend, but I guess unless you've really got something on the ball, good jobs are hard to come by."

"Paul!" Laura said, obviously appalled at his comment.

"I'm sorry," he said, looking first at her and then at Atticus. "I apologize, okay? Now come on," he continued to Laura, "I've got some important people I'd like for you to meet."

"I think I'll stay here and talk to Mr. Gunner for a few minutes, if you don't mind."

"Honey, I said I apologize, and these really are important people. That man is president of a bank; I can't just leave him standing."

"The name is Laura, not honey, and you go talk to him. I'm not interested!"

"But I told him about you, and he would like to meet you."

"That's his problem."

Paul stood there for a few seconds. "Okay," he said, disappointed. "I'll be back to get you in a few minutes." Hesitating at first, he finally turned and walked away.

"I'm sorry," Laura said after he left. "I'm so embarrassed."

"Don't be," Atticus replied. "He's obviously a little overimpressed with himself; he may grow up if you give him time."

"This is the second time I've been out with him. I swore after the first, that would be the last, but I guess I'm a slow learner—here I am."

Atticus smiled.

The lights in the lobby dimmed briefly. "I guess that's our cue to return to our seats," Laura said. "I better find my date. Good luck on Washington Island."

"Thank you," Atticus replied. "And good luck with your data processing consultant."

Laura smiled. "Do you really think I'll need it?"

Atticus winked at her and said, "Yes ma'am; I know you will."

"I'll keep my rabbit's foot handy," she replied, still smiling at him as she walked away.

———————————

When they came out of the theater, the rain had all but stopped. Grace and Bob crossed the street with Atticus just behind. "Our neighbors are having a block party tonight, and we thought we'd stop for a little while," Bob said to Atticus after they reached the shelter of the Helen White Building. "Why don't you join us?"

Atticus frowned. "I think I'll just head for home if you don't mind."

"Shit, Atticus, come with us—just for a little while."

"Bob!" Grace interjected. "Will you please quit badgering him; he wants to go home."

"Oh, all right," Bob said. "Will I see you before you head up to that island?"

"Yes, I'll stop in at your office sometime Monday."

"All right," he said, taking Grace by the arm and starting toward their car. "I'll see you Monday then."

"Good night, Atticus," Grace said over her shoulder.

"Good night," Atticus replied.

—•—•—•—

After leaving Bob and Grace, Atticus eased the nose of his car out into the street, turned on his blinker, and waited for his chance to enter the traffic. The rain started again, so he turned on his wipers. As he sat there waiting, he noticed the silver Corvette go by. As it passed in front of his headlights, he recognized Laura's obnoxious friend, but he was surprised to see he was alone. He looked across the street at the entrance of the theater. Recognizing the purple gown, he spotted Laura standing just outside the lobby entrance. She was up close to the building with her coat draped up over her shoulders. Taking advantage of the next break in traffic, he pulled out, but instead of turning right as he had intended, he turned left and pulled up to the curb in front of the theater. Leaning over the seat, he rolled down the window on the passenger side. "Laura!" he shouted, trying to get her attention over the noise of the rain and traffic.

"Oh, hello," she replied, recognizing Atticus.

"Do you always stand in the rain after a concert?"

She laughed. "No, I'm waiting for a cab!"

"That could take some time on a night like this! Come on, I'll give you a lift!"

She pulled her coat up over her head and ran for the car. Atticus flung the door open, and she quickly slid inside. "Boy, it's really raining again," she said as she pulled the door shut and rolled up the window.

"Where to?" Atticus asked.

"Do you know where the Lake Shore Manor Apartments are?"

150

"Is that the complex across from the park on Lake Mendota?"

"That's it," she replied.

After riding a few minutes in silence, he looked over at her again. "I know this isn't really any of my business," he said, "but apparently your rabbit's foot isn't working very well. Mind if I ask what happened?"

"Oh, nothing really. I just don't like arrogant men who seem to think women were placed on this earth so they would have toys to play with."

"I see," Atticus replied.

"I'm sorry," she continued, "I'm still upset over that—jerk. I went out with him the first time as a favor for one of the girls I work with. I didn't like him then and vowed I would never go out with him again, but he hounded me for over a month, and I finally gave in."

"They call that stalking, you know."

"Tonight was really something else," she went on, "not just because he insulted you—he does that kind of thing all the time—but because of what he pulled after the concert. We were talking with his fat banker friend, along with the banker's floozy playmate, and they invited us to spend the rest of the weekend up at his cottage. Lovely Paul Becker accepted the invitation, can you believe that? He said we would love to go. I set him straight—very fast, and then I told him and his fat friend to get lost! I think I got through to him this time."

Atticus chuckled.

"What's so funny?" she asked.

"I wasn't laughing at you. I was simply thinking about how outclassed Becker was tonight."

"I still feel bad. I don't like treating people like that."

"He'll get over it; scum bags usually do."

"I guess you're right."

When they reached Lake Shore Manor Apartments, Atticus turned left into the drive that went up through the wooded grounds and into the parking area. "This looks like a nice place," he said as they neared the first building. "What building do you live in?"

"I live in the farthest one down. Yes, they are nice. My apartment is small, but it's very pleasant. Would you like to come up for a cup of cocoa or something? I'd offer you coffee but I don't think I have any."

"Thanks," Atticus replied, "but perhaps another time."

He drove up to the sidewalk that led to the third building and stopped. "Well, I guess this is it. I'm afraid you're going to get a little wet again."

"Oh well," she replied, "I won't melt. Thanks again for the ride home." She opened the door and started to get out.

"Laura?"

She paused and looked back.

"I'm sorry your night turned out to be such a bummer. I know it's not much consolation, but for what it's worth, it was a great pleasure for me to escort you home. Your gown is very pretty, and you were, without a doubt, the most beautiful woman there tonight."

She smiled at him. "You're not so bad yourself," she replied.

Atticus returned her smile. "Good night," he said.

She closed the door, waved once, and then hurried up to the building and disappeared inside.

———◆———

Atticus glanced at his watch as he walked up the steps into the DPI building—he still had fifteen minutes before his appointment. He walked through the glass doors that led into the main lobby, and although the bright morning sun was somewhat muted as it fell through the large smoked-glass windows, the lobby was bright and cheery for a Monday morning. After checking the building directory, he boarded the elevator. On the seventh floor, he got off and walked down the hall to Room 708. The printing on the frosted glass window read, "Assistant State Superintendent Thomas E. Kozuszek; Division of Financial Aid; Department of Public Instruction."

Opening the door, he walked in. An elderly woman sitting behind a desk looked up as Atticus entered. "Good morning," she said, smiling at him. "Can I help you?"

"Yes, my name is Atticus Gunner. I called this morning."

"Oh yes, why don't you take a chair? Mr. Kozuszek will be with you in a minute."

Atticus walked over and sat down. While he waited, his mind tumbled over the whole idea of Washington Island for the hundredth time. He still wasn't sure he'd made the right decision. Again and again, the kids were the major hang-up. He hoped he wasn't rationalizing their well-being for the sake of his own selfish aspirations.

"Mr. Gunner, Mr. Kozuszek will see you now."

"Thank you," Atticus replied as he got up and walked toward the inner office.

As he opened the door, Tom Kozuszek looked up from behind his desk and smiled. "Come on in," he said, taking off his glasses and laying them on the desk. "Mr. Gunner, is it?" he said, standing up and extending his hand.

Atticus reached out to greet him. "Yes sir; Atticus Gunner."

"Seems I've heard that name before; have we met?"

"Just briefly; you were talking with Bob Thrison last Saturday at lunch when he introduced me to you."

"Oh yes, you're one of his new assistants, if I remember correctly."

"Well, not exactly; he offered me the job, but I've decided to accept a position on Washington Island."

"Washington Island?" Kozuszek said with a frown. "As the new administrator?"

"Yes," Atticus replied with a smile.

"Have you ever been a district administrator before?"

"No, I haven't, but I am certified."

"Not much up there but trees and seagulls; I hope you realize that."

"Yes, I'm well aware of the geography of the area. That isn't why I came to see you—I was hoping you could fill me in on the financial picture up there, perhaps give me a little background."

Kozuszek sat back down in his chair and leaned back. His cool, steel-gray eyes stared at Atticus. "You're dead serious about this, aren't you?" he said after a long pause.

"Yes sir, very much so."

"That's the smallest school district in the state," he said calmly, leaning forward in his chair, "and it might appear to be a serene and beautiful escape, but you've bitten off one hell of an assignment. Do you realize that?"

"That's the picture I'm getting," Atticus replied, "but I'm a very stubborn man."

Kozuszek leaned back in his chair again and stared at Atticus. Stroking his cheek with his finger, he paused for what seemed an eternity. Finally, he spoke again. "All right," he said with a nod, "sit down. What do you know about power equalization?"

Atticus sat down. "I know the state legislature passed it, and if the governor doesn't veto it, it's coming."

"That's right; do you know how it works?"

"Well, I know it's supposed to equalize the wealth of all the property in the state so as to ensure the same number of dollars behind each student, regardless of where they live in the state, but I have no idea how it's going to be mathematically applied."

"The mathematics isn't important right now," Kozuszek went on. "The idea is, those school districts with a low full property value behind each student, when compared to the state's guaranteed value, will collect the difference from the state; those school districts with a higher full property value will, instead of getting state aid, have to pay their own way, plus pay an additional amount into the state. The result is a balancing out of state funding for all students, regardless of whether they live in a wealthy area or not. You understand?"

"I understand," Atticus replied. "Washington Island, since it's a vacation destination, has a very high land value, while at the same time a very small number of students, thus they're not only going to be paying their own way, but they'll be sending money into the state to help fund places like—say, Milwaukee."

"You seem to be reading it loud and clear, Mr. Gunner."

"There's something I don't understand, though; when I was up there, the school didn't look very wealthy to me. The school building is very simple—somewhat rundown. I didn't see any evidence of elaborate programs. Frankly, things look like they were in short supply, even textbooks. The only evidence of a good program was in the vocational area, and if I understand correctly, that is being developed through federal funds. So what is happening to all this value now? The school sure doesn't seem to be getting it."

"Right again!" Kozuszek replied. "More than 70 percent of the landowners on Washington Island don't live there year round, and many of them don't even claim residence in this state. How supportive do you think they are of raising property taxes to support a school district their children don't even attend? For these people, Washington Island is a tax haven. And, I might add, some of them have rather formidable holdings there."

"But property taxes are determined by the local citizenry," Atticus commented, "and if these rich landowners don't claim their residency on Washington Island, they don't have a voice. Why don't the local people just vote to raise their own property taxes? Seems to me that would be a pretty good bargain, considering that over 70 percent of every dollar raised would not only come from the wealthy, but from people who also aren't in need of any of the educational services."

"Yes, you would think so, but unfortunately it doesn't work that way. First of all, the wealthy people run the show on Washington Island. The year-round people, for the most part, do the service-type work. Indirectly, they work for the rich, and you don't bite the hand that feeds you. Besides, even if that weren't the case, the average year-round islander doesn't make a whole lot of money up there; wages are very low. If he raised the taxes up to where they ought to be, he'd force himself right off the island."

"In other words, what you're telling me is that I'm going to be facing an organized front against any kind of change."

"That's correct; if it costs money, you'll find yourself at odds with the powers that be, and that power reaches well beyond the shores of Washington Island."

"I can't believe all the people up there are puppets to the rich or unwilling to support good education for their children."

"No, you're probably right."

"I've heard there's supposedly a connection with the underworld; is there any truth to that?"

"I suppose that's possible," Kozuszek said with a shrug. "Who knows? I'd be very careful about any comments along those lines if I were you—that could have some nasty repercussions."

Atticus didn't comment.

"Well," Kozuszek continued, "have you had enough? Or are you interested in hearing the rest of the story?"

"I must admit," Atticus said, "I didn't really analyze the negative aid picture, but I think I have an inkling of the rest of the problem; they have financial difficulties, don't they?"

Kozuszek raised his eyebrows. "I really underestimated you. I thought you might be going into this totally blind, but apparently you're not. In a nutshell, that's correct. Over the last six years, they have either set up their operating budget and not levied enough taxes to cover it or set up a budget that is too low and spent beyond it. The end result, of course, has been an ongoing escalating problem of deficit spending."

"Sounds like our politicians in Washington."

"Well, Mr. Gunner, local, state, or federal, a politician is a politician. Everyone wants the services, but nobody wants to pay for them. Short-term borrowing in a public school operation is legal only to alleviate the problems of cash flow," he continued. "The intention is to allow a school district to borrow money that is backed by anticipated receipts, then to pay the loan off when those receipts come in. Because of the island's lack of funding, it can't pay off the notes, so instead they just pay the interest and carry the debt into the next fiscal year. For the last six years, the amount of unpaid notes has increased to the point where, in about three more years, the district will be beyond their borrowing limit and, for all practical purposes, be bankrupt."

"Don't they realize that?"

"Oh, they do! In spite of the fact that old Bill Ploder was as close to being incompetent as anyone could possibly be, the real problem is that the board of education is unwilling to face it. To solve the dilemma would mean a substantial property tax increase, and they're not about to do that."

Again Atticus didn't respond.

"By the way, I see where that job was posted as part-time; what are the rest of your responsibilities?"

"I'm going to be the island cop."

Kozuszek stood up and glared at Atticus in disbelief. "Are you kidding me?

"No sir, I'm not."

"And you accepted that kind of an offer? I don't even think that's legal."

"Yes sir, it is—I've checked. In order to hold a district administrator's position, I must hold a valid license, but there is no requirement for the school board to hire a full-time administrator. The situation is certainly far less than ideal, and I won't argue to support its validity, but we both know laws aren't necessarily made to be fair or even proper. The job is what it is, and the choice of whether or not to accept it is up to me."

"You realize, of course, if you blow it, the chances of you ever getting another administrative position in this state will probably be zero."

"Yes sir, I do, and I'll certainly keep that in mind." Atticus stood up. "Thank you for the information; you've been most helpful." He shook Kozuszek's hand and left without further comment.

CHAPTER 6

The Hersoff Place

By the time Atticus and the girls reached Gills Rock, the sun was well above the trees, flooding the small fishing community with the warmth only a summer morning can bring. Within the hour, they were aboard the ferry, along with a large entourage of tourists. Inger, being her usual jubilant self and filled with curiosity, bombarded her father with a myriad of questions. Even Stacie, far more reluctant to adjust to the whole idea of making this trip, got caught up in the mystique that seems to go along with one's first trip to Washington Island.

After arriving on the island, Atticus worked his way slowly through the crowd at the ferry dock. Between cars, bicyclers, and people walking, progress along the narrow drive was slow. For Stacie and Inger, it was all part of their first impression, and they loved it. The girls' enthusiasm certainly helped to relieve Atticus's anxiety. Downtown, he stopped at the general store. They went inside to get groceries and ice; when they were finished they loaded the items into the car and headed for Jackson Harbor.

Arriving at Spencer's dock, Atticus pulled up behind the barn and stopped. "Well, this is it," he said, shutting off the engine.

Inger hopped out of the car immediately and headed around the barn toward the dock.

"Inger!" Stacie called out after her. "You have to help unload!"

"Yeah, in just a minute," she replied over her shoulder.

"Inger, come on!" Atticus barked. "There'll be plenty of time to run around after we get things unpacked."

Inger stopped; she gave a couple of rocks a disgruntled kick and walked back to the car. Stacie stepped away from the car so she could see out beyond the barn. "Stacie," Inger snapped, mimicking her sister, "you have to help unload!"

"Don't worry about it, dodo!" Stacie replied, making a face at her.

"Okay you two," Atticus said as he grabbed a bag of groceries out of the back seat, "no fighting." Then he handed Inger the bag. "You can put this on the boat, okay?"

Inger took the bag and started back toward the dock. Picking up another bag and a gallon of milk, he handed them to Stacie. "Okay, your turn," he said. Finally, he grabbed the last bag along with the ten-pound bag of ice and followed.

Atticus looked around as he walked past the barn, but there was no sign of Spence. The *Moonhawk* sat silently behind the *Jane*. All was quiet except for the sound of children playing on the city dock across the harbor.

Inger was already on board as Stacie and her dad walked out onto the dock. "Hey Dad!" Inger shouted, standing close to the hatch cover. "Someone left you a note!"

Following Stacie on board, Atticus set his items down on the seat next to Inger's bag. "Let me see it," he said.

Inger handed him the note.

"What does it say?" Stacie asked as Atticus unfolded it.

He read it out loud: "Atticus, contact me as soon as you can. I found a house for you to rent, but the owner wants to meet with you before she leaves on the last boat tomorrow—Butch."

"Who's Butch?" Inger asked.

"He's the president of the school board," Atticus replied as he refolded the note and stuffed it into his shirt pocket.

Atticus undid the paddle lock and opened the hatch as the girls scurried off back to the car. Grabbing the bag of ice, he went below. The air inside was warm and musty from being closed up. He put the bag of ice down and went forward to open the hatches. As he did, he looked around. Coming back into the galley, he leaned down and looked under the cockpit liner. Satisfied, he opened the ice chest and emptied the ice into it.

———◆———

Back at the car, Inger crawled into the back seat and started to hand things out to Stacie. "Do you like it here?" she asked nonchalantly.

"Oh, it's okay," Stacie replied. "Do you?"

"Yeah, I think it's neat."

"This is the first time you've seen the boat; what do you think of her?" Inger asked.

"It's beautiful, but a boat is just a boat as far as I'm concerned."

"Well I think she's beautiful," Inger replied.

"That's because Dad likes it. It's an awful long ways from Madison ya know," Stacie said.

"It's not that far."

"That's because you slept all the way."

"Well, so did you," Inger replied abruptly.

Stacie threw the last sleeping bag on the pile. "I'll take as much of this stuff as I can," she said. "You get the kerosene out of the trunk and bring the rest."

Inger got out of the car, taking the keys with her. "Stacie?" she said, closing the door.

"What?" Stacie replied as she finished picking up as much as she could carry.

"I think this job is very important to Dad. Maybe we shouldn't be too quick to judge it; maybe we should wait and see."

"I know," Stacie replied again, and then she started to walk back toward the boat.

———————

After loading everything on board, and with the girls down below arguing over who would sleep where, Atticus looked up; Spencer was coming down the dock. "Well, how you doing there, Spence?" he said, standing up.

"Just fine," the old man replied, cocking his hat back on his head as he always did. "Anybody bother your boat?"

"Doesn't appear so," Atticus said as he stepped off onto the dock.

"I didn't think anybody would bother her here; I've been keeping a pretty close eye on things."

"I appreciate that," Atticus replied, extending his hand to greet the old man. "You been keeping yourself busy?"

"Oh yes," he said with a big grin. "Say, Butch has been looking for you; I think he was expecting you back yesterday."

"We got held up."

"I guess he's found a place for you to rent."

"So I understand. Do you have any idea where it is?"

"Well," Spencer hesitated. "I think you better wait and talk to Butch about that."

At that moment, Stacie and Inger appeared from below and stood in the cockpit, watching.

"Girls, I'd like for you to meet someone," Atticus said, motioning for them to come over by him.

The girls stepped off the boat and went over by their father without saying a word.

"This is my older daughter, Stacie," Atticus said, putting his arm around her shoulders. "And this is Inger," he continued, tousling her hair.

"I heard you had a couple of good-looking young ladies with you, but I didn't realize they were your kids."

"Yep, I'm afraid so," Atticus said, smiling at both of them again. "This is Mr. Nordman. He owns this dock."

"Just call me Spencer," he replied, smiling. "Tell me, are you both sailors like your father?"

Sensing their reluctance to respond, Atticus answered for them. "Inger is," he said. "But Stacie's more of a city girl; she doesn't care much for sailing."

Just then, Butch came around the corner of the barn, walking briskly. "I was beginning to think you weren't coming back, Gunner," he barked.

"I tried to stay away," Atticus replied with a grin. "But I couldn't find a decent job, so I had to come back."

Both men grinned at each other as they reached out to shake hands.

"And these must be your daughters," Butch said, smiling at them. "My name is Butch Gorpon."

"This is Stacie, and that's Inger," Atticus replied.

Butch shook each of their hands. "You girls going to stay for a while and help the old man get settled in?"

"I guess so," Stacie replied, trying to muster a smile.

"Well, that may be sooner than you think," he said, turning his attention to Spencer. "Did you tell Atticus about it?" he said, smiling at the old man.

"Nope!" Spencer replied. "I left that for you."

"Wait a minute," Atticus said. "I don't like the sound of this. What did you do?"

"There, you see," Butch said, looking at Spencer again. "I told you he'd be happy about this news."

Atticus simply looked at Butch.

"Okay," Butch said, sitting down on one of the dock pilings. "How about the Hersoff place?"

"Are you serious?" Atticus replied.

Butch nodded. "Cynthia is on the island right now. She's heard about you and approached Hepper yesterday. She said she wants to rent her place to you, and she wants to see you before she leaves."

"Butch, after everything you've told me about that place, what makes you think I would want to rent it?"

"Hey, it's a beautiful place! It's big; it's private; it's on the lake; and it's completely furnished. You're not worried about it being haunted, are you?"

"Haunted?" Inger said, her ears perking up.

"Yep," Butch replied with a quick nod. "I mean—well . . ."

"Yes, Butch," Atticus interjected. "Come on, we're waiting; I want to see you talk your way out of this one."

Butch gave Atticus a sickly smile and then looked back at Inger. "It's not really haunted, honey," he said. "That's just sort of an old island story."

"Is that one of the places you told us about?" Stacie asked her father.

"Yes, I'm afraid it is," Atticus said, turning his attention back to Butch. "Butch, look, it's got nothing to do with whether or not it's haunted, but if what you told me about this Cynthia is even half true, she's got to be one weird broad, and if there is anything I don't need right now, it's involvement with more weirdos."

"I hope he's not referring to us," Butch said, smiling at Spence.

"You know what I mean," Atticus uttered. "Besides, what would I do rambling around in a great big house like that? I probably couldn't even afford to heat the place."

"Well, you got daughters that will be coming to see you," Butch said.

"Dad, I'd like to see this lady," Inger interrupted. "Let's just go and look at the house for the fun of it; right, Stace?"

"It's something to do," Stacie replied.

"There!" Butch said with a nod. "Listen to your daughters."

"Okay," Atticus replied, shaking his head. "But Gorpon, if you're getting me involved in another situation . . ."

"It's all of that; that's for sure," Spencer said, shaking his head.

Butch looked over at Spencer. "Hey, just whose side are you on anyway?"

"Well, she's nothing but trouble," he said, looking back at Butch, "and you know it! I wouldn't advise anyone to do business with her."

"Okay," Butch said to Atticus. "I'll admit the woman is—well, strange; but you don't have to put up with her. She seldom comes to the island. All you have to do is send her the rent once a month. Besides, I've looked around and there aren't many choices. Here they are," he said, holding up three fingers to emphasize his point. "There are two summer homes—they're nice, but you can't move into either one of them until September, and you'll have to move out again the following May. Reason being, people want their places available during the summer months. There's the old Putman cottage out on East Point Road; you can have that year-round, but there's no indoor plumbing. There's the hotel, or any of the resorts, but they'll cost you $500 a week during the tourist season; take your pick."

"Okay, you've made your point," Atticus replied. "And I'm not really interested in living on the boat, so what is she asking for her place?"

"That's the part that is totally unbelievable, even for me," Butch said. "Would you believe $125 a month?"

"$125 a month! There's got to be something wrong; why so cheap?"

Butch shrugged his shoulders. "I don't know," he replied. "You'll have to talk to her to get the answer to that question—by the way, she's only going to be here today, so if you're interested, you better get over there soon." Butch patted Spencer on the shoulder as he turned and started to walk away. "Nice meeting you, girls," he said over his shoulder, "and I'll talk to you later, Atticus. You know the way over there, right?"

"Yes, I know the way," Atticus replied.

———•—•—•———

Driving into the cool shade of the tall maple trees on the west side of the island was a welcomed relief from the hot midafternoon sun. Coming to the old wooden sign marking the entrance of the Hersoff place, Atticus turned left into the driveway. Just as he remembered, the wild grass grew tall along both sides of the drive, leaving only the tire trails to mark the way. The path cut across a small meadow and then off into the woods.

Sitting on the edge of their seats, eyes glued to the trail ahead, the girls searched through the foliage for the first hint of the old estate. Then almost without warning, the drive broke out of a thick cedar grove and into a clearing. Ahead, standing off on the north side of the clearing, was the huge two-story stone house with a steep pitched roof and three massive chimneys.

Atticus stopped the car. Whether it was the disjointedness of the structure, the obvious lack of maintenance, or the overwhelming disdain of its silent massiveness, it was hard to say, but no one said a word. The main section of the house was stone clear to the top of the uppermost peak, including the gables. Off the back, at the second-story level, a door led out onto a Swiss-style wooden balcony with a massive wooden stairway coming down to ground level. Below the balcony was a flower garden, grown tall with weeds and surrounded by a low stone wall. On the south side of the house was a three-stall garage with three English carriage doors. Next to the garage, attached to the house, was a greenhouse. Several panes of glass had either fallen out or were broken, and the frames were parched from lack of care. The inside of the greenhouse was equally pathetic; once-cared-for plants, left unattended, had grown only to reach the confines of their prison and die, leaving their gaunt remains twisted against the dirty glass.

"What a place!" Inger said.

"You mean dump," Stacie replied.

"No doubt about it," Atticus said as he took his foot off the brake, allowing the car to start moving forward again. "It could use some work."

They drove down into the yard and up behind a dark green carryall truck with Illinois license plates. Getting out of the car, Atticus walked around the carryall and up to the porch door. As he knocked on the door, the girls came up and stood directly behind him.

While they waited, Atticus looked around. Out beyond the house, through what was once the front yard, through the tall grass and brush, out beyond the unkempt cedars, was the open lake, glistening in the midday sun. Behind them, directly across the clearing, standing in the shadows of the tall cedars, were a couple of old rundown sheds, an old dump truck with no doors, and several large stacks of firewood.

Atticus knocked again; trying the porch door, he opened it and walked in. "What are you doing?" Stacie asked in a half whisper.

"We're going in; what does it look like?" Inger replied out loud as she scurried up the steps following her father.

Stacie followed. Walking up behind Inger, she touched her lightly on the shoulder. "Look out!" she snapped.

Startled, Inger jumped.

"What's the matter, Inger? Afraid?" Stacie said in a teasing fashion.

"Stop it, puke face!" Inger replied, making a face at her.

"Okay you two," Atticus said as he knocked a couple of times on the inside door.

They stood there in silence for a few moments, and then Atticus knocked again. The door latch tripped and the door opened. A bony little man with gray beady eyes, a twisted nose, and a jagged purple scar cutting diagonally across his entire face looked up at Atticus and greeted them. "Can I help you?" he said in a soft, raspy voice.

"Yes, my name is Atticus Gunner. I'd like to talk with the owner if I could."

The man's head made a small involuntary jerk as his right eye drifted off to the side. Saliva began forming at the corners of his mouth, and his jaw fell partially open as though he were grasping for words but couldn't quite find them. His body began to quiver. Atticus reached out, grabbing him firmly by the shoulders to prevent him from falling. As the little man slowly regained his composure, Atticus released his grip. "Are you okay?" he asked.

Giving a nod, the man said, "I'll go get Cynthia." Then with a very distinct limp, he made his way across the room, up the open stairway, and finally he disappeared into the second-story hallway.

When he was out of sight, Stacie gave a sigh of relief. "Wow," she said, "that was strange."

"I doubt he can help it," Atticus replied softly.

"What's the matter with him?" Inger asked.

"I don't know," Atticus said as he stepped into the living room just off the entranceway. "I would guess he's probably had a serious accident of some kind, or maybe he has epilepsy."

"What's that?" Inger asked, following her dad.

"A disorder of the central nervous system."

"Can you catch it?"

"Oh, look out, Inger," Stacie said, shaking her hands and pretending she couldn't control her eyes, "I think I just caught it."

"That's not funny," Atticus replied. "And the answer is no," he said to Inger, "you can't catch it."

"What do you suppose happened to his face?" Inger asked, ignoring Stacie.

"Inger, don't ask so many questions," Stacie said softly.

"I can ask all the questions I want," she replied, giving Stacie another dirty look.

"Yes, you can," Atticus said, "but later, okay?"

Atticus looked around; the combined smell of charred wood and mustiness gave the room a rancid odor. The living room was large, with windows facing both the lake and the porch. Curtains hung clear to the floor and were drawn back at the windowsill. There was a large Oriental rug on the floor, with a half-dozen pieces of large furniture placed about the room, all draped with sheets. On the far wall was a big open-hearth fireplace. Inside it were the remains of three or four half-burned logs. The ceiling above the fireplace was stained from years of exposure to smoke and soot.

Looking out of the living room across the foyer was an archway that led into the kitchen. In the center of the kitchen was a large wooden table with eight captain's chairs. Behind the table was a work counter with cabinets above. The foyer itself was void of furniture except for a wooden coat tree that stood off to the side of the front entrance. The open stairs that led to the second floor wasn't quite what one would expect for such a grand old house; it went diagonally up the back wall and was narrow, with a crude two-by-four handrail. Beneath the stairs was a closed wooden door that couldn't be over five feet high; it was constructed of shiplap and held together with strips of wrought iron.

"Scooby-Doo, where are you?" Stacie whispered in a joking manner.

With the girls following close behind, Atticus walked across the foyer and into the kitchen. It was long and narrow with cupboards from floor to ceiling on the far wall. Back in the corner was another door that opened into the three-stall garage; next to it was an old refrigerator. The most striking thing was the brick oven built into the narrow back wall. A piece of plywood was leaning over the face of the cooking hearth, with an electric stove standing in front of it.

"Mr. Gunner?" came a scratchy voice, startling both Atticus and the girls.

Atticus turned; a rather absurd-looking woman stood in the foyer, staring at them. "I'm sorry," he said, "we were just looking around a bit. I take it you're Mrs. Hersoff?"

"My name is Cynthia," she replied. "Please come in the living room and sit down."

Atticus and the girls followed as she led the way. The three of them looked on silently as Cynthia proceeded to uncover a davenport and a couple of high-back chairs. "I have to keep things covered," she said as she laid the dusty sheets back over the tops of the furniture, "otherwise they get so dirty; come, sit down." She motioned toward the old davenport.

Atticus and the girls sat down.

"Well," she said, sitting in the chair across from them, "you've obviously had a chance to look around; what do you think of my house?"

The woman was wearing a light green quilted kimono with furry blue slippers, and judging by the sorry state of her dyed red hair, which was sticking out in every direction, it was obvious she'd just gotten out of bed. She was a short chunk of a woman who Atticus guessed to be somewhere in her early fifties, and although there was absolutely nothing threatening about her stature, there was an aura about her. Whether it was because of what he had been told, or her almost catlike stare, he wasn't sure, but she left him with an uncomfortable feeling. "Well, it was undoubtedly a grand old house at one time," he replied.

"But in need of a lot of fixing, correct?" she said.

"I'm afraid so."

"I take it these are your children?" she went on, looking at the girls.

"Yes."

She paused for a second and then continued, "I imagine the islanders have told you about me?"

"They've made comments," he replied.

"I've been called many things, Mr. Gunner; mostly I've been called a witch, but I consider myself a mystic and a psychic."

"I'm sorry, ma'am, I'm not interested in what you're called; I came here to talk to you about the possibility of renting your house."

"Do you know what a psychic is, Mr. Gunner?" she asked.

"Ma'am, I'm afraid we're not communicating. I'm not interested in who or what you are; what I am interested in is the house."

"Of course you're not—I forget."

Atticus started to get up. "I think perhaps we've made a mistake in coming here."

"Please, Mr. Gunner," she replied, "you haven't made a mistake. If you would grant me your indulgence for just a moment, I'll explain my seemingly strange behavior. It's just that I've been waiting for some time for you to come, and now that you are here, I'm not quite sure how to proceed."

"I beg your pardon?" Atticus replied with a puzzled look on his face.

"Do you believe in the existence of evil, Mr. Gunner?"

Atticus glanced down at the girls.

"Are you worried I might frighten the children?" she asked.

"No," he said. "What I'm worried about is you wasting my time."

"Then please bear with me, you don't believe in psychics, do you, Mr. Gunner?"

"No, I do not."

"Mr. Gunner, evil has reared its ugly head throughout the history of the world; in every form, in every manner, and to every terrible degree possible. And when it does, I believe an appropriate warrior is brought forward to take on this infamous entity. There is a presence that has crawled up out of the cauldrons of history and is lurking somewhere in the shadows of this island, and it is evil. I have been waiting some time now for the coming of a warrior to take on this beast, and the moment I heard of your arrival, I intuitively knew it was you I was waiting for. Now I am sure that statement bothers you. I would even venture a guess that you would like to write me off as a crackpot, but you will not. Why? Because you already have an inkling of what I speak; that is why you are here, and you and I both know it."

Atticus got up and started for the door; he motioned for the girls to follow, but he did not respond.

"Mr. Gunner! The house will cost you $125 a month, completely furnished. There's plenty of firewood stacked out in the yard, free for the taking, enough to probably take you through two winters. You may do anything you choose with the yard and the house. I'll pay for whatever materials you need. There are lawn mowers, hoses, and shovels—most everything you'll need is right out in the garage. Upstairs there are three bedrooms, completely furnished, and a large recreation room with a fireplace and billiard table. You even have your own private beach. The house includes linens, dishes, silverware, things like that. There's a forty-two-cubic-foot freezer out in the garage. The house is yours year-round as long as you need it, and I will not come around to bother you—ever."

Atticus stopped and turned back toward the woman. The girls were so close behind they practically walked into him. "Why?" he asked. "Why would you want to do this?"

"Let's just say I like you."

"If I decide to take you up on your offer, when would you need to know?"

"I'm leaving on the last boat tonight. You may pick up the key from Hepper Greshion. I'll expect you to pay one month in advance, and every month thereafter as you go. I'll leave my address and phone number on the counter in the event you should decide to take my offer. Any questions?"

"No, ma'am," Atticus replied, "we'll make a decision tonight." He turned and once more started for the door.

"Mr. Gunner, I'm very glad to see a Scorpio come into our affairs," Cynthia said.

Curiosity getting the best of her, Inger finally spoke. "What's a Scorpio?" she asked.

"It's an individual born under the astrological sign of the Scorpion," Cynthia said, smiling at her.

Still confused, Inger wrinkled up her nose and looked up at her father.

"Anyone born in November is said to be born under the sign of the Scorpion," Atticus said softly. "My birthday is November third, that means I'm a Scorpio."

"How in the world did she know that?" Inger asked.

"I just know those kinds of things," Cynthia replied.

"Really? Then what am I?" Inger asked.

"Well," Cynthia said, brushing her ratty hair back off her forehead, "judging from what I see—you're active, talkative, inquisitive, and probably very persuasive; I'd say you're a Gemini."

"Gemini?"

"Yes, born somewhere between May 22 and June 21."

"My gosh, Dad, she's right."

"You say you're a psychic?" Stacie asked. "What kind of spirits do you talk to?"

"Well, my father, for one."

"Your dead father?"

Cynthia nodded.

Atticus opened the door. "Okay, girls; time to go." He stepped out and started toward the porch door. The girls cut off the conversation and followed.

As they walked out of the porch and around the carryall, Inger scurried to catch up with her father. "What do you think of her?" she asked, looking up at him.

Atticus just shook his head.

"I think she's totally spaced out," Stacie remarked as she walked around to the other side of the car and opened the passenger door.

Atticus opened the car door and let Inger slide in ahead of him. "She does make you wonder if she's playing with a full deck," he said as he slid in behind the wheel.

"What do you mean?" Inger asked. "You think she's crazy?"

"No, Inger, people always run around talking to ghosts!" Stacie interjected.

"I wasn't talking to you," Inger snapped. "Dad, do you think she's crazy?"

"I don't know, she's certainly strange."

"Yeah, but that doesn't mean she's crazy."

"No, I suppose not."

"Well, I think she's crazy," Stacie said.

"If she's so crazy, how did she guess my birthdate?" Inger said, looking at Stacie.

"Lucky guess."

"She knew Dad's too; was that another lucky guess?"

"Probably."

"Do you think so?" Inger asked, looking at her father again.

"I don't know," Atticus said as he backed the car up and turned around. "She could have gotten that information in a lot of different ways."

"Well, she didn't find out my birthday from anyone, cause I haven't told anyone around here. I think she is just what she says she is."

On the way up the drive, just before they left the clearing, Atticus stopped the car briefly and looked back.

"What are you doing?" Stacie asked.

"Just looking at the house one more time," Atticus said.

"You're not thinking about renting this place, are you?" Stacie asked.

"Well, you heard Butch," Atticus replied. "This place is pretty hard to pass up, considering the alternatives."

"It gives me the creeps," Stacie replied.

Inger turned around, flopping herself facing forward in the seat again. "I think it's pretty neat," she said. "Just imagine, when we come up here to visit, we'd be staying in a real haunted house; how cool is that?"

Atticus stepped on the accelerator and headed back up the drive. "We'll talk about it tonight," he said as he cranked on the wheel to round a sharp curve in the drive.

———— ‑‑◆‑‑ ————

That afternoon, the girls ran well ahead of Atticus as he walked out of the tall grass and down onto Sand Dune Beach. A middle-aged couple was stretched out on beach towels a short distance away, and a group of teenagers was horsing around a hundred yards or so down the beach; other than that, the beach was deserted.

Rolling up their pant legs, the girls waded out into the surf, only to be chased back by one of the endless waves rolling in. The warm breeze felt good as Atticus stood watching them laugh and splash about. It was a pleasure to see them enjoying each other rather than that incessant bickering.

"Hey, Mr. Gunner!" a young man shouted from down the beach.

Recognizing it to be the Shernie boy, Atticus smiled and gave a casual wave.

The lad grabbed his towel, dried his hair, and started walking toward Atticus and the girls. Another young man sitting on the sand with the rest of the group got up and followed. At first, Atticus didn't recognize him, but as they came closer, he realized it was Bill Sorenson, the boy who worked with Quint.

"How you doing, Mr. Gunner?" Ken said, draping his towel around his neck as he walked up to Atticus. "Have you been getting into any more fights lately?"

"No, not lately," Atticus replied. "Have you been sucking on any beer bottles lately?"

Ken smiled. "No, not since that night."

"Good, then it looks like we're both making progress."

Bill Sorenson joined Ken and exchanged greetings with Atticus. Ken asked when Atticus would be starting his new job. Atticus responded by telling him it hadn't been established yet, but it would be soon.

Stacie came back out of the surf, picking up her shoes as she did. She didn't say anything, but there was a definite femininity in her walk that had been all but absent a short while ago; the boys took notice.

Atticus cleared his throat in an attempt to bring his presence back into the picture. "This is my daughter Stacie," he said, "and this is Inger," he added, as she came up on the other side of him.

The boys smiled at Stacie.

"Your daughters?" Ken asked, not taking his eyes off Stacie.

"That's right," Atticus said. "My daughters—with the emphasis on *my*!"

"You mean you're going to be going to school here?" he asked Stacie.

"No, we're just visiting," Inger replied as though the question had been directed toward her.

"Oh," Ken said, just glancing at Inger. "You're here for the summer then?"

"Well, not exactly," Stacie said, smiling at Ken, "but we'll be back real often, I'm sure."

"That's really great—right, Bill?"

"Yeah," Bill said with a big grin on his face. "By the way, my name is Bill Sorenson, and this is Ken Shernie."

"Hi," Stacie replied.

"Would you like to come over and meet some of the rest of the group?" Ken asked.

Stacie looked at her dad.

"Perhaps in a couple of days or so," Atticus replied. "Right now I'd like to finish showing them around."

"We'd be happy to do that for you," Ken replied.

"We'll take good care of them, Mr. Gunner," Bill interjected.

"Them?" Inger responded, perking up. "You mean I can come along?"

"Sure, Squirt; why not?" Bill said. "We might as well show both of you around."

"I really would like to meet some of the kids," Stacie said, looking up at her father again.

Atticus paused and then gave a shy, "I'm assuming one of you has a car."

"I have my dad's Jeep," Ken replied.

"If you're as responsible about driving as you are about drinking, I'm not sure I can trust you."

"I'm not perfect, Mr. Gunner, but if I give my word, you can depend on it, and I give you my word; okay?"

"There you go," Inger interjected. "Can we?"

"I count three others down there; plus the four of you; that's seven total. You going to pack that many people into a Jeep?"

"It's a wagon, Mr. Gunner," Bill said, "and if it means anything, I'll give you my word too. There won't be any fooling around."

Again Atticus paused. "Okay. It's against my better judgment," he said, "but I'm going to let them go with you. However, I want you to understand this, boys, and I mean it: if you pull any stupid stunts, you won't like dealing with me at all; do I make myself clear?"

"Yes sir," they both replied.

"And I want both of you," he said, looking at the girls, "back at the boat by no later than seven o'clock. Is that understood?"

The girls nodded.

"Okay, let's go then," Ken replied.

Stacie smiled at her dad and then started to walk away with the boys.

"See ya," Inger said to her dad as she scurried off to follow.

———◆———

As they ate breakfast, it soon became obvious that the girls' attitude toward the island had blossomed substantially. Last night it was apparent that both of them were totally infatuated by summer life on the island, and Stacie's attitude was influenced by her more-than-casual interest in Bill Sorenson. Not only did they both voice their approval of Atticus taking the job, but they even thought it would be a good idea to rent the Hersoff place. By the time the morning dishes were done, the decision had been finalized, and in less than an hour, they picked up the key from Hepper and were back on the porch at the old Hersoff place. It all happened so fast even Atticus was taken aback by it. After lunch, Bill Sorenson showed up and was soon recruited into the operation of housecleaning by the girls.

The following morning, on the way to the house, the girls insisted that Atticus stop at the store to pick up some food. When they came out carrying four twelve-packs of pop and a shopping bag full of junk food, Atticus decided it was time to investigate what was going on. It seemed, in the process of their recruiting, the girls hadn't really limited it to just Bill. They apparently convinced him they needed all the help he could get, and as a result, he promised to round up at least six or seven island kids to pitch in for the day.

The thought of a mixed gang of teenagers working on a project from which they could gain nothing but horseplay didn't rest comfortably with Atticus. Even more troubling, when they drove into the yard, there was the Shernie boy's Jeep and another vehicle. Along with the vehicles came a bunch of kids sprawled out all over the steps, waiting for Atticus and the girls to arrive.

Atticus pulled up behind the Jeep and stopped. The girls got out of the car immediately; Atticus stayed in the car for a minute. Finally, with the enthusiasm of a bull being led to slaughter, he got out and approached the group.

Bubbling with social eloquence, Stacie quickly introduced each of the young people to Atticus. There was the girl who had waited on Atticus that first night at the restaurant, Joni Greshion. Then there was the girl who was with her that night, Kris Bowen. Stacie introduced both Ken and Bill as though Atticus had never met either of them before. There was Mrs. Bergason's boy, Peter, a tall, dark kid with narrow shoulders and glasses.

And last, but certainly not least, was Nathan Kerfam. Atticus didn't make the connection until later that day, but Nathan was the son of Jody Kerfam, the talkative woman who picked him up that first night on the island. At any rate, on first impression Nathan appeared to be an absolute buffoon. He was short and squat; his pant legs came down to just above his ankles, and the top was cinched so tight around his waist that Atticus wondered how his lower extremities got any circulation. He was wearing high-top tennis shoes with the whole side torn out of one; his shirt was about two sizes too big with the buttons put through to the wrong buttonholes. His glasses had been broken in about six different places and were held together with everything from Scotch tape to rubber bands; they were all twisted out of shape and barely hung on his face.

When Stacie introduced Nathan, it was as though it gave her great pain to do so, and although the introduction did little more than acknowledge his presence, it was followed by a round of heckling from the rest of the boys. Nathan didn't seem to mind because he really didn't have much choice. But there was more to it than that; Nathan was an exceptionally bright kid who was just a little out of step with the rest of his peers, and to survive, he had become the group's outspoken funnyman.

At that point, it didn't take a genius to decipher the look on Atticus's face. Inger was the first to notice. Stacie didn't pick up on it until she finished her last introduction. But from experience, they both knew what to expect next; Stacie stopped talking and sat down on the steps.

Totally oblivious to the situation, Ken, who was also sitting on the steps, stood up. "Well," he said, "let's get going—the sooner we get started, the sooner we get done."

"Why don't you sit back down for a minute?" Atticus said softly.

"Don't sweat a thing, Mr. Gunner," he continued. "We'll shape this old place up in nothing flat; some of us should probably start with the yard. Have you got a lawn mower?"

Stacie reached up and grabbed Ken by the shirt sleeve and pulled him down. "What are you doing?" Ken remarked as he plopped back down on the steps. Stacie glanced at him and then back up at her father. "Oh," Ken said, getting the drift, "you want to say something, Mr. Gunner?"

"I appreciate that all of you are willing to help, but we've got a lot to do here, and I'm in no mood to play chaperone to a funny farm."

"Good play on words," Nathan piped in with a big grin, "but I really don't think you understand the capacity and enthusiasm of us fine young islanders. We're really not as peremptory as one might expect of such a diverse group."

Atticus looked at Nathan. "Thank you for that," he said, "but I think we'd rather go at this project on our own."

"Perhaps you didn't understand," Nathan reiterated with a bit of sarcasm. "What I was trying to tell you . . ."

"Nathan, isn't it?" Atticus broke in, cutting the boy off.

"That is correct!" Nathan replied.

"Nathan," Atticus said, "so I don't have to get peremptory and send that unsavory rear end of yours up the road in a very unhappy manner, I think it would be best if you shut your mouth and listened. Now, did I make myself clear?"

"Yes sir! It's no skin off my posterior if that's how you feel."

Ken spoke up. "Nate, cool it. If Mr. Gunner doesn't want our help, it's up to him."

Atticus looked at Ken but didn't say anything.

"I imagine you're worried that all we'll do is horse around, right?" Ken said.

"Something like that," Atticus replied.

"I don't blame you, but you sure got a lot to do around here. It's going to take a long time with just the three of you to get it done—I'll tell you what; I'll make you a deal."

"I'll bet you will," Atticus replied.

"No, I'm serious! You let us help, and I promise you there'll be no goofing off. The first time we do, you can tell us to hit the road, and we'll be gone."

"That sounds fair enough," Stacie broke in.

"What do you say, Mr. Gunner?" Ken asked.

Atticus stood there for a second, scanning the group. "Once again," he said, "why—why would you all want to do this? I'm curious."

"It's simple," Ken replied, "we like you. Besides, you're going to be both the new sheriff and the new school boss; it's best if we get on your good side."

"Frankly, I don't believe you, but that's not bad thinking," Atticus replied. "And how about you, Bill, why are you here?"

"Ken's just putting you on, Mr. Gunner," Bill said. "You gave him a ride home on your boat; he owes you; it's as simple as that. For the rest of us, we're curious about you, and besides, we like the girls."

"That's the first honest statement I've heard."

"How about it, Dad?" Inger chimed in. "You going to let them stay?"

"Again, it's against my better judgment, but yes, they can stay; but no horseplay!"

"You got it," Ken replied, getting up.

"Yeah, that's what I'm afraid of," Atticus said softly as he started back to the car to get Stacie's bag of goodies. "Don't forget, we're going to be seeing a lot of each other over the next year; you might want to keep that in mind."

———•◆•———

It was just after ten o'clock that night back on the *Moonhawk* when Inger stood up on the end of her bunk to blow out the lantern. Stacie was already fast asleep, and her dad's footsteps could be heard topside. As the darkness of the night drifted into the cabin, she nestled down into her sleeping bag and listened to the frogs sing in the grass along the water's edge. Inger loved sleeping on board the *Moonhawk*, especially on a night like this. As she lay there, she thought about the day's activities. She thought about the island kids, the Hersoff place, and how they'd actually had a lot of fun today in spite of the work; even her dad was impressed. The island kids really did come through. She thought about Nathan Kerfam and how funny he was. Then just as things began to fade, she was awakened by the sound of voices. After a few puzzling moments, she realized it was Mr. Gorpon talking. He was obviously upset; he mentioned a Mrs. Doebuck, and how she had called for a meeting to discuss property taxes and the school, and how she had insisted that Mr. Gunner be front and center at the meeting. All she could remember her dad saying was, "Calm down; I'll be happy to attend the meeting." After that, things faded away as she drifted off.

———◆·◆·◆———

The next morning, ready to move into the Hersoff place, the girls and Atticus loaded all their belongings into the car and headed for the old house to officially take occupancy. As they turned into the driveway, Stacie spotted Joni Greshion walking down the drive ahead of them. Joni stepped off the path and into the tall grass so the car could pass. Atticus drove up alongside of her and stopped. "Joni, what are you doing?" Stacie asked out her window.

"Hi," she said. "I don't have to work at the restaurant today, so I thought I'd come over and help again."

"That's great," Stacie replied, "come on, get in."

"I was hopin' you guys would be here; walkin' down to that place gives me the creeps," Joni said as she opened the back door and slid in. "I don't know what I would have done if nobody'd been there."

Joni was a pretty girl with a round face, warm smile, and big eyes. She had all the characteristics of growing to the heavy side when she became older, but for now she was a shapely young lady. Atticus remembered the night she waited on him at the restaurant and how the boys had made fun of her. Yesterday he picked up on some of the reasons why. Joni certainly wasn't the sharpest pebble on the beach, not to mention, she was extremely naïve. In the short while he observed, it became obvious she had been afforded little experience beyond the confines of the island. Born and raised here, she had only been off the island three times in her entire life, and then never overnight. Yet she was warm and pleasant with a bubbly laugh, and more important, she and Stacie seemed to like one another.

When they got to the house, the girls started unloading the car and putting things away. Yesterday, with the help of the island kids, they had pretty much wrapped up the cleaning inside the house, along with the cleaning of the attached greenhouse, so today Atticus intended to concentrate on the yard. He rolled out the riding mower from the garage and began to check it over. By noon the place was beginning to look like someone lived there. The entire yard, except along the lakefront, had been mowed. Inger, who spent the morning outside with her dad, managed to pull most of the weeds from the flower garden. Stacie and Joni got everything put away in the house, cleaned the porch, and then prepared a picnic lunch for everyone.

Anxious to find any excuse to quit pulling weeds, Inger welcomed Stacie's invitation to help spread a blanket out under the shade of the cedars and to haul the food outside.

Looking over at Atticus, who was busy grubbing brush along the lakefront, Stacie hollered, giving her father notice it was time to eat. Surprised, but pleased, he buried his ax into a stump. Wiping the sweat from his brow, he walked up into the cool shade, where the girls were meticulously laying things out. "Well, what have we got here?" he asked.

"You name it; we got it!" Inger replied. "They even thawed out some frozen strawberries."

Wiping the dust and dirt from his hands onto the front of his sweaty T-shirt, Atticus sat down and grabbed a couple slices of bread to make a sandwich.

"Dad," Stacie said, giving him a disgusted look. "Couldn't you at least go down to the lake and wash your hands? You look like a pig!"

"Oh Stacie," Inger chimed in with a pathetic tone in her voice, "don't be such an old grandma."

"No, she's right, I could stand a little washing," he replied. "Dink," he said as he got up and headed down the bank to the water, "run in the house and get me a towel and some soap."

Inger gave a big sigh but got up and started for the house. "Stacie, you're worse than Mom," she said as she trotted off. Inger brought her father a towel and some soap and went back up by the girls.

After they finished eating, a mysterious lull appeared in the conversation; that's when Stacie came out with her proverbial, "Dad?"

Although Atticus had absolutely no idea what was coming next, he'd been hit with that brief inquiry enough times to know she was about to put the touch on him for something. He replied, just as he had a thousand times before, "What?"

"You know we've really been working hard for the last couple days—haven't we?"

"Yes."

"And as far as I can tell, we've got the house pretty much finished inside."

"You want the rest of the afternoon off," he interjected.

Stacie smiled. "Well, sort of."

"Sort of?"

"Joni would like to take me over to the hotel and show me around."

"Can I go too?" Inger blurted out.

"Just a minute," Atticus said, motioning for Inger to be quiet. "Hotel?"

"Yes, Joni's uncle owns the Sunset Harbor Hotel, and it's just a half mile down the beach."

"You mean Hepper Greshion is your uncle?" he continued, looking at Joni.

"Yes, why?" Stacie asked.

Atticus smiled. "Nothing; I guess I should have made the connection, but for some reason I didn't. I forget, just about everybody up here is related to someone."

"He's my uncle all right," Joni said.

"Well, can I go?" Stacie asked.

"I guess so—you girls clean up the lunch dishes first, okay?"

"What about me?" Inger asked again.

"How about it," Atticus asked Stacie, "can she come too?"

"I suppose; she has to help clean up these dishes though."

"All right!" Inger replied gleefully.

The girls gathered up the remains of their picnic lunch and disappeared into the house. Atticus returned to his brush grubbing project. He'd no more than picked up the ax when Quint's old truck came rambling down the drive and into the yard.

After coming to a stop in front of the house, Quint and his young helper climbed out, slamming the truck doors behind them. "What the hell are you doing there, Gunner?" Quint barked with a big grin as he and Bill walked across the yard.

"Just trying to make the place livable," Atticus replied.

"So I see."

"Hello, Mr. Gunner," Bill said softly as he and Quint approached.

Atticus returned Bill's greeting and then looked back at Quint. "Well, how have you been, you old war horse?" he asked, smiling at Quint. "It's been a while."

"Yes, it has," Quint replied. "I heard you were back, but I've been busier than a pig in shit. By God, I never thought I'd see this place shaped up again as long as Cynthia owned it."

Atticus parked his ax back in the stump again. "I take it she's not one of your favorite people."

"To each his own," Quint said. "Say, where're those daughters of yours I've been hearing so much about?"

"They're in the house; Bill, why don't you go and get them?" Atticus asked.

Without saying a word, Bill turned and headed off toward the house. In a short time, he returned with all three of the girls, and Atticus introduced each of them to Quint, even though he was sure Quint already knew Joni.

In spite of Quint's typical gruff manner, Atticus could sense a feeling of warmth as he responded to the introductions, and then without hesitation, Quint turned his attention toward Bill. "Well, Bill," he barked, "do you want to ask them? Or should I?"

"Ask what?" Atticus questioned.

"Bill and I have to take a little boat trip across the lake tomorrow, and we were wondering if you and the girls would like to pack a lunch and come along." Quint winked at Atticus.

"Across the lake?" Stacie asked.

"Yes, there's a fella over on South Manitoo Island who's hanging up fishin' for a living, and he is selling everything. The price is right, so I bought his nets. We're going over tomorrow to pick 'em up."

"That's quite a trek by boat, isn't it?" Atticus questioned.

"About sixty miles, one way. You'll be back in time for a late supper."

Atticus could tell by the look on Inger's face that she was all for it, but with Stacie, it was different. "Well, what do you think?" Atticus asked, looking at the girls. "Would you like to ride across the lake to the Michigan side and see what the island of South Manitoo is like?"

"Sure," Inger replied without hesitation.

"What about you, Stace?" Atticus asked, looking at her.

"All the way across Lake Michigan?" she replied, trying very hard not to let on how she really felt. "In a fish boat?"

"Oh, it's a big boat," Bill said. "I mean a really nice boat. It doesn't even smell fishy; besides, South Manitoo is a really neat place."

Stacie looked at Joni. "Do you want to go?" she asked her.

"I can't, Stace," Joni replied. "Tomorrow is Sunday, and I have to work at the restaurant."

"Come on, Stace—it'll be a lot of fun," Bill pleaded.

"There isn't anything to do here," Inger added.

"I suppose," Stacie said.

"Good! Now we can go finish our chores," Bill said, turning to Quint.

Quint smiled at Atticus and winked again. "We'll have to leave early," he said.

"What time?" Atticus asked.

"Oh, around seven o'clock."

"We'll be there," Atticus answered.

Quint and Bill left; the girls headed for the hotel with Joni, and Atticus went back to his brush grubbing project.

The next time Atticus looked up, the girls were talking to Hepper Greshion about a hundred yards down the beach. After a few moments, Hepper started to walk toward Atticus, and the girls continued toward the hotel. Hepper waved. "How you doing?" he shouted.

Atticus smiled. "Just fine."

Hepper walked up to the edge of the foliage where Atticus was working. "Well, what brings you down this way?" Atticus asked.

"I have something for you," he replied. "Adrian Fruger gave me this box to give to you. He said the sheriff sent it up for you. It's Bert's badge and gun. I didn't even know Bert had a gun. He never carried it, that I knew of."

"Well, thank you," Atticus replied, taking the box from Hepper.

"I hope you're not going to take this cop stuff too serious."

"Well, I'll certainly try to do what's expected of me."

"We don't need some gung-ho cop type, you know; this isn't the city."

"Why, do I look like a gung-ho cop type to you?"

"What you look like isn't the issue; from what I hear, you're already far too pushy."

"So how is Tom these days? I'm surprised he's not with you," Atticus replied.

"Oh, I asked him to come, but he declined; he doesn't have much time for you."

"I'm sorry to hear that."

"I'll bet you are. To be honest, I can't really blame him, after being knocked around when he was drunk and all. That probably wouldn't have been quite so easy if he'd been sober."

Atticus paused for a second as though he wasn't going to respond, but then he changed his mind. "Look, Mr. Greshion," he said, "I didn't cause what happened that night; Tom did. And I'm certainly not looking for trouble, but if that kind of behavior ever happens again, and I'm there as the island cop, I'll do whatever it takes to stop it. That includes the Cline boys if they're the perpetrators; and you can tell Tom that for me."

Hepper turned without responding and started to walk away.

Atticus spoke up one more time. "Mr. Greshion, my daughters went down to the hotel with your niece; do you want me to come down and get them?"

Hepper stopped and looked back at Atticus again. "They're fine where they're at, Mr. Gunner. It's not a problem; I was just expressing an opinion, that's all. I've got a party of five businessmen coming in tomorrow; the three girls can help me get set up, if it's okay with you. I'll pay each of them, just like I do Joni."

Atticus looked at his watch. "That's fine, but I'd still like them home in an hour or two."

"Very well—oh, I almost forgot," Hepper went on. "The sheriff also sent a vehicle up for you; it's down at the ferry dock; you can pick up the keys in the ferry office. You must have influence down the county too; it's a brand-new Bronco; it's got 'Washington Island Police' painted on the side and everything. You'll be riding in style." With that, Hepper turned and continued to walk back toward the hotel.

Atticus was surprised by Hepper's attitude at first, but the more he thought about it, the more it made sense. From the very beginning, there seemed to be a built-in resentment for any kind of authority, especially if it came from off-island—that bothered him a bit. Then he thought about Cynthia's connections to Hepper; what odd bedfellows they seemed to be.

Looking down at the box in his hand, Atticus undid the tape and opened it; it was a police badge in a leather badge wallet, a one-size-fits-all baseball cap with "WI PD" embossed on the front, a snubnosed .38 caliber pistol in a belt holster, four boxes of high-velocity shells, and a note. He opened the note: "Dear Mr. Gunner, This isn't much of a weapon, you know; most officers are opting for semi-automatic handguns now. At least learn to shoot the damn thing. You may need it some day, even up there. Sheriff Dawson." Atticus refolded the note and put it back in the box with the rest of the items; he then set it down on the stump and went back to work.

CHAPTER 7

Incident at South Manitoo

$\mathbf{Q}$uint eased back on the throttle in order to maneuver his boat into the narrow channel that marked the only safe passage through Fisherman's Shoal. Once clear, he opened her up and swung the bow due east. The gentle swell running out of the south caused the big fish boat to roll slowly as she paralleled to the run of the sea.

Squinting against the bright morning sun, Quint stood off to the side of the big wooden steering wheel. Leaning on the sill of the wheelhouse, he stared off toward the horizon, quietly guiding the wheel. Atticus was sitting on the bench in the back of the wheelhouse. Occasionally the sound of the girls' laughter would drift up from below over the drone of the diesel engine.

Finally, Atticus slid off the bench and walked over next to Quint. "You've been pretty quiet this morning," he said, glancing over at the old man. "You must have had a rough night."

"Nope!" Quint grunted. "Didn't do a damn thing last night."

"You could have fooled me," Atticus replied. "You have the look of a man who may have imbibed a little too much nectar of the gods."

"Shit," Quint mumbled while rubbing the stubble on his face. "It'd take more than one night of drinkin' to put me down."

Atticus smiled.

"I just don't spend that much time runnin' off at the mouth when I'm behind this wheel—besides, it's been some time since I've heard the laughter of young girls on my boat."

"Does their noise bother you? 'Cause if it does . . ."

"No—no," Quint interrupted. "They're just fine—just fine."

Quint remained quiet for some time as they made their way eastward across the open lake. The activities of the girls on board undoubtedly rekindled his memories of a family long since taken from him. Knowing there were some things not even time could heal, Atticus allowed the old man the dignity of his thoughts in privacy.

Kids seem to have an uncanny ability to flourish in pairs, but never in a group of three, particularly if one of the three has the misfortune of being substantially younger than the others. By 10:15, the two older kids managed to embark on a plan to exclude Inger, but she managed to cope for more than half an hour before deciding to abandon the effort and retreat to the company of the adults in the wheelhouse.

Her arrival in the wheelhouse changed things almost immediately. With no hesitation, she moved into an ongoing dialogue with Quint. By 11:15, as the others settled in below for the long ride, Inger was standing behind the wheel, running the boat, and Quint was busy telling her story after story.

It was just past noon when the first glimpse of the Manitoo Islands rose up over the horizon. With the island's high sandy banks glistening in the bright midday sun, it reminded Atticus of the white cliffs of Dover. Still more than an hour out, Atticus called everyone together for lunch.

While they ate, Quint told of his first visit to these islands on an old sailing schooner more than fifty years ago. He told of how the mob used to run booze out of South Manitoo down to Chicago. "It was a rough place back then," he said. "Now the island belongs to the Michigan Power and Light Company. It's mostly deserted except for the few fishermen that still remain, and about thirteen rundown summer homes, all of which are spending out the last years of their existence under a condemnation order. With no new blood coming in, and the old folks fading away, things are pretty much in a sorry state. It's like a place with no future," Quint went on, shaking his head in disgust. "What the hell a big power company wants with an island is beyond me. Doesn't make a God damned bit of sense as far as I'm concerned."

Interrupting his own train of thought, Quint gave navigational instructions to Inger. She adjusted, and slowly they approached the passage between the two islands; North Manitoo to port, and South Manitoo to starboard.

"Since they went to automated navigational beacons and shut down the old lighthouse, even the government's given up interest in the island," Quint went on, looking out the window at South Manitoo. "There are some nice old homes on that island, just deserted and rotting away—it's a damn shame! Even the old lighthouse is all boarded up and falling apart."

"I heard it was earmarked for a state park," Atticus remarked.

"Yeah, so I understand," Quint replied.

"I don't think they're going to let it go to waste."

"No, I suppose not," Quint continued, taking out a new chew of tobacco. "I guess it's just me. Like so many other things—what I knew as a whole way of life is dead and gone forever."

This time Atticus didn't reply; there was no need.

The boat closed in on the island, passing the high sandy bluffs on the northeast shore and then turning west, heading into the island's only public harbor. The place for mooring consisted of a low sandy beach arching down the east shore for about a mile. At the south end of the harbor, up on top of Red Sandstone Point, partially obscured from view by the trees and the rocky outcropping, stood the old government lighthouse. There were only two yachts in the harbor; both were anchored about seventy-five yards off shore. The only docking facility was an old makeshift wooden dock set on pilings, twisted and torn by years of winter ice, with its bleached white planks glistening in the sun; it too was nothing but a remnant of a time long gone.

Quint took over the controls and maneuvered the boat into the dock. Atticus and Bill jumped off to secure the mooring lines. Inger followed without hesitation and scampered off down the dock while her father hollered instructions for her not to go too far. Stacie stood in the open door of the wheelhouse and watched.

"Stace," Bill said, looking up at her as he tied off his last line, "I'll take you down and show you the old lighthouse while Quint and your dad take care of business."

Stacie looked at her father.

"How long is it going to take us here?" Atticus asked Quint.

"No more than three hours," Quint replied as he shut down the engine.

"You heard him," Atticus said, looking back up at his daughter. "Three hours!" He held up three fingers. "Be back in three hours."

"You got it, Mr. Gunner," Bill replied as he and Stacie headed down the dock toward the beach. "We'll be back in less than three hours."

After no more than a half-dozen steps, Stacie stopped and turned around once again. "Dad, do we have to take Inger along this time too?"

Atticus gave a sigh. "No, I'll keep her with me, but remember she is your sister and she doesn't really have anyone else right now."

"Good," Stacie replied, oblivious to her father's comment.

Atticus watched as the two headed down the beach in the direction of the lighthouse. The island truly was a deserted place. The only people in sight were sitting on the deck of the nearest yacht. The only building in sight was a one-story, unpainted shack back at the edge of the sand; it had a porch-like overhang and a wooden boardwalk in front. The faded words "Island Store" were still visible on the old sign hanging diagonally from the overhang; it looked like something out of an old western movie. There was a red gas pump sitting in the sand next to the building and, behind the building, an open forest of tall stately elms.

"Well," Atticus said as Quint stepped off the boat. "Where does this guy live? I don't see much of anything here, not even a fish boat."

"So I noticed," Quint grunted. "Must have sold the God damned thing. He used to tie up right here."

"Where is his house?"

Quint motioned toward the woods. "He lives up the beach back in a little cottage; it's not much better than that shack though." He pointed at the old store.

"Seems like a poor place to live," Atticus said. "If he sold his boat, how in the world does he get off and on this place?"

"I think they still run a weekly ferry," Quint replied as he started down the dock.

Just then, Inger came running up the beach from the same direction Stacie and Bill had gone. "Dad!" she hollered as she ran up to him. "Stacie told me I couldn't go with them; how come?"

Atticus gave a shrug. "Well, because they want to go alone, I guess."

"Where they going?"

"They're just walking down to the old lighthouse."

"That's what I thought," Inger said disgustedly. "Dripnose just wants to be alone with Bill!"

"Well, that's okay," Atticus replied, grabbing her by the back of the neck and pulling her in under his arm. "You can stay with us—we're better company anyway."

Inger squirmed free and ran ahead to catch up with Quint. The three of them walked up the beach past the dunes and dune grass, and into the woods by way of a dirt road.

———•◆•———

Stacie stopped when she and Bill got within full sight of the lighthouse. It was a neat old place, but kind of spooky, she thought. The round stone tower stood high above the trees; the lighthouse at the top, with a sheet metal deck and iron railing rusted brown with long streaks of rust bleeding down the face of the tower, made the structure look strangely harmonious with the surrounding landscape. Attached to the base of the tower was a two-story wood-frame house. Half of the shingles were missing, exposing the rafters, and the lapstrake siding was gray and cracked with age. What once had been the yard was now head-high with a tangle of brush and lilac bushes. From what Stacie could see of the house, all the doors and windows were boarded shut. To the left of the lighthouse was a sandstone outcropping that went down to the water's edge. Behind was what looked to be the mouth of a small inlet. The near side of the property was fenced off with a high wire mesh fence; a big wooden sign bolted to the fence read "Government Property! Keep Out!" Behind the fence, the terrain angled up sharply as it led up the face of one of the island's two bluffs.

"Come on," Bill said as he started to climb up the rocks toward the lighthouse.

"Where we going?" she asked.

"Up the tower."

"Up the tower? Bill, that sign says keep out."

"Don't pay any attention to that—nobody does. Come on."

Bill led the way; they followed a trail around to the back of the property to where there was a hole in the fence. Following Bill's lead, Stacie lay down and scooted through the hole. The smell of lilacs laced the air as she followed him through the tall bushes and up to the back door. Reaching up to the edge of the plywood nailed over the door, Bill sprung one side open and motioned for Stacie to squeeze through. She did, and Bill followed.

The room was dark and dingy and smelled of rotting wood. "Bill," Stacie whispered, "I don't like it in here."

"What are you whispering for?" Bill replied with a big grin. "You afraid of spooks?"

"Don't be a nerd. I just don't like it in here."

"It's the only way up the tower. Come on, and watch your step; some of these floorboards are rotten. If you're not careful, you could end up down in the basement with all the snakes and spiders."

"Very funny," she replied as she followed him across the room into what was once the kitchen.

Off the kitchen was another small room that entered the base of the tower. The open-grid metal stairs circled up the interior of the tower wall to the very top. Stacie could see beams of light shining down the tower's interior. Behind the tower stairs was another stairway that led down to the basement.

Without hesitation, Bill started up the steps. "Watch yourself," he said over his shoulder, "a couple of these stairs are broken; you have to step over them."

Reluctantly, Stacie followed until she reached the very top. Bill took her hand and helped her as she stepped out of the tower and into the lamp room. It was like a whole different world. Stretched out before them to the south and west was the open lake, glistening in the sun. To the east, she could see the faint outline of Michigan's mainland. Below was the blue-green water of the harbor and the white sand of the beach. Not only could she see Quint's boat, but she could see the tops of all the trees along the lower part of the harbor.

"Pretty neat, isn't it?" Bill said.

Stacie continued to scan the panorama. "Yes, it's beautiful," she said.

"Come on, let's go out onto the catwalk; I'll show you the remains of an old sunken boat just offshore."

"Are you sure it's safe?" she asked.

"Sure; just be careful," he said, stepping out onto the catwalk.

Bill carefully made his way over to the railing and looked down. He had no more than looked down when he ducked back. Grabbing Stacie by the shoulder, he moved her back away from the edge. "There are some men down there," he whispered.

"Oh come on!" she replied impatiently.

"No, really," he whispered, putting his hand over her mouth to muffle her words. "Look for yourself."

"If you're lying to me, Bill Sorenson, you're going to get it," she whispered as she moved cautiously to the edge. "And no funny stuff either," she said looking back at him. She peeked over the edge, and just out of sight from the main harbor, a big gray trawler lay at anchor along the rocks at the foot of the lighthouse. Six men were carrying three large wooden boxes from the boat up through the rocks toward the lighthouse.

"What are they doing?" Stacie whispered to Bill, who was now looking over the edge with her.

"Maybe they're dope smugglers," he said.

"I'm sure; right in broad daylight."

"Why not?" Bill said. "Who's going to see them in this deserted place? And what better place to stash it than in an old abandoned lighthouse?"

"They're probably coming to work on the place."

"Yeah, right. If you believe that, you got a problem."

"Come on; we got to get out of here," Stacie whispered, moving back toward the lamp room.

"No way. They'll be here long before we could get down the tower."

"We can't just stay here!"

"Why not? They'll probably stash their stuff and leave."

"What if they come up here?" she asked with a trembling voice.

"They're not going to haul those boxes all the way up here; my guess is they'll put them in the basement."

"I'm scared," Stacie whispered.

"Relax," Bill said, sitting down and leaning against the broken light stanchion. "If we're quiet, they'll never know we're here."

Soon the sound of voices came echoing up the interior of the tower. They couldn't determine what they were saying, but as they waited for them to leave, the minutes passed like hours. After silence returned, they sat quietly, listening in the deathly still for several minutes; finally,

Bill crawled back out on the catwalk and peeked over the edge. The boat was leaving.

"Come on," he said, crawling back inside. "They're gone; let's go."

Stacie gave a sigh of relief and wasted no time following Bill down the tower.

When Bill reached the base of the tower, instead of back-tracking across the kitchen, he continued down toward the basement.

"What are you doing?" Stacie asked, stopping at the kitchen entrance.

"Come on," he replied over his shoulder. "I want to see what they put down here."

"Bill, that's a stupid idea. Come on, I want to go back to the boat."

"Don't sweat it; they're gone."

"That's not the point; we don't belong here; let's leave!"

"In a minute," Bill's voice came echoing back as he disappeared into the shadows.

Stacie squatted by the top of the stairs to wait. She could hear his movements in the darkness below. Bill began pounding on something, and then the distinct sound of nails being pried loose gave out a metallic screech—"Holy shit!" came Bill's voice.

"What's the matter?" Stacie replied.

"Come down here!"

She started down the stairs. "What is it?"

Over in the corner of the basement, she could see the dim outline of Bill standing over one of three wooden crates. "Guns!" Bill exclaimed. "A whole shit pile of guns!"

"Guns?"

"Yes, guns. This box is full of them."

Stacie worked her way over to take a look. The box was stacked full of military small arms; more kinds than she'd ever seen before.

"Bill," Stacie whispered, "come on, let's get out of here. These people, whoever they are, aren't just foolin' around."

Bill picked up one of the handguns and held it up to the sliver of light shining through a crack in the floor above. Then without saying a word, he tucked it under his belt.

"What are you doing?" Stacie exclaimed with a dumbfounded look on her face.

"I'm taking one; what does it look like?"

"Are you crazy?"

"So what? They're all stolen anyway."

"I don't believe you; that's totally stupid."

"Relax; besides, they'll never miss it."

"That's supposed to make it all right?"

"Come on," Bill said, turning back to the box, "let's get this box nailed shut and get out of here."

Bill replaced the lid and hammered the nails back in with the same piece of angle iron he'd used to open it. Suddenly, the light coming from the stairway behind them dimmed; they both turned to look. Standing directly in the light was the silhouette of a man. Stacie was so shocked and frightened she couldn't move. The man said nothing; he just stood there. Then she heard the unmistakable snap of a switchblade locking open as he started to walk slowly toward them.

"Mister, we didn't bother anything," Bill stammered in a feeble attempt to defuse the situation.

"Is that so?" the man muttered. "Come here!"

Bill hesitated for a second and then stepped forward slowly.

"He's got a knife!" Stacie blurted without thinking.

The man lunged forward. He and Bill tumbled backward over one of the boxes. They fell to the floor, knocking the angle iron from Bill's hand with a loud clang. Stacie was so frightened she couldn't even scream. Bill somehow managed to shrug off his pursuer and get to his feet, only to be tackled again. Tripping over a second box, they fell to the floor again. The two rolled over and over, with Bill ending up on the bottom. Stacie saw the blade of the knife flash as Bill tried desperately to avoid being stabbed. Without thinking, Stacie rushed forward, grabbed the piece of angle iron from the floor, and swung it at the man's head with all her might. He looked up just in time to see the cold steel smashing into his face. The impact knocked him sideways and sent him sprawling to the floor.

"Run!" Bill hollered as he scrambled to his feet and started for the steps. Stacie dropped the angle iron and took off right behind him. They ran up the stairs and across the room, squeezed out the door, and ran through the overgrowth toward the fence. Bill dropped to the ground and scooted under the fence. "Hurry!" he said as he grabbed the mesh and held it up for her. Stacie dropped down and slid through the opening too. Just as she slid free of the fence, their pursuer came rushing out of the brush; he grabbed for Stacie's leg but missed. Jumping to his feet, Bill ran up the trail toward the top of the bluff as fast as he could run. "Follow me!" he hollered back to her.

The steep trail was littered with rocks, making it almost impossible to gain footing. Soon Stacie's breath was coming in deep gulps, and her legs began to feel like rubber. Pausing only long enough to find her footing, she pushed herself as hard as she could. Over and over, the same thought kept tumbling through her head: *We're going the wrong way—we're going the wrong way.* It was as though her mind was stuck in rhythm with her gasping for air.

After what seemed an eternity, Stacie managed to reach the summit. Clawing her way up over the ridge, she spotted Bill kneeling on a boulder looking back down in the direction from which they had come. Totally out of breath, she stumbled over to him and flopped down next to him. "We're going the wrong way," she muttered.

Bill said nothing; he just kept watching the trail below.

"Is he coming?" Stacie asked, too exhausted to raise her head.

"I don't know," Bill replied softly. "I think so, but I haven't spotted him yet."

"Is there another way up here?" she asked.

"No, not from the lighthouse."

Then she noticed his left hand. He had a hanky wrapped around it, and it was saturated with blood. "What happened?" she said, sitting up.

"I came a little too close to that guy's knife," Bill replied, keeping his eyes glued to the trail below.

"Oh my God," she gasped. "How bad is it?"

"It's all right—there he is!" Bill exclaimed, interrupting himself. "Come on, we gotta get movin'!"

Stacie glanced over the edge just long enough to spot their pursuer. He was about a hundred yards down the bluff, picking his way up the steep trail in their direction.

"Come on!" Bill said again as he turned to move out.

"Bill," Stacie gasped between breaths as she trotted along behind. "What are we going to do? He wants to kill us!"

"I know," Bill replied over his shoulder. "That's why we have to ditch him."

The trail was smooth and relatively level, making running easy; still, Stacie had all she could do to keep up. Bill, with his long legs, loped along almost effortlessly.

After what seemed an eternity, they came to a split in the trail. She stumbled to a stop behind Bill. The left fork went down to the island's south side beach; the right went across a little ravine and disappeared into the woods.

"This is it," Bill said as he caught his breath. "That creep's not far behind, so listen carefully. That trail leads down through the old village and back to the harbor," he said, pointing to the trail that went into the woods. "I want you to hide down in that ravine; I'll head down this other trail to the south beach. When our friend comes along, I'll make sure he sees me. After he takes off to follow me, you head down that trail and back to the boat—you understand?"

"Yes, but how are you going to get rid of him?"

"Don't worry about me; I'm the fastest runner on Washington Island. I can run circles around that jerk. I'll lead him to the other side of the island, ditch him, and then double back through the woods."

"Are you sure?"

"Yes, I'm sure. Now get going." He gave Stacie a nudge.

"But what if he spots me?"

"Make sure he doesn't!" Bill said.

Stacie worked her way down through the tall grass and into a large clump of bushes. When she glanced back up at the trail, Bill was gone. Finding a place with good cover, she lay down. Startled by the sound of footsteps along the trail, she flattened to the ground as far as she could and froze.

The man stumbled up the trail until he was directly above Stacie, and then he stopped. She wanted desperately to get up and run but continued to lie perfectly still. Her pursuer stood and looked around. All Stacie could hear was the beating of her heart. Then looking off toward the beach, the man gave a grunt and took off in that direction; soon his footsteps faded down the hill.

Stacie got up and clawed her way out of the bushes. She hurried back through the tall grass to the trail, headed into the woods as Bill had instructed, and ran as hard as she could. Following the top of the bluff, she made her way through a stand of big hardwoods. Then the trail angled down a gentle slope toward the village and harbor below. As she hurried along, she glanced continuously over her shoulder. All kinds of horrible scenarios rolled through her mind.

After thirty minutes, the trail leveled off along the valley floor. Eventually, it turned into a single-lane dirt road, and ahead through the trees she could see some old buildings. She wasted no time as she hurried along the road and into the deserted village. A single row of eight huge square framed houses, set well apart, stood along both sides of the road, with the tall trees silently shading their graying remains. Although the picket fence along the road had fallen down and was rotting away, there was enough left to get a good picture of what it must have been like at one time. The harbor was clearly visible through the trees now, and Stacie could see Quint's boat at the far end of the inlet. Leaving the road, she cut between the last two houses and headed into the tall dune grass along the beachfront.

Glancing back, she spotted Bill loping through the tall grass toward her. From the grin on his face, it was obvious he had given his pursuer the slip. "Thank God!" she blurted out. "You don't know how worried I was!"

"No sweat," he said as he came running up to her. "He's probably still stumbling around on the beach on the other side of the island."

"Are you sure?" Stacie asked, scanning the edge of the woods behind.

"I'm sure he's not on my trail, if that's what you mean."

"I'll feel a whole lot better when we get to the boat," she said. "Is there any other place with people on this island?"

"Nope!" Bill replied as he picked up the pace along beside her. "This harbor is the only place left with people."

"Then sooner or later, he's going to come here looking for us."

"We'll be gone by then."

"I hope so," she replied. "Come on, we got to get my dad to look at your hand."

"It's okay," Bill said, "besides, the bleeding has stopped."

"Bill, you still have to have someone look at it!"

"And what am I supposed to tell your old man when he asks how it happened?"

"How about the truth?"

"No way, Stacie! Look, even if we told the truth and they caught the guy, maybe even confiscated all those guns, you think this guy is in this all alone? We'd be in a whole lot of trouble! Those people aren't fooling around; I say we keep our mouths shut."

Stacie stopped and looked at Bill. "I'm scared!" she said. "Why did we have to go snooping around there anyway?"

"Look, if we can get out of here without that guy seeing us—there's no way he's going to know who we are, or where we're from. Come on," Bill said as he started to walk again. "We'll go back to the boat and stay out of sight until we leave."

"And what about Inger?" Stacie asked as she hurried to catch up. "She's not stupid; she's going to spot that hand right away. And what are you going to tell her? She'll know you're lying."

"You just leave that to me," he said. "I'll handle Inger."

"What did you do with the gun you stole?"

"I don't know," Bill replied, "I think I lost it when we crawled under that fence."

"Good! At least we don't have to worry about someone finding that on you."

They hurried down through the tall grass, past the old store, and out onto the beach.

Inger was sitting all alone up in the wheelhouse, totally bored, when she spotted Bill and Stacie hoofing their way down through the sand toward the dock. Ducking down, she watched as they scampered up onto the dock and headed straight for the boat. Knowing for certain something was up, Inger knelt down quietly by the companionway to listen. Without hesitation, they went below.

"Looks like no one's here," Bill said.

"I don't know if that's good or bad," Stacie replied.

"They should be along pretty soon," Bill said as he plopped down on the starboard bench.

"I hope so. In the meantime, I've got to find some kind of clean bandage for your hand. Has Quint got a first aid kit on board?"

"Yeah, it's up in the wheelhouse behind the radio."

"I'll get it," she replied, heading for the steps.

Unable to avoid being discovered any longer, Inger popped up, startling Stacie. "What are you guys up to?" she blurted out with a big grin on her face.

Stacie almost fell backward off the steps. "Inger, what are you trying to do?" she barked. "I figured you'd be sneaking around here someplace."

"Well, you're right."

"Look out," Stacie said, pushing past her. "I have to find the first aid kit."

"What did Bill do to his hand?" Inger asked.

"I don't know; you'll have to ask him."

"What did you do to your hand?" Inger asked, bouncing down the stairs and over to where Bill was sitting.

"Oh, I cut it on a sharp piece of metal," he replied, holding his hand up.

"Holy man!" Inger said, looking at the blood-soaked hanky still wrapped around it. "I better go get Dad! Man alive, you must have really cut it!"

Glancing back, Inger saw Stacie coming down the companionway stairs as fast as she could; her face was as white as a sheet. "He's coming," Stacie mumbled, looking straight at Bill.

"Where?" Bill replied.

"Down the beach; right toward the dock."

Bill jumped up and hurried over to the porthole to get a look.

"Who's coming?" Inger asked, following them to the window.

"Inger," Stacie said, catching hold of her wits, "go upstairs; if that man comes up to the boat, pretend you're all alone; it's just you, Dad, and Quint; no one else is along; you don't even have a sister—you understand?"

"What's going on?" Inger asked.

"We'll tell you later," Bill said.

"No! You'll tell me now!"

"Inger," Bill pleaded. "He's going to be here in a minute."

"Now!" Inger repeated, refusing to move.

Stacie glanced at Bill and then back at Inger. "We found a big box of guns over in that abandoned lighthouse," she said. "That man caught us looking at them and tried to kill us with a knife; that's how Bill got his hand cut. He's been chasing us all over the island."

Inger scurried up the companionway steps without saying a word. "What happens if he doesn't believe me?" she asked when she got to the top of the stairs. Knowing neither Stacie nor Bill had an answer, she continued forward and stepped out of the wheelhouse. Working her way along the catwalk up to the bow, Inger began to fiddle with the mooring lines. Trying very hard not to look up or appear as though she expected anyone, she pretended to be busy.

The man stepped up onto the dock and walked out toward the boat. "Hey kid," he said in an abrasive tone, "I'm looking for a boy and a girl; are they here?"

Trying with all her might to contain herself, Inger looked up. "Who you looking for?" she asked, pretending not to have heard clearly.

"A boy about this tall," he replied, holding his hand up about Bill's height, "and a girl; have you seen them?"

Inger shook her head.

"Is there anybody else on the boat?" he asked, walking past Inger and looking inside the wheelhouse.

"Just my dad, my uncle, and me," she replied.

"Where are they?" he asked without looking at Inger.

"They're up buying some fish nets."

The man stepped up into the wheelhouse.

"They should be back any moment now," she said as her heart began to pound.

He walked over to the companionway, bent down, and looked below.

Inger's heart froze; she couldn't think of a thing to say. Then the man stood up, looked around the wheelhouse one more time, and stepped off the boat. "Where you from, kid?" he asked, looking up at Inger.

"The mainland," she replied.

"Michigan side?"

Inger nodded.

He walked around and looked at the back of the boat. As he did, Inger remembered that the name of Quint's boat, *Ellie May*, and where it was from was written across the back of the boat. "What did you do to your face?" she blurted out in an attempt to divert his attention.

He didn't respond, and then after a few moments he looked back up at her again. "If you're from Michigan, how come it says 'Washington Island' on your boat?"

"My uncle just bought it and hasn't changed the markings yet," she replied.

The man grunted and then turned and walked away.

Inger stood there for a moment and watched as he stepped off the dock and headed up through the sand toward the store. Giving a big sigh, she stepped back into the wheelhouse. "He's gone!" she blurted out as she scurried down the companionway steps.

Bill and Stacie, who were hiding under a piece of canvas up in the bow, crawled out. "Holy shit," Bill said as he hurried over to the porthole again. "That was close—you did a fantastic job, kid!" Bill grinned at Inger.

"But why did you tell him we were from Michigan?" Stacie asked.

"I didn't see you out there saying much of anything," Inger responded. "I didn't want to tell him where we were really from."

"Well, he certainly knows you were lying now."

"Hey, stop the wrangling," Bill said as he stepped away from the porthole. "The guy obviously bought it or he wouldn't have left—Inger, you did good."

"I was afraid if Dad and Quint showed up before he left, that jerk might start putting things together."

"What do you mean?" Stacie asked.

"I mean that's the guy dad beat up and threw off the *Moonhawk*."

"Are you sure?" Stacie replied.

"Believe me, I'm sure."

"What are you guys talking about?" Bill asked.

"I'll tell you later," Stacie replied, still looking at Inger. "Inger, we can't tell Dad about this, okay?"

"I know," she replied as she headed up the stairs and back into the wheelhouse. "I just hope we don't get into a lot of trouble for this one."

As she reached the top of the stairs, Quint's voice came booming through the boat. "Hey there, lass, where in the hell are those other two scamps?" he roared as he threw a box of nets down on the dock next to the boat.

"They're down below," Inger replied as she jumped off the boat.

"Well, tell Bill to get his ass out here and start loading these nets."

"He can't; he cut his hand over at the old lighthouse. I think it's pretty bad too."

Just then Atticus and two other men walked up to the boat, each carrying a box of nets. They set them down on the dock; both Quint and Atticus thanked them, and they left.

"Now what in the Sam Hill is all this about Bill cutting his hand?" Quint asked as he stepped up into the wheelhouse.

"What's going on?" Atticus asked Inger as they followed Quint on board.

"Bill cut his hand," Inger replied.

"How bad?" Atticus asked.

"I think you better look at it, Dad."

They followed Quint below. Bill was sitting on the port bench; Stacie was standing there, watching everyone approach.

"What the hell did you do?" Quint asked, looking at the hanky wrapped around Bill's hand. "Whatever it is, it looks like you did a right fine job of it."

Atticus walked up next to Quint, asked where he kept his first aid kit, and sent Inger after it. "I think we better take a look at that," he said as he sat down next to Bill. "Let's get that rag off."

"Okay, but take it easy," Bill said anxiously. "It really hurts if I move my fingers.

Atticus took Bill's arm and carefully unwrapped the hanky. Inger came down with the first aid kit, opened it up, and set it down on the bench next to her father. "How did this happen?" Atticus asked, glancing up at both Stacie and Bill.

"Without realizing it, I grabbed hold of a sharp piece of metal on that old fence by the lighthouse," Bill replied before Stacie could respond.

"I see," Atticus said as he dropped the blood-soaked hanky away.

Stacie flinched and turned away.

"Yeah, did it up fine," Quint said, looking over Atticus's shoulder.

Atticus surveyed the damage. A deep slash went down the middle of Bill's hand and halfway up his index finger. "That must have been one sharp piece of metal," Atticus said softly.

"Yeah, it was," Bill replied without looking down at it. "How bad is it?"

"Well, you're going to have to get some stitches when we get home, that's for sure. But the bleeding seems to have stopped, and I don't think any tendons are cut. We'll put some antiseptic salve on it, wrap it up, and get you home, but I think you're going to live," he continued, patting Bill on the shoulder. "You sure that's how you got that cut? It looks an awful lot like a knife cut to me."

"Oh no; that's how it happened; right, Stacie?"

Stacie nodded.

———•◦•●•◦•———

In less than twenty minutes, they cast off and were underway; this time, hoping to cut a little time off their trip home, they headed around the south end of the island. Stacie sat below on the starboard bench with her arms wrapped around her knees, looking out the porthole. Her dad and Quint were up in the wheelhouse with Inger at the helm. Bill was stretched out across the way on the portside bench. All that could be heard was the drone of the diesel and the hiss of the water sliding beneath the hull.

As the old lighthouse slid past the porthole, Stacie stared out at it and thought about the day's events. Even though she felt reasonably safe now, she still wondered if that man would figure out where they were really from; if he did, what he would do? There were many things she didn't tell her father, but she had never out-and-out lied to him, especially over something as serious as this. She wanted desperately to tell, but if she did, Bill and the rest of the island kids would never trust her again; besides, she'd promised not to tell anyone. Then there was Inger; she's never been able to keep her mouth shut for very long about anything; what would happen if she told? With her mind a jumble of thoughts, she leaned back onto a pile of nets and soon slipped off into a troubled sleep.

CHAPTER 8

A Visit from Laura

Atticus put on his new law enforcement cap, pulled the bill down over his eyes, and looked in the mirror. He turned partially to the side to get a better profile, adjusted the cap again, then stood there admiring himself.

Stacie, who was standing behind him watching, rolled her eyes and shook her head. "Somehow I just can't picture you as a police officer," she said.

"Neither can I," he replied, "but it's pretty dashing, don't you think?"

"Yeah, right," she chuckled.

"I thought you were going to some kind of school meeting tonight?" Inger asked as she came out of the kitchen.

"I am."

"Then why the police hat?"

"Well, I understand there are going to be some pretty important people there, and I thought this might give me a little more of an official look; besides, it goes with my new set of wheels out there."

"Dad, people are going to laugh at you," Stacie said.

"Hey, you don't laugh at the new top gun."

Stacie chuckled. "Yeah, but you're not a police officer, and you're certainly not a top gun!"

"Well, sweetie, that's where you're wrong—I'm afraid I'm the only gun in town; that makes me top gun."

"Does that mean you're a policeman everywhere?" Inger asked.

"No, just on Washington Island, and for me, that's quite enough."

"A police officer/school administrator," Stacie said, shaking her head. "Boy, that's got to be a first."

"Yes ma'am, that it is," Atticus replied in a western drawl while pinning the badge to his shirt.

————•◆•————

The girls were busy bickering over who took the longest in the bathroom as Atticus started the Bronco and drove toward the main road. He was quiet as they made their way across the island. At Joni Greshion's, he stopped, gave the girls instructions, let them out, and then went to pick up Butch.

The meeting was at the Doebucks', and the purpose, or so Atticus had been told, was to discuss the impact of the new state-proposed power equalization tax formula. Atticus was sure the real purpose was for the Doebucks to test the waters with the new administrator and to straighten him out if necessary. No doubt the Doebucks didn't like the outcome of their first encounter with him, and wanted to make sure he got properly reoriented.

Atticus wasn't uneasy at all about discussing the new tax proposal with anybody, or explaining his opinion of the concept, but as he thought about the unexpected twist he was bringing with him—the badge—he smiled; after all, the authority of the island constable is quite different from that of a school administrator. He wasn't quite sure how it was going to play out, but he was actually looking forward to his first trial run. Besides, he had a little get-even plan stirring in the back of his head.

Turning into Butch's drive, Atticus stopped behind the old station wagon and tapped on the horn a couple of times. Shortly, Butch came rambling out of the front door, letting the screen slam behind him. One stubby hand was negotiating a toothpick, and the other was holding a light brown leisure jacket over his shoulder. With no tie and his shirt open three buttons in usual Butch fashion, he sauntered up to the passenger door and opened it. "What the hell are you doing dressed as a cop?" he asked as he slid into the Bronco.

"Well, I have to start sometime," Atticus responded as he backed out onto the road again. "I figured tonight was as good a time as any."

"Jesus Christ, Atticus, this is a school meeting, not some kind of cop coming-out party."

"Really? You could have fooled me; I thought it was more of a administrator-bashing affair than anything."

"Well, you're going to get your eyes opened, that's for sure. Just do one thing for me, will you?"

"And what might that be, most honorable Boss Man?"

"Just save your opinions until you find out a little more about the politics from my side of the trench."

"In other words, keep my mouth shut."

"That's right; think you can handle that?"

"I'll do my best, but what if I get pressed for an opinion?"

"You're a college man; talk around the issue; just don't offend anyone. I know you haven't been too successful at that so far, but just try, okay?"

"Got any other good ideas?"

"Atticus, God damn it, I'm serious!" Butch said, looking at him with a serious expression. "You continue to take on the Doebucks, and you'll be biting off more than you can chew!"

"Don't tell me you're afraid of the Doebucks! I didn't think you were afraid of anybody."

"It's not that I'm afraid, it's just—well, you don't attack a bear in his own den; at least not that one. Why in the hell are you being so obstinate, anyway?"

"Just trying to figure out where you're coming from," Atticus replied with a shrug. "I'm trying to figure out if you're a man or just another politician."

"You mean an islander, or school board president."

"Something like that."

"In this case, my friend, it's one and the same. I don't think this tax proposal is good for the school or the island, and the Doebucks have got the political clout to block it if anyone has. There! I don't give a shit what you've been told; Madison bureaucrats don't always have the right answers."

"And you think the Doebucks have?"

"What does it matter? If their interest serves our interest, I don't really give a shit what their motives are."

"That's where we have a parting of the minds. That kind of thinking is just a marriage of convenience; your interest may serve theirs, but never the other way around. Don't kid yourself, Butch. They don't care about you or the school, and never will."

"Look," Butch said, holding up his hand, "let's just drop it; I don't want to argue with you. Just humor me by listening tonight, okay?"

"I'll try," Atticus replied.

"By the way," Butch said, looking at Atticus again, "how did your trip to South Manitoo go yesterday?"

"Just fine."

"Did you see the old lighthouse?"

"Not up close, but the Sorenson boy took Stacie over to see it. As a matter of fact, he cut his hand bad enough that his folks had to take him over to Doc Burnett to get it stitched up."

"Knowing him, I'm not surprised," Butch replied. "He was probably climbing around where he didn't belong."

"I suspect you're right," Atticus said as he turned east to head across the island. "Stacie wasn't too willing to supply many details."

"By the way," Butch continued, "the Bronco is a nice touch; Sheriff Dawson must really like you."

Atticus smiled at Butch and tipped his hat. "Speaking of the sheriff, I've been meaning to ask you something," Atticus went on. "As head of the police committee, you must have known old Bert Federman pretty well; did you ever know him to drink too much?"

"No, Bert didn't drink."

"The police report ruled it a drunk driving accident, isn't that correct?"

"Yes, it did."

"If you say he didn't drink, and the police report said he did, how is it the report went unchallenged?"

"Look," Butch replied, "the coroner's report said Bert had a blood alcohol content three times the legal limit, and the sheriff said everything at the crash site pointed toward an accident; who am I to go up against that? Besides, could be he was a closet drinker; I don't know. I certainly didn't know him that well."

"Where did the accident happen?" Atticus asked.

"Over here on the east side, about three miles north of Bondin's Rock, or I should say Baynard's estate."

"Really? Who reported the accident?"

"Actually, it was Baynard who called it in."

"That's interesting. Butch, did Federman ever indicate to you that he thought something fishy was going on?"

"Yeah, he did once. On our way out of a meeting, he said he didn't like what he saw happening on the island, but one thing led to another and I never got a chance to ask him what he meant by that comment."

"Butch, you told me this Baynard character runs some kind of a separatist camp out there on his property. You also said Doebuck took him under his wing; what exactly did you mean by that?"

"A group of islanders raised a protest against Baynard's hate rhetoric and militant attitude; they even formulated a group to work toward getting him off the island. Old Man Doebuck came to his defense, and the issue died on the vine, especially after Adrian Fruger backed off and sided with Doebuck."

"Adrian Fruger was part of that group? That's also interesting."

"Yes, it is; you may not like all of Adrian's money, but he's a straight shooter, Atticus."

"There has to be some kind of a connection between Baynard and Doebuck; what is it?"

"I don't know, other than Doebuck's defending Baynard's right to be different."

"Do you think this Baynard guy will be at the meeting tonight?"

Butch shrugged. "I don't know."

"If you spot him, point him out to me, okay?"

"Sure, but why?"

"If he's there, I'm going to engage him in conversation; I want to get myself invited out to his property to see what's going on."

"That'll never happen," Butch replied. "Baynard doesn't allow anybody on his land."

"You were invited out there to work on that trawler, weren't you?"

"That was different; he didn't have much choice. And they watched me like a hawk; I wasn't allowed to look at anything but the boat engine."

"Well, I just might be able to push him into the same kind of a situation."

Butch shook his head. "If you manage that, I want to be with you."

"I'll see what I can finangle."

"Ya know, Gunner, I thought we hired you to run the school."

"You did, but you also hired me to be the island cop."

"You seem to be taking this cop job a whole lot more serious than the school job."

"Don't underestimate my magnetic personality; I'll do what I was hired to do."

Butch shook his head again. "Gunner, has anyone ever told you that sometimes you just seem to bubble over with bullshit?"

"Yes, as a matter of fact they have; my former wife being one of them, not in the same terms of course, but . . ."

"No wonder she's your former wife."

"Yeah, you're probably right."

When they reached the Doebucks', Atticus drove under the big gate and up into the yard. "It looks like we're not the first to arrive," he said as he pulled up behind about fifteen cars.

"That's for sure; the brass is all here," Butch replied as he opened the door and got out. "Now remember, behave yourself."

They walked up to the house and rang the bell. Atticus's favorite bodyguard answered the door. The man shook Butch's hand, invited them in, and then smiled at Atticus. "My oh my, looks like our guest of honor has arrived," he muttered, "and wearing his policeman's costume, no less."

"Well, thank you," Atticus replied. "I think it looks good, don't you?"

The bodyguard just scoffed at Atticus and closed the door. Without further comment, he directed the two men toward the sun porch at the back of the house. They started across the room, but after a few steps, Atticus stopped. "Ah—by the way," he said to the bodyguard, "what does Mr. Doebuck call you, Mr. Bodyguard, or Dipwad?"

"It's none of your God damned business what he calls me," the man replied.

"No, you're right; I don't even care. But what I do care about is that it's against the law in the state of Wisconsin to carry a concealed weapon, unless you have a permit, and I doubt you do. So you're either going to give me that gun you've got under your suit jacket, or you're going to put it in the drawer of that table over there until I leave. If you don't do either, I'm going to walk into that meeting and raise absolute hell about the fact that you're toting a weapon."

"You must be dumber than you look."

"No, actually, I think I'm smarter. You and I both know you're not going to shoot me here, and you also know, if I walk in there and start shooting off my big mouth, Mr. and Mrs. Doebuck are going to get very upset; I would even venture to say he'd probably find it easier to replace you than to face all the hell I would raise." Atticus smiled.

Butch, who had been watching with a dumbfounded look on his face, turned without saying a word and started walking across the living room; Atticus followed. "Jesus Christ, what are you doing?" he whispered over his shoulder.

"Wait!" the guard blurted out. He walked over to the table by the door, opened the drawer, and slid his handgun inside. He locked the drawer and turned back toward Atticus. "You win this time, Gunner," he said, glaring at Atticus.

"The key," Atticus replied.

The guard threw him the key, and Atticus walked past Butch. "You're crazy," Butch whispered.

Atticus winked at him. "Someone else accused me of that not too long ago. He was so convinced I was crazy, he jumped off my boat to get away from me."

"This isn't your boat," Butch replied.

"Same principle," Atticus replied, mustering a big smile as they walked into the large glassed-in room off the back of the house.

There were about twenty-five people standing around in small groups, most holding a cigarette in one hand and a drink in the other. Mrs. Doebuck, who was across the room, spotted Butch and Atticus almost immediately; she waddeled over. "Mr. Gunner, how good of you to come," she said as she approached the two men. "Come in, come in." Then she turned her back to them and clapped her hands. "People; people!" she said, continuing to clap her hands. "I'd like to introduce two more of our guests if I may! This is Mr. Gorpon, a dear friend and president of the school board—someone I'm sure you all know! And this is Mr. Gunner, our new school administrator, and . . ." she looked at Atticus, "island policeman."

She then took Atticus by the arm as though he were a small child and continued to introduce each of the other guests in the same flamboyant fashion. And even though each of the introductions was always made relative to her interest, Atticus was especially curious about a few of them. Mr. Baynard of the old Bondin Place was indeed there; she introduced him as a new island resident and Detroit businessman. Then there was Adrian Fruger, who Mrs. Doebuck introduced as a "dear friend, lifelong island resident, and spokesman for the people of the island."

In spite of that nauseating introduction, Atticus's first impression of the ferry tycoon was favorable. He was a distinguished-looking man with an air of saltiness; he was of medium build with silver-white hair and bushy eyebrows to match. He sported a deep weathered tan, and his steel-gray eyes sparkled when he smiled.

Then there was Dr. and Mrs. Burnett, the island physician and his wife. When Atticus had first come to the island he didn't realize there was such a thing as an island doctor, or that the island could even support one; it was only later that he discovered the Burnetts were longtime island residents. The dear doctor was handsomely subsidized by local tax dollars, but most noteworthy, his presence on the island was only contractually required during the spring, summer, and fall months, when the summer residents were more likely to be present. If anyone carried an air of aristocracy out for all to see, it was the Burnetts.

Beyond that, there were several other island residents introduced, three of which Atticus deduced to be relatively wealthy summer residents, and the others, either employees of the ferry line or members of the town board. The last seven men were from off-island: three state assemblymen, one of whom Atticus recognized to be the majority whip; a Republican state senator whose reputation for beating an indictment for fraud preceded his introduction; and finally a group of three lobbyists, who seemingly had no vested interest in the island at all. The only connection Atticus could surmise was that they were present to demonstrate the influence of the Doebucks. Notably absent, however, was Mr. Doebuck.

Butch of course knew all the island people, and before long he was engaged in a robust conversation about trap shooting with some of the summer people; it appeared that Butch was the island's undisputed champion and had been for some time. Atticus stood silently by, passively participating with an occasional smile and false attentiveness. Eventually he drifted away from the group unnoticed and meandered over to the snack table. Pouring himself a cup of punch, he watched the goings-on from the relative separateness of the sidelines.

Atticus didn't notice Mr. Baynard, who had also drifted over to the table and was pouring himself some punch, directly behind him. "How do you do there, Mr. Gunner, or am I to address you as Sheriff?" the man said in a very snide tone.

Atticus turned to face the man. He was a stout, gruff-looking man with a round face, bald as a bowling ball, wearing heavy black rimmed glasses, and sporting an American flag tie with "Love It or Leave It" printed diagonally down the front of it. "You may call me anything you like," Atticus replied.

"Atticus; that's a Jew name, isn't it?" the man shot back.

"No, actually it's not; does that make a difference?"

"Just curious, that's all. He held his stubby hand out for Atticus to shake.

This was a man Atticus immediately disliked, but he smiled and shook his hand. "I was hoping to have the opportunity to meet you tonight," Atticus said, feigning enthusiasm. "I'd like to make arrangements to come out and talk with you tomorrow if that's possible."

"Why would you want to do that?" he replied with a frown.

"Sheriff Dawson is having some problems collecting insurance on the car Bert Federman was driving when he was killed. It appears the state lost the accident report or something, and the sheriff doesn't want to reopen the case just to get it resolved. So instead, he asked me if I could meet with you and clarify some questions." That statement was, of course, a total lie, but Atticus had his motives.

"I already told them everything I knew, Mr. Gunner; I have nothing more to add."

"Yes, I'm sure you did," Atticus replied, "but like I said, it's either a little time with me, or the sheriff will be parked up here in front of your gate until you talk to him. I don't think you want that; I know I sure don't want them up here nosing around."

"Gunner, it sounds to me like you're trying to bite the hand that feeds you!" He smiled at Atticus. "I like that; sure, I'll meet with you; how about if I stop by the school?"

"No, I don't think that will work," Atticus went on. "I'd like to talk to you out by your place if you don't mind."

"Sorry, I don't let outsiders on my property, especially representatives of the state."

"I work for Washington Island, not the state, Mr. Baynard," Atticus said.

Baynard took a sip of his punch and then looked at Atticus again. "I've been told you don't like taking shit from anyone," he said with a smile. "I like that in a man. Okay, I'll give you a half hour tomorrow morning; be at the gate at ten o'clock."

"I need a witness, so I'd like to bring Butch Gorpon along if I can. He's been out to your place before; he worked on a boat for you."

"Butch Gorpon? Sure; he's a friend of the Doebucks, and any friend of theirs is a friend of mine. But I want you to know, we're only discussing the Federman accident, and I don't know a whole lot about that; I just happened to be the one who reported it."

Atticus glanced away, just in time to see Mrs. Doebuck approaching, with Butch at her side. "Well, Mr. Gunner, I see you've met Mr. Baynard," she said, waddling up to him.

"Yes, ma'am," Atticus replied, glancing at Butch. "He tells me he's a close friend of yours."

"Yes, he is," she said with a smile. "A young administrator should learn to mingle with the natives."

"Oh," Atticus commented, "I didn't realize he was an island native."

"Deary—that's just a figure of speech," she replied. "But you'll find we're all pretty much one family here. Come; the meeting's going to begin, and I'd like for you to sit next to me; that way, if you have any questions, I can help."

Again Mrs. Doebuck clapped her hands and the room became silent. "People—I think perhaps we should commence," she said. "So—if everyone will find a seat, we'll begin."

The various groups began to disperse as everyone sat down.

"Oh, Mr. Gunner," Mrs. Doebuck said loudly, looking back over at Atticus. "I have a place for you right here." She motioned toward the empty chair next to her. "And Mr. Gorpon can sit on the other side of you."

Atticus walked over and sat down next to her without further comment. Butch came and sat on the other side; he whispered into Atticus's ear, "Did you have any luck with Baynard?"

Atticus gave Butch a thumbs-up. "We're to be at Baynard's gate at ten o'clock tomorrow morning; can you make it?"

"I don't know how in the hell you managed that, but I wouldn't miss this for the world."

"By the way, where is Old Man Doebuck?" Atticus whispered.

"Probably in Chicago; he seldom gets involved in island affairs."

"Without his bodyguard?"

Butch shrugged. "Maybe he was left behind to keep tabs on the old lady, or maybe he left him here just so you could piss him off."

As soon as everyone was settled down, Mrs. Doebuck spoke again. "Because of substantial concern over the proposed power equalized school property tax being proposed by the state, I thought it would be appropriate to gather some of the more responsible island residents, along with some lawmakers, to discuss the issue. So Adrian, if you'd like to open the meeting, the floor is yours."

Adrian Fruger pulled a prepared statement from inside his coat pocket and unfolded it in his lap. Putting on a pair of reading glasses, he cleared his throat. As he spoke, his voice was even and steady. Atticus felt some of his concerns were legitimate, but given just a passive knowledge of Adrian Fruger's landholdings, island business interests, lifestyle, and even his potential gross income from the ferry line (which was a common topic of discussion throughout the island), Atticus found it difficult to relate to the picture he painted of himself; a picture of a struggling, hard-working man, whose sole purpose in life was to keep open the main gateway to the outside world. But even that wasn't what bothered Atticus the most; it really wasn't a crime to make a profit, or even to get rich while doing it, but Atticus didn't trust him. He was too aloof, too fatherly, and most of all, too powerful. The very thought of his control over every islander, summer or native, was quite awesome. No wonder everyone rang his bell rather than rattle his cage; he truly was king of the island.

Following Adrian's presentation, there was a round-robin discussion; just about every islander, including Butch, added their two cents' worth in support of Adrian's opinions.

Finally, Baynard, who'd been completely silent, raised his hand. Mrs. Doebuck quieted down the others and recognized him. Baynard cleared his throat and said, "I know I am a newcomer to this community, but I for one would like to hear what our new school administrator has to say about this idea."

"Yes," one of the town board members chimed in. "I'd like to hear that myself."

"I'm just here to listen," Atticus replied.

"This is a state idea, is it not?" Baynard asked Atticus.

"It is a proposal coming from the state legislature," Atticus replied.

"And you mean to tell us you don't know anything about it?" Baynard continued, pressing Atticus, while at the same time smiling at him.

"I am aware of the theory behind it," Atticus replied.

"Well, if you understand it in theory, then you certainly must have some opinions," Baynard continued.

Atticus glanced over at Butch and then looked back at Baynard. "Yes, I have some impressions."

"But," Butch interjected, "he would rather wait until he learns more about the island before giving them."

"Nonsense," Mrs. Doebuck said, giving Butch a scolding glance. "Let Mr. Gunner speak."

Atticus paused for a long moment and then went on. "I'm not going to insult your intelligence by saying school finance is too complicated for the average person to understand, but if you are truly interested in what I think, you're going to have to grant me some indulgence. School finance is complex, and I underwent substantial schooling to learn it. I can't address your concerns without some elaboration. I'll attempt to answer your questions and give you my opinions."

"You sound like a politician," one of the islanders broke in.

"Wait a minute," Butch replied, "he said he'd answer questions and give us his opinion if we're willing to let him; what's unfair about that? All he's asking is that we give him enough time to fully explain. That's what we hired him for. If we didn't need someone with special training to help us through this, we could have hired anyone off the street. Is that what we want?"

Adrian Fruger raised his hand. "Edna, I'd like to hear what Mr. Gunner has to say," he said calmly.

Mrs. Doebuck nodded to Atticus. "Go ahead, Mr. Gunner," she said.

"All right," Atticus replied as he stood up. "I'll try to make it as brief as possible. Our country was born out of the desire to free our people from the tyranny of absolute power and religious oppression. Our founding fathers declared a complete separation of church and state, thus guaranteeing our right to practice religion as we see fit. They also established a representative democratic government whereby our people were guaranteed the right to govern ourselves. We fought a war of independence to confirm those freedoms. That's basic American history that you all know.

"But what folks seem to forget is that in the process of becoming a democratic society, it was also recognized that in order for our country to survive, it was essential to have an educated population. Thus the concept of public education was born. And the assurance of that education is, by declaration, a federal responsibility. However, the federal government has delegated that task to the individual states, and our state in turn delegated it to the local municipalities. To pay for it, local governments were forced to put it on the property tax rolls.

"Why property taxes?" Atticus went on. "Because the value of property was easy to assess; property couldn't be hidden or moved; the tax assessed was easy to enforce by local governments; and finally, the services rendered were seen to have a direct benefit to the local community.

"As time moved on, however," he continued, "and education began to play a more dominant role in our society, as knowledge expanded and became more specialized, as science and technology started to mushroom, as the need for specialized educational institutions grew beyond the abilities of local communities to support, the transition of educational responsibilities has begun to swing back toward the state and federal government. Unfortunately, change in the system of funding education has not kept pace with the transition of responsibility."

As he continued to talk, Atticus looked straight at Adrian Fruger. "Although states are now looking at new ways to expand educational opportunities and services, the politicians are still hung up on property taxes as a primary source of funding. They're trying to find a way to equalize the tax burden across the state on the basis of property value. Unfortunately, property value is not necessarily a true measure of one's ability to pay. Just because one lives in an area of high property value, it does not automatically follow that one's ability to pay is commensurate with that of his property value.

"So where does that leave us here on Washington Island?" Atticus asked rhetorically. "I firmly believe, somewhere in the middle. I'm not in favor of sending property tax money to Madison so they can equalize the burden in Milwaukee or someplace else, but I also recognize the fact that educating our kids here on Washington Island costs money, and we are going to have to tax ourselves enough to get the job done. If you're unwilling to pay for good teachers, you're not going to have good teachers; if you're unwilling to pay for the appropriate tools of learning, your kids will fall behind and not be able to compete with those who do have them; if you're unwilling to keep up your facilities and provide an environment conducive to good learning, it won't happen. It is as simple as that!"

Excitedly, Dr. Burnett stood up. "Mr. Gunner, the money we are spending to educate our kids right here on the island has absolutely nothing to do with this issue; we're doing just fine!"

"Oh but it does, Doctor," Atticus replied, feeling the hairs on the back of his neck bristle. "You have the lowest property tax rate in the entire state. The taxes you're raising aren't even enough to balance the school budget, and I might add, the budget is already grossly inadequate when considering your needs."

"What about people who don't even own where they live? People like you get off scot-free."

"I'm afraid that's wrong too, Doctor. If a rental property owner isn't collecting enough rent to cover the tax on the property he's renting, he's a poor businessman."

"Don't get funny with me!" the doctor snapped back. "I don't intend to take that kind of smart-alecky talk from anyone, especially from the likes of you!"

"Mr. Gunner, thank you," Mrs. Doebuck interjected. "I think we're drifting away from the topic at hand; if I could perhaps redirect the subject?"

Atticus sat down and watched as the topic swung back just as though he had never spoke. After a moment, as the crowd continued to talk back and forth, he got up, walked around in back of Butch's chair, and whispered in his ear, "Come on, let's go."

Butch looked up. "Right now?" he whispered back.

Atticus nodded and started to walk out.

Butch got up and followed Atticus across the room. "We can't just walk out," he whispered again.

"We just did," Atticus said as he threw the key on the table next to the door and stepped out into the night air.

"I sure as hell hope you don't think you changed anyone's mind in there tonight," Butch said as he caught up to Atticus. "That's the second time you bailed out on Mrs. Doebuck. She's not going to be happy about that."

"The first time they pushed me out without a parachute. This time I left by my own initiative, and that's the way I like it."

"Well, regardless, we didn't make any friends in there tonight."

"I'm sure you're right, but the majority of those people weren't here to gain information; they were here to simply help promote a witch hunt."

"Not the islanders, Atticus."

"That depends on who you include as islanders."

"You know who I mean."

Atticus didn't respond.

They both got into the Bronco. Atticus started the car and headed down the drive.

———◆•◆•◆———

A guard wearing a paramilitary uniform was standing at Baynard's gate as Butch and Atticus drove up the next morning. He had an AK47 draped over his shoulder and was holding a tight leash on a guard dog.

Atticus rolled down his window. "I'm Atticus Gunner," he said, "and we're here to see Captain Baynard."

"He's expecting you," the guard said as he opened the gate. "When you get up to the house, stay in the car until someone comes out to get you; otherwise, you're dog meat."

Atticus rolled up the window. "Friendly chap," he said to Butch as he stepped on the accelerator.

The Bronco bounced and bucked as they drove over the tops of rounded boulders embedded in the rough terrain. When they came out of the woods and onto the big open rock bearing its namesake, not only did they have full view of the open lake, but standing up on top of Bondin's Rock was the old estate's manor. And even though it was run down from years of neglect, it was still an impressive sight; it was as close to old England as one could get without actually being there. Butch pointed off to the left at the natural weather-safe inlet, where he had worked on the trawler.

As they pulled up to the front of the old estate, Atticus was surprised at the lack of people; he was expecting more of a gathering of skinhead types, but there weren't any. There were a few men clad in military-type uniforms walking the grounds, but that was it.

Someone wearing a uniform came out of the manor and down toward the Bronco. It wasn't until she motioned for them to get out that Atticus realized it was a woman. They got out and followed her up to the entrance. She went directly inside; both Atticus and Butch followed.

Walking across a large open foyer, they approached a set of closed wooden doors; she opened one and motioned for them to enter. As she stepped aside, the two men entered what had obviously once been a large study. Except for a big desk in front of two floor-to-sealing windows, and two wooden chairs, the room was empty. Captain Baynard was sitting behind the desk; he looked up as Atticus and Butch approached.

As Atticus glanced around, he noticed a large flag adorning a silk-screened picture of Hitler hanging on the wall behind them. Over in the corner, back behind a partially closed curtain sporting black-on-red swastikas, were three leather chairs; a man was sitting in one of them. He was mostly obscured by the shadows from the curtain.

"Mr. Gunner and Mr. Gorpon," Baynard said with a big smile, "welcome to my humble abode. Sit down, please."

Atticus and Butch sat down. The woman who had led them in opened the door and came back into the room. She walked up and took a formal parade rest stance behind Atticus but said nothing.

"Well, gentlemen, you left rather abruptly last night," Baynard continued. "Mrs. Doebuck was not at all happy about that. And you, Butch, I imagine will be hearing from Munster when he gets back from Chicago."

Butch glanced over at Atticus but said nothing.

"But my word is my word, so here we are. Now, Mr. Gunner, how can I help you with the Federman accident?"

"I just have a few questions, sir," Atticus replied. "I understand you reported the accident; how did you learn of it?"

"I was down at the gate talking with the guard when Federman came driving past in an erratic manner; a few minutes later, we heard the crash."

"What exactly did you hear?" Atticus asked.

"First we heard the screech of tires and then a loud crash."

"Is that how you stated it to the investigating officer?"

"Yes."

"When was that, Mr. Baynard? That night?"

"You mean with the investigating officer? No, it was the next day."

"Did you go down to the crash site that night?"

"No, I did not."

"Why not?"

"I didn't really think it was any of my affair."

"Was there any snow or ice on the road that night, Mr. Baynard?"

Baynard chuckled, looking at Butch. "Your schoolboy here obviously hasn't spent a winter on the island yet," he said. "The roads were covered with ice, and there was at least a foot and a half of fresh powder everywhere."

"In the woods?"

"Especially in the woods."

"So you're telling me you heard the tires squeal on ice-covered roads, and a loud crash coming through the snow-filled woods from three miles away; is that correct?"

Suddenly, a voice barked from the back of the room. "Captain, all the issues involved in that crash have already been resolved. Trying to trip you up on your testimony is completely irrelevant. What Mr. Gunner is trying to do is beyond me, but this interview is over; say no more."

"And you are?" Atticus said, turning toward the shrouded figure.

"That's none of your business," he replied. "Connie, show these men out!"

With that, the woman slid her weapon off her shoulder and assumed the ready stance. Baynard stood up and gave the woman a nod. She took the muzzle of her weapon and pushed it into Atticus's back from behind.

Her intent being obvious, Atticus stood up; Butch followed suit. "And from this am I to assume you're going to shoot us?" Atticus asked as he walked toward the door. "You and I both know that's not going to happen, so why are we playing this game?"

"No, we may not shoot you this time," the man from the back of the room said, "but I can assure you we have some dogs here that are very hard to control, so don't get too smart, commando boy."

Without saying another word, Butch and Atticus walked out and back down to the Bronco with their armed female guard in tow. As they drove back down toward the gate, Butch looked over at Atticus. "Every bit of common sense tells me I should be scared shitless," Butch said, "so why am I pissed off instead?"

"Because we're beginning to see just how phony some of these people really are," Atticus replied. "That must have been some investigation. In less than two minutes Baynard was already tripping over his own bullshit. And who was the Gestapo-type dude in the shadows; do you know him?"

"No, I've never seen him before, but then I couldn't get a good look at him either."

"The only things I got a good look at were his shoes," Atticus said, "and they were very expensive shoes, I might add; but whoever he is, he's got control over Baynard."

⸺•◆•⸺

Things were extremely busy at the ferry dock the next morning. Not only was there the hustle of lots of tourists coming and going, but Stacie's island friends were there in the Jeep to see the girls off. They drove down to the dock and up alongside the boat, hooting and hollering as Atticus and the girls boarded. "Stacie, when are you coming back up to the island?" Ken hollered.

"In two weeks," she replied as she hung out the car window.

"Too bad you can't stay; Quint is taking us snorkel diving up by the Boils Sunday!"

"Maybe next time," she replied. "Are you going, Bill?"

"No," Bill said, holding up his hand as his explanation.

The ferry gave a long blast on its horn and started backing away from the dock. "Good-bye, Stacie; good-bye, Inger!" Joni hollered as she waved at the girls.

The girls waved back. "See you in two weeks!" Inger replied, happy to have been acknowledged.

⸺•◆•⸺

Atticus rolled over to greet the bright morning sun flooding in through the open bedroom window. The sound of the gentle surf tumbling over the rocks down at the water's edge was soothing. He could do with more sleep, but he was famished; he hadn't had a bite to eat since leaving Madison, so he rolled out of bed.

It wasn't until after he finished breakfast that he really started to notice the absence of the girls. The old house seemed quiet. It was always like that after spending time with his daughters, but it seemed even more so on the island.

Walking out through the porch and into the yard, he gave his shoulders a stretch and wandered over to the shore to look out over the open water. It was Sunday, a perfect day to work on the *Moonhawk*.

After putting his car back in the garage and grabbing a few rags and a pail from the house, he jumped into the Bronco and headed for Spencer's dock by way of the island store.

Things were extremely quiet down by Spencer's; not a soul around. Atticus went directly out onto the dock, climbed on board the *Moonhawk*, and unlocked the hatchway. After opening the boat, he returned to the car to retrieve the things he'd purchased at the store; he climbed back on board and made his way below. He put the canned goods in the storage bin next to the sink, dumped the ice in the ice chest, placed the things that needed to stay cool on top of the ice, and closed the lid; then he folded the bags and threw them into one of the lockers.

"Hello there!" a woman's voice came from out on the dock. "Atticus, are you there?"

Somewhat startled and not really recognizing the voice, Atticus went up onto the companionway step and stuck his head out of the open hatch. Standing on the dock, dressed in a pair of Levis and a white blouse, was Laura Bock. "Hello," she said, smiling up at Atticus.

Atticus was completely dumbfounded. "Laura! What in the world are you doing here?" he asked.

"What does it look like I'm doing?"

"Where did you come from?"

"Where do you think I came from? Madison."

"Yes, but why?"

"To see you."

"Yes, but . . ."

"Have I come at a bad time?"

"No—no," Atticus stammered as he stumbled up the steps and over to the safety rail. "Come on board," he said, extending his hand to her. "How in the world did you find me?" he asked as he helped her over the safety rail.

"Well, when I stopped at the store, they not only knew you, but they knew where I could find you. So—here I am."

"I apologize for gawking but . . ."

"I figured you'd be surprised."

"That's an understatement. Stunned is a better word—you mean to tell me you drove all the way up here from Madison to see me?"

"That's right."

"Why didn't you call first?"

"It wouldn't have been a surprise then," she replied, still smiling at him.

"That's ironic," he said. "I was just in Madison yesterday—I took the girls home. I tried calling you, but there was no answer so I headed out for up here."

"What time did you call?"

"I don't know; about four."

"I left to come up here at three; I must have just missed you."

"That's incredible!" Atticus said, grinning at her. "How long can you stay—on the island, I mean?"

"I have a room at the Island Inn; so I guess you're stuck with me until tomorrow. You didn't tell me you owned a boat," she said, looking around. "Especially something like this; it's absolutely beautiful."

"I didn't really tell you much of anything. Actually, I'm not over being stunned that you're here. Really, why did you come all the way up here?"

"Why did you try calling me?"

"I almost didn't, and I probably shouldn't have, but I couldn't get you out of my mind."

"I had those same thoughts, so I decided to do something about it; I came up to see you."

"Ah look," Atticus said, motioning around, "I was going to do some work on the boat, but heck, that can wait. Why don't we take her out for the day? You couldn't ask for a more perfect day, and I bought enough food this morning to feed an army."

"That sounds perfect."

"Good! Well, why don't you grab whatever you need from your car, and I'll write a little note so if anyone comes looking for us, they'll know where we are, and we'll be off."

"You've got yourself a date."

Atticus started below but stopped at the hatchway. "Laura," he said as she walked away. She stopped and looked back at him. "I'm really glad to see you."

"I know," she replied, and then she turned and continued down the dock toward the car.

——•◆•——

As the morning slipped away on board the *Moonhawk,* Atticus and Laura talked about the island, the school, and the island kids; they discussed their mutual acquaintance with Butch Gorpon; and they chatted about Laura's involvement with the vocational project. They talked about the girls, and about Laura and her family. They sipped wine and had lunch. They even found time for some horseplay: they both slipped on the foredeck and fell into each other's arms. It was then that the first compulsion to kiss her flooded over Atticus. He could sense the willingness in her eyes, but he managed to refrain and pulled away as though nothing had happened.

Midafternoon found them on Rock Island, where they spent the rest of the day hiking. By the time they finished eating supper and got underway again, evening had settled in with a waning moon peeking up over the horizon.

The air was still warm as Atticus steered the *Moonhawk* around the breakwater and headed back toward Jackson Harbor under power. Laura was below. The boat's running lights twinkled against the shimmer of the water in the fading light. When she returned topside, she made her way back to where Atticus was standing. Leaning back against the stern rail beside him, she watched as he gazed off silently toward the blinking buoy in the distance. He smiled at her but said nothing. "You're very quiet," she said softly.

"Sorry," Atticus replied, turning his attention back to her.

"What were you thinking?"

"Oh—I don't know; nothing really."

"That's not true, Atticus; what were you thinking?"

"Well," he said, leaning back against the rail and steering with his foot, "I guess I was thinking how beautiful it is out here tonight; I was thinking how wonderful today has been, and how sad I am that it's about over." Laura reached over and put her arms around his waist and pulled herself close. Atticus put his arm over her shoulder. She laid her head against his chest. "And," he continued, "I was thinking how much I'm going to miss you after you leave tomorrow. You know, it probably sounds strange to you, but I haven't felt like this for a very long time—that's the part that troubles me the most."

"Why?"

"It's hard to put into words; you're young, you're very beautiful, and from the moment I laid eyes on you in Madison, something triggered in me. Yet I know how unrealistic it is that anything could ever develop between us."

"You talk as though you've got one foot in the grave."

"Laura, there's more than just a couple years between us."

"Are you afraid of that?"

"What I'm trying to say is, for you to get involved with someone like me means you would be taking on a whole lot of excess baggage; baggage I couldn't possibly leave behind. And for me to expect you to do so would be very unrealistic."

Laura lifted her eyes and looked up at him. "I'm not sure I want to admit this," she said softly, "but the moment we talked in Madison, I was immediately infatuated, but you needn't worry, I would never consider coming between you and your daughters. That doesn't necessarily mean, however, that nothing could ever happen between us."

Atticus kissed her softly on the nose. "Are you sure you know what you're doing?" he whispered.

"Are you?"

"I don't know," he replied, kissing her on the nose again. "It's all moving so fast; I'm not sure I'm ready for this."

"It feels too right to be wrong," she said, laying her head back against his chest.

"That's the part that scares me; I don't think I've ever been so comfortable with anyone before—or horny."

"Atticus Gunner!" she said, jabbing him in the ribs. "You are a dirty old man."

Atticus laughed and slid away. "I told you," he said, still chuckling. "What you see is what you get."

Laura piled on top of him and once again they were wrestling and laughing as they rolled off the seat and onto the cockpit floor. Holding her hands in back of her to keep her from jabbing him again, he tilted her chin up, looked deep into her dark brown eyes, then released her arms and kissed her slowly on the lips for the very first time.

Suddenly, Atticus broke free, jumping to his feet and looking around. "Holy shit!" he barked as he dove back for the tiller, swinging it hard to port. The rumble of gravel scrubbing lightly on the boat's keel echoed up through the hull as the boat came about; finally, all went quiet again as they slid free and moved off into deeper water. Straightening out the tiller, Atticus gave a sigh of relief. "Excuse the language," he said.

"What in the world happened?" Laura asked.

"We just about put her up on Fisherman's Shoal," Atticus said as he once again headed toward the red blinking light at the mouth of Jackson Harbor. "That would have truly changed the complexion of the whole day."

"I guess maybe you shouldn't have been fooling around, huh?"

"Me!"

"It's not my fault you don't know where you're going," she said, still joshing him.

Atticus reached over and pulled her in close. "What time do you have to leave tomorrow?" he asked in a more serious tone.

She looked up at him. "In the morning."

"Right away?"

Laura gave a nod. "The eight o'clock boat," she replied softly.

"Why so early?"

"I have to get back."

Atticus moved the tiller to the left to follow the channel marker as they entered the harbor.

"Are the girls coming up next weekend?" she asked.

"No."

"I don't suppose you'll be coming down to Madison then."

"I wish I could, but I think I'd better hang around here. I'm supposed to be the island cop, you know."

Atticus throttled down the engine as they glided on past the city docks. In a short time, he was maneuvering the *Moonhawk* slowly in along Spencer's dock and up behind the *Jane*. Even though the moon was far from full, mooring was easy, and soon Atticus was snapping the lock on the companionway gate.

Laura was sitting on a pylon, waiting, as he stepped off the boat. Reaching out to take his hand, they started walking slowly down the dock toward their cars. "You look like you're running out of steam," Atticus said as they walked along.

Laura smiled at him. "I know," she replied. "I didn't realize I was so bushed until I sat down."

"It's been a long day with lots of fresh air and sun."

"What time is it?" she asked.

Atticus held his watch up to the moonlight. "Ten after ten," he said. "Would you like for me to escort you back to the inn?"

"No, I can find it."

They strolled around Spencer's old barn to where the vehicles were parked and stopped at Laura's car.

Laura put her arms up around Atticus. Reaching down under her chin again, Atticus tilted her face up to his and kissed her softly. "When will I see you again?" he asked.

"I don't know," she replied. "We'll have to figure out something." She laid her head on his chest. "I don't want this day to end," she said.

Atticus smiled. "Well, it's Sunday night; we could always go down and hit one of the bars."

"Okay!" she said, looking up at him.

"I was just kidding," Atticus replied.

"But just for a short while, okay?"

"Are you serious?"

"Yes; I don't want to go back to the inn just yet."

"All right," Atticus replied, "you're on." He stepped back and kissed her hand. "Let me take you to *le Casbah*, and with a police escort no less."

She laughed. "Now Atticus," she said as he walked toward the Bronco, "no ripsnorting honky-tonk joint; someplace quiet, okay?"

"In that case, how about my house?"

"That's too quiet."

Atticus smiled.

———— ••• ————

As he rolled into uptown, things were popping in usual fashion for a Saturday night. There were cars parked in front of all the bars up and down both sides of the street. The largest congestion seemed to be centered at the bar where he, Butch, and Quint had had their encounter with the Cline boys. Not wanting a repeat, Atticus pulled into the parking lot of the first bar on the north end of the strip. Laura pulled up as Atticus was getting out of the Bronco. "I think everybody on the island must come here," she said as she crawled out of her car.

"Just about," Atticus replied as he took her by the hand. "Come on; let's see how the other half lives."

As they walked through the door, one of the two young men shooting pool in the back of the room looked up. "Hey, Mr. Gunner," he said, grinning at Atticus. "What's up?" It was Ken and Bill; Atticus smiled at them.

"Friends of yours?" Laura asked softly as Atticus helped her with her chair.

"Would you believe students?" he replied.

"Well, at least we're drinking pop this time," Ken said as he walked over. "You impressed?"

"Yes," Atticus replied as he sat down, "I am."

Bill walked over to the table and stood behind Ken. "Hi, Mr. Gunner," he said softly.

Atticus nodded. "Hello, Bill, how's that hand?"

"Just fine," Bill replied, holding up the big white bandage. "In another week or so, it'll be as good as new."

"Glad to hear it," Atticus said.

"What happened to your hand?" Laura asked, smiling at the boy.

"Oh, nothing much," Bill replied with a shrug. "Mr. Gunner can tell you about it some time."

"He cut it climbing around an old lighthouse tower with Mr. Gunner's daughter," Ken chimed in. "Are you a teacher?" he went on, looking at Laura.

Laura shook her head. "Sorry," she said, smiling at him.

"Crap! I knew we couldn't be that lucky," he replied.

"This is Miss Bock," Atticus interjected. "And these," he went on motioning toward the boys, "are students and friends of my daughter Stacie; Ken Shernie and Bill Sorenson—oh, and this is Nathan Kerfam," Atticus went on, motioning toward a third teenager approaching from the obscurity of the other side of the pool table.

"Hey there, Mr. Gunner," Nathan said, pulling up his already too high pants, "just came over to say hi—and to tell you, ma'am," he said, looking at Laura, "you're the most beautiful woman I think I've ever seen, but more important, I think I'm falling in love with you."

Atticus looked at Laura and rolled his eyes. "Thank you, Nathan, for those kind words," he replied, "but now if all of you will please excuse us?"

"You mean you want us to leave?" Ken inquired.

"Exactly," Atticus replied.

Laura could hardly keep a straight face.

"He's a very selfish person, you know," Nathan mumbled to Laura out of the side of his mouth as he walked away.

"I apologize for them," Atticus said as they all went back over by the pool table.

"I think they're very charming," she replied.

Atticus shook his head. "Yeah, they're about as charming as a broken leg. Now what would you like to drink?"

"7UP."

In spite of the cars out in front, there were only four people sitting at the bar, none of whom Atticus recognized. He walked up to the bar and ordered two 7UPs and then withdrew a couple of dollars from his wallet and laid them on the bar. When the bartender returned with the drinks, he slid them over in front of Atticus. "The drinks are on the house," he said as he pushed the money back over to Atticus. "Your money's no good in here, Mr. Gunner."

Atticus looked at him with a puzzled look. "You know me?" he asked.

"Yes sir, I think just about everybody does by now."

"And why the free drinks?"

"Just because—and by the way, Mr. Gunner, if you want me to kick those kids out of here, just say the word; they're underage."

"No, that's not necessary; just no booze or beer; okay?"

"You got it, sir."

Atticus smiled at him. "Thank you." He picked up his money and the drinks and went back to the table.

Suddenly the door opened, and two men came stomping into the bar, arguing. "Hey Gunner!" one of them barked as he spotted Atticus over at the table; it was Quint.

"I think we picked the wrong bar," Atticus whispered to Laura. Then he looked up at Quint. "Well, you old war horse," he said, smiling at the old man as he came walking over to the table, "what are you up to tonight?"

"Not a hell of a lot. I thought you were going south for the weekend."

"I ended up with company instead."

"So I see," Quint said, looking at Laura while at the same time rubbing the stubble on his face.

"Laura, this is Quint Jebson, the toughest old salt on the island," Atticus said.

"How do you do?" Laura replied.

"Just fine, thank you, ma'am. Boy, you sure are a pretty one," he went on, still rubbing his face, "skinny but pretty."

"Well, thank you," Laura said, smiling at Atticus. "That's the second compliment I've received in here tonight."

With a puzzled look on his face, Quint looked at Atticus. "The second what?"

Atticus pointed his thumb over his shoulder at the pool table. "Nathan," he said.

"Oh yeah, our boy Nathan," Quint responded. "That reminds me why I came down here. If those damn kids are going with me in the morning, they're going to be heading for home shortly."

"You're taking those kids fishing with you?" Atticus responded.

"No—no," the old man said, "every year I take 'em out to find an old sunken wreck so's they can do some snorkel diving on it; this year I'm taking 'em up by the Boils."

"The Boils?" Laura interjected, looking up at Quint. "Seems to me I've read about that place somewhere. Isn't that supposed to be a really dangerous place?"

"Well, not many people go there, that's for sure," Quint replied, "but I know the area pretty good; I been fishing there for years—it's supposed to be nice tomorrow, so there shouldn't be any problems."

Atticus looked up at Quint. "Now that you mention it, I remember the kids mentioning that last week when they asked my daughters to go with. What the heck are the Boils anyway?"

"For Christ's sake, man; sailing around up in this neck of the woods and you've never heard of the Boils? I don't think I'd go sailing with this guy if'n I were you," Quint replied, grinning at Laura.

"I'll remember that," she said, giving Quint a nod.

"Listen, you old half-baked lizard," Atticus interjected, "why can't you just give me a straight answer like a normal human being?"

Quint laughed. "Ma'am, you tell him to take a look at his chart tomorrow; that's if he's got one." Quint bent down and whispered in Laura's ear. "Actually, he's okay; a little rough on anyone who riles him, but okay." Then he straightened up and walked back to where the boys were playing pool.

"What did he mean by that?" Laura asked.

Atticus shrugged. "Who knows; that's just Quint."

"I take it you know him pretty well."

"Yes; next to Butch, probably better than I know anyone else on the island."

"I can tell he likes you."

Atticus looked back at Quint talking to the boys. "He's rough looking and rough talking, but he's probably got the biggest heart of anyone I've ever met," Atticus replied. "Well," he went on in an attempt to change the topic, "I see they have pizza here; would you like me to order one?"

Laura shook her head. "I have to go home," she said. "I hope you won't be too upset with me, but if I don't go pretty soon I'm going to fall asleep right in this chair."

Atticus got up. "Come on," he said, sliding his chair back into the table. "I'm not too excited about sitting here anyway; let's go."

Atticus followed Laura toward the door. "Don't you want to say good-bye to your friends?" she asked him over her shoulder.

"No, I'd just as soon slide out of here, real quiet like."

"That's not very nice."

"I know, but no one has ever accused me of being very nice."

She laughed as she continued through the door and out into the night. When she reached her car, she turned to Atticus. "Well," she said, looking up at him, "I guess this is really the end of a very lovely day."

Just then the three boys came rambling out of the bar and over toward Bill's old pickup. "Hey Mr. Gunner, take her easy!" Ken blurted out.

Atticus acknowledged the boys by giving them a short wave.

"Why don't you come with us tomorrow?" Ken went on as he reached for the door of the pickup.

"Maybe some other time," Atticus replied.

"Don't be stupid, Ken," Nathan said from behind. "Can't you see he's got better things to do?"

Ken motioned Nathan to get into the truck ahead of him, and then he followed. "I guess you're right," he responded to Nathan as he slammed the door shut and hung his arm out the window. "Can't say that I blame him; man, if I had a fox like that!"

Bill started the engine and took off like he was going to peel out, but remembering Atticus, he eased back on the throttle and drove out of the parking lot like a normal person.

After they disappeared, Laura reached up and kissed Atticus. Then she opened the door of her car and got in. She rolled down the window and started the engine. "Good night," she said. "I'll see you in a few weeks—call me."

"I'll do that just as soon as I know what my schedule looks like," Atticus replied.

Laura waved and drove out of the lot. Atticus stood there and watched as she disappeared into the night.

CHAPTER 9

The Bell Rings Once; Four Times

Scattered clouds drifted silently across the night sky at the Hersoff place. The lights from inside the house glowed warm against the colorless night. Atticus was sitting on the couch in front of the fireplace. He was punching figures into his hand calculator. On his lap was a note pad, and on both sides of him were piles of papers. Taking off his reading glasses and laying them on the cushion next to him, he rested his head back against the couch for a moment. Finally, he looked at his watch; it was ten minutes after midnight.

The day had been one of solitude since Laura left on the early boat. In spite of the fact that Atticus was very busy for the entire day, he still spent a great deal of time thinking about her. He called the kids early in the evening and then settled down and returned to his school work.

As far as school was concerned, he had a number of things he needed to get prepared for. First and foremost, he had two interviews set up for tomorrow. The first was with a high school English teacher by the name of Frank Seamy, a young single guy out of Chicago. The second was for the industrial arts teacher, Brian Karmel from Iowa. He was also single and had applied through Butch before Atticus was in the picture. There were some things about this guy's background that he didn't like, but because Butch liked the man, and because they needed a person on board as soon as possible, Atticus agreed to go along with an interview. In addition to the interviews, he had over ten sets of credentials to go through for the open elementary teaching position. And finally, the thing he dreaded the most, the annual report, due at the state department by the beginning of next month.

The annual report was a beastly task, especially considering the fact that all the information needed was not readily available. He would have to go through Mrs. Boomer for a good share of it, and their working relationship already left a great deal to be desired; whether it was Atticus she disliked, or just men in general, he wasn't sure, but it was a problem that was beginning to eat at him.

The silence was shattered by the stark ringing of the telephone. Atticus walked over and picked up the receiver. "Hello, Gunner residence," he said softly into the receiver.

"Atticus? Butch—I get you out of bed?"

"In another ten minutes you would have; why? What's up?"

"I just called the Sorenson place; Bill said you talked to Quint last night; did he say anything to you about today?"

"Just that he was going to take some of the boys up to the Boils to do some snorkeling, why?"

"Dick Shernie called me a little while ago; they're not home yet."

"My God, it's after midnight."

"I know; that's not like Quint, and I'm worried."

"Did you call the Coast Guard to see if they've heard anything from him?"

"Yes, they've heard nothing. I decided to call Spence; we're taking the *Jane* out to look for them; can you come with us?"

"When are you leaving?"

"My wife is making a big thermos of coffee, and Spence said he'd bring some sandwiches, so we should be ready in about twenty minutes."

"I'll meet you at the dock."

"It's supposed to rain; bring some warm clothes."

After Butch hung up, Atticus stood there for a moment with his hand on the receiver. Regaining his presence of mind, he put on his shoes, grabbed his coat and hat, and headed out the door.

———◆———

Atticus arrived at the dock ahead of Butch and Spence. He went on board the *Moonhawk* and retrieved his flashlight, binoculars, and rain gear, just in case. As he was locking the latch, he heard Butch and Spence coming around the barn. Spencer's lantern swung in the darkness as they walked out on the dock.

"Are you ready?" Butch asked Atticus as they approached.

"About as ready as I can be at one o'clock in the morning," Atticus replied as he stepped off the *Moonhawk*.

"Especially for something like this," Spence said. "It reminds me of the night you went missing."

"Yeah, but Quint should be better prepared," Butch replied as he stepped on board the *Jane*, "and there hasn't been any weather."

Atticus ignored the unintended jab as he followed the two men onto the *Jane*.

Spence put down the picnic basket and headed below. He hung the lantern on a hook directly over the big, single-cylinder diesel in the midsection of the old boat.

"I can't believe they're missing," Atticus commented as he walked around to the other side of the engine.

Spence cocked his hat back on his head. "It's not like that old dog to not call in or anything." He shook his head slowly. "I got a bad feeling about this."

"Especially when it involves the Boils," Butch added.

"You know how to start her up?" Spencer asked Butch.

"It's an old Palmer, isn't it?"

"That's right."

Butch looked her over. "Light the head torch, let her heat up, crack the petcock, give her a spin, and hopefully she'll kick over," Butch replied.

"Very good; you do know something about diesel engines. And if you do her right, she'll kick off every time. Now come on, young feller," Spence went on, turning his attention to Atticus, "let's you and me get this old tub ready to get underway."

The two men went up into the wheelhouse. As the old man threw the main and turned on the running lights, Atticus went forward to cast off. As Atticus undid the bow line, he heard the old diesel give a loud *pop*, sputter a few times belching black smoke from her stack, hammer as though she were going to fall apart, and then smooth out to a steady *thump—thump—thump*.

Soon they were underway with Spencer at the helm. The big engine's flywheel gave out a low steady whine as she thumped away in a slow, rhythmic beat. They made their way out of the harbor, through the cut in Fisherman's Shoal, headed north up the east side of Rock Island, and finally out into the open water toward the Winter Islands about twenty miles to the northeast.

All three men stood silent for a long time. The light from the instrument panel cast ominous shadows on the ceiling above. Finally,

Butch reached back and picked up the paper bag his wife sent along. "How about some coffee?" he said, opening the bag and pulling out a large thermos and three cups.

"There're sandwiches in that picnic basket if anyone wants one," Spence added.

"You want a sandwich?" Butch asked Atticus as he handed him a cup of coffee.

"No thanks, not right now."

"I guess I'm not hungry either," Butch replied as he handed Spencer a cup.

"What the hell could have possibly happened?" Atticus asked. "Engine failure?"

"Not likely," Butch replied. "I just worked on his engine not more than three weeks ago; besides, he would have called in if that had happened."

"Maybe his radio didn't work for some reason," Atticus added.

"That's also unlikely."

"Why?" Atticus continued.

"Because of the way Quint is. There's never anything on his boat that doesn't work; everything is kept in tip-top shape; right, Spence?"

Spencer nodded but said nothing.

Atticus thought about the attempted sinking of the *Moonhawk*, but said nothing. He leaned back on the small seat in the back of the wheelhouse and looked out the window into the night. "There's another boat," he said, noticing lights behind them on the horizon.

Both Spence and Butch looked back. "That's got to be Captain Jack," Butch replied. "He's got Bill Sorenson, his dad, and Dick Shernie with him."

"And you think there's tension on this boat?" Spence said, turning back to the wheel. "Imagine what Dick is feeling."

"I know," Butch replied. "I tried to talk Dick out of coming, but if it were my kid, I guess I'd be there too. Does your radio work, Spence?"

"Last time I tried it," he said as he reached up and turned it on.

Butch took the mike off the hook and called for the *Becce Lee*. Captain Jack responded immediately. They exchanged location confirmation and Butch reaffirmed the search plan. The *Becce Lee* would swing out wide around the ten-mile buoy and come in along the upper banks of the Boils. The *Jane* would stay in close, work its way up into the cut between Little Winter and Big Winter islands, and then swing east out along the lower edge of the Boils. If either boat found Quint or spotted anything, it would radio the other. If neither of them found anything, they would call the Coast Guard to start a formal search. Captain Jack asked Butch if there was anything he'd have to look out for along the upper banks; Butch assured him the water was calm, so there should be no surge; but to be on the safe side he reminded him to stay out of the shallows and in deep water.

"Just what are the Boils anyway?" Atticus asked as Butch hung up the mike.

"The Boils is a ten-mile-wide slab of the Canadian shield that protrudes up from the bottom of the lake at about a 45 degree angle. The top of it comes to within six to ten feet of the surface of the lake. It starts at the southeast corner of Big Winter Island and runs straight out to the east. On this side of that slab, she drops straight down to the bottom, eight or nine hundred feet in some spots; that's called the Trench. It starts out about fifty or sixty feet wide just off Big Winter and spreads to about four miles wide at the outer end. On this side of the Trench, starting in the cut between Little Winter Island and

Big Winter Island, going out into the lake about three miles, are boulders; hundreds, maybe thousands of granite boulders; boulders of all different shapes and sizes, some just beneath the surface, and others standing as high as thirty feet in the air; that part of the Boils is called the Peppers. And the islands, they too are something different; if you notice the cliffs of Washington Island or Rock Island, they're made up of sedimentary limestone, but not the cliffs on Little and Big Winter Island, they're solid red granite. Some time eons ago, powerful geological forces pushed the whole area straight up from the bowels of the earth."

"It sounds like a beautiful place," Atticus said.

"Yeah—hauntingly beautiful," Butch went on, "the lake thermals moving over that slab, especially in the spring and fall, cause the water to churn, makes it look like it's boiling. That's where it gets its name, but that's not how it got its reputation. Any weather, coming from any direction, pushes water over that slab. And when that happens, it becomes one hell of a wave-making machine; killer waves—ask old Spence here. The Boils is no place to be in a blow, right, Spence?"

"The Boils is no place to be anytime," he said matter-of-factly.

"Tell Atticus."

"That was a long time ago," Spence replied.

"What happened?" Atticus asked.

"Go ahead and tell him," Butch reiterated.

Spence glanced over at both of them and then cocked his hat once again. "Well," he said, "it's almost fifty years ago now; I was fishing with my father and brother; we headed up toward the Boils along with three other commercial fishing boats from the island; it was a Saturday morning, a bright and beautiful Saturday morning."

Spence told how they pulled in along the south shore of Little Winter and started setting nets.

"About ten in the morning, the weather started to change," Spencer said. "It turned windy and cold. We were in the lee of the island, so Pa decided we were going to finish. The wind started to blow something fierce, but we'd been out in worse, so we kept right on going. When we got done setting, we decided to head for home. We soon found out how the Boils got its name. We no more than came out from the lee of the island when we ran into the worst seas I've ever seen. It was a good thing we were running with them, cause there was no way we could have went against 'em. Some of those waves were forty-footers if they were an inch. They were so huge that if they caught the boat just right, she'd take off and surf down the front side of the wave like a kite—Pa did a beautiful job of handling the boat for the first hour; then it happened. A huge gray beard came up out of nowhere off our port stern; I only saw it for a second, but she looked like a mountain. She had a wall of water plummeting down her face like a landslide. It caught the *Jane* . . ."

"The *Jane*?" Atticus interrupted.

"That's right, the *Jane*," Spence went on. "The boat you're standing on right now. That monster from hell caught us and rolled us over and over sideways. My brother says we went over three times; I counted twice; Pa never said. If we hadn't been empty and closed up tighter than a drum, we'd a met our Waterloo that day. Way it was, our portside gate got staved in, and it took every window out of the wheelhouse. The old Palmer never lost a beat though; she kept right on running. If she hadn't, we woulda never made it home. The way it was, we damned near froze to death pumping water just to keep her afloat. I froze my left hand; that's how I lost this finger." Spence held up his scarred paw.

"The worst of the whole deal was, of the four boats out from the island, we were the only one to make it home. No, the Boils is no place to be—ever, as far as I'm concerned."

Atticus said nothing.

"The only other man who's been in the Boils during a blow and lived to tell about it is Quint. Hell, I think he's been there at least three times," Spence continued. "If you want to hear tell of the Boils, talk to Quint. He can tell you stories that'll make your flesh crawl."

Butch looked over at Atticus. "Quint says, when you're in close to the Boils during a blow, she hisses like a snake, and in the Peppers, she wails like a woman scorned."

"But that's all irrelevant to this situation; there was no storm; not even a breeze," Atticus said.

"That's how this big lake is," Spence replied, "especially the Boils; it likes to grab you when you least expect it."

The very first hint of dawn was beginning to show when the ghostly outline of Little Winter Island loomed up off the port bow. Atticus could see the salutes of hundreds of boulders strewn out from her shore; they stood off to the east as far as he could see.

"I'm not going to take her in too close," Spence said, falling off to the northeast.

They slid on past the southeast corner of the island, paralleling the Peppers along the port beam. Soon Big Winter could be seen; it was an awesome sight in spite of her less-than-mile-wide span. The island was flat on top and covered with huge pine trees, but the 150-foot reddish-gray granite cliffs made her appear totally inaccessible. The cliffs were jagged and rough with no apparent refuge. The only possible anchorage was in the narrow channel between the two islands, and that was so strewn with boulders that lying in there was extremely risky;

especially in a surge. The whole area did indeed look completely out of place in comparison to all the other islands; it was as though it had been pulled from some mystical location and placed there by mistake.

"Now you know why people steer clear of this place; not even the sport fishermen come here," Butch said to Atticus. "The government had a lighthouse on the north point of Big Winter, but it's so forbidding, even they gave up on it. Now they've got automatic navigation buoys to ward off the lake's commercial traffic; the whole area is void of human activity."

"Is there a safe anchorage at all?" Atticus asked as he continued to stare at it.

"There's a small narrow inlet on the southwest corner," Butch replied. "There's also a way in from this side, but it's tricky and would take too long; besides, Captain Jack will be able to see in there when he comes down the west side."

"I can see why Quint is so intrigued; it's absolutely beautiful," Atticus said.

"Yes," Spence replied, "like a black widow is beautiful."

"Slow her down, Spence," Butch interjected, "we're going to have to move in amongst the Peppers if we want to cover the area. This is where they're most likely to be. At least this is where a good share of the wrecks are, the accessible ones that is, and I'm assuming that's what they came up here for."

Spence throttled the old Palmer down. Moving carefully, he steered the *Jane* past the first big boulder and into their midst.

"We'll go out front to watch for the deadheads," Butch said, starting down the steps. He motioned for Atticus to follow. "Watch for our signals," he said to Spence over his shoulder.

"I don't like this," Spence replied. "I wish the sun was up so we could see."

"We'll be all right," Atticus said softly as he moved past Spencer to follow Butch. "Just take her slow."

Hurrying down the steps into the lantern-lit interior, Atticus moved forward past the throbbing Palmer to the portside gate, which Butch swung open wide. Out on the catwalk, hanging onto the handrail along the cabin roof, he followed Butch forward to the bow. Once there, he climbed up on the bowsprit next to Butch, where they had a full view of everything forward. Butch pointed off the starboard bow. "See that big boulder just beneath the surface?" he said. "That's what we have to keep our eyes open for; that's what we call a deadhead." Atticus watched as the dull gray menace just beneath the surface slid silently past.

They proceeded forward slowly, working their way east away from the islands. Wisps of fog rose up off the water and drifted slowly north through the silent army of granite centurions. A dull gray morning emerged, bringing with it little optimism. Once their hopes soared, only to be cast aside when what they thought to be the fleeting outline of a drifting boat turned out to be nothing but another strange configuration of rocks.

———————◆◦◆◦◆———————

It was a little after eight o'clock by the time they reached the outer limits of the Peppers, and with the emergence of morning came a light drizzle. "Damn the weather!" Butch muttered as he came up the steps into the wheelhouse, unbuttoning his raincoat. "Get the weather on the radio," he said to Spence, "let's find out what it's supposed to do today."

"I already have," the old man replied as Atticus came in behind Butch. "There's a big cold front moving in slowly from Canada. She's supposed to be like this all day, then turn cold and windy tomorrow."

"Of all the God damned luck," Butch said, walking over to the window and looking out. "Where in the hell could they be?"

Atticus took off his raincoat and hung it on a hook next to the starboard window. "Let's have some coffee," he said.

"Sounds good," Butch replied, without turning around.

"Spence; how about you?" Atticus asked.

"Sure, I need something to keep me awake. I guess I'm getting too old for this kind of thing."

Atticus poured each of them a cup, including himself. "Here," he said, handing Spence his. "You been standing at that wheel all night; let me spell you for a while."

"I guess so; we're out of the rocks," he replied, taking the cup and stepping aside.

Atticus had no more than taken over when the radio crackled; the call letters for the *Jane* tumbled forth from the small speaker. Butch reached over and grabbed the mike.

"Butch?" came a voice from the radio.

"Yeah, go ahead," Butch replied.

"I think we've spotted something."

"What?" Butch asked.

Everyone stared at the radio waiting for a response. Finally, Butch squeezed the mike again. "For Christ's sake, man, what the hell is it that you see?"

"I'm not sure," came the voice again, "we're coming alongside it now. I think it's a life ring floating in the water."

"Is there anything printed on it?" Butch asked.

"Wait a minute—yeah—*Ellie May*."

Butch lowered the mike; his face turned gaunt. Spence reached over and put his hand on Butch's shoulder, and then he took the mike from his hand. Without saying a word, Butch walked over to the window and stared out at the horizon. Atticus glanced over at Spence; he didn't have to ask who the *Ellie May* belonged to.

"I'll take the wheel," Spence said softly to Atticus. "Go sit down, lad."

Atticus walked back to the bench and sat down.

Once again the radio crackled. "Butch, are you there?"

Spence raised the mike to his mouth. "This is Spencer—over," he said softly.

"Spence, we retrieved the life ring, but we got troubles. Dick went crazy when he saw the name; we've got him quieted down, but he sure doesn't look good. Over."

Butch turned around and walked back over to Spencer. "Let me talk to him," he said.

Spence gave Butch the mike. "Jack, this is Butch. Where are you now?"

"We've been working our way back toward Big Winter; I can just see it on the horizon off our starboard bow now—over."

"Turn her around and head for home. We're going to call in the Coast Guard; it's their baby now."

"It doesn't look good, does it, Butch?"

"No—no, it doesn't look good at all."

Atticus went below to the open gate. Standing there, he gazed for a long time out across the water. It was raining hard now; thousands of droplets popped as they hit the flat surface of the lake. A single gull winged silently past, inches above the water. The only sounds audible were the throb of the Palmer and the patter of rain on the cabin roof above. The *Jane* slid past another boulder off the port side and then turned northeast, continuing her search along the Peppers. The morning had risen to a very sad day.

———————•◦•———————

It was Saturday morning, and once again it was gray, windy, and cold. Atticus was standing quietly in the living room with his hands in his pockets, looking out the front window at the windswept lake. He was wearing a dark suit in preparation for the funeral. The entire week had been as depressing as the weather. By noon Wednesday, the search had been called off. Two Coast Guard cutters, a Coast Guard chopper, two private planes, and a dozen private boats, including the *Jane*, systematically combed the entire sector for two and a half days, turning up nothing more than the life ring, not even an oil slick. By three o'clock Wednesday afternoon, Quint Jebson, Ken Shernie, Nathan Kerfam, and a young man from off-island by the name of Bradly Wader had all been officially declared lost at sea.

While the island went into shock, word spread across the state. When Atticus talked to Laura on the phone Thursday evening, it had even been picked up by the national media. Afraid the girls would get the news before he had a chance to talk to them, Atticus decided to call shortly after talking to Laura. The phone call was awkward, painful, and devastating, but at least they knew and he could pick it up from there when he went down to Madison to see them; maybe by then more would be known about what had happened.

The incident struck Atticus with a real sense of loss. In the short time he knew Quint, he had developed a deep connection with the old man. In spite of all life had thrown at him, Quint had possessed that rare combination of dignity and true grit. He had relished in the romance of a way of life that was rapidly fading, and he had done it in a way that should never be forgotten. The world would move on, letting what had happened fade rapidly into the past, but there was no doubt in Atticus's mind that old Quint would truly be missed by those who knew him.

Equally painful was the kinship Atticus felt with the Shernies and Jody Kerfam. He couldn't dismiss the fact that his daughters, except for what could have been a flip of a coin, had narrowly missed the same fate.

Then there were the questions; questions that ran over and over in his mind. What could have possibly gone wrong? If there'd been an explosion, some kind of wreckage would have been left behind. They could have capsized and gone down, but there were no seas that day. They could have hit something, but there was no oil slick. They simply disappeared, so fast that Quint could do nothing; so fast that neither Ken nor the Wader boy, who were both excellent swimmers, with wet suits, could make landfall of some kind; so fast that the dual bilge pumps on Quint's boat couldn't slow the sinking enough for Quint to even get off a distress call. No matter what scenario he conjured up, it never came to an acceptable conclusion. Deep within the pit of his stomach, Atticus had that sick feeling that something very dark and evil had happened out there on the lake that day, and that it had nothing to do with the Boils.

The week had truly been a busy one; for three straight days, Atticus had been involved in the search; on Thursday he was asked if he would take charge of making arrangements for the multiple funeral; he even managed to hire Frank Seamy for the vacant high school position that day. But with Brian Karmel, the industrial arts candidate, it was a different story; Karmel was extremely upset over the fact that Atticus couldn't find the time to meet with him.

The clock on the wall struck nine; Atticus glanced at his watch; it was time. He put on his coat and went out to the Bronco.

———————•··•··•———————

On the way to the church, Atticus thought about the funeral. There would be no caskets, no pallbearers, no trip to the cemetery, no final good-byes; at least not in the traditional sense. Today there would be a simple eulogy, some prayers, and the singing of a few songs. Following the service, the church bell would toll once for each soul lost, in the traditional manner for those lost at sea.

Upon arriving, Atticus walked across the parking lot toward the front of the church. Cars were rolling into the lot one after the other now. He entered the church behind four people he'd never seen before. Once inside, he spotted Butch and his wife sitting in the very last pew; he worked his way in and sat next to them. Both Butch and Karen acknowledged his presence; Butch with a nod and Karen with a smile. Sitting silently, Atticus watched as the people continued to file in. In the background, the somber sound of organ music filled the room. On the altar were four large candles, along with a host of flowers. Atticus could see the anguish in the faces of the immediate families as they made their agonizing trek to the front of the church. Soon Reverend Watson entered, and the service began. As the reverend spoke, Atticus found his mind drifting back to the encounters he'd had with Ken, Nathan, and especially Quint. The realization that his memories had no future upon which to expand struck hard. Finally, the congregation recited the Our Father. Following the prayer, stillness fell over the church. In the silence, the church bell tolled slowly four times. With a lump in his throat, Atticus swallowed hard to keep the tears back.

———————•◆•———————

Butch and Karen were waiting in front of the community center when Atticus arrived for the luncheon following the funeral. "That's the one good thing about a funeral on the island," Butch said as Atticus approached, "the Ladies Aid puts on a tremendous feed."

"That's good," Atticus replied, "because it looks like half of Chicago is here."

"Well, both the Shernies and the Waders are from Chicago," he said, "even Jody Kerfam's people are Chicagoans."

"Yes, that's what I understand," Atticus responded with a smile.

They walked together up to the front door. Atticus pulled the door open for them to enter. Karen put her hand on top of her head in an attempt to keep her hair from blowing in a gust of wind as she hurried in. Butch motioned for Atticus to go ahead, and then he too entered.

The hall was already filled with people. There were a dozen or so long tables covered with white linen. Up front was another long table covered with an assortment of hot dishes, sandwiches, cakes, and pies. Some folks were already sitting at the tables eating, while others were filling their plates.

Butch and Karen were captured by some summer Chicago friends and whisked off into the crowd. Atticus decided to work his way out of the main flow of traffic. As he excused himself through the crowd, he felt a tug on his shirtsleeve; turning, he was met by Spencer, standing directly behind him. "Hey there, young fella, you look lost," Spence said, grinning up at Atticus.

"That I am," Atticus replied.

"Food'll draw 'em every time," Spence said, still grinning.

Atticus smiled at Spencer. "You know, I hardly recognized you without your hat."

"Well, you know how women are about funerals," Spence replied. "I had to wear my Sunday duds—by the way, this is Sylvia, my boss."

"Oh, Spencer," the little woman standing next to him said, "he always fusses whenever I make him wear something other than those bib overalls," she went on, smiling up at Atticus. "Anyway, I've heard a great deal about you, and it's a pleasure to finally meet you."

Atticus smiled down at her. She was a petite woman in her late fifties or early sixties, with silver-white hair and a warm smile. There was a sparkle in her eyes and directness in her actions; together they seemed to demand both respect and admiration. "How do you do?" Atticus replied, extending his hand to her. "I've heard a great deal about you too, and I'm looking forward to working with you."

"I've been on the island so long, I'm afraid my teaching style may seem a little old-fashioned," she said.

"What is a long time?"

"On the island?" she replied, smiling first at Spence and then back up at Atticus. "Spence and I have lived here all our lives," she said. "We were married when I was twenty. I started my first year of teaching at the age of seventeen, right out of high school. They couldn't find a teacher that year, so I was recruited. After that, I went off the island for two years while I attended County Normal in Sturgeon Bay. Then I came back and have been teaching here ever since."

"How many students did you have at the ripe old age of seventeen?" Atticus asked.

"Nine," was her reply, "first grade on up."

"You mean there were only nine children on the island at that time?"

"Oh, goodness no," she replied. "Back then you couldn't just hop in a car and drive from one side of the island to the other; it was an all-day trip, usually by horse and buggy, and that was in good weather. The roads were nothing more than dirt trails back then. So, there were three schools operating—seems hard to imagine nowadays, doesn't it?"

"Yes, it certainly does."

"Well, that's enough about me; tell us about yourself. I understand you have two lovely daughters."

"Yes, Inger and Stacie."

"Those are beautiful names; are they going to school down in the Madison area?"

"Yes."

"I certainly hope I'll get a chance to meet them sometime."

"Oh, I'm sure you will," Atticus replied.

Just then, a middle-aged couple came up and greeted both Sylvia and Spencer. In a short while, two more people approached Sylvia and started a conversation with her. Before long, Sylvia and Spence drifted into the crowd just as Butch and Karen had. For a brief moment, Atticus spotted the Doebucks and Adrian Fruger and his wife. Joni and her brother Allen were eating at one of the tables with the rest of their family, including Hepper. Greta Bergason smiled and greeted Atticus as she made her way past him through the crowd. Dr. Burnett and his wife were talking with some off-island people on the other side of the room, and Reverend Watson and his wife came in the door and disappeared into the crowd.

Spencer was more inclined to let his wife do the talking in large gatherings and only entered into the conversation when addressed directly; as a result, he spent most of his time watching people. Right now he was watching Atticus work his way through the crowd alone, eventually reaching the door. He nudged Sylvia to get her attention and then nodded toward Atticus. "I'm afraid Mr. Gunner feels a bit like an outsider," she said quietly to Spencer. "Go over and get him. Have him come and eat with us."

Giving her a nod, Spence started through the crowd toward Atticus. By the time he reached the door, Atticus had wandered outside and was standing on the sidewalk, looking up at the sky. "I imagine she's blowing pretty good out there today," he said as he walked up behind Atticus.

A bit startled, Atticus turned his head quickly. "That's for sure," he replied. "If this keeps up, these people might not get off the island this afternoon."

"Oh no," Spence said, stepping up next to Atticus. "It may get a bit bumpy, but they'll get off; you needn't worry about that. How about coming inside and grabbing a bite to eat with us?"

Atticus smiled. "Thanks," he replied, "but I'm kind of thinking about heading for Madison myself."

"Madison?"

"Yes, I told the girls what happened, but there are a lot of details they don't know, and I can't handle that over a telephone."

"You can't do that on an empty stomach either; besides, Sylvia said I was supposed to come and get you. You can leave after you've had something to eat."

Atticus smiled. "All right," he said, "let's go get something to eat."

CHAPTER 10

The Doves Coo, While an Eagle Screams

The trip down to Madison after the funeral was a short one. With the girls' expanded summer activities and their desire to be on the island during the upcoming summer carnival, it was decided their next trip to the island would be in three weeks, rather than in two, as was originally planned. Atticus was disappointed in the time delay, but the truth was he really needed an escape from everything; he was feeling overwhelmed. During his short visit with Laura, it was decided she would come up to the island the following weekend, and they would spend an entire week on the *Moonhawk* away from everything and everyone. Other than working on the annual report for school, things were very quiet right now for Atticus, and although he made a conscious effort not to think about the disappearance of Quint and the boys, it was always lingering in the back of his mind. Needless to say, Atticus was elated over the prospect of spending some time with Laura again.

The week of waiting was finally over; after what seemed an eternity, he and Laura would finally have their week of sailing. The *Moonhawk* was loaded and ready to go. Atticus meticulously laid out his plans. He even managed to borrow a dinghy to pull behind so they could do some out-of-the-way exploring. This afternoon they would make the five-hour sail northwest to Escanaba and stay at the yacht club. Tomorrow, they would sail across Big Bay De Noc to Fayette and bum around for the day, and then on Monday, head for the Mackinac Straits and Mackinac Island. On Wednesday, they would head for the Beaver Island group to do some more exploring and gunkholing. Finally, depending on time, they'd sail south to the Manitoo Islands and back across the lake, arriving back on Washington Island a week from today. The plan did not include the Winter Islands or anywhere near the Boils; he thought about it, and very nearly came to including it, but decided it would be best to give it a wide berth for now.

Arriving at Butch's house, Atticus swung the Bronco into the drive and up along the picket fence. Butch, who was tinkering with his lawn mower in the back yard, looked up. "You need a job?" he asked Atticus as he got out of the Bronco.

"No thanks," Atticus replied, "I got all the jobs I need."

"I didn't think you stopped by to help."

Atticus smiled and said, "No, I just stopped by to ask you for a favor."

"That figures; what?"

"I'm going to take off for a few days and do some sailing," Atticus went on, "and with Spence off the island, I wondered if you'd let him know when he gets back."

"Where are you going?" Butch asked with a puzzled look on his face.

"Well, I'm going to head on up to Escanaba, then over to . . ."

"Never mind," Butch interrupted. "You're going out there to nose around."

"No, Butch, I'm not."

"Bullshit, Atticus; going out there all by yourself, especially to the Boils, is plain stupid."

"Butch, I am not going out there to look for trouble, nor am I going to the Boils."

"Right. You're just going out there to sail around for a few days. You must really think I'm stupid."

"Forget it," Atticus replied. "I didn't mean to make a federal case out of it. I'll be back a week from today."

Butch looked away, shaking his head. "Damn! You are bullheaded," he said. "Look, I can't let you go out there alone; if you insist on going, I'll go with you."

"Butch, any other time, you'd be more than welcome, but not this time."

"Why?"

"Because I'm not going alone."

"You're not going alone? Who you going with?"

"The Bock girl."

"The Bock girl; are you sure that's a good idea?"

"Why?"

"You've already got a number of people up here on your case; important people, I might add. Isn't that a little like throwing gas on a burning fire? They're not going to look very favorably on that kind of behavior from their schoolmaster, or their cop."

"Butch, for Christ's sake, this is the twentieth century."

"They may not see it that way."

"No, they probably won't, but that's not going to change my mind."

Butch shook his head again. "No, I guess it wouldn't."

Atticus made no response.

"Yes, I'll tell Spence," Butch said.

"Thanks," Atticus said.

"Be careful out there; I still think the whole idea is a bad one, but I'll try to keep your whereabouts as quiet as possible."

Atticus got back into the Bronco. "If you need me, give Vivian a call; she'll know how to get ahold of me."

"Vivian? Well, so much for keeping it quiet." Butch shook his head again. "Be safe out there, Gunner; especially considering you have a passenger along. We don't need any more bad news."

Atticus smiled at Butch. "Hold down the fort my friend, and I'll see you next weekend."

Butch waved him off and went back to his lawn mower.

———◆———

It was midafternoon by the time Atticus turned down the drive to the Hersoff place. Laura would be arriving at any time now. He drove into the yard and up to the house. He got out of the Bronco and went over to the front steps to sit in the warm afternoon sun to wait for her. The long-range forecast for the entire week was for warm, beautiful weather. Glancing at his watch, he leaned back and rested his head against the porch door. Ten minutes passed, and then the silence was broken by the rumble of a car coming down the drive. Atticus looked up to see Laura's car come rolling out of the trees and into the yard. She honked as she pulled to a stop beside the Bronco. As Atticus got up to greet her, she scurried out from behind the steering wheel and ran to meet him. After throwing her arms around his neck, Atticus picked her up and spun her around. Finally, he put her down and held her at arm's length. "Let me look at you," he said. "Yes; you're just as pretty as I remember."

"You're prejudiced," she replied, still smiling at him.

"I may be, but I'm not blind."

They looked into each other's eyes silently for a moment. Laura reached up and swept his hair back off his forehead. "It seemed like today would never get here," she said softly, her eyes still searching his. She glanced up at the house. "You didn't tell me you lived in a mansion," she went on. "This isn't at all what I expected. I pictured a quaint little cottage or something."

"Well, you know how we big island tycoons are," he said, taking her by the arm and starting toward the front steps. "We live in big houses."

"Really, Atticus, how can you afford this?"

"That's a long story," he replied. "Would you believe a hundred and twenty-five a month?"

"How in the world did you swing that?"

"I'll tell you about it sometime. Right now, I'll give you a quick tour, and then we've got to get going. We have to make Escanaba tonight."

"Did you have any trouble arranging things at school?"

"No," Atticus replied as he opened the porch door. "Actually it went better than I expected. I still have to reschedule one of the interviews I had set up the day of the disappearance; he showed up for the interview, and of course I didn't."

"Well, given the circumstances, I'm sure he understood."

"It was the industrial arts man, and no, he was very indignant about the whole thing."

"There's a shortage of certified industrial arts teachers, you know."

"I know," Atticus replied, "but maybe I'll just take my chances and look for someone else."

"How many positions do you have left to fill?"

"Three; the IA teacher, high school math/science, and a lower elementary."

"I'll spread the word. Maybe we can help you."

"Good—well, enough about school. This is my humble abode; pretty nice, huh?"

"Interesting," she replied, looking around the foyer.

"It can use some work, but it's more than I ever expected. Upstairs there are three bedrooms and a big recreation room."

"Really?"

"Yep. Now we've got to go," Atticus said, taking her by the hand and starting back toward the door.

"Atticus . . ."

"I'm sorry, but you can see it when we get back."

"Well," she said, following him along, "I sure hope I'm not rushing you or anything."

"Laura, we'll never make Escanaba if we don't get going. There is one thing I did forget, however." Atticus tilted her chin up and kissed her.

As he pulled her in tight, Laura wrapped her arms around his neck and kissed back; it was a long kiss. Finally, as he released her, she looked into his eyes. "You're right," she said softly, "I guess I can see the house when we get back."

———— ·•◆•· ————

The compass gave off a deep red glow; while above, a blanket of stars filled the night sky. The blink of a far-off beacon gave an occasional flash on the dark horizon. With everything up close falling prey to the darkness, the sound of the wind whispering through the rigging along with the swish of the waves seemed to dominate the senses aboard the

Moonhawk. Both Laura and Atticus were settled back, fully enjoying the ride in the unusually warm night air. The eventual rise of the moon brought with it the passing of a lake freighter with its deck lit up. And through it all, it was Atticus who did most of the talking; he was in his glory, pointing out the constellations and talking about sailing. All the while, Laura just sat there, tucked under his arm and smiling up at his undaunted enthusiasm.

A little after ten o'clock, the lights of the Escanaba waterfront appeared. Dropping the sails, Atticus guided the *Moonhawk* slowly into the open breakwater at the yacht club. Inside, he shifted the gear lever into neutral, allowing the boat to drift while he looked the situation over. Every slip and most of the mooring floats were occupied by boats of every size and configuration. Dockside was crowded with people, and from the clubhouse came the faint but clear sound of country music drifting through the night air. "They must be celebrating our arrival," Atticus said, grinning down at Laura. Atticus moved the shift lever forward again and guided the boat slowly over to the nearest empty float. "I think we'll dock right here," he said, reversing the thrust to bring the sloop to a standstill.

While Atticus shut down the engine, Laura grabbed a mooring line and went forward to tie it off. After completing her task, she started below to light the lantern and turn the power off. As she passed Atticus attending the sails, she jabbed him in the ribs from behind. Responding playfully, Atticus dropped what he was doing and went after her; the chase was on. They ran around the deck, laughing like children. By the time Atticus caught up to her, she had made it into the cockpit. There he brought her down tumbling into the starboard seat. Then as before, the thrashing and squealing soon went silent as the opportunity finally gave way to its candid purpose. "Atticus, please," she whispered in his ear. "If we don't stop soon . . ."

Atticus stopped; his breathing subsided. Finally, he got off of her and slid over. As he did, she sat up. Laura smiled at him and then leaned down and kissed him lightly on the lips. "I'll go light the lantern and turn off the running lights," she said.

After Atticus finished with all the tie-downs, he too headed below. "Are you ready to go?" he asked as he came down the companionway ladder.

Laura looked out from the forward cabin, where she was organizing her things. "Where are we going?" she asked.

"Well, I have to check in with the harbormaster so he knows we're here, and I promised I'd call the girls. If you'd rather not face that mob, you can wait here."

"No, I'll go with. Should we turn out the lantern and stuff?"

"No, they'll be fine," Atticus said, extending her his hand. She took it and together they went back up on deck.

Atticus went over to the stern rail to retrieve the dinghy. He pulled it up alongside and lowered the boarding ladder, climbed down, and got in. He positioned the small craft while holding onto the ladder, looking up at Laura. "Okay," he said, "your turn." She climbed down and got into the back of the dinghy. Atticus pushed away and rowed the fifty yards over to the waterside dock next to the dinghy rack.

Laura stood by, looking around, while Atticus pulled the small boat up onto the dock. Finally, she helped slide the dinghy over next to the rack and then, taking Atticus by the hand again, followed him up the steps and onto the main dock.

As they approached the end of the dock in front of the clubhouse, a robust-looking man wearing a yachting cap and carrying a clipboard approached. "Are you Gunner?" he asked as he walked up to them.

"That's right," Atticus replied.

"Good!" He extended his hand to Atticus. "I'm Topper, the harbormaster. I saw you come in and was hoping it was you. You're the last one on my list."

"I'm sorry," Atticus said, shaking his hand. "We got a late start."

"No need to apologize. You and your wife staying more than the night?"

"No, just tonight," Atticus replied, glancing over at Laura.

"Okay," he said, flipping through the papers on his clipboard. "Let's see—*Moonhawk,* isn't it? Thirty-two feet?"

"That's right."

"That'll be twenty-two dollars."

Atticus took out his wallet and gave the man his money. "By the way," Atticus asked, "what's the occasion?"

"Summer Regatta Dance," the man replied, putting the money in his shirt pocket, "and it's open to any guest of the yacht club, so help yourself."

"Can you tell me where there is a phone?" Atticus asked.

"Down in the main bar," he said, pointing toward the far end of the clubhouse.

Atticus took Laura by the hand again. "Stick close," he said to her as he started to work his way through the crowd.

"Just lead the way, husband," she replied.

Atticus looked back at her over his shoulder, and she grinned.

When they reached the end of the building, they entered the open door with a flashing beer sign above it. Looking around, Atticus led the way over to a small table in the corner. The place was full of people. Just off to the right, two large French doors were propped open, with people coming in and out of the ballroom. The music was so loud, the vibrations pulsated in the smoke-filled air. "I have to find the phone!" Atticus shouted into her ear. "Do you want to come with me?"

Laura shook her head. "I'll wait here!"

Atticus nodded and then disappeared into the crowd.

"Did you find the phone?" Laura asked Atticus upon his return.

Atticus nodded as he sat down.

"How did it go?"

"Just fine; Stacie had fallen asleep on the couch, but Inger was still up watching TV and waiting."

"That's sweet," Laura said, smiling at Atticus.

"Their mother didn't think so."

"Why?"

"She chewed me out for not calling earlier."

"It is kind of late."

"Yes, I know. Ordinarily, it wouldn't have been such a big deal, but the girls are kind of uptight about my sailing since the death of Quint and the boys."

"I can understand that. Do they think you're all alone?"

"No, I told them I was taking a friend from Madison."

"At least you didn't lie. Are they a little more at ease now that they know you made it here without mishap?"

"Yes, they're fine; I don't have to call in again until we get home. Well," Atticus went on, "you've had a long day; do you want to go back to the boat?"

"I'm not tired," she replied.

Atticus grinned at her and started to get up. "Good, let's go see what's happening in that dance hall."

Once inside, they moved out of the main lane of traffic and stood on the sidelines and watched. The floor was crowded. After a few minutes, Atticus leaned his head down next to hers. "Want to try it?" he asked. Laura looked up and gave him a nod. Atticus held out his hand; she took it and put her other hand on his shoulder; they were off.

Laura was an excellent dancer; she was as light and graceful on her feet as she was lovely to the eye. Atticus felt like a million bucks dancing with her. He swung her around and around on the fast ones, and he held her in close on the slow ones. They danced every dance for the next hour and a half. Finally, at two o'clock, the lights went on and the band stopped playing.

Laura took Atticus by the arm and held it in close as they left the hall and walked out onto the dock. "Atticus," she said, looking up at him, "I don't think I've ever had a better time than I've had today."

Atticus smiled back. "Neither have I," he replied.

"We really are very good together, everything seems so natural—I've never known anyone quite like you before."

"I think you're overtired," Atticus replied with a grin.

"I really mean it."

"That proves it," Atticus said. "You are definitely overtired."

———◆———

Atticus pulled on the oars with long, steady strokes. A light fog was drifting in over the water. The light from the lantern on board the *Moonhawk* still glowed through the cabin window. Looking back, the clubhouse was all but empty now; just four people were standing on the dock, talking next to a big sailboat.

When they reached the *Moonhawk,* Laura crawled up the ladder and took the painter from Atticus, and then he followed. After everything was secure, Atticus opened the hatch for Laura to go below. "Your sleeping bag should be in the hanging locker in the forward cabin," he said as he came down the steps behind her.

"Are we going to bed?" she asked, turning toward him.

"It's three in the morning; tomorrow is going to come pretty fast."

"But I'm not tired, are you?"

"No, I'm not, but we will be tomorrow if we don't get some shut-eye."

"All right, I've got an idea," she said. "Why don't we get ready for bed, turn off the lantern, and sit out here in the main cabin until we get tired?"

Atticus smiled at her. "Turning off the lantern and sitting out here sounds like a good idea to me, but I don't know about the getting ready for bed."

Laura reached up and kissed him lightly on the lips. "All right, Captain," she said smiling at him, "no getting ready for bed."

"I don't know why I can't ever learn to keep my mouth shut," he replied with a grin.

Atticus watched as she walked into the forward cabin and opened her locker. Then he pulled out his sleeping bag and rolled it out on the quarter berth. Opening his travel bag, he grabbed a clean T-shirt. Finally, he reached up and snubbed out the light; everything went black.

Laura made her way out to where Atticus was standing. "This is more like it," she said softly.

Atticus took her by the shoulders and kissed her. When he finally released her, he sat down on the quarter berth, putting one leg up and patting the seat for her to follow. She sat down facing him, scooted up close, and leaned back on his knee.

Her soft brown eyes twinkled in the pale light. Atticus reached out and gently touched her cheek. There was something very special about her, something more than the obvious. Everything about her was perfect; her eyes, the way she walked—but tonight there was something about the way she looked at him. A feeling came over him; something deep within the inroads of his past; a memory . . .

"Well," he said, trying to shake it, "does your mother know about me yet?"

"Yes."

"And what did she say?"

"She told me you were well educated, good looking, very debonair; the kind of man a woman could fall for."

"I'll bet she did; what else did she say?"

"She said you would love me and then break my heart. She told me to find a man closer to my age; someone without children. She also told me I was very pretty and should have no problem attracting anyone I choose."

"Sounds to me like your mother gave you some pretty solid advice—so what did you tell her?"

Laura reached over and brushed his cheek. "I told her she was too late."

This time Atticus didn't respond.

"Atticus, you don't like to talk about yourself, do you?"

"Why do you say that?" he replied.

289

"Because you never do. Oh, I know you talk, but I mean, about yourself."

"There's not much to tell; what would you like to know?"

"Tell me about the women in your life."

"The women in my life!"

"Yes, I don't mean affairs or one-night stands; tell me about the women you've loved."

"There are no women in my life other than my girls, and now you."

"Atticus, that's not true. There is someone out there."

"What makes you say that?"

"Because of the way you are around me; your caution, your bashfulness, your uncertainty to commit, and none of those behaviors really match your personality."

"You're very intuitive."

"What was her name?"

"It was a long time ago—I mean, I was just a kid. I was too young for it to have been anything more than a case of puppy-love gone bad."

Laura looked at him. "That's not true, is it?"

Atticus looked away again. Finally, he took a deep breath and leaned his head back against the bulkhead. "Her name was Judy," he said as though it pained him to speak the name.

"Tell me about her," Laura said, laying her head against his chest. "Where is she now?"

"I have no idea," he said, shaking his head slowly. "Laura, it was a long time ago. Life has moved on."

"Judy what?"

"Judy Chaterfield," he replied.

"Tell me about Judy Chaterfield."

Atticus hadn't heard her name spoken in a very long time. "We were just kids when we met," he whispered. "I was sixteen, and she was fourteen. We were so young, our relationship never even came close to being consummated. But that spark for some reason went very deep. For whatever reasons, that very rocky romance lasted seven years off and on; long enough to burn deep impressions into a young man's psyche. It was put on hold while I ran off to Oregon for a year, and then to Florida for another year. While I fiddled, Rome burned. She grew up and went off to college, leaving me behind. At any rate, since that time I've never looked back, and until now I've never spoken her name."

Atticus glanced down at Laura. "I've never told another living soul what I just told you," he said quietly. Then he paused again. "My former wife is a good woman," he continued. "She deserved a lot better than what she got. There was even a time when I thought we were happy. The truth of the matter is, she suffered the consequence of a ghost she knew nothing about.

"I do however, love my daughters dearly, and although I'm probably not the best of fathers, I'll never turn my back on them again." Again Atticus paused. "She was very bitter over the divorce," he whispered, "and rightfully so—at any rate, that brings me to the here and now; a divorced middle-aged man with two kids, a tour in the army, seven years of college, and a boat called the *Moonhawk* that I don't deserve; pretty impressive stuff, huh?"

He looked down at Laura and smiled. She was fast asleep. "One thing is for sure," he continued, knowing full well that he was talking to himself, "I'm excellent at putting women to sleep." He lowered his leg so as not to disturb her, slid his arm underneath her, and carried her quietly into the forward cabin.

As he laid her gently down on her bed, she opened her eyes slightly. "What are you doing?" she whispered.

"Putting you to bed," Atticus replied softly.

"I can't sleep with my clothes on."

Atticus grinned. "Would you like me to undress you?"

She attempted a feeble poke at him as she rose sluggishly to a sitting position. "I can manage myself," she replied.

"Very good; then I'll see you in the morning." He turned and started to walk out.

"Atticus?"

He stopped and looked back. "What?"

"What would you have done if I'd said yes?"

"To undress you?"

Laura nodded.

"I'd like to think I would have declined, but the truth of the matter is, I don't know." Atticus smiled at her again. "Good night." He walked out of the cabin.

Atticus held his watch up to the cabin window so he could see the time; it was 4:15. He stripped down to his undershorts and laid down on his sleeping bag, folding his hands behind his head. Dawn was just beginning to show. After fifteen minutes, unable to relax, he decided to go for a short swim. He got up quietly, retrieving a towel from his locker, opened the companionway gate, and went up on deck.

The water was bone-chilling cold as he stepped off the boarding ladder and slipped beneath the surface. He glided through the inky blackness about ten yards before resurfacing. Shaking the water from his eyes, he swam silently around the *Moonhawk* and back to the boarding ladder.

The dip only lasted a few minutes, but he felt 100 percent more relaxed as he crawled back on board. Picking up the towel, he dried himself, and then he took off his shorts, hung them over the boom, and wrapped a towel around his midsection.

After making his way back down into the main cabin, he reached up and closed the gate quietly. It was then he noticed Laura standing in the forward passageway. "I'm sorry," he said softly, sitting down on his bunk. "I didn't mean to wake you."

"I couldn't sleep either," she replied.

Laura walked over and sat down next to him. She was wearing a plain nightie that came down to just above her knees. It wasn't a see-through garment by any means, but the combination of the faint glimmer of dawn shining through the window from behind, and the way it clung to her in all the right places, made her grace and beauty easy to observe. "Atticus," she said, "do you believe in destiny?"

Atticus didn't respond.

"What happened in your past happened for a reason. Just as your girls were meant to be, so were we." Laura turned around to a kneeling position next to Atticus. As she raised her knee to straddle him, she reached out and touched his face. She kissed him on the lips. She pressed gently against his chest, and Atticus leaned back against the bulkhead; there was no way to stop what was happening. She reached down, undid his towel, and let it slide to the floor.

————•◦•◆•◦•————

Heading west by southwest across the big lake, the *Moonhawk's* bow rose to each windswept wave and then plummeted down the back side on its way to the next. Even though the sun was beginning to burn away the morning haze, the blustery wind had a stinging bite. Atticus pulled his coat collar up around his neck to keep out the chill. His back to the wind and spray, he held tight to the tiller as the sloop plunged ahead at a solid nine knots.

Too wet and cold in the cockpit, Laura had retreated to the warmth of the cabin. There she lay on the starboard berth, watching Atticus brave the elements up at the helm. It was Saturday morning; they were on their way home. Beaver Island, where they spent the last two days bumming around its sparsely populated beaches, had been a perfect culmination of their week together. They hadn't covered every location on the trip, but it made no difference; it seemed perfectly fine as long as they were together.

The way things turned out, heading for home from Beaver Island forced Atticus to pass parallel to the Boils. He charted a course that would take them north around Big Winter Island. This not only put them safely out of harm's way, it also took them down the west side of the Winter Islands in the relative safety of deep water.

By noon, the situation improved substantially; the wind tapered off to nothing more than a moderate breeze, and the frothing spray from the waves, which had made things miserable on deck, finally lessened with the drop of the seas to a low rolling swell. The sun, too, which was now burning bright and hot, helped warm things up.

Laura took the helm while Atticus went below to change clothes. He stripped off his damp Levis and slipped on shorts. As he gathered up his wet things, he leaned over to the open companionway gate.

"Hey Laura!" he shouted, looking up at her. "You got any wet clothes you want dried?"

Laura looked down and smiled. "No," she replied, shrugging her shoulders. "I didn't get wet this morning!"

"Oh, that's right," Atticus muttered in a kidding fashion, "I forgot; you spent the entire morning hiding down here!"

Laura, who was sitting on the rim of the cockpit in her swimming suit and steering with her foot, simply shrugged her naked shoulders and grinned.

Atticus finished gathering his things and went back up on deck. He went over to Laura, kissed her quickly on the lips, and then headed for the foredeck.

"Is that the best you can do?" she asked as he walked away.

"You just keep her on course," he replied as he stepped up onto the cabin roof and down to the portside of the boat. "I'll take care of you later."

"Promises, promises, all I ever get are promises."

"That's not a promise," he said, grinning back at her as he hung his things on the safety rail. "That's a fact!"

"Hey, Atticus, what's that?" she asked, pointing off to the horizon.

To the south, where the sky met the water, the horizon was dancing. Still further off to the southwest, little protrusions that looked like a line of toy soldiers standing in a long column raised what looked to be their heads above the dancing horizon.

Atticus looked off to where Laura was pointing. For a long moment, he said nothing. Finally, he spoke. "That's the Boils," he replied, continuing to stare off at it. "The dancing horizon is waves, and those protrusions are the Peppers."

"Is that where Quint and the boys were lost?"

Atticus gave a nod. "Yes—that's the place."

"We're not going there, are we?"

"No," he replied, shaking his head. "We're going around to the northwest of it."

"The way the horizon is dancing, that must really be rough water."

"Yes, I imagine she's churned up pretty good today," Atticus said as he came back into the cockpit.

———◆◆◆———

Within the next hour, both of the Winter Islands appeared on the horizon, and by early afternoon, they were rounding the north end of Big Winter, about a half mile off its cliff-laden coast.

To avoid spilling any of the lunch she had prepared, Laura waited until well after Atticus had set the new tack before she made her way up the ladder and into the cockpit. Carefully, she put the tray down on the windward seat. "Are you hungry?" she asked as she reorganized the drinks so they wouldn't tip over.

Atticus was bent down, looking under the sails, and didn't respond.

"Here," she said, holding a sandwich out to him. He still didn't respond. "Atticus?" she repeated.

"Oh great," he replied, somewhat startled. "Thanks." He took the sandwich.

"I'll tuck your drink into the seat cushion here next to you, okay?"

"Fine," he replied. He took a bite from the sandwich and then looked away again.

Wondering what he was so preoccupied with, Laura bent down so she could see under the sails. To her surprise, Big Winter Island, with its towering red granite cliffs, seemed to be just off the port bow. "Aren't we coming in awfully close to that island?" she asked.

"Yes, I know," he responded as he swung the tiller to port, bringing the bow into the wind.

The *Moonhawk* lost its forward drive and rapidly came to a standstill. Dead in the water, she began to wallow and roll in the pitch of the seas; the empty sails fluttered and snapped in the wind. "What are you doing?" Laura asked.

"We're going into that island for a look-see," Atticus replied. "Come here and watch the tiller for a minute."

"Atticus, we're spilling our drinks and everything," she said as she made her way back through the pitching cockpit to take hold of the tiller. "What am I supposed to do?"

"Just keep her nose into the wind," he replied.

Laura sat down with the tiller in one hand and her drink in the other as Atticus hurried forward. Suddenly, as the boat made a quick heave to starboard, the tray of food she had so meticulously prepared slid off the seat cushion and went crashing onto the cockpit floor. "Atticus Gunner!" she barked. "The next time you do something like this without telling me first, you're going to get it! And I mean it!"

Atticus dropped the mainsail and then the genoa. Tying off the ropes, he jumped back into the cockpit and hurried below to throw on the blower switch. In less than two minutes, he was back at the helm, starting the engine. Soon the prop was churning, and the *Moonhawk* regained steerage.

As things settled down, Laura gathered up the food strewn all over the cockpit floor. She took everything below and then came back and sat next to where Atticus was standing. "I'm sorry," he said, looking down at her.

"Sorry doesn't cut it," she replied. "You never tell me what you're thinking. Sometimes I think you even forget I'm along—besides, I thought you said we weren't going to come in here."

"I guess I was pretty inconsiderate."

"Yes, you were."

Atticus made no reply.

Finally, she looked up at him and shook her head. "I'm sorry," she said. "I didn't mean to bark at you. I know you didn't mean to do that; it's just that sometimes your inattentiveness makes me so frustrated."

"I'll try to be better," he replied.

Laura looked up at the high rugged cliffs as they crawled along beneath them. "So this is where Quint and the boys went missing."

"Well, not exactly," he replied. "It was somewhere on the other side of the island; at least that's the speculation."

"You intend for us to go on that island?"

"Yes, if you're not afraid."

"Atticus Gunner, I'll go anyplace you go, but it's not a very hospitable-looking place, is it? How in the world are we even going to get in close enough to try?"

"There's a harbor just around the point here, or at least so I've been told."

As they approached the rocky point, Atticus throttled back the engine. Rounding the point, the narrow opening between the two islands came into full view; to the left was Big Winter Island, with its towering red granite cliffs shining in the midday sun, and to the right, Little Winter Island, not nearly as domineering or high, but rocky and covered with scraggly old cedars clear down to its boulder-laden shores. Ahead through the canyon-like cut between the two islands, at a distance of about three-quarters of a mile, laid the beginning of the Boils.

One hand on the throttle and the other on the tiller, Atticus guided the *Moonhawk* slowly in amongst the boulders. Protected on both sides by the two islands, the seas subsided to a gentle but constant surge. Laura stood silently at the stern rail and watched. In the distance, the muffled roar of the surf pounding through the Boils on the far end of the cut echoed down the canyon. Overhead, the moan of the wind clawing its way through the trees was suddenly shattered by the piercing scream of an eagle somewhere off in the rugged wilderness above.

Laura looked over at Atticus. "What do you hope to find here?" she asked.

"I don't know," he said, giving a shrug, "I just have to see it."

"I think this place is spooky," she replied, shivering.

"Imagine what it's like during a storm."

"No thanks."

"There's the harbor," Atticus said, pointing at a large open crevasse in the southward cliff of Big Winter Island.

A pie-shaped slab of rock that once filled the gaping hole in the cliff had broken loose some time in the past and dropped straight down into the water, wedging itself between two large boulders. Its final resting position left it standing with seventy feet of its mass protruding up out of the water. The opening itself was thirty feet wide and hosted a water depth of forty feet. Along the left side of the huge granite slab, a rusty steel-framed dock was anchored to the rock four feet above the waterline. Half-rotted planking bolted to the steel framing led back to a trailhead and up a steep path. The path itself finally disappeared behind some rocks as it meandered its way back and forth up the face of the cliff.

Pushing the tiller to starboard, Atticus swung the bow toward the jagged opening. Easing the throttle into neutral, he guided the *Moonhawk* ever so carefully into the opening. As he approached the dock, he gave a couple of quick reverse thrusts to stop the boat. Laura hopped off, holding onto the bow sprit until Atticus retrieved the docking bumpers and mooring lines. After he finished securing the sloop, he went back on board to shut things down.

"Looks like we're not the first to have visited here," Laura said as Atticus stepped off the boat again.

"What makes you say that?"

"There's a cigarette butt," she said, pointing down between two of the planks.

He bent down, picked it up, and smelled it. "My guess is it's only been here for a couple days," he said softly.

"How . . . you . . . know . . . that . . . kemosabe?" she said in a deep voice.

"I'll kemosabe you," he replied, looking up at her.

Laura grinned.

"You better get some tennis shoes on if you're going with me," he said.

"Do I have to change out of my swimming suit?"

"No, we're not going to be gone that long. Hurry up!"

Laura went below to get her shoes. Atticus looked again at the cigarette butt; the printing on it was in Turkish. He rolled it over a couple of times in his hand and then crumpled it and threw the pieces into the water.

Laura reappeared. "I'm ready," she said, stepping off the boat.

Atticus smiled.

"What's so funny?" she asked.

"Nothing; it's just that I've never gone hiking with a beautiful woman in a bikini before, that's all—kemosabe."

"You want me to change?"

"No, you're fine; let's go." He took her by the hand as they started down the dock. When they got to the narrow trailhead, Laura went ahead, leading the way.

They followed the trail as it climbed up into the rocks and twisted back out along the face of the cliff. About halfway up, they stopped to rest at an outcropping. Standing in the bright sun, they looked down into the shadowy precipice. From this vantage point, they could see the entire channel. To the right was the narrow opening through which they had come. To the left was the entire rock-strewn channel, all the way out to Lake Michigan. They could also see the entire expanse of the Boils; veiled in a frothy whitewash of waves and foam, it arched out into the lake clear to the horizon. Behind it, between the Boils proper and the Peppers, lay the Trench; narrow at the mouth of the pass, its deep blue hue expanded ever wider until it finally disappeared into the deepness of the lake itself.

Laura turned to Atticus, who was looking out over the expanse. "It's beautiful, isn't it?" she said over the muffled roar of the pounding surf below and the moan of the wind clawing through the pines above.

Atticus didn't respond.

"Atticus?"

"Oh, I'm sorry," he replied, his thoughts returning from a long way off. "What did you say?"

"Are you okay?" she asked.

"Yes, I'm fine."

"No, you're not; what is it?"

"I'm fine; let's go."

"Atticus, what's going on? Sometimes it's like you're a thousand miles away."

"It's nothing really."

"Yes, it is, and I'm not leaving here until you tell me what it is."

Atticus leaned back against the rock. "Laura, have you ever heard of the five senses?"

"You mean like seeing, hearing, smelling, tasting, and feeling?"

"Yes. Well, some people say there's another; a sixth sense; a presence we cannot see, we cannot hear, we can't smell or taste, but that we somehow experience its existence from time to time."

"You mean like God?"

"No—not exactly. Anyone who looks up at the night sky would be hard-pressed not to realize there is something out there that is far greater than us; a God by some definition. But this is different—it's like looking out at the Boils and being overwhelmed by its awesome power, and at the same time feeling a sense that there is something else present; something out of place; something that doesn't belong, but you don't know what it is."

"Atticus, that's spooky."

"Yes, it is. And I had that feeling just now; I also had it when we approached the island today; I had it the night I was here with Butch and Spencer. Actually, I've had it several times since I arrived on Washington Island."

"Maybe you're taking the disappearance of Quint and the boys too hard. Maybe you're taking your job as island cop too seriously."

"You could be right," Atticus said as he reached out and put his hands on her waist. He drew her in close. "Yes, it is beautiful out there, and so are you," he said, changing the subject. "You know we've crossed a line on this trip, and there's no going back."

"Yes, I know," she replied as she put her arms around his neck. "I love you, Atticus Gunner, even if you are crazy, and I wouldn't go back if I could."

Atticus kissed her, and as he did, he slid his hand down inside the back of her swimsuit bottom, feeling the firm nakedness of her buttocks. He pulled her in close. "I think we should wait until we get back to the boat," she said softly, brushing her lips against his.

Atticus kissed her on the nose. "I know," he replied.

———•◆•———

The island proper was relatively flat at the top and covered with the most magnificent stand of mature pines Atticus had ever seen. Because of the thick blanket of pine needles covering the entire forest floor, and the absence of undergrowth, other than an occasional fallen tree, it was like walking through a park. The canopy was thick, except for the occasional patch of brightness caused by the wind swaying the treetops and exposing an opening for the sun to filter through.

They continued to make their way in the direction of the interior. At the top of a knoll, they stopped; ahead, nestled in a shallow valley, stood what appeared to be an old barn. Laura looked over at Atticus. "What in the world is that doing in a place like this?" she asked.

"I imagine that's an old outbuilding," Atticus replied. "There was a lighthouse on this island at one time, and its keeper probably raised his own livestock."

"So where is the lighthouse?"

"I think it's on the north end of the island, and if the charts are correct, I don't think there's anything left but part of the tower."

"How far is that from here?"

"I don't know. It can't be very far; this island isn't that big. Come on," Atticus said, as he walked ahead, "let's go down and look around."

Laura caught up to him, and together they walked down the hill. As they approached the building, Laura took Atticus by the hand. "The place isn't as rundown as it looks from up there," she said.

"No, it sure isn't," Atticus replied. "Looks like someone repaired the roof and even replaced the windows."

"Who owns this island anyway?"

"The US government; it's supposed to be part of the national forest system."

"Is it going to be made into a park or something?"

"Not that I know of."

"Then why in the world would someone want to fix it up?"

"That's a good question."

"Maybe the government is going to use it to store some equipment or something."

"That's possible, but have you ever known the government to just fix a few shingles on a project?"

Atticus walked up to the front of the building and slid open the big door. Together, they stepped inside. With the exception of six makeshift double-deck bunks built into the far wall, two orange crates with plywood laid across the top, and a dozen cheap folding chairs, the building was empty.

They walked to the far end. Laura sat down on one of the bunks while Atticus looked around. "Do you suppose someone actually slept here?" she asked.

"Looks that way," Atticus replied as he knelt down by one of the orange crates. He picked up several cigarette butts from the floor and looked at them; they were all American except for one; it was the same as the one found down by the dock.

"This place gives me the creeps," she said, "what if they come back? Let's get out of here."

"Well, I don't think we have to worry about someone coming back right now, but you are right about one thing; this place is a little creepy. Let's head back to the boat."

———◆———

By the time Laura and Atticus arrived back at the top of the cliff, the wind had shifted from the southeast to the northwest and dropped to a light breeze. A northwesterly would make the sail home much easier, but without the wind blowing up the face of the cliff, the midafternoon sun radiated off the rock like an oven. As a result, their return trek down the trail was almost unbearable.

The minute they reached the dock, Laura took off her shoes and ran out to the boat. Throwing her shoes on board, she dove off the dock into the water. She popped back up to the surface and turned toward Atticus. "Come on in, the water is beautiful," she said.

Atticus climbed on board, lowered the boarding ladder, and then, after a quick look around, stripped down naked and dove in.

Looking up through the crystal-clear liquid, he swam up toward Laura's dangling legs as they treaded water above. Surfacing directly behind her, he touched her as he came up. As he threw the water from his face, Laura turned around and put her arms around his neck. "Doesn't this feel great?" she said, smiling at him.

"Fantastic!" he replied, pulling her in close.

"You're naked," she said, somewhat surprised, as she brushed against him.

"So I am."

"Aren't you afraid someone will see us?"

"Now who's going to see us?" he said as though it were the furthest thing from his mind.

"I guess you're right," she replied.

Atticus slid his hands up her back and undid her bikini top. She allowed him to slide it off; he then reached down to take off her bottoms; again she cooperated until her legs were free. Atticus threw them up onto the boat, and then he pulled her in close and kissed her. They slid beneath the surface; finally, in need of air, she let go, separated, and came back to the surface. "Let's go onto the boat," she said as Atticus broke the surface behind her. She swam the short distance over to the boarding ladder. As she climbed up the ladder, the water slithered from her back and down her long, beautiful legs. Totally obsessed by her lovely nakedness, Atticus reached for the boarding ladder and followed her eagerly on board.

———•◆•———

It was dusk by the time they got underway again. Atticus was at the helm, and Laura was sitting tucked under his arm. Heeled mildly to port and running in an even swell off the starboard stern, the *Moonhawk* rolled slowly as she made comfortably for home port. All was silent except for the gentle creak of the rigging and the whisper of wind and water. Neither Atticus nor Laura had made more than minimal conversation since leaving Big Winter Island. Finally, Atticus looked down at her. "How you doing?" he asked.

"Fine," she said, pressing her head against him.

"What's wrong?" he asked.

"Oh, nothing really, it's just that it's about over, and I don't want it to be."

"I know," he said softly. Atticus reached down and raised her chin. He kissed the corner of her mouth gently and then the end of her nose. "What happened to all that destiny stuff?" he asked.

"It's still there," she replied, smiling up at him.

"Good; we're going to need it, because the real world is waiting for us at the very next stop."

"Yes, I know."

"Tomorrow morning we are going to have to get up early and head for Madison. When we get there, I have to pick up the girls and head straight back for the island."

"Yes, I know."

"If you could come up next weekend, you could meet them. The summer carnival will be going; it might be a good time to break the ice."

"Okay, I want to meet the girls."

"Well, that was a lot easier than I thought it would be."

"That's because when it comes to you, I'm very easy. And somehow I feel that wherever you are, I'm supposed to be there too."

Atticus smiled. "You're beginning to sound like my landlady."

"What do you mean by that?" she asked, looking up at him.

"Nothing," he replied. "Nothing at all."

CHAPTER 11

The Carnival and the Cop

Atticus walked over to the stove and opened the oven door to peek in. Taking a quick look, he closed it, wiped his hands on the apron tied around his waist, and went back over to the sink. As he finished breaking up the lettuce for the salad, he glanced at his watch; it was twelve noon. The kids would be home anytime now. Lunch was to be homemade pizza and salad, something he didn't usually do, but this was a special occasion. As usual, he'd procrastinated; he hadn't told the girls that Laura was coming up for the weekend, and it was now Friday, just four hours before her arrival.

While Laura's weekend visit was an unknown to the girls, the sailing trip he and Laura had made was anything but; truth be known, it was in all likelihood the main topic of gossip all over the island, especially amongst the kids. Atticus didn't find out until much later, but the girls had no more than arrived last Sunday when Joni told them all about it. The incident was totally void of any confirming details, but as it goes with gossip, there was no lack of speculation.

Atticus glanced out the window as he heard the girls approaching the house. Soon the screen door slammed. "Hi Dad," Inger said as she walked into the kitchen.

Directly behind Inger were Joni and Stacie. "Can Joni stay for lunch?" Stacie asked as she walked over to the sink to wash her hands.

Atticus hadn't really planned on an additional guest, but—"Sure," he replied, putting the salad on the table. "Grab another dish out of the cupboard."

"I hope it's not too much of a bother, Mr. Gunner," Joni said as she followed Stacie's lead and went to the sink.

"I smell pizza," Inger said, pulling out a chair.

"The hands!" Atticus said, giving her a nod.

Inger got up and went over to the sink.

Soon they were all seated and Atticus brought the pizza out of the oven.

"What's the occasion?" Stacie asked as he placed it on the table.

"No occasion; just felt like making pizza." Atticus proceeded to cut it into slices.

"Dad, we saw the carnival arrive this morning," Inger said as she put a slice on her plate. "Do you think we can go down there this afternoon and watch them set up?"

"You don't even have to take us," Stacie chimed in. "Bill's going and said we could ride with him."

"That's not exactly a place for kids," Atticus replied.

"Oh, we'd stay out of their way," Joni said.

"And what about Inger?" Atticus went on, glancing at Stacie.

"They said I could come along," Inger interjected.

"I would expect you to watch her, Stacie."

"I'm not a baby," Inger replied.

"No, you're not a baby, but you tend not to be afraid when you should be."

"I'll watch her," Stacie said, "but you have to tell her to mind what I say."

"Inger?" her father said, looking at her.

"What?"

"Don't *what* me; can you mind your sister?"

"Yes."

"Well, I'll trust you guys this time, but—" Inger grinned from ear to ear, and Stacie and Joni smiled at one another. "There are a couple conditions, however," Atticus went on. "First of all, understand if there are any problems, of any kind, there will be two girls that won't be going to the carnival tomorrow. Second, I want you both back here by no later than three o'clock; okay?"

"Three o'clock!" Stacie said. "That hardly gives us any time, Dad; why so early?"

"Because I want both of you to meet the four o'clock boat with me."

"What for?" Inger asked.

"Because we have company coming for the weekend."

"Company?" Stacie asked. "Who?"

"She's a friend of mine."

"She?" Inger asked, looking over at Stacie.

"Yes, a young lady by the name of Laura Bock."

No one said a word.

Atticus glanced around the table. "All right," he said after a moment or two, "I think someone knows something I don't; what's going on?"

Again no one said anything. Finally, Inger glanced at Stacie again. "Is that the woman you went sailing with?" she asked as she nonchalantly started to eat.

"Now I get the picture," Atticus said as he leaned back in his chair. "I knew there was a reason I should have talked about this sooner. What's the island saying, Joni?"

"I didn't say anything bad, Mr. Gunner. I just told them what other people are saying."

"And what might that be?"

Joni gave a shrug. "That she's your lover, and that you took her sailing for a week."

"I see," Atticus replied.

"Is she?" Inger asked, looking at her dad again.

"Would you believe me if I told you no?"

Inger gave a shrug. "Are you going to marry her?"

"Do you think I would come to a decision that serious in a week's time?"

"You took the job up here in that period of time," she replied.

"That's not exactly true," Atticus said. "Besides, there's a big difference between taking a job and marrying someone. No, I do not plan to marry her. Yes, I did take her sailing. She works in Madison. I met her when I was down there on school business. She's a very nice person, and I really enjoyed being with her, so I asked if she would like to go sailing, and she accepted."

"Is she your girlfriend?" Inger asked.

"Yes, I guess you could say that; she is a friend, and she most certainly is a girl. That's why I asked her to come up this weekend; I do like her, and I think the two of you will too."

"There were Bock girls that used to live down the road and babysat us when we were little," Stacie replied. "Is she part of that family?"

"Yes, this is the older sister," Atticus replied.

Nobody said a word.

"What happens if we don't like her?" Stacie finally asked.

"Well, what the two of you think is very important to me."

"Yeah, but," Inger said, picking up her piece of pizza after deciding she really was hungry, "what happens if she doesn't like us?"

"She will like you," he replied. "But if she didn't, that would be a very different story."

The topic was dropped, and everyone started to eat.

"There is one more thing," Atticus said after about five minutes. "Laura is company this weekend, and I will expect her to be treated as such. After she leaves, you may express your opinions, but until then, keep them to yourselves. Understood?"

"Where is she going to sleep?" Stacie asked. "I don't want to give her my bed."

"Does one of us have to give up our bed, Dad?" Inger chimed in as though she had missed something.

"No," Atticus replied, "you don't have to give up your bed. There's the old roll-away up in the recreation room; I thought we could open that for me and then she can have my bed."

Again the topic was dropped.

When the girls finished lunch, Atticus excused everyone by telling them he'd do the dishes. He received no argument, and certainly did not expect one; the girls were on their way out the door before Atticus even got the milk put away. "Hey Stacie!" he barked as the screen door slammed shut behind her.

"What?" came the reply.

"Remember what I said; three o'clock, and don't forget to watch your sister!"

Stacie acknowledged she would—and then the three girls scurried across the yard and cut through the woods toward the hotel.

———•◆•———

By the time Atticus finished the dishes and got the ham ready to go in the oven for supper, it was a little after two. By three o'clock, he had gotten the house picked up and ready for Laura. The girls returned home, and by 3:40 they were on their way to the ferry dock.

The week had been a busy one. Atticus worked through Thursday and had a budget meeting with the board Wednesday night. Between taking his turn at making meals and running roughshod over two active daughters, he didn't have a whole lot of time to think about the weekend. It wasn't until now that it really hit home that Laura would be here in a very short while.

The incoming ferry was rounding the last channel marker when they arrived at the ferry dock. Atticus and the girls got out of the Bronco and started down the dock toward the embarkation ramp. Judging from the load of people on the boat, and the crowd at the dock, it was obvious that the big weekend was drawing people by the numbers.

Walking into the crowd with both girls at his heels, Atticus made his way toward the front of the dock. Laura was standing at the railing, near the bow of the approaching ferry. Spotting Atticus and the girls, she started to wave.

"There she is," Atticus said, pointing and waving back.

"The lady with the long hair?" Inger asked.

"Yes; remember her name is Laura," Atticus replied.

Neither Stacie nor Inger waved; they just stood there with a sober look on their faces.

Atticus finally lowered his arm and turned toward the girls. "I take it we're going to do everything we can to spoil this, is that correct?"

They didn't respond.

"I was hoping you would at least give it a chance," he said, turning away again.

Atticus watched patiently as the cars unloaded one by one. The passengers greeted family and friends as they arrived. Finally, it was Laura's turn; coming down the ramp, she drove slowly through the crowd toward Atticus and the girls. When she got close, she pulled off to the side and stopped. Atticus walked over to the car, grinning all the way. The girls followed but stayed well behind. "Hello," he said as he approached, "you're right on time."

"I'm always on time," she replied, smiling back at him.

Atticus winked at her. "Good," he said. "Ah, here, I want you to meet my daughters. This is Stacie, and this is Inger," he said as they approached reluctantly.

"Hello," she replied warmly, "your dad talks about both of you all the time."

The girls managed a slight smile.

"Well, look," Atticus continued, but stammering a bit, "we can get acquainted back at the house."

"Maybe the girls would like to ride with me," Laura interjected. "That way if we get separated, they can show me how to get there."

"Inger can ride with her," Stacie responded, looking at her father. "I'll ride with you."

"Inger?" Atticus asked, in hopes of a more favorable response.

"Okay," she replied soberly.

"Good." He looked back at Laura. "We'll meet back at the house then."

Laura gave him a nod while she smiled at his awkwardness.

———•◆•———

Inger went around the front of Laura's car. She opened the door, climbed in, and slammed it shut behind her. Sitting way forward in the seat with her hands on the dash, she stared out the windshield. Laura sat quietly while they waited for Atticus. Finally, watching Inger out of the corner of her eye, she spoke. "I hope you're not as nervous about all this as your father is," she said.

Inger glanced over at her. "I'm not nervous," she replied.

"Good," Laura said, "because I think I'm going to need some help."

Inger said nothing.

"I bet you guys like it up here, huh?" she went on.

"Yeah, it's okay," Inger replied.

"Is the carnival all set up yet?"

"They're setting up today."

"I can remember when I was a kid; I always wanted to go and watch them set up in the little town where I lived, but I never could."

"We were down there today," Inger replied.

"Really?"

"Yeah," Inger said, glancing over at her again. "It was really cool."

"They really have some strange people traveling with them, don't they?"

"That's for sure," Inger replied, looking over at Laura, a little more relaxed. "They had this great big fat lady with tattoos all over her body. You should have seen her."

"I can remember when I went to one of the carnivals; they had this poor guy with three arms in one of the sideshows."

"Really?" Inger asked, sliding back in the seat a bit.

"Yeah, really; I don't think they can do that kind of thing anymore; it's really cruel."

"Well, they had this little guy with stubby fingers; they called him the Midget. But you should have seen him climb around those rides while they were putting them together; he could climb like a squirrel."

Atticus came driving out of the parking lot; Stacie was sitting next to him in the front seat. He honked as he headed down the road. Laura started her car and followed. As she rounded the bend, she looked over at Inger again. "What all do you guys do up here, anyway?" she asked.

"Oh, we got lots of friends, we go swimming and stuff. My dad's got a sailboat—oh, that's right," Inger said flatly, "you know all about the sailboat."

"Yes," Laura replied, "I went sailing with your dad last week."

"Yeah, I know," Inger said matter-of-factly.

"He told me he really missed not having you along."

Inger made no comment.

"Actually, I think the only reason he asked me was because you and Stacie couldn't go."

"Stacie doesn't like sailing much," Inger replied.

"Really? Oh, I think it's great."

"Yeah, so do I," Inger said, looking out the window.

◆

In a short while, they turned into the drive leading down to the Hersoff place. Finally, coming into the yard, Laura pulled up beside Atticus and stopped. The muffled jingle of the phone ringing in the house could be heard; Stacie rushed out of the Bronco and ran inside to catch it.

As Laura got out of her car, it was the first opportunity Atticus had to really look at her. She was wearing sunglasses, a dark blue medium-length skirt, and a white blouse. Her long, slender legs were firm and shapely, and her breasts filled out her blouse in a most alluring manner. Her long ash-blonde hair piled up on top of her head accentuated her femininity. Although every night since she left, Atticus had replayed in his mind the intimate moments of their week together, he seemed to have forgotten just how beautiful she really was. He wanted desperately to pick up where they had left off.

"Dad?" came Stacie's voice.

"What?" Atticus replied.

"Can we go swimming in front of the house with Joni and Allen tonight?"

"No, not tonight," Atticus replied.

"Why not?"

"Because we have company tonight."

"It's going to be a lovely evening," Laura said as she handed him a suitcase. "Why not let them go swimming? I don't mind—really."

Atticus looked first at Laura and then at Inger, who was watching. "Well, all right," Atticus replied after a moment or two, "but only after we get through eating."

"Oh and Dad," Stacie continued, "can Joni spend the night?"

"Stacie!" Atticus replied, a bit upset.

Laura looked at Atticus as if to tell him to calm down.

Atticus picked up on the message, but he still shook his head in disgust. "Okay," he replied, "yes, Joni can stay the night."

"That means you'll have to take Allen home," Stacie went on.

"Yes, I will take Allen home," he replied.

Stacie disappeared back inside to tell Joni the good news, and Inger couldn't help but grin.

"Ya know," Laura said, looking at Inger, "I think I'll come swimming too, if that's all right."

"Sure," Inger replied, even more surprised.

"Maybe we can even talk your father into joining us; what do you say?" Laura asked, winking at Inger and then smiling at Atticus.

Atticus looked at Inger's beaming face and then back at Laura. "Why is it I'm beginning to feel outnumbered?" he replied, shaking his head again. "All right, swimming for everyone it is."

"Can I take your other suitcase?" Inger asked Laura.

"Sure," Laura replied.

Inger took the overnight bag, Laura slammed the trunk shut, and the three of them started toward the house.

———— •◆•• ————

Stacie, being the older, had always been more cognizant of what was going on at the time of the divorce. Atticus worried that bringing the added pressure of Laura into Stacie's life might complicate things even more. Interestingly, while his fears were not without substance, Laura managed to turn it around almost completely. Whether it was Laura's age, or her ability to cross the generation span between Atticus and the girls, or whether it was her nonjudgmental presence, or possibly her openness, or all these things, it's hard to say; but whatever it was, from the moment she walked into the lives of the Gunners, things were never the same again. Her presence filled a void that neither Atticus nor the girls were capable of; for Atticus, she provided the female companionship that the girls could not; for the girls, in the absence of their mother, Laura provided the adult female friendship and counsel that Atticus could not.

The next morning, Inger and Laura were the first to rise; they allowed Atticus and the two older girls to sleep while they went for a hair-washing dip in the lake. When they returned to the house, Laura sent Inger to wake both her father and the girls. While Atticus showered, and Inger gleefully harassed her sister and Joni until they got out of bed, Laura found her way around the kitchen and prepared breakfast.

As had been agreed the night before, they would get ready and head for the carnival as soon as everyone was fed and had their chores completed. By 11:45, Laura was upstairs, changing from a sweatshirt to a blouse while Atticus waited in the foyer. "I'm sorry," she said, hurrying down the stairs, "I didn't mean to keep you waiting."

"No problem," he replied, smiling up at her. "I'm sure everything will still be there when we arrive." Together, they walked out the door and toward the Bronco. The girls came bounding out of the house and up to them. Atticus opened the front passenger door, and Inger darted in ahead of Laura. "Hold it," Atticus said, motioning toward the back seat, "company rides in front."

"Oh yeah," Inger replied without dispute, crawling over the seat into the back with Joni and her sister.

"There we are, ma'am," Atticus said, motioning to Laura. "The front seat is all yours."

Laura grinned at him as she got in.

Atticus closed the door and walked around to the driver's side. He got in, but before starting the car, he turned toward the girls. Stacie looked at Joni. "Lecture time," she whispered softly. The situation was not intended to be funny, but it was so obvious, Laura had all she could do to keep a straight face.

"Yes, this is lecture time," he said, looking at Stacie, "and I expect the three of you to listen. Stacie, you are not to run off without telling us where you are going; understood?"

Stacie gave a nod.

"You are also to look after your sister."

"Oh Dad, does she have to come with me every time?"

"Yes I do, puke face," Inger replied.

"And you mind Stacie!" Atticus said, looking at Inger.

Inger just rolled her eyes.

"Don't roll your eyes at me," he said. "Do you understand?"

Inger nodded as she took a deep breath.

"Dad, you tell her that every time," Stacie responded, "and every time she does the same thing."

Atticus looked at Joni, who had remained quiet through the entire conversation. "Do you and Allen have these kinds of problems?" he asked.

She nodded.

"And what do you do to solve them?"

"I beat him up," she replied matter-of-factly.

Atticus shook his head. "I'm sorry I asked," he replied. Then he looked back toward the front, glancing over at Laura in the process; she was grinning again. "I hope you took note of my profound skills as a father," he said as he started the Bronco.

Laura just continued to smile.

The topic was forgotten as quickly as it arose; all three girls were laughing and carrying on as though nothing had happened by the time they reached the end of the driveway.

————◆•◆•◆————

Coming down the big hill this side of Jackson Harbor, it was obvious that something big was going on. There were cars and people everywhere; automobiles were parked bumper to bumper on both sides of the road three quarters of the way up the hill; some were parked down in the ditch, while others were parked clear up on the embankments along the road.

Taking advantage of being the island cop, Atticus drove the Bronco down the hill and through the crowd. Tapping on the horn once or twice, he made his way to Spencer's dock and up to the barn, and even though the area was marked "Private Property," there were several cars parked in the yard.

The girls were more than champing at the bit to get started, so after he parked the Bronco, Atticus reluctantly let them go on ahead, but only after making them promise to meet on the *Moonhawk* in an hour and a half. As they rushed off to join the festivities, Atticus gave a big sigh and then looked at Laura. "It looks as though this is about as alone as we're going to get," he said, taking her by the hand and starting to walk toward the road. "This is one event I'm expected to be seen at, so I hope you don't mind walking around for a while."

"Actually, I think I'm almost as excited as the kids; I don't mind at all."

The small village was almost unrecognizable; there were several rides scattered along the road that went past the drive to Spencer's dock, and a big Ferris wheel was erected out past Quint's cottage. On both sides of the road, down past Spencer's and out onto the city dock, were games and concession stands, one after the other, even a sideshow or two. The smell of brats, cotton candy, and popcorn tantalized the senses, while the sounds of carnival music and the smell of diesel exhaust filled the air. The carnival tractor trailers, trucks, and campers were parked everywhere.

Hand in hand, Atticus and Laura strolled down the midway through the wall-to-wall people and past the tents. They bought some cotton candy and played a couple of games. Atticus won a doll by throwing darts at balloons; they even stopped to watch a barker give his pitch for the girlie show. When they got to the tilt-a-whirl, Laura spotted the girls standing in line to get on. After getting their attention, they stood and watched as all three squealed and screamed to the thrill of the ride. Inger was especially funny, with her hair flying; she would wave, grinning from ear to ear, each time they spun around.

After the tilt-a-whirl, the girls came running up to Atticus. Mostly it was to beg for more money, but they also informed Atticus they had seen Butch and his wife, and that Joni had to work at her uncle's food stand starting at three o'clock. After agreeing to meet at the *Moonhawk* when Joni went to work, the girls were off again as quickly as they had appeared.

The afternoon passed quickly. When the girls rejoined Atticus and Laura, they went to Hepper's concession stand, where Joni was working, and had supper. They ran into Butch and his wife, and later they sat with them and watched the blessing of the fleet ceremony and the water show that followed. They also ran into Bill Sorenson, and although Atticus didn't pay a whole lot of attention at the time, he did notice that Bill and Stacie didn't seem quite as close as they once had been. Atticus just passed it off as the whims of young infatuation.

At Laura's encouragement, the four of them went for a ride on the Ferris wheel and then through the fun house, and they finally ended up at the shooting gallery, where Stacie won a prize. When they all went on the Ferris wheel, Inger was running at full throttle, but by the time they got to the shooting gallery, she had bogged down to little more than a rough idle. Atticus sat down at one of the picnic tables with Inger straddled between his legs. She leaned back against her father, all but out of it. Stacie managed to drag Laura off to another ride, and by the time they returned, there wasn't an ounce of spark left in Inger.

"How is she?" Laura asked as she walked up to them and knelt down by Inger.

"I'm afraid she's pretty much cashed in her chips for the day," Atticus replied, "too many rides and too much junk food."

"She'll be all right," Stacie said as she sat down on the picnic table next to them.

"I don't know," Atticus replied, "your sister is looking a little green at the gills."

"So what do you want to do?" Laura asked Atticus.

"I'm not sure; I should take her home, but I also need to stay around here."

"But the fireworks and the dance haven't even started yet," Stacie interjected. "What about them?"

"I know," Atticus replied.

"I'm supposed to meet Joni when she gets off work; she was going to watch the fireworks with us."

"Yes, I know," Atticus replied again. "I think I'll just take Inger to the *Moonhawk*; she can sleep there until we go home. We'll have to stay there and watch her though," he said to Laura. "Do you mind?"

"Not at all," Laura replied.

"Well, can I stay here until Joni gets off then?" Stacie asked.

"Not without an adult," Atticus replied as he stood up, carefully scooping Inger up in his arms.

"But Dad, you promised," Stacie said; the tears starting to flood her eyes. "Can Laura stay with me then?"

"I really don't mind staying with her," Laura said. "She has been planning on this all week, you know."

"Laura, I didn't intend to turn this weekend into a babysitting job."

"It's not a problem. Why don't we take Inger to the boat, and then I'll go with Stacie? We'll come back to the boat for the fireworks; after that, you can do your rounds, or whatever it is you have to do, then we'll all go home."

"Are you sure?"

"She doesn't mind, Dad; I know she doesn't," Stacie interjected. "And Inger will be just fine on the boat."

"I really don't mind," Laura replied again with a smile.

Atticus gave a big sigh. "Well, all right. It's not exactly what I had hoped for, but given the situation, I guess it will work." Carrying Inger, he started for Spencer's dock, as Laura and Stacie followed.

After Laura and Stacie left for the carnival again, Atticus managed to get Inger into bed in the forward cabin. He retrieved a glass of water from the well next to Spencer's barn. After putting the water on the bulkhead table, and a pail on the floor close by, he opened the porthole windows, sat down on the quarter berth across from her, and leaned back against the bulkhead. Inger never stirred, and Atticus soon concluded she was more overtired than sick.

Startled back to consciousness, he opened his eyes to the sound of footsteps running out on the dock toward the boat. Poking his head out of the open hatch, he could see it was Laura and Stacie, and they were in a hurry. He glanced at his watch; it was 9:55, a little early for the fireworks. He stepped off the boat to meet them.

Stacie ran up and threw her arms around his chest. "What's the matter?" he asked, looking first down at Stacie and then up at Laura as she approached.

"We saw a man," Laura replied.

Atticus frowned as though he hadn't heard right. "You what?"

"We saw a man," she reiterated. "Stacie, tell your father what you told me."

"What in the world is going on?" Atticus asked, looking down at Stacie again.

Stacie started to cry.

Atticus looked back up at Laura.

There was a serious expression on her face. Finally, she answered for Stacie. "We were walking through the crowd near the beer tent when we accidentally bumped into this man," she said. "Stacie's face turned absolutely white; the next thing I knew, we were running through the crowd away from him. I didn't know what was going on at the time, but Atticus, there are some things going on that you don't know about."

Atticus took Stacie by the shoulders and slowly forced her to release the grip she had around his chest. "What's going on, Stace?" he asked in a soft but firm voice.

Stacie was sobbing so hard she could hardly talk. Laura gave Atticus a tissue, and he blotted the tears from her cheeks. "Now, from the beginning; this has something to do with South Manitou and Bill's hand, doesn't it?" he said.

Stacie nodded, and then she told her father all about the events at the lighthouse, adding that the man tonight was the same man who had chased her and Bill all over South Manitou; she told how he came to the boat, and how Inger managed to cover for them. She explained about the guns and how Inger identified him as the same man he had thrown off the *Moonhawk*. When he asked why she didn't tell him all this before now, she said they were afraid.

Atticus looked at Laura. "Did this man see her?"

"Yes, he had to," she replied, "but I don't think he recognized her."

"Are you absolutely sure it was the same guy?" he asked Stacie.

"Yes, absolutely!" Stacie replied.

"Was Bill with you tonight when you ran into this guy?"

Stacie shook her head no.

"Is Bill still at the carnival?"

Stacie gave a shrug. "I don't know; why?"

"If he spots Bill, he may not be as lucky as you were."

"What are we going to do?" Stacie asked her father.

"Right now, I want you to stay on the boat; Laura will stay here and keep her eyes open; I'm going out to look for this man."

"But Dad, what if he figures it out and comes looking for us? He knows this boat!"

Atticus grabbed the compressed air horn canister off the radio shelf and handed it to Laura. "When I leave, you latch the hatch cover closed. If anyone approaches the boat, anyone at all other than me, blow that horn out one of the windows; believe me, no one will stick around with that thing going off. Plus, I'll be back here pronto."

"Atticus, I'm afraid," Laura said. "What's going to happen if you find him? This isn't something to fool around with."

"I'll be fine," Atticus replied as he scurried up the companionway ladder. Halfway up, he paused just long enough to grab his ax handle from the hook. "Now remember what I said!" Without further hesitation, he was up and off the boat.

———————◆———————

By the time Atticus reached the beer tent, the fireworks had started and most everyone had vacated the tent. There were still a few people left inside, but by no means a crowd. As he approached, he stopped in the shadows just outside the doorway. Amazingly, there he was, as bold as life, standing at the bar. Equally interesting was the fact that he was talking to Hepper Greshion, and they seemed to be engaged in a serious conversation.

"Mr. Gunner?" a man whispered from behind. Atticus turned to face him. "You probably don't remember me," he said softly. "I'm the man who owns the bar where the kids play pool; remember? I don't want to get involved in any way, but . . ."

"Yes, I do remember you," Atticus interrupted, "but if you don't mind, I'm kind of busy right now."

"This is important, Mr. Gunner; I've known Quint for years. He used to come in my bar almost every night; oftentimes he'd even eat supper there."

"And?"

"You see that man talking to Mr. Greshion?"

"Yes."

"He's wearing Quint's pocket watch."

"How do you know that?"

"I just got off from tending bar, and he pulled it out to check the time as I served him a drink."

"How did you know it was Quint's?"

"Like I said, I've known Quint for years; he's shown me his watch many times; it's engraved. And when that man pulled out his watch, I saw the engraving; that's Quint's watch, I'm sure of it."

"Was Hepper there when he opened the watch?"

"Yes."

"Did Hepper see it?"

"I don't know; he must have."

"Would Hepper know Quint's watch?"

The man shrugged.

"Have you told anyone else this information?"

"No, sir."

"Can you keep it between the two of us?"

"Yes, sir; as a matter of fact, I don't want anyone else, other than you, to even know I saw it."

With that, the man was gone as silently as he'd appeared.

Atticus took a couple of deep breaths and then walked into the tent and up to the bar; Hepper was to the left of the man, Atticus to the right. Atticus laid his club gently on the bar in front of himself.

"What can I get for you, officer?" the bartender asked Atticus.

"Nothing," Atticus replied, and then he looked over at Hepper. "How are you doing tonight, Mr. Greshion?"

Hepper looked over at Atticus and returned a cool but pleasant smile. "Just fine, Mr. Gunner, and yourself?"

"I'm doing fine. Who's your friend?"

"He's a guest at the hotel."

Atticus nodded and paused for another moment. "I saw the three Cline boys leaving the island with your freight truck Friday afternoon—business venture, I suppose?"

"Yes, they went down to Chicago to pick up a freight order for me."

"It must be some pretty important freight to take them away from the island on carnival weekend."

"Well, you know how business is."

"No, I'm afraid I don't know much about your business, but I suspect, as time goes by, I'll learn."

The smile disappeared from Hepper's face. "Are we just exchanging pleasantries, Gunner, or is there something specifically you want?"

"Well, now that you mention it, yes there is; I need to talk to your guest here—alone. So if you don't mind, I'm going to have to ask him to leave with me."

"Emil doesn't speak English very well. Perhaps I can help translate for you."

"I'm impressed; I didn't know you spoke a foreign language. But there you go—see, I've already learned something more about you."

"I'm not fluent, but I know enough that perhaps I can help."

Atticus picked up his ax handle and lowered it to his side. "Oh, I think we'll do just fine without you. You see, I happen to know your friend here speaks perfect English. Now—Emil, is it? What do you say you and I walk out of here quietly?"

The man, who hadn't said a word or moved a muscle until now, turned his head and looked at Atticus. The scar that cut diagonally across his face twitched as he glared. "Tell me, asshole," he mumbled to Atticus, "is this where I'm supposed to be scared shitless?"

"Emil!" Hepper barked. "This isn't the time for a confrontation! And you, Gunner, just who in the hell do you think you are? This man has done nothing. You think you can harass someone just because you're the island cop?"

"Shove off, Greshion," Emil said over his shoulder. "I don't work for you. Besides, I've got a score to settle with this prick."

"Then you're on your own!" Hepper barked as he turned and stormed out of the tent. "You're a fool!" he said without looking back.

By now, the other four or five people in the tent, along with the bartender, had also departed. Atticus and the scar-faced Emil stood alone at the bar.

It's uncertain who made the first move, but there was a long moment of stillness and then all hell broke loose, but it lasted for less than a minute; in a matter of seconds, Emil was sprawled out on the ground. He had two black eyes, a broken nose, a messed-up face, a cracked rib, and a broken wrist. His open switchblade was lying on the ground halfway across the tent.

Unscathed, Atticus laid his club back down on the bar. He knelt down and frisked his fallen opponent for more weapons. Finding nothing, he grabbed Emil by the shirt, slid him up to a sitting position, and leaned him against the bar; with each move, Emil moaned in agony. Atticus reached into Emil's front pocket, pulled out the pocket watch, and ripped it loose from the man's belt loop. Atticus opened it and looked at the inscription. Finally, he knelt down and held the watch so Emil could see it. "Where did you get this watch?" he asked.

"I found it," Emil mumbled.

"You're a liar."

331

Emil just rolled his head back and forth, mumbling, "I need a doctor."

Atticus slapped him across the face with the back of his hand. "I said, where did you get this watch?"

There was no answer.

"Who do you work for?"

Again there was no response.

"Who owns the *Kamora Moo*?"

Again nothing.

Atticus took a deep breath and let it out slowly. He tucked Quint's watch into his pocket and stood up. "Barkeep!" he barked.

"Yes sir!" came the answer from the shadows on the far side of the tent.

"Is the Coast Guard boat still over at the city dock?"

"Yes sir, as far as I know."

"Send someone over to get the captain and two of his crew. Tell him we also need a medic."

"Yes sir."

People were starting to gather out in front of the tent. Some were even pushing inside the entrance to get a better view. Suddenly, Butch came pushing through the crowd and into the tent. "Atticus, what the hell is going on?" he said as he approached. "Hepper Greshion just confronted me and said you were raising drunken hell over here!"

"Yeah, well, you know me, Butch; that's what I do: raise drunken hell." With that, he retrieved the watch from his pocket and handed it to Butch.

Butch looked at it. "This is Quint's," he said, looking back at Atticus. "Where did you find it?"

"Our friend here was wearing it."

Butch looked at the watch again.

Atticus bent down and picked up Emil's switchblade. Throwing it, he stuck it into the ground next to Butch's feet. "He was wearing that too," he said. Then he walked over and picked up his club. "The Coast Guard is on their way over here to retrieve this man. I want them to haul him down to Sturgeon Bay and turn him over to Sheriff Dawson to hold for me. Can you handle that for me, boss? I would do it myself but I've got family to attend to."

"What should I tell them?" Butch asked as Atticus turned to walk out.

"Tell them he assaulted an officer with a deadly weapon, or he's guilty of possession of stolen property; you can even tell them I want him held on suspicion of murder; they may all fit." Atticus walked off into the crowd.

———•◆•———

Tuesday morning at 10:50, Atticus pulled into the parking lot across from the Bertom Building in Green Bay. The FBI office was on the fourth floor. He had an appointment at 11:15 with Sheriff Dawson and Agent Paula Smith.

Walking across the street, he felt surprisingly calm. The girls and Laura were safe in Madison now, Butch was solidly behind him at last, and although he hadn't had a chance to talk with his prisoner, knowing he was safe and sound behind bars in Sheriff Dawson's jail gave Atticus a feeling of confidence; at last the entire parade of bizarre events seemed to be heading in a common direction.

As he walked into the office, an attractive African American woman in her midthirties came out of the back room and over to the reception area. She picked up a folder on the desk and smiled at Atticus. "Good morning," she said. "I take it you're Mr. Gunner."

"Yes ma'am," Atticus replied.

"I'm Agent Paula Smith. If you'll just follow me," she said, motioning to Atticus. "Sheriff Dawson is waiting in the other room."

Atticus followed her across the room. She opened a door and stepped inside; Atticus followed. "Sheriff, Mr. Gunner is here," she said. "Make yourself comfortable," she said to Atticus. "I'll be back in just a few minutes." Agent Smith then exited the room, leaving Atticus standing there.

The sheriff smiled at Atticus but said nothing.

It was a plain room with a big square table, six chairs, and a picture of Abraham Lincoln on the wall. Atticus walked over, pulled out a chair next to the sheriff, and sat down. "Good morning," he said.

"I wish it were," the sheriff replied, "but I'm afraid you're not going to be very happy after I tell you what happened."

Atticus looked at the sheriff for a moment. "What are you talking about?" he asked. "What's going on?"

"They relieved me of your prisoner, Atticus."

"What do you mean?"

"They came in last night with a federal warrant and took him."

"Took him where?"

"I don't know; I tried to find out, but they wouldn't tell me."

"You mean the FBI?"

"That's right."

"Can they do that?"

"I checked with the DA, and apparently they can."

Atticus sat there for a few minutes and then finally got up and walked over to the window, looking out at the street below.

In a short time, Agent Smith and another man walked into the room and closed the door. Atticus walked back over to the table and sat down next to the sheriff again.

"I imagine the sheriff has told you what happened," Agent Smith said as she sat down directly across from him. The other man sat at the end of the table.

Atticus looked first at the man and then back at Agent Smith. "I came here with the hopes of getting this thing going in the right direction, but right now I don't understand what's happening; I hope you can enlighten me."

"Mr. Gunner," the man said, "I'm Special Agent Barker out of the FBI's Milwaukee office. In a nutshell, Mr. Gunner, you inadvertently stumbled into a federal investigation, and we had to step in before you screwed things up."

The only way to adequately describe the look on Atticus's face was one of total bewilderment. "You're kidding me," he replied.

"No, sir, I'm afraid I'm not."

Atticus looked back at the woman. "What kind of an investigation?" he asked her.

"I'm afraid we're not at liberty to discuss that," Agent Barker replied.

Atticus looked back at him. "What did you say your name is?"

"Special Agent Barker."

"Well, Special Agent Barker, I was talking to her; do you mind?"

"Sir, I'm afraid that's the only answer she's going to be able to give you too."

"What Special Agent Barker told you is correct," Agent Smith interjected. "I can tell you this, however: the case to which Agent Barker is referring has international implications."

335

Atticus leaned back in his chair; Agent Barker leaned forward in his. "I think it's important, Mr. Gunner, that we establish an understanding," Agent Barker said. "This is beyond your expertise, and we don't want you going back to the island to play detective; if you do, we will prosecute you. Is that understood?"

Atticus didn't respond, but it was obvious he was getting agitated.

"Wait a minute," Agent Smith interjected. "Accusations and threats are not going to get us anywhere. Mr. Gunner, we understand your anxiety and your frustration, and we will do everything in our power to keep you informed when it's appropriate, but for now, we want you to go back to the island and keep your eyes and ears open, but do not attempt to become involved. Can you do that?"

"Where's my prisoner?"

"He's in a place where he can do no harm," Agent Barker replied. "That's all we can tell you."

Atticus stood up.

Agent Barker also stood up. "We'll stay in touch through the sheriff," he said, closing his folder.

"Yes sir, I'm sure you will," Atticus replied.

———◦———

As they walked out of the Bertom Building, Atticus said nothing. Finally, Sheriff Dawson, who had been quiet through the entire meeting, stopped. "Gunner, where are you parked?" he asked.

"Right next to your squad car," Atticus replied. "Sheriff, what did you make of that meeting?" he continued as they walked along.

The sheriff shrugged. "I don't know; I think you should be relieved. It's out of your hands now, Atticus; besides, you don't have the personnel or the expertise to deal with something like that. You did your job; now it's time to let it go and let them do theirs."

"I suppose you're right," Atticus replied. "Tell me something: Did they ask you anything about me before I got there?"

"They asked me what kind of a person you were."

"What did you tell them?"

"The truth."

"And that is?"

"I told them it was a mixed bag; some islanders say you're the best thing that has happened to the island in some time; others say you're pushy and a hothead. Mr. Gorpon thinks you're nobody's fool, and I would have to agree with that. There is one thing everyone on the island agrees on, though."

"And what is that?"

"It's not a good idea to piss you off."

"Did they ask you anything else?"

"No."

"You know what bothers me?" Atticus continued.

"I didn't think anything bothered you, Gunner."

"There have been five unexplained deaths on that island in the last six months, and as far as I'm concerned, not one of them has been resolved; not even old Bert Federman's death."

"That's all that bothers you?" the sheriff snorted. "You should be in my shoes for a few months. You just got that little island to babysit; I got the whole damn county."

"Oh, there's plenty else up there that bothers me, but I'm sure you're right; my problems pale in comparison to what you're dealing with in the rest of the county."

"Atticus, if you want my advice, just run the school. That's what they're really paying you for anyway."

Atticus chuckled. "If you only knew the truth," he said as he stopped by his car.

"And what is the truth?"

"Some day I'll tell you about it," Atticus said as he opened his car door.

This time, the sheriff chuckled. "You can start by telling me where the Bronco is."

"I'm on my way to Madison, and I don't take the Bronco on personal business."

"Yeah, I've heard about your personal business; you better go a little easy on that too, my friend."

Atticus got in his car without responding and rolled the window down. "I'll talk with you later, Sheriff," he said as he started the car and backed out of the parking space.

CHAPTER 12

Hardball; Some Step Aside

It had been over two months since Atticus had his encounter with the FBI. Most of the summer shops were closed for the season now. Except for a few weekenders, the tourists and summer residents were gone too. For Atticus, up front and foremost in his thinking was the knowledge that the primary reason he was sent to Washington Island did indeed have some substance. The thing that haunted him most was the deaths of Quint and the boys. The fact that things had been so abruptly pulled out from under him by the FBI bothered him immensely. Still, deep down inside he knew that it was not over by any means. This beast would raise its ugly head again, and when it did, he had every intention of being there.

Atticus buttoned up his jacket as he stepped out of the house into the cool evening air. The gray dinginess of dusk had settled in, giving everything a somber hue. Fall was in the air, he could even smell it as he climbed into the Bronco and headed for school.

As he drove, his mind drifted back to the phone conversation he'd had with Paula Smith just one week after his visit with them. She'd told him that two days after the carnival incident, Emil was released in Chicago under diplomatic immunity status, and three days later, he was killed in an automobile accident. She just wanted to make sure Atticus was updated, and as a result of the circumstances, there would be little reason for them to pursue the issue any further.

The hole left by the death of Quint and the boys was beginning to glaze over on the island. Stacie and Bill, who were both strongly affected by the deaths, as well as by the South Manitoo affair, had recovered but never regained the close friendship they'd once enjoyed.

Throughout the summer, Laura had become a regular guest on the island, or at least until the ferry ran less frequently. In the brief passing of the summer, she had managed to capture not only his heart, but those of the girls as well. Joni Greshion and her brother had also become regular guests at the Gunner household. Although much of what they did rotated around Laura, Joni and Stacie had become the best of friends. Inger? Well, Inger was still Inger: active, spunky, and always independent. In many ways, she was closer to Laura than to Stacie; Atticus surmised it was the mutual attraction of their boundless energy.

Other than the loneliness that was beginning to creep into his life, the only immediate problems Atticus encountered these days were related to school. The first of these wasn't anything insurmountable, at least not yet, but it did cause some friction between Butch and him. It happened one weekend while Atticus was off the island; Butch hired the industrial arts teacher. The kicker was he hired Brian Karmel, the individual Atticus refused to interview because of his attitude during Quint's funeral. A problem of far greater consequence, however, was the school budget. Here they were, four weeks into the school year, and the board had not yet adopted a budget to present to the electorate for approval. This was in spite of the fact that Atticus had managed to get a handle on the finances and developed strategies to correct the many problems facing the district. It wasn't that Atticus didn't have support; both Butch and Greta backed his ideas, even though they included the necessity of a substantial tax increase, but Nordien, with her twisted and simplistic view of reality, along with constant prodding from Vivian, made the going almost impossible. Not only did Nordien constantly attempt to discredit Atticus and his ideas through misrepresenting figures, but she made numerous innuendos about how it seemed as though he was more interested in satisfying the state than serving the island. If that wasn't enough, she also managed to throw in a few snide, but well-placed, comments about Atticus and his sinful relationship with a woman almost half his age. Finally, but very much part of the same problem, was Vivian's backhanded, backstabbing performance; as far as Atticus was concerned, her role in all of this was of major concern and needed to be dealt with soon.

Tonight would officially turn the first stone of his future on the island, probably his future as a school administrator. Tonight was the final board meeting prior to the annual school district meeting; that's the meeting where the budget would be presented to the district electorate and voted on. Tonight the school board would have to set their proposed budget in order to be ready for the big event. If he prevailed, it would probably be a strong indicator of his success at the annual meeting and beyond; if he failed, his professional future on the island, or anyplace else for that matter, would be very much in question. And that didn't even take into consideration the possibility of his contract with the Morgan Group collapsing. A strong performance by Atticus was more critical now than it had ever been; to make it any further down the road, this was a hurdle he could not fail to clear.

As he pulled into the school parking lot, Butch was just getting out of his car. Atticus drove up next to him and parked. As he shut off the engine, he could see the lights were on in the meeting room. Vivian and Nordien were sitting at the table, talking. Greta hadn't arrived yet.

Butch walked up to Atticus as he got out of the Bronco. "Christ, I was hoping we'd be the first ones here," Butch said quietly, "but it looks like the two assholes beat us to it."

As Atticus closed the truck door, he glanced again at the school. "Yes, it looks like they're hard at it, doesn't it?" he replied.

"I don't know which is worse," Butch went on, "that God damned pushy Vivian, or poor stupid Nordien. At any rate, you can bet they're up to no good."

"Yes, I suspect they're planning my demise."

"I don't understand you, Gunner; aren't you worried?"

"A little."

"A little?"

"Well, Butch," Atticus continued, "I have a well-founded, comprehensive understanding of the financial status of this school. I'm also well educated on the overall operation of a public school district. What I have for the board, and the people of this community, is the correct information; those two don't."

"I know you're right; it's just that someone needs to bring them down."

"I have every intention of doing just that," Atticus replied. "First of all, I intend to take on the budget issues; if we're successful there, and we get a budget proposal, I can assure you they won't go unscathed. I'm afraid I don't have any choice but to play hardball tonight."

"What have you got planned?" Butch asked.

"Well, you know me, I'm full of surprises," Atticus replied with a quick smile. "What I need first is leadership from you."

"What exactly do you mean?"

"I want you to run that meeting like our success depended on it, because it does."

"I can handle that," Butch replied. "Besides, they've only got one vote, and if need be, I'll remind Vivian she's not a member of the board. I'm not worried about that; we'll get through this meeting. What I'm worried about is the next meeting and beyond."

"Let's take it one meeting at a time, Butch," Atticus said as he started to walk toward the school.

Butch shook his head in disgust. "Why don't we wait out here for Greta to arrive?" he said. "I need to talk to you privately anyway."

Atticus stopped and turned toward Butch.

Butch looked at him for a moment and walked back over to the front of his car. "Atticus," he said, leaning against the front fender, "I know you know this is going to be a tough budget to sell, but I'm not sure you realize just how tough. I have to say something, and don't get me wrong; your personal business is none of my affair, but it does have me worried. Do you realize what's really going to happen here, Atticus? They're going to come at you from every direction, and they're going to be throwing any kind of crap they can find. And in my experience, if you throw enough shit, some of it is likely to stick. I'm talking about the Bock girl; are you ready for that?"

"Butch, that's what I meant about leadership. This is a budget meeting. Keep it there; don't let them turn it into a witch hunt. You do that; I'll take care of the rest."

"I don't like Vivian Boomer, you know that, and I certainly don't agree with Nordien's kind of logic, but there are a whole lot of people out there who are going to jump on their bandwagon with whatever they throw at you. Some of those people are very influential."

"Yes, I know," Atticus replied.

"Well, I sure hope you're prepared to defend yourself."

"Butch, I don't think my moral character is really as big of an issue as you might think. I think the real issue is that I'm an outsider, and some of these people see me as a threat to their pocketbook; maybe even more. If you can shut down the mud-slinging, I can handle the rest."

"I don't know," Butch replied. "There are a few people who think like Nordien, and she thinks you're an evil son of a bitch." Butch smiled and added, "And she's probably right."

Atticus grinned back at him. "Yes, maybe she is right. And that brings me to another topic; what do you know about Nordien?"

"What do you mean?"

"I mean her past; she strikes me as a person who's got something to hide. What's her story?"

"Well, she's no innocent angel, if that's what you mean; at least she wasn't when she was back in high school."

"What happened in high school?"

"She got involved with a merchant marine, spread her legs for him once too many times, and ended up pregnant. He up and took off; soon after that her folks sent her away. While gone, she secretly had her baby and gave it up for adoption."

"You know that for sure?"

"Oh yeah; it's a fact. It's one of those things everyone on the island knows, but no one ever talks about."

"Is she married now?"

"No, she's still at home living with her mother; her dad passed away some time ago."

"That's a pretty sad story."

"Yeah—well, she's got religion now."

"Yes, she does," Atticus replied. "Butch, I need two more things from you. First, I'm going to have a little talk with Nordien tonight after the meeting, and I'd like you to stick around; you don't have to do or say anything, I just want you there as a witness. Second, I'd like for you to meet me in my office at 7:15 tomorrow morning; same thing, only this time it will be with Vivian. Can you do those two things for me?"

"By God, you do plan to play hardball, don't you?"

"I'm afraid that's the name of the game right now."

Just then Greta's old Chevy came rolling into the lot and parked on the other side of Butch's car. Both Butch and Atticus greeted her as she got out. Together, all three of them started for school.

"Seems Nordien and Vivian are working on their own tonight," Butch said to Greta as he walked along beside her.

"So I see," she replied. "Nordien usually calls me for a ride. I was wondering why she didn't tonight. Now I guess I know."

When they got to the school entrance, Atticus opened the door to let them pass and then followed them into the meeting room. Greta and the two women exchanged greetings; Butch said nothing. As Atticus walked over to his place at the table, Vivian laid his meeting folder in front of his chair. Atticus greeted her; she responded with a quick nod. Nordien conversed briefly with Greta, glanced once at Butch, and completely ignored Atticus. Soon everyone was seated, Butch to the right of Atticus, Greta to Atticus's left, and Nordien facing him at the other end of the table. Vivian was seated in a chair behind and to the left of Nordien; removed, but still present.

Butch wasted no time calling the meeting to order. He asked Atticus if there were any further changes to the proposed budget; Atticus responded that there were none. Butch then informed the others that if there were no further changes to the proposed budget, he would be happy to entertain a motion to accept the budget as presented, especially considering that it had all been discussed before.

Nordien was the first to speak. "Mr. Chairman," she said, "I would like for the board to consider an alternative budget that I have prepared with the expert help of Mrs. Boomer. You have a copy in your folder."

The board members opened their folders, retrieved their copy of the proposal, and started looking through it. Atticus opened his folder; there was a copy of the agenda and his budget proposal, but nothing else. He closed his folder but said nothing.

"Nordien," Greta said, leaning forward in her chair after a few minutes, "this proposal is $70,000 less than last year's actual expenses, and the suggested levy is down almost three mills; the entire proposal is contrary to everything we've discussed. Are you sure you thought this through carefully?" Her voice was calm but very serious.

"Oh yes, it's well thought out—and I support the idea that we cannot continue to spend more than we budget, or tax less than we spend, but that doesn't mean the only solution is to follow Mr. Gunner's outrageous ideas. If you give me a few minutes to explain, I'll prove it to you."

"Jesus Christ, Nordien," Butch blurted out in a very disgusted manner. "Just how many years have you been on the school board anyway?"

"Nine years," she replied.

"Well then, if you're so damn good at school finance, how is it you didn't come up with this solution a long time ago?"

"Because we're too busy listening to the wrong people—and swearing about everything doesn't help either!"

"Yeah, right!" Butch replied. "Jesus is going to show us the way, right?"

"He would if you'd let him," she said, looking at Butch.

"Butch, she has a right to be heard," Greta interjected. "What do you have, Nordien?"

"Thank you," she replied. "Well, first of all, if the board would meet regularly one night a week, and stop in school regularly to help take care of things, I don't think we would need an administrator. Therefore, I propose first that we eliminate the position of school administrator. That way, Mr. Gunner would be able to spend more time as island constable; if that's not acceptable to him, he could resign completely and leave the island. That action will save a substantial number of dollars that we would have otherwise paid him in salary."

"Second," she went on, "we all know one must sacrifice to live on the island; that's all part of what it takes to live here. I don't think we should go backwards with any of the teachers who have been here for some time, but I propose we reduce all the new teacher salaries by 20 percent; that would save another substantial amount; besides, I think it takes a couple of years before one learns what is expected of a teacher and begins to earn his or her salary.

"Third," she continued, full of exuberance, "I know we need new textbooks, but we could buy one book in each discipline; the teachers in turn can copy what they need from it and distribute it to the children. Science textbooks, on the other hand, should be consistent, and I have found a source for brand-new books, and I might add, at one-tenth of the cost Mr. Gunner has proposed.

"Finally," she said, "I know we can't continue to operate in a deficit. If we adopt my proposed budget, not only will we reduce our need to borrow, but because as a school we can borrow money at 3 percent, I propose we borrow the full amount allowed by law, and reinvest it for a higher return; right now the going interest rate is 9 percent; that would gross a substantial amount for us. Not only will we wipe out our deficit in seven years by doing that, but we'll be able to lower taxes in the process, and that would make everyone happy."

She leaned back in her chair and glanced back at Vivian with a grin. "There," she said, "very simple, and we didn't have to go to college to figure it out!"

No one said a word. Finally, Butch looked at Atticus. "Do you care to respond?" he asked as though he were lost for words.

"Well," Atticus replied, "I wasn't provided a copy of her proposal, so . . ."

Nordien interrupted him. "I didn't think it involved you," she said, "so why waste the paper?"

"As I was saying before I was interrupted," Atticus went on, "I wasn't provided with a copy of Nordien's proposal, so I can't respond to any of its detail, but I can certainly respond to her main points." He paused for a moment and then went on. "However, what I have to say will be very blunt."

"It certainly can't be any more blunt than what we just heard," Butch replied. "Go ahead."

"Very well," Atticus said. "I'll take it point by point, starting with the first. Can you eliminate my job? The answer is yes. There is no requirement for you to hire an administrator. As a matter of fact, there was a time when most school districts were run by the board of education, but that was some time ago. There are some questions you need to ask yourself before taking that route, however; do you understand school finance well enough to run the district; how is your knowledge in school law or employee relations? Do you know anything about insurance requirements for the district? How about school board liability? Do you know anything about the state statutes that govern the operation of a public school district? How about federal law, such things as nondiscrimination? Do you understand the nature of contractual obligations? If you did, then you would also know that by eliminating my job, you wouldn't save a dime this year. Why? Because you have a contract with me. That means if I don't quit, or you fire me without just cause, you'll have to pay me whether you keep me on the job or not."

"You mean to tell me," Nordien interjected, "you'd force the island to pay you even if they didn't want you here?"

"Absolutely, unless my performance as an administrator is unacceptable and you can substantiate justifiable reasons to let me go."

"No one is accusing you of being incompetent, Mr. Gunner," Nordien responded, "but we do think your performance is unacceptable."

"In what way?"

"It's your moral character we're most concerned about."

"Perhaps you could explain to us what moral character I have demonstrated that you find unacceptable?"

Butch hammered loudly on the table with his gavel. "That's enough," he said, "we're getting nowhere, and that's not part of the agenda. We're here to discuss the budget, not the administrator's moral character."

Atticus eased back into his chair. "Thank you," he replied softly. "I'm sorry for the diversion. I do have more comments about her proposal. Point number two; I realize it takes special considerations to live on the island. There are many conveniences elsewhere that one must sacrifice to live here; that's a given. But your teacher salaries are already low; to impose another 20 percent cut would make it impossible to get and retain any qualified teachers. That doesn't even take into consideration the contractual obligations we already incurred when we signed contracts with these people."

"We wouldn't if they willingly accepted it," Nordien said, avoiding Atticus by looking at Butch.

Atticus leaned forward again. "And you honestly think our new teachers are going to willingly take a 20 percent cut in pay just so they can come to Washington Island?" He shook his head. "Especially after signing a contract that states otherwise?"

"Yes," she replied in the same haughty manner. "I think they would, Mr. Gunner, especially after we explain our problem to them."

"And what might that be?" Atticus asked.

"Taxes are too high."

"Nordien," he said, gesturing slightly to emphasize his point, "no one likes taxes, but taxing yourselves to provide services in your own community, services that would not be provided without local taxes, such as educating your children, those kinds of taxes are essential. And to that point, are you aware that the rate of property tax for education on this island is the lowest in the entire state, by a substantial amount? Or are you aware that better than sixty cents of each tax dollar raised comes from people who really don't care if you do or do not educate your children, because they don't even have children in the district?"

Nordien made no response.

Atticus went on. "Point number three; textbooks. We don't provide textbooks simply for the convenience of teachers; we provide them for the benefit of the children. This school district is so small we don't have the time, or the people, to develop well-planned sequential curriculum guides. That's why we need well-done, sequentially developed, current textbooks. Not only will that give scope and sequence to our instruction, but it gives us a means by which to be consistent and provide predictability, something by which the school board and parents can judge what is being taught. If we were to allow teachers to simply teach what they please, there would be no consistency. Further, you can't simply buy one textbook and copy it for distribution; that would violate the copyright laws and therefore be illegal. Finally, I have studied and reviewed textbooks until I'm blue in the face. If there is a source for general science books at one-tenth the cost I proposed, I'd like to know what it is."

"I have a copy right here," Nordien replied, reaching down into her satchel. She flopped it down in front of her on the table.

"May I see it?" Atticus asked.

"Certainly," she replied, sliding it over to him.

Atticus picked up the book and opened it to the table of contents. After a few moments, he looked up at Nordien. "Is this the book you're proposing as the school's general science text?" he asked.

"That's right," she replied.

"And of course this is the one text you want every student to get a copy of."

"Correct," she replied again.

"I wonder how the parents would respond to that," he said as he slid it over to Butch and Greta to look at. "Especially considering it's a religion book, not a general science book."

"That is a science book!" she replied sharply.

"No, Nordien," Atticus said, "that's a book on creationism."

"That is the true science, not that evolutionary garbage those atheists down in Madison would like us to believe."

"That's your opinion, and you have every right to it," Atticus replied, "but your religious preference has no place in a public school curriculum, not even on Washington Island."

"That's because you're one of them!"

Atticus ignored the comment. "I have one last point to make," he said, looking back at Butch. "I don't know if any of you have ever heard of the term 'arbitrage,' but it pertains to the process of collecting public taxes for the express purpose of reinvesting them for profit; it too is very much against the law. This entire proposal exemplifies the need for proper counsel and direction. If you were to accept Nordien and Vivian's budget plan, rather than resolve your problems, you'd compound them a hundredfold."

"I don't agree!" Nordien blurted out. "Just because Mr. Gunner is a smooth talker doesn't mean this board should go stupid and follow what he wants. He is evil and does not represent the values of this community! I propose we . . ."

Again Butch hammered the gavel. "Nordien!" he barked loudly. "I've heard enough of your crazy ideas for one night! I'm going to call for the question. I move we accept the budget as presented by Atticus, and that we prepare to present it at the annual meeting for approval by the people of this district."

Greta looked over at Nordien. "I'm afraid I'm going to have to second that," she said, as though she didn't want to hurt Nordien's feelings.

Butch tapped the table with the gavel. "All in favor signify by saying aye."

Greta and Butch both responded in the affirmative.

"Those opposed?"

Nordien said nothing.

"The meeting is adjourned," Butch said, tapping the gavel on the table one last time. Immediately everyone rose except Nordien and Vivian; Nordien was busy gathering her things and putting them back in her satchel. Greta left immediately. Butch lingered by the door. Vivian gathered her things but remained seated, waiting for Nordien.

Atticus got up from his chair and walked over to Nordien. "Before you leave, I'd like to speak to you privately, if you don't mind," he said softly.

She looked up at Atticus. "I have nothing to say to you."

"No ma'am, I'm sure you don't, but I have something to say to you, and I think you'll want to hear what I have to say; it's very important for you."

Nordien stood up and Vivian followed. Nordien turned to walk away but paused for a moment, turning back toward Atticus. "Important?" she said. "What could you possibly say that I would consider important?"

"It's personal, ma'am."

"I'll stay here with you, if you like," Vivian whispered to her.

"No Vivian, you will not stay," Atticus replied. "This is between Nordien and me; I want you to leave."

"Then what is Butch doing here?" Nordien snapped.

"He's here because as president of the board, I want him to hear what I have to say."

Vivian glared at Atticus and then strutted off toward the door. Butch opened it for her and followed her to the outside door to make sure she really did leave.

When Butch returned, he walked over to the table and sat back down in his chair. Atticus sat down on the tabletop at the opposite end of the table and motioned for Nordien to have a seat.

"I'll stand if you don't mind," she replied.

"Suit yourself," Atticus replied. "Nordien, you don't like me; we both know that," he went on.

"That's an understatement," she replied.

"Yes, and I'm well aware that you're going to do everything in your power to disrupt the operation of this school as long as I'm here."

"That's also correct; getting rid of you has become my main goal."

"Well, I'm not going to leave, so it seems we've got a problem. I say *we* because I think you need to know I'm also going to do everything I can to get rid of you. I'm not sure you realize it, but as an elected public official, everything about you is open for scrutiny. I can come after you with anything I find: personal issues in your present, or your past—especially your past. Now, if that's okay with you, and I think you know exactly what I'm referring to, then let's bring it on. However, if it's not okay, and you do not want me to expose your past, I want your written resignation from the board, submitted to Butch by no later than ten o'clock tomorrow morning. I say ten o'clock because shortly after that, I'm going to start the ball rolling, and there will be no turning back after that. Do I make myself clear?"

"I beg your pardon?" she replied, obviously stunned by his comment.

"We're dealing with the education of children here," Atticus went on, "not some personal quest you have to cover up your past. If you want to do that, do it on your own, not in a public school."

"Are you threatening me?"

Atticus didn't respond.

"You wouldn't dare!"

"Try me."

She stood there for a moment, glaring at him. Shaking, she finally spoke. "You bastard," she said. There were tears in her eyes. "You dirty bastard!" Without saying another word, she turned and walked briskly out.

After she left, Atticus took in a deep breath and let it out slowly. He looked over at Butch. Butch looked away and said nothing. "Hardball isn't much fun, is it?" Atticus said as Butch got up from his chair. Butch shook his head and started for the door. "Don't forget; my office tomorrow morning at 7:15."

Butch nodded and walked out.

———◆———

Butch looked at his watch as he walked into school; it was 7:15 on the button. Atticus was sitting behind his desk as Butch walked into the office. Vivian wasn't there yet, but there was a shoebox on the top of her desk. Atticus was writing something on a piece of paper; he signed it, folded it in half, and placed it on the desk in front of him. "Good morning," Butch said. "This is a little early for you, isn't it?"

"Normally yes, but not today," Atticus replied. "There's fresh coffee in the pot if you need some."

Just then, Vivian came walking in and closed the door. Surprised to see Butch and Atticus there, she raised her eyebrows as she hung up her coat.

"Vivian, do you have your school keys with you?" Atticus asked without greeting her.

"Yes, of course I do. What did you do—forget yours at home again?" she replied.

"May I have them?" he asked.

She dug into her coat pocket and pulled out her ring of keys and handed them to Atticus.

Atticus started going through the keys. "Let's see—this, this, and this; these are all the school keys, aren't they?"

"Yes," she replied with a confused look on her face.

Atticus separated them from the ring and then handed the ring back to her minus the keys he had taken off.

"What are you doing?" she asked.

Atticus picked up the slip of paper in front of him and handed it to her. "That's your official notice; you're fired. I took the liberty of removing all your personal belongings from your desk and put them in that shoebox. You may take the box and leave; your services are no longer needed."

Vivian was obviously stunned. She opened the paper, looking first at Atticus and then over at Butch. "You're firing me?"

"That's correct," Atticus replied.

"You can't do that."

"I'm afraid I just did," Atticus said.

"He can't do that without board approval," she said, looking at Butch.

Butch said nothing.

"I'm sure you and Nordien have a copy of my contract hidden away someplace; if you read it carefully, you'll see I have express permission to fire you, and that's exactly what I'm doing."

"But why? Who will pay the bills and stuff?"

"I'm sure you know exactly why I'm firing you. As to your duties, you needn't worry about them; they're no longer your responsibility. In that box, you'll also find a check to cover payment for your unpaid services, and a statement as to the status of your various fringe benefits. Now, I would like for you to leave."

Vivian looked at Butch again. "Are you just going to sit there and let him get away with this?" she asked.

"I'm afraid he's on solid ground, Vivian," Butch replied. "Besides, this is one action I'm in total agreement with."

"And if I refuse to leave?"

"I'll call the constable and have you removed," Atticus replied. "He's a very close friend of mine you know."

"You make me sick!" she replied. "Nordien is right; you are evil!" She grabbed her coat and stormed out the door.

Atticus looked over at Butch. "Out number three," he said.

"How do you know that was the third out?"

"Just a wild guess."

"Well, you're right; Nordien's written resignation was stuck in my screen door when I got home last night. So you got rid of the two thorns in your side, and you got a proposed budget; the big game is yet to be played, however; you do know that?"

Atticus got up and poured himself a cup of coffee. "Yes, I know that."

Butch got up and buttoned his coat. "Any more surprises this morning?"

"No, I'm afraid that's it," Atticus replied. "We can only provide one surprise a day here at Washington Island School; that's all we're allotted."

"By the way," Butch went on, "I finally did something I've wanted to do for some time."

"What's that?" Atticus replied as he sat back down at his desk.

"I bought a boat."

"A boat?"

"Yep."

"What did you get?"

"A twenty-eight-foot Whaler with twin 250-horse Mercs."

"You ought to be able to tear up the lake with that."

"That I should."

"When will you have it?"

"In about three weeks—should have it well before duck hunting begins."

"Well, congratulations."

"Thanks. When I get it, I'd like for you to come with me on her first trial run."

"You got a date."

"By the way, who is going to do Vivian's job now?"

"I am, until I find a replacement."

Hearing a noise, Butch reached over and opened the office door. Standing with his ear almost up to the door was Brian Karmel, the new industrial arts teacher. Startled, Brian, a small man with beady little eyes and a scruffy short beard, stepped back. "Sorry," he said. "I just came in early to talk to Mr. Gunner before he was off on another one of his numerous adventures."

"That's okay," Atticus replied, "Butch was just leaving. Did you catch everything, or is there something you missed that we can fill you in on?"

"Excuse me?" Brian stammered.

Butch looked over at Atticus. "Never mind," Atticus replied. "Come on in. I'll see you later, Boss Man," he said to Butch.

"Yeah, later," Butch said as he stepped aside for Brian to pass. Butch looked back at Atticus as he pulled the door shut. Atticus smiled at Butch and gave him a wink. The door closed and Butch walked out, shaking his head.

CHAPTER 13

Two Kinds of Scary

Because Lake Michigan cools slower than the mainland, winter arrives later on the island. Nonetheless, the bright shades of fall were well under way now, and before very long, the gales of November would be howling their way across the big lake. The *Moonhawk* had been moved from Spencer's dock to Pickle's dock, where she now lay waiting to be taken from the water for the winter.

Saturday was an unusual day to schedule an annual meeting, but such was the case. Tonight, ready or not, Atticus would face the island people, and anxiety seemed a constant companion. On the positive side, after three long weeks, Laura was to arrive on the noon boat. It would only be for a short visit, she would leave tomorrow, but it seemed an eternity since they'd had the opportunity to be alone together, and Atticus was elated.

Yesterday, Butch took delivery of his new boat. Last night, he called and wanted Atticus to go with him on the maiden run this morning. It wasn't that Atticus didn't want to go, but with Laura coming and the meeting tonight, going for a boat ride was the furthest thing from his mind. But he had promised, and as a result, he was now in the process of getting ready for that adventure.

It would be cold and rough out on the lake today. Atticus slipped into his down jacket, grabbed his wool cap and winter gloves, and headed out the door. The tops of the big maples standing in the yard, tinged by Thursday's frost, displayed a deep chestnut red in the bright morning sun. A gust of wind swirled past his feet, tumbling the few fallen leaves helter-skelter as he hurried across the yard toward the Bronco.

Just as he was about to open the truck door, Bill, Joni, and another girl came rumbling down the drive in Bill's old pickup. Yanking on the wheel, Bill swung next to where Atticus was standing and slid to a stop. "What are you outlaws up to this early in the morning?" Atticus asked as Bill rolled down his window.

"We came to talk to you," Bill replied with a big grin on his face.

"I'm not in the market to buy anything," Atticus replied.

"No, we're serious," Joni interjected from the far side of the seat.

"You look serious," Atticus replied, still in a joking manner.

"We heard you're going to have some trouble tonight," Joni said.

Atticus leaned over so he could see her better. "What kind of trouble?"

"At the meeting."

"Where did you hear that?"

Bill gave a shrug. "People are talking," he said.

"What people?"

Again Bill gave a shrug.

"We thought we could get a bunch of kids and show up at the meeting to back you up," Joni said.

"That's a nice gesture," Atticus replied, "but I don't think that would be such a good idea. That kind of thing can backfire very easily."

Bill got a puzzled look on his face. "You mean you don't want our support?"

"Bill, it isn't that I don't appreciate your support, but I think it would be far more effective if you expressed that support at home to your parents and encouraged them to come to the meeting and support the school."

"You sure you don't want us there to cheer you on?" Joni went on.

Atticus smiled and shook his head. "Not tonight."

"Okay," Bill replied, "but don't say we didn't warn you." He ground the old truck into reverse.

"If you change your mind, give me a call," Joni blurted out as Bill roared backwards to turn around. "By the way," she went on, leaning over Bill and poking her head out his window, "when are Laura and the girls coming up?"

"They'll all be here for Halloween weekend," Atticus replied; he didn't want to advertise the fact that Laura was coming this weekend. "And Bill, slow that damn truck down; I don't want to be peeling any of you off a tree someplace!"

Bill roared the engine again and popped the clutch, throwing Joni back into her seat. Looking out the rear window of the cab, she grinned and then gave Atticus a thumbs-up as they roared off. Atticus watched, shaking his head as they thundered off up the drive in a cloud of dust. Atticus reminded himself it was time to have a little heart-to-heart with Bill about his driving.

———•◆•———

Approaching the first driveway this side of the ferry dock, Atticus wheeled a hard left. He drove down the gravel drive between two of the gift shops and out onto the flats by the old potato docks. Swerving around a couple of old fish boats up on wooden skegs, he came to a stop.

Butch, who was at the far end of the dock down in his new boat, heard Atticus drive in and stood up. He watched as Atticus got out of the Bronco and started to walk toward him. "Jesus Christ, man," he barked as Atticus approached, "I was beginning to think you weren't coming."

"Seeing how cold it is, that thought did cross my mind," Atticus replied. Butch gave a grunt and went back to work installing the compass at the helm.

Pausing by the edge of the dock, Atticus looked down at the new boat. If you loved power boats, she was a beautiful thing; twenty-eight feet long, snow white from stem to stern, with a high bow and generous freeboard. Beneath the foredeck, she housed a cuddy cabin, and in front of her standing helm was a windshield. At the back, behind the open cockpit, were twin 250-horsepower, six-cylinder Mercury engines. They gleamed bright in their shiny black shrouds. "I'm not much on power boats," Atticus said, "but even I have to admit—that's one nice piece of machinery!"

Butch grinned. "That's exactly what I said when I first saw her; she is sweet, isn't she?"

"May I have permission to come on board, sir?" Atticus asked as if making a formal military request.

"Don't be an ass," Butch replied with a grunt, "and untie that rope on your way."

Atticus undid the rope and stepped down into the cockpit. Butch hit the switches and the big twins came to life. "Where are your life jackets?" Atticus asked as Butch pulled the dual levers into reverse and began churning slowly away from the dock.

"Down in the cabin," Butch replied with a nod.

Atticus slid open the cabin door and reached in, pulling out two vests. Putting one on, he held the other out for Butch; Butch waved it off. "I don't need that," he said. "If we went down out there this morning, we'd freeze to death before we could swim a hundred yards."

"Now that's a comforting thought," Atticus replied.

"Besides, this boat is unsinkable."

"That's what they said about the *Titanic*."

Butch chuckled.

Once clear of the dock, Butch moved the levers forward slowly until the engines re-engaged into forward gear. Rolling the wheel hard to the left, he brought the bow around until they were headed down the channel toward the open lake. With the engines throbbing barely above idle, and a gurgling sound belching from the boiling water behind, the sleek new boat slid smoothly down past the ferry dock.

"She's going to be cold and rough out there," Atticus said as he looked out past the horn buoy toward the open lake. The five-foot swells rolling past the outer banks were emerald green with frothy white tops cascading down their flanks. "I'd go damn easy out there if I were you."

Butch chuckled again. "That would defeat the whole purpose for this run," he said with a big grin. "I have to find out just how well she's going to handle the big lake."

Atticus looked over at Butch with a puzzled look.

Butch grinned again. "Relax," he said, "I'll get you back safe and sound in time for the big meeting tonight." The words had no more than fallen from his lips when he leaned forward on the throttle. Immediately, the big twins dug in. The bow rose toward the sky as the big Whaler crawled up out of the hole and lunged forward. Within seconds, they were screaming down the channel at full tilt.

Maintaining a white-knuckled grip on the grab rail with one hand, Atticus reached up with the other and worked his cap down over his ears. The cold wind bit at his cheeks, so he leaned forward to gain more benefit from the windshield. They roared out of the harbor channel past the horn buoy, but instead of swinging right out into the big swells as Atticus expected, Butch turned to port, heading down between the outer banks of Detroit Island and the east side of Plum Island.

"I'm going to take her out around the lee side of Plum!" Butch shouted over the loud whine of the engines. "As soon as she's round the point, I want you to take the helm for a minute. That starboard engine isn't running quite right, okay?"

"They sound just fine to me!" Atticus replied as he braced himself against the rough pounding of the choppy water.

Butch shook his head.

After they rounded the point into the relative smoothness off the east side of Plum Island, Butch turned the helm over to Atticus and started back toward the stern. Atticus had no choice but to take the wheel; soon, the offensive scream mellowed out. Butch closed the access panel on the engine shroud and worked his way back forward. Giving Atticus a tap on the shoulder, he took over the helm again. "Can you tell the difference?" he shouted, the wind practically washing his words away.

Atticus gave a nod.

"Now we'll take her out in the rough stuff!" he barked.

Pounding past the east side of Plum Island, Butch turned the boat to the right. He headed straight out into Death's Door Passage, where the crisp fall wind was clawing its way untethered across the open water. Ahead, the froth of wash tumbling off the prancing waves sparkled with a glimmering whiteness against the jaded sea. Atticus had all he could do to suppress his fear. He looked over at Butch; he wanted to say something but all he could muster was, "You crazy bastard!" He held tight.

Roaring out from behind the island's protection, the big Whaler hit the first wave head on. The boat catapulted into the air and then came down with a tremendous swat as it burst into the next wave. Green water careened back over the boat in every direction. The impact knocked Atticus to his knees. Behaving like a kid on his first roller-coaster ride, Butch gave out a squeal of pure delight. One hand on the throttle and the other on the wheel, he cut the power and took the next couple of waves off the port bow. Varying both the thrust and direction, he plowed on like a drunken man trying to negotiate a high-speed obstacle course, only in this case the obstacles were themselves on the move. The boat heaved first this way and then that; an almost constant wash of spray sent its icy wetness flying through the air. It wasn't until they were a quarter mile or so out that Atticus began to realize that what he'd mistakenly taken for reckless insanity was, in reality, the application of an exceptional skill; Butch not only had the uncanny ability to read the seas, but he seemed to know exactly what the boat could endure.

When they finally rounded the big horn buoy from the opposite direction and entered the relative placidness of the choppy channel, Atticus eased his death grip on the grab rail. As they approached the ferry dock once again, Butch pulled back on the throttle and the Whaler dropped down to a crawl. Atticus leaned back against the starboard rail and took what seemed like his first normal breath. "Gorpon," he said after a moment or two, "excuse my language, but you son of a bitch."

Butch laughed. "I wondered what you would think."

"Wondered! You knew damn well what I would think."

Again Butch laughed. "Well, what the hell," he replied, still sporting a big grin. "I don't get an opportunity like that very often—I was beginning to think there wasn't anything in this world that really shook you up; besides, you needed a diversion."

"Some diversion," Atticus replied, "and what the hell gives you the idea that nothing scares me?"

Again Butch chuckled as he guided the boat back in along the potato docks and brought it to a stop. Taking a rope, Atticus crawled up onto the dock and tied it off. "Well," Butch went on, "the worst that can happen to me after tonight is they can vote me off the board, and I'm not so sure that wouldn't be the best thing for me anyway. But you've got everything riding on this, and you seem to be as solid as a rock. Not only have you got the island to face, but you got that damn Kozuszek coming all the way up from Madison."

"What are you talking about?" Atticus asked as he stood up.

"I'm talking about Kozuszek coming all the way up here to little old Washington Island to observe our annual meeting!"

"Where did you hear something like that?"

"You don't know about it?"

"I haven't got the slightest idea what you're talking about."

"Atticus, for Christ's sake, this isn't new news; it's well over a month old and all over the island. He called the school to talk to you. Apparently, you were in class or something, so he talked to Vivian. He told her he would be coming up to the island to observe the annual meeting. Vivian told Nordien; Nordien told Greta; and Greta told me. I assumed Vivian told you."

"No, this is the first I've heard of it. That certainly resolves any pangs of guilt I was having over firing Vivian."

"So now that you know, what do you suppose he's coming up here for?"

"I don't know," Atticus replied, "it's not to present us with an award, I can assure you that. I would suspect some of our influential friends have managed to stir up a little political controversy under the superintendent of public instruction, and he's sending his number one deputy up to take care of it."

"So what are we going to do about it?"

"Nothing I can do," Atticus replied. "When is he supposed to get here?"

Butch shrugged. "By the way," he continued, "how are you doing finding a replacement for Vivian?"

Atticus shrugged.

"Well, Greta told me she would be more than happy to take over Vivian's duties until you find a replacement for her. The extra work for you is interfering with some of your police duties, especially the way some of the kids are beginning to drive around the island lately."

"Point well taken," Atticus replied. "She can take over Vivian's job anytime she wants."

"It's 10:30," Butch said after looking at his watch. "You want to come over to my place for breakfast?"

"Thanks, but no thanks," Atticus replied. "Laura is coming here on the noon boat. Besides, I want to go down and check on the *Moonhawk* at Pickle's dock. He's supposed to take her out of the water sometime next week."

Butch laughed. "That'll be the day. You'll be lucky to have her out by Thanksgiving."

"Boy, you're full of good news today. I was told he's pretty good."

"Oh he is; he's just not very punctual, that's all."

"Maybe I better have a little talk with him."

"That won't do much good," Butch replied as he crawled up out of his boat. "Pickle will get her out when he feels like it; no sooner, no later."

"Do you suppose she'll be all right there?"

"Which side of the dock is she on?"

Atticus paused for a moment to get his bearings. "On the east side," he replied. "Why?"

"Can I get a ride over to my car?" Butch asked. "It's over by the boat ramp."

"Sure," Atticus replied.

"Well," Butch went on as they walked toward the Bronco, "Pickle's got a concrete dock but he gets a pretty good chop running past his place when there's a northeaster blowing. If that happens, you better get down there and move your boat to the other side of his dock or she'll take a real beating."

"I'll keep that in mind," Atticus replied as he opened the driver's door and climbed in. Butch walked around to the other side. "By the way," Atticus went on as Butch climbed in, "where are you keeping your boat?"

"I think I'll keep her right here until after duck season."

"Who owns this old dock anyway?" Atticus asked as he started the Bronco.

"Adrian."

Atticus smiled. "Surprise, surprise. By the way, do you think our island tycoon will be at the meeting tonight?"

"Oh yeah," Butch replied with a nod.

"You think he'll be a problem?"

"That's not Adrian's way. If he has a problem, he'll have someone else do his talking."

"Such as?"

"Doc Burnett."

"That also figures; the status seeker."

"Well, that may be," Butch replied, "but it would be well to remember, Adrian Fruger and Doc Burnett are two of the most influential people on the island. You turn them against you, and you got a real serious problem."

"Yes, so I'm learning—what about the Doebucks? Will they be there?"

"No, they're off the island now. They never participate in anything like this anyway. You can bet they made their feelings known through the political channels though, especially Mrs. Doebuck. That's probably what's bringing Kozuszek up here."

Atticus pulled in by the boat ramp and stopped next to Butch's old station wagon. "Who else will be there?" he asked. "I mean, that might be a problem?"

Butch laughed as he gave another shrug. "That could be just about anybody, but the rest of them will be regular islanders, like me. Jody Kerfam will be there, representing the island paper. Tom Cline and his brothers will be there, and of course you're their favorite person, but you already know that. There's Hepper Greshion, he'll be there; I never really saw him as a problem, but for some reason he doesn't like you either. I imagine your teaching staff will be there; Sylvia and Spence, of course. Then you've got Vivian and Nordien; I don't think they'll say much, but they'll vote against anything you propose. The rest of the people are just regular folks; how they vote will depend on how you come off. Oh, I forgot your industrial arts man; he doesn't seem to like you much either; what's that all about?"

"That's about a creepy little man who's more interested in what I'm doing than in what he's teaching, but that'll resolve itself in time. I hope you and Greta are behind me."

"I believe in education, and I believe in you, and so does Greta. You have our complete support; you know that." Butch got out of the Bronco.

"I wonder if Baynard will be there."

"That's another one you won't have to worry about," Butch replied. "He and a bunch of his cronies went off-island Wednesday, and as far as I know, they haven't come back yet."

Atticus watched as Butch walked over to his car. Once there, Butch opened the door, looked back at Atticus, and gave him a nod, and then he got in. Atticus continued to sit there for a few minutes after Butch drove off. Finally, he started the Bronco and took off toward Pickle's dock.

———————

Noon found Atticus standing by the ferry dock, waiting for Laura's arrival. The anticipated hostility over the school budget, mixed with the complications of Tom Kozuszek coming to witness it all, generated the worst possible scenarios in his mind. Every insecurity Atticus ever had came bubbling to the surface. He felt like a young warrior, about to get his first taste of combat and, at the eleventh hour, second-guessing his capabilities. It wasn't until Laura came walking up to him, with her overnight bag in one hand and her suitcase in the other, that his mind snapped back to reality. "Atticus Gunner, are you just going to stand there, or are you going to help me?" she asked, looking at him in the strangest way.

Startled, Atticus fumbled for words. "Oh—I didn't—I mean, I'm sorry," he replied apologetically. He took the suitcase from her while at the same time giving her a peck on the cheek. "I guess I'm so wrapped up in this school thing that I—anyway, I'm sorry."

"Wow, you must really be worried," she said. "I don't think I've ever known you to be that preoccupied, especially after being apart for so long."

Atticus smiled at her and held out his elbow for her to take. "You're right," he replied. "Truth of the matter is, you're about the only positive thing I've been able to think about the entire time."

She took his arm and stretched up, returning his kiss on the cheek.

"How was the crossing?" he asked.

"A little bumpy but beautiful. The trip up the peninsula this morning was absolutely gorgeous; the trees were every color of the rainbow, and the air is so crisp. It's so beautiful up here in the fall, I wish I could stay forever."

Atticus smiled at her.

"Tomorrow I want to go someplace and romp in the woods; okay?"

Atticus continued to smile at her. "Tomorrow we'll go for a romp in the woods," he replied.

Holding his arm tight, Laura pressed her cheek to his shoulder and smiled back as they started to walk toward the truck.

"I've been so darn busy I haven't even had a chance to call the girls this week," Atticus said.

"Well, I did, and they are both looking forward to coming up for Halloween. As a matter of fact, I even have their mother's permission to pick them up and bring them with me."

"That is amazing; how did you manage that?"

"Very simple," Laura replied, "it's you she dislikes, not me."

Atticus continued to smile but said nothing.

"I was just kidding," she went on with a big grin. "The truth is, she was very pleasant when I talked to her."

"Speaking of pleasant, do you realize we are all alone this weekend? I mean just the two of us."

"Yes, that thought did cross my mind," Laura replied.

"Good, then I suggest we go home and unpack."

"Is that what you call it now?"

"Ma'am, I can assure you I have nothing but the most honorable of intentions," he said as he opened the back of the Bronco and put her suitcase in. After Atticus got behind the wheel, Laura slid over next to him. Just as Atticus was about to turn the key, he froze. "Oh my God, I almost forgot," he blurted out. "Did you see Kozuszek on the boat? I forgot to look."

"Kozuszek? You mean Tom Kozuszek?"

"You do know him, then?"

"Yes, he's a good friend of my boss; they go golfing together all the time. I'm not a personal friend of his, but I know who he is, and he knows who I am. Why would he be on the boat?"

"He's coming up here to observe our annual meeting, or so I've been told."

"He's coming all the way up here to observe your annual meeting? I've never known him to attend a local school board meeting; this must really be a special occasion."

"Yes, you might say that. You're sure he wasn't on the boat?"

"Atticus, there were only three cars on the boat; I think I would have noticed if he was there."

"Yes, of course you would," Atticus said as he started the Bronco.

When they arrived at the Hersoff place, Laura immediately got out and walked down by the lake. Atticus walked up behind her. "Atticus, I miss being here," she said. He put his arms around her from behind. She turned toward him. After a long, passionate kiss, she took him by the hand and started leisurely toward the house. "I'm afraid it's going to be a very long winter," she said.

"You've got no idea how much I've thought about that," he replied, "but for right now, I'm going to have to stay focused on tonight; I hope you understand."

"What all is going on?" she asked.

Atticus shook his head. "I don't really want to go into it right now," he said. "This is one of those occasions where you simply have to watch as it unfolds. Tomorrow you can ask me all the questions you want."

———◆———

The afternoon went by quickly; four o'clock found Atticus and Laura at the ferry dock once again. When the boat arrived this time, Atticus noticed there was only one car on board. He waited for the car to disembark and pull over to the side of the parking area and stop.

Laura hung back a little. "Do you want me to wait in the truck?" she whispered.

"No," Atticus replied as he started to walk toward the car. "You're with me."

A man stepped out; it was Kozuszek. "Hello, Mr. Gunner," he said calmly as they approached. "And I see Miss Bock is here too. I was told she had an extended interest up here."

Atticus knew exactly what he meant, but he wasn't sure if Kozuszek was addressing Laura or himself. He reached out and took the man's extended hand; Kozuszek managed a slight smile, but his steel-gray eyes were as cold and hard as ice. In an attempt to break the tension, Atticus asked if he was aware there would be no more boats today. Kozuszek informed him he was, and that he had made arrangements to stay the night. Atticus then asked if he would like to come to the house and perhaps have a bite to eat and relax some before the meeting. Kozuszek thanked him but suggested, given the circumstances, that might not be the best idea.

Atticus paused for a moment and then looked at Kozuszek straight on. "And just what might those circumstances be?" he asked.

"I'm here at the request of the state superintendent," Kozuszek replied.

"I didn't think this was a social visit."

"No, you're right," he went on. "It seems the state superintendent has received a threatening call requesting that you be removed as the district administrator."

"Wow, that must have been a pretty important call; who was it?"

"I have no idea," he replied.

"And you're the hatchet man who asks no questions but is bound by duty."

"I know Miss Bock wouldn't get involved with someone who really thinks like that, so I'm going to assume you're just spouting off."

"And what would you say under similar circumstances?"

"Probably the same thing."

"Well, it seems very apparent that I've managed to ruffle a few feathers on more than just the island," Atticus said.

"That you have."

"The state superintendent doesn't have the authority to fire me from this job, so I imagine you're up here to acquire my resignation."

"Mr. Gunner, I came up here because I was told to, but I'm here as an observer. We'll talk about your future after the meeting."

Atticus turned and walked away.

"Good luck, Mr. Gunner," Kozuszek said.

Laura held back; she smiled at Kozuszek. "Tom, I won't apologize for Atticus," she said, "but he is under a lot of pressure right now; I'm sure you realize that."

"Yes, I realize that," he replied, returning her smile, "but you needn't worry about him, Laura; he's a fighter. And from what I've observed, he's got the brains to go with it."

———◆———

It was 7:30 when Atticus and Laura arrived at school. There were already fifteen or twenty cars in the parking lot. Atticus pulled into the first open space and turned the engine off. Inside, the science room was lit up and all the worktables, except for the big one in the front of the room, had been pushed back against the wall to make room for the folding chairs. Butch was standing up front next to the table, talking with Adrian Fruger, and Greta was in the back of the room, talking with a couple of parents. Atticus just sat there, looking into the meeting room for a minute or two.

"Well," Laura finally said, looking over at him, "are we going in?"

"I guess we don't have much choice, do we? Tell me, why do I feel like I'm going on trial here?"

"In a way, you are."

Atticus snickered a bit. "Yes, I guess you're right—well, let's get on with it."

"You'll knock 'em dead," she said as she opened her door.

"Let's hope so," Atticus replied as he got out. He walked around the front of the Bronco. "Come on," he said, holding his hand out to her. "We'll go in through the office."

"Why?"

"So we don't have to parade through the crowd," he replied.

Laura wasn't sure what difference it made, but rather than belabor the point, she took his hand and followed as they hurried around to the front of the school.

Atticus paused again at the front door. "Two things," he said; "first of all, don't be surprised if someone makes an unpleasant remark about the two of us; second, when we get inside, I'll have to leave you alone; I hope that won't be a problem."

"Atticus, I'm not a child," she replied.

Atticus looked at her and then nodded. "Sorry," he said, "I guess I'm a little on edge."

"You'll do just fine; now let's go."

Taking the key from the inside pocket of his suit jacket, Atticus opened the outside door and entered the dark front hall. He made his way over to his office door. Atticus flicked on the lights. They walked through the office to the other door that led directly into the science room, where the meeting was being held. He paused for a moment and then opened it. Stepping into the back of the meeting room, Atticus glanced at Laura. Taking her by the hand again, he began to make his way through the crowd, greeting people politely as they went along.

Atticus headed toward Sylvia and Spencer, who were standing over by the coffeemaker, talking to Frank Seamy. Sylvia looked up as they approached. "Well hello, Atticus," she said.

"Hello," he replied, "I'm glad to see you could make it tonight."

"I never miss an annual meeting," she said.

Atticus directed his attention momentarily toward Spencer. "And I see Sylvia's got you in those Sunday duds again."

"Oh yes," Spence replied, grinning at Atticus, "never fails, funerals and school meetings."

Atticus smiled and then glanced over at Frank. "I thought you were headed for Chicago this weekend."

Frank gave a shrug. "I thought I'd better stick around."

"Well, I'm glad you did," Atticus replied. "By the way," he went on, glancing at Laura again, "I don't think any of you have met Laura. Laura, this is Sylvia and Spencer; I know you've heard me mention their names many times."

"Yes I have," she replied; "how do you do?"

"And this is Frank Seamy, our new English teacher."

"Hello," Laura said, smiling at him.

Sylvia smiled warmly at Laura. "I'm glad to finally meet you," she whispered. "Atticus here never says a word about you, so the only thing I know is what the kids tell me."

"I hope it's not all bad," Laura replied. "From what Atticus tells me, the people must think I'm a monster."

"Oh gracious, don't pay any attention to that; some of them don't even like themselves."

"Well, I think I better mingle a bit," Atticus broke in as he looked about. "Maybe you could stay with these folks; do you mind?"

"No, not if they don't."

"We'll take good care of her; you just go ahead," Sylvia replied, glancing first at Laura and then at Atticus.

"Well, wish me luck," Atticus said, smiling at the group.

Spencer gave a nod. "Go get 'em, boy," he replied reassuringly.

Atticus smiled at the four of them again and then moved off toward the front of the room. Approaching Butch, who was still talking to Adrian, Atticus walked up and interjected himself into the conversation. "Good evening," he said.

"Oh, there you are," Butch replied, turning his attention to Atticus. "You remember Adrian Fruger, don't you?"

"Oh yes," Atticus replied. "How are you tonight, sir?"

"Just fine," the man replied.

"I imagine it's a relief to have things slow down after a busy summer," Atticus went on.

"Yes, it's nice to relax, but it's also expensive to run empty boats."

"Yes, I'm sure it is," Atticus said, and then he excused himself and stepped over to the front table.

"Are you about ready to start?" Butch asked Atticus over his shoulder.

"Anytime you are," Atticus replied. "I just want to check my folder to make sure I have everything."

"Well, give me a nod when you're ready."

Atticus opened his folder and shuffled slowly through his papers; everything seemed to be in order.

"Good evening, Mr. Gunner," came a voice from off to his left.

Atticus looked up; Tom Kozuszek was standing there with his coat draped over his arm. "Hello again," Atticus replied. "Would you like for me to introduce you around?"

"No, that's fine," he replied. "I'll just find my way to an inconspicuous spot in the back, if you don't mind. I just wanted to wish you good luck again."

"Thank you."

Kozuszek smiled and walked away.

Atticus looked one more time around the room; Nordien was in the back of the room, conversing with a woman Atticus had never seen before. Brian Karmel was also in the back, talking to the island doctor and his wife; somehow Atticus figured that for a match. Other than Sylvia and Frank, he didn't see any other teachers.

Big Tom Cline was present; not only could he see him towering above the rest of the crowd, but he could hear his loud voice as though he were standing right next to him. Baynard wasn't there, and the Doebucks weren't either; that was a good sign. Jody Kerfam was, but Atticus didn't see her as a threat; she was working part-time as an aide for the school now. Hepper was talking with the same people as Nordien; Atticus assumed that not to be good news. The rest of the people were parents; some Atticus recognized, and some he didn't. There were no kids present. Vivian was there, of course. He spotted Reverend Watson and his wife. After another moment or two, he took a deep breath; ready or not, he was anxious to get on with it, so when Butch glanced up at him, Atticus gave him the nod.

Excusing himself from Adrian, Butch walked back over to the table. "Did you see Kozuszek back there?" he whispered to Atticus.

Atticus nodded.

"I'd like to know what that son of a bitch is up to," Butch went on softly.

"I don't know, but let's get on with it," Atticus replied.

Butch tapped the gavel on the table and asked people to please be seated. The room became relatively quiet as people shuffled to find a seat. Atticus watched as Laura sat down in the very end seat of the fifth row from the back. Next to her were Sylvia, Spence, Frank, and finally Tom Cline. In the very back was Kozuszek. To his left were the doctor and his wife, Brian Karmel, and finally Reverend Watson and his wife. Adrian Fruger sat down in the front row, directly in front of Atticus. Atticus sat down. To his right was Greta, an empty chair, and then Butch at the podium.

Butch called the meeting to order; he read out loud the purpose of the annual meeting from the statute book, announced the ground rules for participation, and then asked Greta to read the minutes from last year's meeting.

Greta stood up, read the minutes, and sat down again.

Butch went back up to the podium. "We will now hear the presentation of the budget by our new administrator," he said, looking over at Atticus. "Mr. Gunner." Then he sat down.

Atticus opened his folder, took out his papers, and got up from his chair. He stood there for a moment, took a deep breath, and cleared his throat. "I wish this was a more pleasant occasion," he said. "I wish I were here to bring you good tidings—but I'm not. I'm here to ask you to levy a tax upon yourselves; I'm here to tell you how I'd like to spend your money over the next school year. Having said that, I know I'm going to frustrate you, probably make you angry, but I hope you'll listen to what I have to say before coming to a conclusion."

Atticus walked back to the blackboard behind the table and picked up a piece of chalk. "I'm going to start with something a bit unusual," he said. "I'm going to give you a brief financial history of the Washington Island School District." Across the top of the board, he wrote the dates of the last four school years. "Four years ago, you set a budget of $152,000." He wrote the figure on the board. "You set a levy to match that amount." He wrote that figure directly under the first. "You spent $163,000 that year." He paused for a moment. "As you can see, you spent $11,000 more than you took in on taxes. In addition, you were already carrying over $27,000 in unpaid short-term notes from the previous year. So in essence, at the end of the school year four years ago, you were $38,000 in the hole."

"Three years ago," he continued, "you set a budget of $154,560. Again you set your levy to match the budget." He wrote the figures on the board. "And again, including the interest you paid on the short-term borrowing, plus the interest you had to pay on the notes carried forward, you spent $175,560. In other words, you now had a total deficit of $59,000, all in unpaid notes."

"I'd like to know just where in the hell you're getting those figures from!" came a booming voice from the back of the room.

Atticus turned around.

Tom Cline was on his feet. "I've never heard any figures like this before!" he barked. "What are you doing, making them up as you go?"

"No, Mr. Cline, I'm not," Atticus replied. "These figures have all been taken from the audited annual reports submitted to the state by this school district."

"Anyone can twist figures around," he said. "It's been my experience that when liars figure, figures lie!"

"These figures have been fully analyzed by your school board; I'm sure they'll confirm them as being correct."

"Confirmed, hell, mister; if you spent half the time working on an honest school budget that you spend horsing around with your pretty girlfriend here, we wouldn't have to be listening to garbage like this!"

Sylvia Nordman rose to her feet. "Mr. Chairman," she said calmly.

Butch recognized her with a nod.

"As you know, I've had a good many of you as students over the years," she went on. "Tom is no exception. He was, however, a very poor student in arithmetic. Would you care to tell the folks about your success in fifth grade arithmetic, Tom?" She paused, waiting for a response, and then continued on. "I didn't think so," she said. "Tom failed arithmetic in fifth grade, and I spent the entire following summer tutoring him, and under protest, I might add. He never returned to school the following fall. To my knowledge, he hasn't been back to school since." Pausing again, she turned her attention back to a very embarrassed Tom Cline. "I hardly think you're in any position to make judgments about anyone's ability in arithmetic, Tom." A chuckle came from the crowd. "I suggest you sit down and shut your mouth. There are a number of us who would like to hear what Mr. Gunner has to say."

Cline glanced around the room sheepishly and then sat down.

Sylvia looked back up at Atticus. "You may proceed, Mr. Gunner," she said flatly as she returned to her seat.

Stunned over this tiny woman's ability to demand respect from the likes of Tom Cline, Atticus returned to the blackboard without saying as much as a word.

"Mr. Gunner!" came another voice from the back of the room.

Again, Atticus turned around.

A little man in the very back row stood up. "My name is John Findly; I own the mercantile here on the island," he said. "I'd like to ask a question."

"Go ahead, Mr. Findly," Atticus replied.

"Being in business, I deal a lot with the banks. I oftentimes borrow money on a short-term basis, but I don't understand what that has to do with school. And what do you mean when you say deficit?"

Atticus walked back over to the table. "That's a good question," he said as he sat down on the corner of the table. "Public schools receive money from three different sources: the federal government, the state government, and local property taxes. Federal monies usually come in the form of grants; for example, the equipment in your vocational shop was paid for by a federal grant. State money comes in the form of general educational aids; we don't get state aids here on Washington Island. So what's left to run our school district? Local property taxes; that's it. As a property taxpayer, you pay your tax bill in halves, twice a year. But as a school district, the bills we have to pay come due more frequently than that. We have to keep up with the heat, the electric, school bus costs, payroll, and things like that. And even though we may have tax dollars coming to cover those costs, we don't always have the cash on hand when we need it. To help alleviate that problem, the state passed a law which allows schools to borrow against their anticipated receipts, which in our case is anticipated tax money. The idea, of course, is to pay off those short-term notes when we receive our tax monies. Unfortunately, if a district under-projects its expenses or its receipts, it comes up short. What happens then is the district usually ends up carrying some of the unpaid notes into the next budget year; that's called deficit spending. Does that answer your question, Mr. Findly?"

Findly gave a nod.

"Mr. Gunner, I don't think it's necessary to follow your example through all four years," Adrian interjected as Atticus turned back toward the board again. "I think we've got the picture. Just tell us what our deficit is, as of right now."

Atticus turned around once again. He paused for a moment and then took another deep breath. "Eighty-seven thousand dollars," he said.

At first Adrian didn't respond; it was as though he wasn't sure he heard right. "Are you telling us we're $87,000 in the hole, above and beyond anything we might consider for a budget tonight?"

"That's correct," Atticus replied.

The room exploded. Butch pounded the gavel on the table. "Please, please!" he said. Still the noise continued. He hammered again. "People, we must have order!" Slowly the room quieted down.

"Unfortunately," Atticus went on, "that isn't the only kicker. The law also states that a school district can only borrow up to 50 percent of its anticipated receipts. With what we need to borrow to operate, on top of the deficit we are already carrying, we'll hit that ceiling by the end of December, one year from now."

"And what does that mean?" Adrian asked.

"That means the bank would be forced to cut us off; with no other alternative available to us to get the money we need, we would be unable to meet our expenses; in essence, we'd be bankrupt."

Again the room became noisy, and again Butch had to pound on the table several times to quiet things down.

Again Adrian raised his hand. "If that were to take place, what would happen?" he asked.

"I'm not sure," Atticus replied. "Mr. Kozuszek, the finance director at the Department of Public Instruction, is here tonight; perhaps he can tell us. Mr. Kozuszek, has anything like this ever happened anyplace else?"

Kozuszek, who was leaning silently back in his chair, leaned forward. "Yes," he said with a cautious nod, "it happened once in my time with the department, about ten years ago; it happened to a small school district over in the western part of the state."

"And what did the state do?" Atticus asked.

"They disbanded the school board, terminated the existence of the school district, liquidated its assets, and attached the district's property and jurisdiction to a neighboring school district."

Dr. Burnett raised his hand and then stood up without waiting to be recognized. "I'm not convinced that this isn't some kind of a pre-orchestrated scare tactic," he said, "but regardless, so what if the state did close us down? What's to stop us from starting a private school of our own? We don't get anything from the state anyway."

Again talking erupted sporadically about the room, but Atticus held his hand up to quiet things down. This time the people responded. "Nothing would stop you from doing that," he replied, "but don't do it thinking such a move would solve your financial problems; it would not."

"Why wouldn't it?" the doctor said with finality in his voice.

"Because," Atticus replied calmly, "if the island were attached to another school district, you'd have to share in the property taxes to support that district, whether you sent your children to their schools or not. And the operation of a private school here on the island would be an additional cost, not replacing what you have now."

"Well then, we just might refuse to pay those taxes," the doctor said.

"A government could not survive if it allowed its citizens to pay taxes only when they felt like it," Atticus went on. "If you did that, they would confiscate your holdings. No, Doctor, I'm afraid this is a problem you can no longer run from. It has to be faced whether we like it or not."

"Then I'd like to know just how in the hell the school board allowed us to get into a jam like this?" the doctor replied.

"I can't speak to the quality of the administrative counsel the board has received in the past," Atticus replied, "but I do know they've been under tremendous pressure to keep property taxes down at any cost. Unfortunately, keeping taxes down at any cost and meeting their obligations were incompatible goals."

Again Adrian Fruger spoke up. "Mr. Gunner, some time ago, at a meeting to discuss this power equalization concept, you spoke in favor of it. I'd like to know just where that thing is legislatively now, and further, if implemented, what impact would it have on our present situation?"

"Mr. Fruger, I'm afraid I'm going to have to correct you; I did not say I supported the power equalization concept; I simply explained it. It's my understanding that the concept has run into substantial resistance throughout the state, and as a result, it is no closer to becoming a reality now than it was the night of that meeting. On paper, it seems a beautiful concept; the idea that all children should receive equal educational opportunities, regardless of where they live, is an honorable concept, but the idea has one serious flaw: it assumes property to be an equitable measure of wealth, and it is not! After having been here for a while now, I've come to realize that no place demonstrates that inequity more than here on Washington Island. Because of the nature of where we live, our property is very desirable for recreational purposes; wealthy people are willing to pay a premium price for it. But for the people who live here, it's a different story; this is their home; this is where they live year-round; they don't simply recreate here during the summer and then run back to their high-paying jobs in the winter. The true island people make the sacrifices necessary to keep this place going year-round, among which is a generally lower income. As to the impact of power equalization on our present situation—it would be disastrous. I do not and will not support it, and I intend to express that opinion wherever and whenever I can!"

The room erupted in applause.

"I suggest our unwelcomed guest from DPI take that message back to the bureaucrats in Madison," came a voice from the crowd.

Kozuszek made no response.

Raising his voice above the noise, Adrian spoke again. "Mr. Gunner, just how fast would our deficit have to be paid off and still allow us a reasonable opportunity to maintain the operation of our school?"

The noise subsided in anticipation of Atticus's response. "If we approve a realistic budget and set a proper levy," Atticus said, "you could adjust the payoff over the next three years. If you stretch it out further than that, you'll hit the borrowing limit before you gain enough to recover."

"And just what kind of levy would we need to do that?" Adrian went on.

"Before I go into that," Atticus replied, "I think we should go through the proposed budget; you need to understand the entire picture. I'm not going to lie to you; the levy we're proposing reflects a substantial increase."

"Well, get on with it then," Adrian said with a strong sense of directness.

Atticus opened his folder and pulled out the budget figures. Without hesitation, he turned to the blackboard and wrote out the total proposed budget figure, and then he circled it with a swing of the chalk. "This is the total dollar cost of the budget we are proposing," he said, turning back to face the room. "It represents a 22 percent increase over what was budgeted last year. That does not include the $87,000 deficit or any payoff thereof. It does, however, include the cost of interest we will have to pay on that deficit, and it also includes the interest we will have to pay on the money we must borrow in order to operate the school this year. It's the burden of the deficit that accounts for the biggest share of the increase, but there are other increases; let me point them out to you."

Again Atticus walked back to his folder on the table. Laying the budget tally sheet on the table, he opened the folder again. Spreading the remaining papers out on the table, he began to explain. Account by account, he proceeded through the budget proposal in the same fashion as he had with the board weeks prior. When he finished, no one spoke. He gathered up his papers and put them back in his folder. "There," he said, looking back up at the crowd, "you have the entire picture now."

"What's all this going to cost?" asked Findly.

Again Atticus went to the board. "Your present mill rate on the assessed value is nine mills," he said, writing the number on the board. "The proposed budget I just presented to you, plus paying off one third of your deficit, will raise your tax rate to seventeen mills."

No one said a word.

Finally, Adrian spoke up again. "Mr. Gunner, that's practically a 100 percent increase," he said. "Do you realize what kind of a burden you're asking these people to endure?"

"Yes sir, I do," Atticus replied.

Adrian turned his attention to the board members. "Do you agree with these figures?" he asked.

Butch looked briefly over at Greta and then rose to his feet. "As president of the board, I guess it's my responsibility to respond," he replied, clearing his throat. "We don't like the figures any more than you do, but what Atticus has presented is an accurate and honest representation of the way things are; we agree with the proposal."

Still the room remained quiet.

"Very well," Adrian said after pausing for a moment, "I move we adopt the budget and levy as proposed by Mr. Gunner, but with one stipulation. Should Mr. Gunner be wrong about anything he has presented here tonight, or should his promises not come true, Mr. Gunner is to be given his walking papers and we elect a new board of education."

"I second that motion," replied the doctor.

Butch cleared his throat once more. "All right, people, you've heard the motion made by Adrian, and seconded by Dr. Burnett. All those in favor, signify so by raising your right hand." He paused to count the hands. "Those opposed? Motion carried. This meeting stands adjourned!" He rapped the gavel once more and then laid it down on the table.

"Point of order!" Vivian cried out.

"This meeting stands adjourned!" Butch stated again as he rose from the table.

The people began to rise immediately and file out of the room.

Atticus stood there almost stunned; he couldn't believe it was over. He wasn't sure of the exact count, but he only saw four people vote against it: Vivian, Tom Cline, Hepper Greshion, and Nordien.

Greta stood up and pushed her chair in next to Atticus. "You did an excellent job, young man," she said to him.

"Thank you," Atticus replied.

"I hope you can deliver now."

"I'll certainly give it my best."

"I'm sure you will," she said. "Good night."

"Good night," Atticus replied.

Just then, Butch came up from behind and put his hand on Atticus's shoulder. He whispered into Atticus's ear, "I'm surprised, no one said a word about your job as island cop; not even Hepper."

Atticus turned and grinned at Butch. "Well, I guess that's because I'm such a damn good cop; what is there not to like?"

Butch just rolled his eyes. "Yeah, right," he replied.

When Atticus turned front again, Laura and the Nordmans were approaching the table. Laura was grinning from ear to ear. Sylvia was the first to speak. "I told you they would come through when they understood what you were saying," she said while reaching out to take his hand.

"Yes, you did," Atticus replied, "but I think the credit rests more with you; I've never seen anyone command such respect before. Thank you."

"Nonsense," she replied, shaking his hand gently with both of hers. "You just needed the opportunity to be heard, that's all. Right, Spence?"

"Absolutely, my boy," he said. "Besides, Sylvia wasn't about to let the likes of Tom Cline talk down such a nice young lady as you have here."

Atticus smiled.

"Well, I'll see you bright and early Monday morning," Sylvia went on, patting the top of his hand again. "Good night." Then she and Spencer moved off to join the others on the way out.

Atticus looked at Laura; she was still smiling. "And what are you grinning about?" he asked.

"Nothing," she replied, "I'm just proud of you—that's all."

Atticus smiled at her and winked. "Come on, let's get out of here," he said.

Kozuszek, after watching the room clear, finally got up. With his coat still draped over his arm, he walked toward the front of the room where Laura and Atticus were getting ready to leave. Atticus spotted him as he approached and paused. "You did an excellent job tonight, Mr. Gunner," Kozuszek said as he walked up to them.

"We got our budget," Atticus replied.

"Yes, you did."

"And now that I've publicly bashed power equalization," Atticus went on, "I imagine, as far as Madison is concerned, my future is on pretty shaky ground."

"If I were to have asked you for your resignation tonight, would you have given it to me?"

"I wouldn't even have considered it."

"I didn't think so."

"So where does that leave us?"

"That leaves me going back to Madison to tell the state superintendent that you did a brilliant job tonight."

Atticus smiled.

"I will also tell him your views on power equalization, however."

"I'm very sorry about that," Atticus replied.

Kozuszek smiled. "Yes, I'm sure you are. Well, good night."

"Good night," Atticus replied.

"By the way," he said, turning his attention to Laura, "I'm assuming you'll be back in time for our meeting with your boss Monday?"

"Yes sir, I'll be there," she replied.

Kozuszek turned and started to walk away. "Good night again," he said over his shoulder.

"You have a meeting with him Monday morning?" Atticus whispered to Laura.

Laura nodded.

Atticus winked at her. "You're a very lucky woman," he said.

Laura looked at him. "Yes I am—come on; let's go home."

CHAPTER 14

Night of the Grim Reaper

It was extremely dark for only 6:30 in the evening, and although it wasn't particularly cold for late October, the wind was blowing out of the northeast at near gale force. The rain careened across the road in sheets as the wipers on the Bronco slapped back and forth at full force across the windshield. Atticus didn't know why, but he could sense something more than the onset of miserable fall weather. It was a lousy night for a party, but trying to stay on the positive side, Atticus thought of how fortunate he was. Had the weather hit yesterday instead of this afternoon, Laura and the girls might not have made it over to the island.

Wearing his police cap and coat, he glanced over at Frank, who was sitting quietly and looking out the window as Atticus drove. "It never fails," Atticus said as he cranked on the wheel to avoid a fallen branch in the road, "it always seems to rain on Halloween."

Frank glanced over at him and grinned, his painted clown face glowing in the reflection of the dash lights. "I guess that's Wisconsin," he replied, squinting to see through the deluge. "The storm is supposed to pass over us by late tonight," he went on, "if that means anything."

Flicking on his high beam, Atticus slowed down as he approached the upcoming intersection, and then he turned right and headed down the main road toward the school. The annual Halloween party was an island tradition that included everyone, adults and kids alike. This year, the planning honors had fallen to Atticus; he in turn managed to commandeer Frank. The two of them had spent just about every night this past week getting things ready for the big event.

The party was to be held in the gym at the community center. There would be bobbing for apples and games of every description. The island band was to provide live entertainment for dancing, and there would be a costume contest.

When they arrived at the community center, a number of cars were already in the parking lot, and the band was unloading their equipment from the back of an old panel truck in the pouring rain. Atticus pulled in next to Brian Karmel's vehicle and parked. Together the two men got out of the Bronco and ran inside.

When the crowd finally began to arrive, Frank stood by the door stamping everyone on the back of the hand, while Atticus stood on the other side of the entrance and silently watched for problems. The sound of music filled the air, and the indirect lighting from the lanterns, along with the fog from the dry ice drifting across the floor, gave everything a mystical look. Atticus couldn't believe all the people who were showing up; it seemed as though every kid, plus their parents, had come. It was a good feeling to see the effort made pay off in such a communal way.

The rain had let up temporarily, but the wind was still blowing hard when Laura and the girls arrived. Atticus watched from the entranceway as the three of them got out of Laura's car and walked briskly across the lot toward the center.

When Inger spotted her father standing in the doorway, she darted out ahead of the others. "Hey Dad, how do I look?" she cried out through her protruding vampire teeth.

"You look absolutely frightening!" he replied as she approached. "How do I look?" He pulled his cap down over his ears and made a face.

"Stupid," she said, grinning from ear to ear.

Atticus kneeled down and gave her a quick hug.

"Dad, is Joni here yet?" Stacie asked as she and Laura approached.

"I think so," he replied.

"Good; I'm going to go find her, okay?"

"I suppose," he replied.

"Can I go too?" Inger chimed in.

"Yes, come on, Squirt," Stacie replied. And the two of them disappeared inside.

Holding her hair from blowing in the wind, while at the same time swirling around for Atticus to see her outfit, Laura was also smiling. "Well, what do you think?" she asked. She was dressed in a full-length, strapless blue gown. Her hair was combed out, and the silver glitter in it sparkled like twinkles of light. Her dark brown eyes appeared exceptionally deep and piercing from behind the white face mask she was wearing. "Well?" she said, swirling around again.

"You, my princess, are absolutely beautiful," he replied.

"Why thank you, Sir Cop-a-lot," she said smiling again.

Atticus held his elbow out to her in a kidding manner. "And if Friar Frank here can guard the entrance to Shorewood Forest without my assistance, I'll escort thy fair maiden into yon castle."

Reverend Watson and his wife, who were coming up the walk directly behind Laura and the girls, overheard the entire exchange between Atticus and Laura. Mrs. Watson tried not to smile but failed. The reverend looked at Frank as he held his hand out to be stamped. "Tell me, Friar Frank," he said in a sober kind of way, "does your boss behave like that at school too?"

Frank looked up at him. "Yes sir," he said with a smile, "fact is, you never know what he's going to say or do next."

The reverend just shook his head and started to walk away. As Mrs. Watson passed by, she smiled at Frank; Frank smiled back and winked.

The bad weather may have put a damper on the traditional trick-or-treating, but it certainly didn't hamper the party. Everyone, young and old, seemed to be having a good time. The dancing, the games, the food, and even the costume contest were all a great success. It was Atticus's responsibility, along with Frank's, to maintain crowd control and run the games, so periodically he would have to excuse himself from the others in order to tend to his duties. But in spite of the interruptions, he and Laura, along with the girls, managed to spend a good share of the time enjoying themselves as a group.

A little after ten, Atticus, Laura, and the girls were dancing the schottische behind Butch and Karen when Thor Henderson, the director of the community center, came up and tapped Atticus on the shoulder. Atticus excused himself and went with Thor off to the side of the dance floor. "What can I do for you?" he asked Thor.

Thor cupped his hands up to his mouth and leaned over to Atticus. "I was standing over by my office door when the phone started to ring. It rang and rang, so I finally went in and answered it. Do you know Old Man Trundle?"

Atticus shook his head.

"Well, anyway, he said he had to talk to you. I told him you were busy, but he insisted; said it was an emergency. I told him I'd have you call him back, but he insisted on waiting. So he's on the line in my office."

Atticus nodded. "Okay, thanks. I'll take it."

Atticus walked into Thor's office. He closed the door, walked over to the desk, and picked up the phone. "Hello," he said, "this is Atticus Gunner."

"Mr. Gunner, this is John Trundle; you have to come quick—there's been a plane crash!"

"A what?" Atticus asked.

"A plane crash! I saw it; it went right over my house! It must have just taken off from the airport. It was a big two-engine job; I heard it sputtering and then it went down. It crashed into the woods on the east side, north of the park."

"Are you sure?"

"Yes sir! I saw the fireball! I can still see the glow in the sky right from my house. I'm heading over there right now. You need to come fast!"

"Mr. Trundle, I'm on my way; don't try to approach the site on your own, you understand?"

"I'll stay back, but you best bring some help!" There was a click on the line as Trundle hung up. Atticus paused for a moment and then hurried back out onto the dance floor.

Spotting Frank talking to some people, Atticus hurried over and interrupted. "Excuse me for the intrusion," he said, "but I need to talk to Frank here for a moment; would you excuse us please?" With that, he led Frank over to the back wall.

"What's up?" Frank said as they walked away.

"Butch is out there dancing with Karen and another couple. I'm going to take you out on the floor so you can take his place; I need to talk to him."

"What?"

"Just do it; I'll explain later."

Frank gave a shrug as Atticus led him out on the dance floor.

As Butch and his group came around, Atticus approached them. "Mrs. Gorpon, I need to talk to your husband for a minute," he said bluntly. "Frank will take his place for a few minutes, okay?"

"I hope you're better at this than Butch is," she replied to Frank as he stepped in.

"Ma'am, I am an expert at the schottische," Frank replied.

Atticus led the somewhat confused Butch off the floor. "Do you know John Trundle?" he asked Butch over his shoulder as they made their way through the crowd.

"Yeah, why?"

"I just talked to him on the phone. He said there's been a plane crash over on the east side."

"A what?"

"That was my reaction," Atticus replied, "but he sounded pretty convincing; said a big twin-engine job tried taking off from the airport, flew over his house, lost power, and crashed into the woods on the east side. He also said he saw a fireball."

"Who in the hell would try to fly on a night like this?" Butch replied.

"I can't imagine, but let's not get everyone excited just yet," Atticus said. "What we don't need is a bunch of people tripping over each other to get out there for a look-see; besides, we're not even sure there was a crash. To be on the safe side, however, maybe we should get Doc Burnett, and the three of us quietly check it out."

"Okay, I'll tell Karen we're leaving."

"Butch, find the doctor too," Atticus said. "I have arrangements to make before we go, so I'll meet the two of you out by the Bronco."

Butch gave a nod and disappeared in the crowd.

Laura and the girls came around the floor again. Atticus motioned to Laura; she excused herself and came over to him. "Your daughters are not very happy about pulling me off the floor," she said jokingly. "What do you need?"

"I have to leave with Butch for a while," he said.

"Leave?"

Atticus took her by the arm and led her back away from the crowd. "There's been a plane crash over on the east side," he said. "We have to check it out."

"A plane crash? Oh my Lord!"

"The word will get out soon enough," he said, "but keep it as quiet as you can, okay?"

"What do you want me to do?"

"First of all, I may not get back before the dance ends, so find Frank and tell him; he may have to wrap things up here without me. That also means you may have to take the girls home alone."

"They're going to ask where you are; what do I tell them?"

"Tell them the truth, but they're to keep it quiet, especially Inger."

Just then, Atticus spotted Butch and the doctor approaching the front doors. "I've got to go," he said.

"Be careful," Laura said as Atticus hurried off.

———•◆•———

When they reached John Trundle's place, he was sitting in his pickup at the end of his driveway; his lights were on and the engine was running. He waved as Atticus pulled to a stop. "It crashed down in the woods over those trees!" Trundle pointed over the top of his truck. "I could see the glow of fire before it started to rain again! Follow me—I'll show you!" John pulled out onto the road and headed down toward the east shore. Atticus stepped on the accelerator to follow. The rain was coming down hard again.

Approaching the east shore, Trundle turned right. They drove down the mud-laden gravel road, through the woods, past the darkened homes of summer residents, and into the big maples of East Shore Drive. Finally, looking out through the naked trees, the glow of fire could be seen off to the left and down by the shore.

Pulling over to the left side of the road, the three men peered out into the pouring rain at the burning debris. What remained of one wing, an engine, the right landing gear, and a good part of the tail section laid half buried in the mud about fifty yards down the hill.

"Jesus Christ!" Butch said. "It's a big twin-engine job—or should I say, what's left of it."

"It's that old DC7 I saw land at the airport this afternoon," Doc said as he opened his door and pulled his collar up. The doctor took a flashlight out of his coat pocket and walked around to the front of the

Bronco. He stood by the side of the road and shined his light at the debris trail down through the woods.

Atticus and Butch grabbed a flashlight, and Atticus took the first aid kit from the Bronco and followed the doctor. John joined them, and the four men hurried down through the brush toward the crash site. "You say it landed this afternoon?" Atticus asked the doctor, half stumbling and half sliding as they hurried along.

Doc Burnett nodded. "Yes; the pilot had to make two passes before he could manage to bring it down."

"I wonder how many people were on board?" Butch asked.

"I saw four men get out and leave in one of Baynard's vehicles," the doctor said.

"Did you say Baynard?" Atticus asked.

"Yes," the doctor replied.

"From what I hear, he's been on the island most of this week," Butch interjected.

Atticus made no further comment.

The four men looked inside the broken fuselage; there were no signs of bodies. "I think it would be best if we spread out," Atticus said, wiping the water from his face.

They spread out, shining their lights into the brush and along the ground as the wind howled through the trees above. Atticus hadn't taken more than a dozen steps when John cried out, "Hey Doc, over here!"

All three men hurried over to where John was shining his light up into a tree. Atticus looked up; plastered into the crotch of a tree, about seven feet above his head, was the battered torso of a man with one arm dangling down lifelessly. The gold watch on his wrist sparkled in the beam of light. The corpse's clothing, slicked down by the piercing rain, clung to the decapitated body like a second skin.

"I'm afraid that poor devil's beyond any help we can render," the doctor said.

Again they spread out. Paralleling one another as best they could, they began working their way toward the shore. Just as Atticus approached another section of the plane, he spotted a second body; overtaken by the finality of death, the corpse's mouth hung open in helpless submission. The rain tattered off the cold gray face and bled away the crimson red that saturated the ground near the stub of his severed arm. "Here's another!" Atticus managed to blurt out after swallowing away a nauseous feeling. Again the others converged, and again the doctor pronounced the person dead.

Light from a car filled the blackness as it approached the area and stopped. Two men got out and shined their flashlights down into the woods. Atticus hollered to them for identification; it was Tom Cline and one of his brothers. They too started down the hill to join the search.

Again the darkness retreated as still another set of car lights appeared. This time the gears ground loudly as the second visitor pulled to a stop; Atticus knew it was Jody Kerfam.

"Tom," Atticus shouted as he and his brother came down the hill. "We got dead people down here! Go back up to the road and set up a perimeter; keep everyone moving along, and don't let anyone come down!"

Tom was disgruntled but responded with an affirmative. He and his brother turned around and headed back up toward the road. In the meantime, Jody got out of her truck and hurried down the hill toward the crash site.

Atticus worked his way down to the edge of the hardwoods where the dense stand of shoreline cedars began. In the darkness, he lost sight of both Butch and John, but he could still see Doc Burnett's light flashing through the trees. "Mr. Gunner," came the doctor's voice through the wind, "over here—quickly!" Shining his light through the cold rain, Atticus spotted the doctor kneeling on the ground next to a big cedar tree; he hurried over to him.

"Here," the doctor said as Atticus approached, "shine your light down here. This one might be alive!" Atticus held his light so the doctor could see. A man was lying face down in the brown matted leaves. "I'm going to have to turn him over," the doctor said. "Help me." Atticus bent down, and together they rolled the man over carefully. As Atticus attempted to straighten out his legs, the doctor wiped the wet leaves and mud from the man's face. Then the doctor put his ear down to his chest. When Atticus shined his light into the man's face for the first time, he gasped; it was the same man he had thrown off the *Moonhawk*; the very same man who had pulled the knife on him in the beer tent; the man the FBI said had died in a car crash.

"What's the matter?" the doctor asked.

"Nothing," Atticus replied. "I thought for a moment I recognized him, that's all."

"Do you?"

"No."

"Well, I'm afraid he's dead too," the doctor said flatly.

Cars were beginning to arrive at regular intervals now. Most of them would continue on as instructed, but occasionally one or two would stop and the people would get out. Although no one ventured down to the crash site, they stood around gawking like sheep, shining their lights down into the woods.

"Hey Doc, we found the nose section!" came Butch's voice through the wind from the other side of the cedars.

The doctor started through the trees toward the shore; Atticus followed. As the trees gave way to the open rocks along the shore, he could hear the roar of the surf. Although barely visible in the darkness, the run of huge storm waves came crashing into the rocks one after the other. Occasionally, spray caught by the wind would rain down clear up into the cedars. Leaning into the wind, Atticus and the doctor made their way toward the dim outline of the plane's nose section down by the edge of the rocks.

Meanwhile, Jody worked her way down to within twenty yards of the first section of the wreckage. Slipping and sliding as she went, she approached the fuselage as carefully as she could. Her foot hit something that went skidding out in front of her. She shined her small penlight on it; it was a leather pouch. As she reached down to pick it up, it fell open, spilling papers on the wet ground. She gathered up the loose papers. Holding them tight so as to keep the wind from snatching them from her, she leafed through them.

When Jody was growing up, her father had served in the English diplomatic service, and from the age of four to sixteen, they lived in Afghanistan; during that time she had become fluent in the languages of the area. These papers were written in Pashto, a Persian dialect of Afghanistan. It had been some time since she'd had an opportunity to visit the languages of her childhood, but she had little trouble translating the words.

There were several pages, but it was all part of one document addressed to the Northern US Mafia Cartel, and was signed with multiple signatures under the heading of the Afghan Freedom Fighters. As she read on, the document explained how even though there were constant rumblings of the collapse of the Soviet Union, they were convinced of a planned invasion of Afghanistan, through Pakistan, by the Soviets. And the Afghan Freedom Fighters were determined to be ready when it happened. Further, in their quest to arm themselves, they were prepared to trade heroin for cash.

Jody stopped. "My God," she whispered out loud, "what in the world is going on here?"

Suddenly, the light from a flashlight shined on her from behind. "Jody, is that you?" came a man's voice.

Jody quickly stuffed the papers back into the leather pouch, snapped it shut, and tucked it up under her coat and stood up. "Yes, it's me," she replied, turning to face the voice. "And you can stop shining that light in my eyes, Tom!" she barked.

"You're not supposed to be down here," he said.

"And why not?"

"Because hotshot Gunner doesn't need you in the God damned way, that's why. It'll all still be here in the morning; you can take your pictures then. Now come on," he reached out and grabbed her by the arm. "You're going back up on the road. And what's that you got under your coat?"

"It's just my camera case," she replied as she stumbled along. "I don't want it to get wet."

<hr />

Ahead, wedged between two huge boulders, and hanging precariously out over the edge of the water, was the entire nose section of the plane. As Atticus and the doctor got close, they spotted Butch and John down in the rocks trying to peer inside the torn fuselage.

"There's someone in there!" Butch hollered above the roaring surf.

Without warning, a huge wave rose up out of the darkness and slammed into the cliff with a thunderous explosion; water came crashing over the rocks and through the crevasses. The deluge careened into the hole where Butch was kneeling. Atticus and the doctor were immediately up to their knees in rushing water. The wreckage twisted violently to the right with a loud grinding sound and then settled back into almost the same position it was before, but Butch and John had disappeared. Atticus reached out and grabbed the doctor by the arm. "You okay, Doc?" he barked as the water subsided.

"Yes, I'm fine," the doctor muttered, "but we can't stay here!"

Redirecting his flashlight, Atticus panned the area in an attempt to find the others. John was just getting back on his feet down at the far end of the big boulder; he looked like a drowned rat. Again he panned the area, but still there was no sign of Butch. "Butch, where are you?" he shouted anxiously; his words faded into the roar of the surf.

"Over here!" came a muffled reply.

Atticus swung the light; Butch was picking himself up out of the rocks. Atticus worked his way over to him. Wiping the water from his face, Butch attempted to get back to his feet. "Banged the shit out of my leg," he said. As he started to stand up, he moaned and dropped back down. "Son of a bitch!" he barked. "I must have turned my ankle too!"

Atticus put Butch's arm over his shoulder. "We've got to get you to high ground," he said as he lifted him to his feet.

"We've got to get that guy out of the wreck," Butch mumbled. "Another wave like that last one and the whole nose section will be history."

"I'll get him out," Atticus replied as he struggled to get Butch up the face of the rocks. The doctor grabbed Butch by the arm from above and pulled him up onto a high ledge; Atticus let loose and immediately went back down toward the wreckage.

———◆◆◆———

After Tom finished helping Jody back to her truck, he left and went back down the road. She crawled inside and started the engine to warm her feet. As she sat there, she opened the leather pouch again, but by now her penlight had lost too much power to be of any use. She threw it in the seat beside her, turned on the headlights, and got out of the vehicle with the papers in hand. Bending over in front of the headlights in the pouring rain, she continued to translate.

Sensing the presence of someone, Jody looked over her shoulder; she saw nothing in the rainy darkness, but a cold shiver ran down her spine nonetheless.

———◆◆◆———

Atticus knelt down and panned his light into the interior of the wreckage. Three seats were torn loose and thrown forward into the control cabin. Buckled into the pilot's seat and slumped over was a motionless body. Bringing the light back to his immediate surroundings, Atticus began to crawl through the debris and down into the ankle-deep water toward the pilot. Atticus felt his neck to see if there was any sign of life; there was a weak pulse. He pushed the debris back out of the way and undid the pilot's restraining belt.

A light flashed in from the back of the fuselage. "How are you doing?" came a stranger's voice. Atticus didn't respond. The visitor slithered down the interior and up next to Atticus; he spoke again. "Is he still alive?" he asked.

"Barely," Atticus replied without looking up.

Another huge wave hit with a thunderous explosion. Again the water careened up over the rocks and blasted into the fuselage. The nose of the wreckage heaved violently, throwing Atticus back into the tangle of wire and debris. The water in the cockpit swirled back; the fuselage dropped back down, but this time at twice the angle it was prior to the last big wave. Simultaneously, the backwash from the wave sent water careening back into the cockpit from the open end of the wreckage. Atticus braced himself as the cockpit filled with water. He held his breath in the inky blackness until the water began to drain away and his head emerged once again.

Atticus took a couple of deep breaths to regain his composure. He then panned his light about to reassess the situation. His visitor was pinned between the back of the pilot's seat and the cabin bulkhead; he was choking and coughing but apparently okay. The pilot had been washed from the seat and wedged down between the controls; his face was totally submerged in about two feet of water.

Again Atticus pushed the debris away and dropped to his knees next to the pilot. Lifting the man's face from the water, he cradled him on his lap and felt for a pulse; there was nothing; he tried again. Giving a deep sigh, Atticus released the body and sat motionless for a second. Finally, he directed the light over toward his visitor again. "Agent Barker?" he asked in complete surprise.

Barker nodded, still coughing and struggling to regain his breath. "Man, I wasn't expecting that," he muttered. He coughed again. "What kind of shape is the pilot in?"

"He's dead," Atticus replied.

"Matt, you all right in there?" came another man's voice echoing down the fuselage.

"Yeah, we're okay, Chief!" Barker replied. "Come on, let's get this guy out of here," he said to Atticus. "I'll take one arm, you take the other."

As they grabbed hold of the pilot's lifeless body and began to drag him out, Barker paused. Pointing his light back down into the cockpit, the beam caught a shiny object. He crawled back and retrieved an aluminum suitcase. Placing the suitcase on top of the dead man's chest, Barker motioned for Atticus to lead the way out.

When they finally cleared the wreckage and reached high ground, they laid the body out on the rocks. There was a group of three men waiting. One of the group stepped forward, retrieved the suitcase, and started to open it. An older man, the one Barker had called Chief, asked the third man, "Dick, did you and Paula get everyone cleared out of here?"

"Yes sir," Dick replied, "everyone but that character over there." Then he shined his light up toward the edge of the cedars, where Butch was sitting on a rock in the pouring rain. "He refuses to leave."

"You go tell him that this area has been restricted by the Federal Bureau of Investigation, and that either he gets the hell out of here, or I'll have his ass hauled off to jail!"

"I already did that, sir," Dick replied. "He told me to go to hell; he refuses to leave without Mr. Gunner."

The chief turned and looked back at Atticus. He was a tall man in his early forties, wearing a yellow raincoat and a brimmed hat pulled down over his eyes. Dick shined his light on Atticus.

"He's with me," Atticus said, assuming he was expected to respond.

"Hey Chief!" the other agent called from where he was looking into the suitcase. "You better come and take a look at this; I think we just hit the jackpot!"

Barker and the others walked over; Atticus followed.

"There's got to be at least a million dollars here," the young man went on as he looked up at his boss. "Looks like they made their buy tonight in spite of the weather."

The chief turned to Atticus again. "Do you have any idea what's going on here?" he asked.

Atticus shook his head. "How did you people get here anyway?"

"We came on the island four days ago, masquerading as a hunting party," Barker interjected.

Atticus didn't respond.

"We've also been very busy looking out for your interests," the chief said.

"Oh really?" Atticus replied.

"Did I say something funny?" the chief replied.

"About as funny as the rest of the night," Atticus said.

"Then what's the wise-ass attitude supposed to mean?"

"If you're so damn busy looking out for my interests, why did you people lie to me about the man I arrested?"

"We didn't have much choice, Gunner," the chief replied. "We had to keep him under unhampered surveillance; he's the only real inside lead we have. You and your family aren't in any danger, I can assure you."

"Really? And where is he now?"

"Gunner, I hear you're not to be underestimated, but his whereabouts is none of your business, and if I have to, I'll take the wind out of your sails."

"Yes sir," Atticus replied, "and with the full power of the federal government behind you, I doubt you'd have any problem." Atticus started to walk away. "By the way," he said over his shoulder, "just in case you're interested, the man under your unhampered surveillance is lying up there in the woods—or should I say, what's left of him."

The chief glanced over at Barker and then looked back at Atticus as he continued to walk away. "Gunner, my name is Inspector Dampit; I'm the Central Division Chief, Barker's boss, and I don't remember giving you permission to leave."

"I don't remember asking for it," Atticus said as he walked over to Butch. "I work for Washington Island; I don't work for the FBI."

"You do now," the chief replied. "At least for tonight; I'm commandeering your services."

"Can he do that?" Butch whispered to Atticus.

Atticus shrugged. "I better go down there long enough to find out."

"Go ahead, I'll be fine," Butch said.

"Backup or no backup," the chief was saying to Barker as Atticus approached, "we've got to move on it now."

"Chief, there's no way you could get a chopper in here tonight," Barker replied. "And the nearest Coast Guard cutter is three hours away."

"I know that," he replied. "We're going to handle it on our own. Dick, go tell Paula I want security maintained on this site until the state crime lab gets here, and I mean secure!"

Dick gave a nod and started up the hill toward the road. After taking just a few steps, he turned back toward the chief. "What about that character over there?" he asked, referring to Butch.

"I'll take care of him," the chief replied as he turned his attention back to the young agent by the money. "Will, pack up that money and bring it along." The chief then turned and started walking toward Butch. "Gunner," he said over his shoulder, "what do you know about the terrain around Baynard's place?"

Atticus shrugged.

"Pretty rough, isn't it?"

"Yes," Atticus replied, "you could say that."

"Do you think we can get in there by surprise?"

"No! Besides, the way you guys came in here tonight, everyone on the island knows you're here by now, including Baynard."

"So this guy is with you," the chief said, pointing at Butch and ignoring Atticus's last comment.

Still shaky and on one leg, Butch stood up.

"That's right," Atticus replied.

"What about by water?" the chief asked Atticus.

"On a night like this?" Atticus replied.

The chief turned to face Atticus. "Let me explain to you a little bit about what's at stake here," he said. "Baynard and his friends are part of an organization called the Aryan Purists. We think sizable heroin shipments are being brought into this country via the Great Lakes and then sold to a drug syndicate. Our sources informed us that such a transaction was to take place here sometime soon. It appears to have taken place tonight, or at least was attempted. I think there's a good chance they haven't completed the deal yet even though Baynard may have the goods. If he knows, which you say is a strong possibility, that the money never made it off the island tonight, he's undoubtedly a very nervous man right now. If we can get to him before he figures out what to do, we just might be able to bust this thing wide open."

"I have a power boat," Butch said.

The chief looked first at Butch and then over at Atticus.

"If anyone could make it in there, he could," Atticus replied.

"Getting in there is the easy part," Butch continued, "but if you're right, Baynard's not only going to be nervous, he's going to be dangerous."

The chief looked over at a short muscular man standing up on a rock; he had on a blue rain jacket with "ATF" written in bold white letters across both the front and back. He was also wearing a baseball cap with "CIA" written across the front. He had been silent the entire time, and this was the first Atticus was even aware of his presence. "What do you say, Pope?" the chief asked the man.

The man gave a shrug but made no response.

"Mr. Gorpon, I want you to take the island squad car to your boat. Will, you and Barker ride with him. Gunner, I want you to ride with Pope and me; we'll follow them."

Atticus looked at Butch. "Are you sure you can handle this?" he asked.

"I don't like Baynard's kind of business," Butch replied.

"What about the ankle?"

"I'll survive."

Atticus put Butch's arm over his shoulder, and together they started to follow the others up toward the road.

When they reached the top of the hill, the entire area had been cleared of vehicles except for the Bronco and a gray Chevrolet. Dick was down the road, talking to some people in a pickup; Paula Smith, who was standing in front of the Chevy, greeted the group as they approached.

"Paula, what arrangements have you made to take care of the bodies down there?" the chief asked her.

"There are no body bags on the island," she replied, "so we sent the doctor with one of our cars to get some blankets. We've made arrangements to set up a temporary morgue in the fire station. The volunteer firefighters will help us make the transfers."

"Very good," the chief answered. He then motioned for Atticus to get into the back seat of his car. "Paula, you and Dick keep things secure here until we get back," he continued as he climbed into his car. The man in the ATF jacket walked around and got into the passenger front seat. "By the way," the chief said, looking over his shoulder at Atticus, "this is Damon Pontiff; he's with ATF."

Atticus already surmised two things about Pontiff: first, he wasn't simply one of the boys; and second, for some reason, he didn't like him. "Tell me, Mr. Pontiff," Atticus said. "Why did Inspector Dampit call you Pope?"

Pontiff turned his head and looked back at Atticus. "Pontiff?—Pope?" he said, shaking his head as though he had just spoken to an idiot.

"Sorry," Atticus replied. "I didn't make the connection."

Once again Pontiff turned and looked back at Atticus; he grinned. "Gunner, I'm disappointed. Somehow I figured you to be quicker than that."

"Yeah, it's funny how first impressions work; I was just thinking the same thing about you."

Pontiff turned again; this time he wasn't smiling. "Let's make one thing clear, schoolboy: stay out of my way."

"I'll keep that in mind," Atticus replied. "But just one more question, if I may: What's with the CIA cap? Is that wannabe or has-been memorabilia?"

Pontiff didn't respond.

"I'll take that as both," Atticus replied.

CHAPTER 15

The Sinking of the Kamora Moo

Dampit slid to a stop behind the Bronco at the end of the potato docks. Everyone piled out of the vehicles. He went immediately to the rear of his car, opened the trunk, and began handing out flak vests. Throwing one over to Atticus, he instructed him to put it on. He then hurried over to the end of the dock and threw one down to Butch, who was already making ready to get underway.

Atticus put the vest over his head and snapped it shut.

"Pope, distribute the hardware!" Dampit barked to Pontiff. "Matt, you and Will help Gorpon with the boat."

Atticus hurried over to the boat and started to untie the mooring lines. Pontiff came around and gave Matt and Will each a Beretta plus a belt of six clips. Pontiff then went back to the car and took a weapon and clip belt for himself. As he stood there strapping on the belt, the chief came by, reached in the trunk, and took an ammo belt and Beretta for himself. "Don't forget Gunner," he said as he walked away.

"Gunner?" Pontiff asked.

"You heard me," he replied over his shoulder, "Gunner."

"If you want to give him a gun, go ahead, but I'm not about to."

Dampit stopped and turned around. "Pontiff, I'm in charge," he said. "If you don't like the way I run things, then get the hell out of here!"

Atticus stepped forward. "Inspector, I'd just as soon not carry a weapon if you don't mind."

"Fine, then stay behind," he replied as he started for the boat again. "I don't need another observer."

Atticus watched the chief crawl down into the boat; he walked over to Pontiff. "Give me a weapon," he said flatly.

Pontiff reached into the trunk. "Sorry, we don't have any squirt guns," he said sarcastically as he held out a different kind of weapon to Atticus. "Know how to use this, schoolboy?"

"I'll figure it out," Atticus replied as he reached for the piece.

Pontiff withdrew it. "I didn't ask if you could figure it out; I asked if you knew how to use it."

Atticus glanced down at the weapon. He paused for a moment before he spoke. "Heckler and Koch MP5," he said, "fires a 9mm Parabellum; weighs 5.4 pounds unloaded; 100 rounds per minute; muzzle velocity, 1,312 feet per second; maximum range 220 yards."

Pontiff stood looking at him and then handed the weapon over to Atticus without further comment. Atticus reached into the trunk, grabbed a clip belt, and walked away.

Once everyone was in the boat, Butch backed away from the dock and swung the big Whaler around. Able to see only the faint outline of the shore on both sides, he headed northeast up the center of the channel between the two islands.

By now the rain had stopped, and the wind had let up some, but the frigid foggy air drifting rapidly over the water felt cold and clammy against Atticus's wet clothing. Crouching down to get out of the wind as much as possible, he leaned back against the rear cockpit combing. Pontiff was to his right, ahead were Will and Matt, and up front with Butch was the chief. No one said a word.

Dampit looked over at Butch. "No lights, and when we get in close, cut your speed," he said. Butch gave a nod without taking his eyes off the channel.

The chop progressively worsened as they came closer to the northeast end of the channel. Bringing the boat in close to shore, Butch cut the throttle. When they rounded the point, the wind picked up. A heavy surge coming in from the open lake caused the boat to rise and fall as it navigated over the oncoming swells. Across the half-mile-wide inlet was Bondin's Rock, but with the black heavy sky hanging low over the horizon and wisps of fog drifting across the water, Butch had all he could do to see the outline of the other shore. Easing back further on the throttle, the big Whaler headed slowly across the pitch-black inlet.

As they proceeded, Butch studied the opposite shore; finally he spoke. "Something's wrong," he said to Dampit. "I know we're still a ways out, but even at this distance we should be able to see lights from Baynard's place."

"Maybe they've cleared out," Pontiff responded.

"Or they're waiting for us," Atticus added just loud enough for the others to hear.

"I want everyone to be quiet and stay down," Dampit said.

They came in toward the big rock searching the darkness for some indication of movement. When they got within thirty yards of the shore, Butch eased back even more on the throttle. Swinging the boat to starboard, he paralleled the rugged coast. They slid slowly past the big house; it stood dark and silent. Except for the muffled thunder of heavy surf out along the reef, all was quiet; no sign of life.

Just as Butch turned the boat around to head back past the estate one more time, a sound rose up above the thunder of the surf; it was the loud drone of twin diesels. Suddenly, from the other side of Bondin's Rock, a big gray trawler came rambling out into full view; lit up like a Christmas tree, she was moving out under full power. Turning north by northeast, she burst out into the open lake. Wallowing in the heavy seas, she rambled off into the windswept night.

"I should have known!" Dampit barked. "Damn! Butch, how seaworthy is this thing?"

"Just say the word," he replied.

"How much fuel have you got?"

"Enough to chase that big tub to hell and back."

Barker looked at Atticus and then back at the chief. "That's crazy!" he exclaimed in total disbelief. "We can't go out there on a night like this in an open boat."

The chief looked off into the wild night; he watched the trawler's rolling lights slowly diminish as she put distance between them. Finally, he looked over at Butch again. "Can we catch 'em?" he asked.

"We can sure as hell try," Butch replied.

"Then give her hell!"

Barker glanced back at Atticus again with a look of horror; Atticus simply held tight. Butch rolled the wheel to port and at the same time leaned on the throttle. The big Whaler stood up on her haunches as she wheeled around and burst into a full gallop out along the lee side of Bondin's Reef. The sea was rough and choppy, but nothing compared to what was on the outer banks. Even in the darkness, one could see the endless procession of huge storm waves crashing into the rocky outcropping. Butch dropped his speed to half throttle as they approached the open water at the end of the reef. Rounding the point, the nose of the Whaler plunged into the trough of the first big wave. The bow sliced into the water, a heavy wash careening up over the boat. Committed, they plowed forward.

Hunched down in the relative security of the cockpit, the men remained silent as Butch pressed on under the watchful eye of the chief. The constant procession of huge rolling seas coming up out of the black and shapeless night, along with the bite of a northeast wind, seemed more than one could possibly endure in an open boat. Occasionally, a break in the heavy black clouds exposed the waning moon, along with a blanket of twinkling stars. The marine radio on the console was turned on to monitor the airwaves; it hissed almost continuously with only an occasional navigational check made by some distant freighter.

❖

By 1:30, the weather began to improve. As the wind subsided, it switched from the northeast to the east, but with it came a noticeable drop in the air temperature. The waves, on the other hand, seemed to be getting worse; for the second time in the last fifteen minutes, they had taken green water over the bow. Butch was forced to slow the boat to a crawl in order to keep from being swamped. There was little indication that they had closed the distance between them and the trawler; in fact, it seemed to be increasing.

Finally, after a long silence, Dampit spoke. "Where in the hell could they be headed?" he asked.

"If they hold this course much longer," Butch replied, "right into the gates of hell!"

"What do you mean?" Dampit asked.

Butch pulled on the wheel as they slid off the back side of another huge wave. "They're headed straight for the Boils," he replied.

"The Boils? Isn't that the big reef off the Winter Islands?"

"That's right," Butch replied. "Only a crazy person would go in there on a night like this; and I don't care what kind of a boat they've got."

"There must be someplace for them to hole up around there then."

"There's no place to hide in the Boils," Butch went on as he glanced again at the compass.

"Maybe they don't know it's there?" Barker inserted.

"They know," Atticus replied. "They're headed for Big Winter Island."

Butch, who was still studying the compass, looked up at the chief. "Atticus might be right," he said, "they've changed course. Now they're headed northwest; that would take them around the southwest side of Little Winter. From there they could get into Big Winter; even on a night like this."

"Why would they want to go there?" Dampit asked.

"I don't know," Butch replied. "All that's there is an old abandoned lighthouse and some rundown buildings."

"But it's in the middle of nowhere, and dangerous to get to," Atticus added. "A good place to hide."

"I take it you've both been there," the inspector said.

"Yes, we have," Butch replied, "but apparently Atticus has been there a little more than I realized."

———◆———

The lights from the trawler had long since disappeared by the time they approached the southwest point of Little Winter Island. Protected from the rage of the Boils, but close enough to hear the heavy breakers tumbling into the rocky coast on the windward side of the islands, Butch veered to the west and headed up the leeward shore of Little Winter. Completely protected from the wind, the wave action diminished to a surge along the black granite cliffs of the small island.

Butch finally looked over at Dampit. "Well, Inspector," he said softly, "up ahead is the channel that separates Little Winter from Big Winter Island. If they're here, that's where they'll be."

"Can we get close enough to see without being spotted?" he asked.

"I think so," Butch replied.

"All right," Dampit said as he looked around at the others, "no need to tell you gentlemen, keep a low profile and no talking."

Slowly they slid along the base of the cliff. The idling engines gurgled as they churned slowly along. Finally, the outline of many boulders emerged ahead; beyond, the black cliffs of Big Winter Island rose up toward the sky. Butch cut the engines. They drifted in silently.

Sitting up on the edge of the cockpit, Atticus and Barker helped to ease the boat past a boulder just off the port side. Once clear, they pushed off gently toward the next. As they came out from behind the next rock, Dampit held up his hand and ducked down. "What do you know?" he whispered. "There's Big Winter Island, and there's our trawler."

Dead ahead, at a distance of about two hundred yards, the trawler was tucked back into the open crevasse on the other side of the channel, the very place Atticus and Laura had docked the day they were there. It was tied to the old metal dock. All the deck lights were on, and a couple of bright lanterns glowed from the dock. The words *Kamora*

Moo written across her stern were clearly visible. Two men were busy draping camouflage netting over the boat, while four others unloaded canvas-covered bales off the boat and onto the dock. The surge caused the big boat to rise and fall slowly as a ghostly shadow of the trawler swung back and forth on the sheer granite cliffs. The moan from the wind above, and the distant thunder of surf along the outer banks of the Boils, echoed down through the canyon in a weird wailing moan.

Atticus could hear Quint's voice whisper in his ear as though he were sitting right next to him: "When you get up in close to the Boils during a blow, she wails like a woman scorned."

"Yes," Atticus said softly, "it does."

Pontiff looked over at Atticus. "Did you say something, schoolboy?" he whispered.

"No," Atticus replied. "I was just thinking out loud."

The inspector glared back at them, especially Atticus. He motioned to move the boat back out of sight. Atticus and Barker pulled them back. "Is there any other way to get on that island?" Dampit whispered to Butch after they were out of sight.

Butch thought for a moment. "There's a trail that comes down the cliff on the west side," he said. "It comes down to a low ledge that hangs out just above the water, but there is no way we could tie up there."

"Can you get us in close enough to drop us off?" the inspector asked.

"Yes."

"Then let's do it."

They carefully pushed their way back out of the rocks. Butch started the engines; with the lights off and the motors running as quietly as possible, he headed out from the island giving the channel entrance a wide berth. Finally, he swung the boat back in toward the island again.

He came back in along the high cliffs on Big Winter's west side out of sight from the cut between the two islands. Idling along, he searched for the ledge. "There it is," he exclaimed, pointing ahead. Guiding the boat ever so carefully, he came in along the outcropping.

Dampit reached out and took hold of the rock in order to keep the boat from smashing up under it with the rise and fall of the water. "Pope, help me hold the boat steady," he said. "Gunner, you've been here before, so you're our guide. Will, you and Barker go with Gunner. Pope and I will reconnect with the three of you at the top of the cliff. Wait for us there. Now get going!"

Atticus scurried up onto the ledge; Will and Barker followed. Dampit turned back toward Butch before climbing out of the boat. "Gorpon, I want you to go back in the rocks where we were and wait," he said. "Make sure you're not spotted. When you hear gunfire, get on the horn and call the Coast Guard. Give them our location and tell them it's a priority-one call; they'll ask for a confirmation number; it's F0044. Can you handle that?"

Butch gave a nod. "F0044," he repeated.

Dampit crawled up onto the outcropping. Pontiff followed and pushed the boat away. They started up the steep trail.

"Good luck," Butch said as he backed the boat away slowly.

"When it's over, we'll signal you from the boat landing," Dampit said. Butch gave a nod, turned the boat, and disappeared into the night. Dampit hurried up the trail behind Pontiff.

———◆◆◆———

Atticus and the others were squatting down behind some rocks at the top of the cliff. At first Atticus was nervous, but then a strange calmness came over him. He squeezed the MP5's cold pistol grip tight; it felt comfortable. For a brief moment, he was back in the forest of East Germany. It was then that it struck him; he hadn't really had time to think before now, but this was the target of the Morgan Group; this was why he'd been hired. His mind flashed back to Attorney Markup and the whole interrogation about his experience with the Nighthawks and his success at hunting former Nazis. He even thought of Cynthia and her comments about the presence of evil; he wondered if she was connected to the Morgan Group in some way. He thought about Bert Federman; Old Bert had stumbled onto something, and they had gotten rid of him. He even thought about Quint again. And although he had absolutely no evidence of foul play in the disappearance of Quint and the boys, deep down inside he knew there was a connection there too; he just hadn't found it yet. Baynard and his group were neo-Nazis, there was no doubt of that, but intuitively Atticus knew this little venture was by no means the heart of the real issue; no matter what transpired tonight, it would only scratch the surface of what was really at play.

Then there was Pontiff. Why had he taken such an immediate dislike for him? Suddenly it dawned on Atticus: they were both here for the same reason. Pontiff was a Nazi hunter. Maybe he and Atticus were more alike than either of them would care to admit. It's not the first time that competing warriors made tenuous bedfellows.

Inspector Dampit came crawling up over the edge of the cliff. "Gentlemen," he said as he joined the group. "I don't want anyone hurt, but I don't have to tell you, we're on our own; so take no chances, and if hell breaks loose, play for keeps. Any questions?"

"What's the plan?" Pontiff asked calmly.

"Well, as I see it, we've got an advantage," Dampit replied. "They don't know we're here, so they probably feel safe. That means we should be able to take them by complete surprise. We don't have enough ammunition to sustain any kind of extended gunfight, so if we must fight, we must be fast and lethal; any questions?"

There was no response.

"Okay gentlemen, load 'em!" Dampit continued. He took a clip from his belt and slammed it into the receiver of his Beretta, then rammed a shell into the firing chamber.

Everyone else did the same, except for Atticus.

"Gunner?" the chief asked.

Atticus glanced back at him. "Sorry," he replied. Then he too slapped the bolt lever back and loaded his weapon.

"You still with us?" the chief asked.

"I told you we shouldn't have brought him along," Pontiff interjected. "He's real brave with his club, especially when his opponent doesn't have a weapon, but this is a little different, isn't it, schoolboy?"

"Cool it, Pope!" the chief replied, never taking his eyes off Atticus. "He's the only one who knows anything about this place; that is, unless you've been here before, Pope."

Pontiff made no response.

"Gunner, I know your background," the chief went on. "I know you can handle yourself; so what's going on?"

"Just getting my bearings," Atticus replied.

"Where are these buildings Gorpon was talking about?" the chief asked.

"There's only one to be concerned about, and it should be just about straight in from here," Atticus replied.

"All right, lead the way," the chief said softly.

Atticus moved out; the rest followed. He picked his way through the rocks and headed into a stand of huge pines. The blanket of pine needles on the ground was wet and slippery underfoot, but it made moving quietly an easy task. The predawn light made it easy to make out the silhouette of each massive trunk as the big trees swayed in the wind.

At the top of a hill, Atticus gave the signal to stop. Pontiff came up next to Atticus and knelt down next to him behind a fallen log. Down below, in a shallow valley, they saw the lights shining from the windows of the old shed.

"You actually found it, schoolboy," Pontiff whispered. "I'm amazed."

Atticus looked over at Pontiff but said nothing. Inspector Dampit appeared from behind a tree and moved up next to Atticus. "Pope," the inspector whispered, "I want you to go down and have a look-see, and just a look-see, and then report back here."

Pontiff laid his gun against the log, drew his knife, winked at Atticus, and disappeared into the darkness.

Atticus mouthed some words just above a whisper. "Here we come to save the day; Mighty Mouse is on his way . . ."

"It's obvious that you two don't like one another," the inspector said, "and he may well be the biggest asshole you'll ever meet, but don't ever underestimate him."

Again Atticus didn't respond.

After about ten minutes, Pontiff reappeared just as silently as he had left. "There are two people in the building," he whispered to the chief, "Baynard and a woman. Baynard is sitting at a table doing paperwork; the woman is just sort of wandering around."

"What about weapons?" the inspector asked.

"The woman is wearing a handgun; I don't think Baynard is armed. There's an assault rifle hanging on the corner of one of the six bunks in the back of the room; I assume it's his."

"Hold it," Atticus whispered, touching the inspector on the shoulder; he pointed toward the building. Someone came out of the large open front entrance and disappeared into the woods; it looked like Baynard.

"How far is it to the harbor from here?" the inspector asked Atticus quietly.

"It's about a half mile to the face of the cliff. I would guess that's where he's headed."

"Okay," the inspector went on, "we'll wait for a few minutes to make sure he is indeed headed for the boat. Pope, when we move out, I want you to take out the woman in the shed."

Pontiff gave a nod.

"I want her alive," the inspector said, "but be quiet about it."

"I have no problem taking her out quietly, but alive? That may be a problem."

"Alive," the inspector repeated.

Pontiff didn't respond.

"The rest of us will go down and position ourselves on the trail just this side of the cliff. I'm sure they'll be hauling their goods up here to stash; when they do, we'll hit them. Okay, let's move out; Gunner, lead the way."

Atticus moved out.

Crouched behind a big boulder at the edge of the cliff, Atticus watched and waited silently for the first sign of movement on the path below. The others were stationed back in the woods along both sides of the trail. They were waiting for Atticus to signal the approach of their prey. Once they passed his location, the plan was to close in from uphill. Atticus was to stay out of it unless one of them managed to break back toward the boat. He looked at his watch; it had been about twenty minutes since they left Pontiff. The early dawn light was just beginning to glow on the horizon. He heard nothing and wondered if Pontiff had managed to subdue the woman, and if he had, was she still alive.

As Atticus watched the trail below, a ground squirrel scurried across the cold wet rocks. Then he saw the heads of men bobbing above the rocks as they trudged their way up the twisted path below; each was carrying a small bale on top of his head. His heart jumped. Ducking back behind the rock, he took out his flashlight and pointed it back up toward the woods; he blinked it three times. A light blinked back. He snapped his weapon off safety and waited.

Before long, the sound of voices could be heard coming up the path. Pressing down close to the rock, Atticus remained completely still. Watching along the edge of the boulder, he counted each person as they passed; there were six. Four of them were carrying automatic weapons.

After the sixth man disappeared up the trail, Atticus realized that Baynard wasn't with them. He lifted up to look down the path again. What happened next only took an instant, but it seemed like an eternity. As Atticus lifted up to look down the trail, Baynard was just coming out from behind a rock on his way up the path; their eyes met immediately. First there was a look of complete disbelief as they both realized what was happening, and then Baynard swung the muzzle of one of the three AK47s he was carrying directly at Atticus.

Atticus dove for the dirt; the silence was shattered by the rapid succession of automatic weapon fire. Bullets splattered into the rocks around him; several hummed past his head as they ricocheted off the hard granite surfaces. He rolled down into the tall grass behind another boulder. The silence shattered again with the sound of more gunfire; this time from up in the woods. Scrambling, Atticus crawled around to the other side of the boulder and rose up slightly; Baynard was gone. Again he froze; his heart was pounding. He scanned the area again and again. Finally, Atticus spotted him about forty yards down the trail; he was behind a big boulder with only the very tip of his weapon exposed.

Atticus slithered over the top of the rock and then brought his weapon up, tucked it up under his chin, flipped the lever to single fire, and made ready to squeeze the trigger. Flat on his stomach, legs apart, he waited and watched through the tall blades of grass as they swayed in the wind. The gunfire up in the woods stopped, leaving a heavy silence. Finally, the tip of Baynard's weapon dropped out of sight; cautiously he appeared from behind the rock. Atticus placed his cheek against the cold steel and aimed carefully. Baynard began moving backward down the trail, slowly at first, and then he turned and ran. Atticus followed him in his sights but was unable to squeeze the trigger.

After Baynard disappeared around the bend, Atticus continued to stare at the empty trail through his sights. When he could no longer hear Baynard's footsteps, he lowered his piece and clicked it back on safety. Finally, as though it just dawned on him that Baynard was getting away, he took off running down the trail after him.

As Baynard hurried, he discarded the two heavy AK47s he'd been carrying for his colleagues. He still wasn't sure what had happened, but something had certainly gone wrong; very wrong. He felt certain he had dropped the man up in the rocks, but from the pattern of gunfire up in the woods, he was also certain his colleagues had not fared as well.

Rounding the last bend, Baynard headed out onto the dock. Laying his weapon down, he climbed on board the trawler and began throwing the camouflage netting off the boat as fast as he could. When he finished, he jumped off and untied the mooring lines, picked up his weapon, and climbed back on board.

As Atticus came running out onto the dock, the big trawler was swinging away from the dock in an attempt to turn around. Running with all his strength, Atticus jumped for the passing stern rail. He missed the rail and came crashing down on the stern board platform. The impact not only caused him to lose his weapon, but he lost his hat as well; still, somehow he managed to hang on.

———•◆•———

Watching the drama unfold before his eyes, Butch knew he had to do something. As the trawler turned and headed in his direction, he cranked the engines and throttled out directly into the middle of the channel. Once there, he turned on his big spotlight and flashed it directly at the oncoming trawler.

———•◆•———

In his panic to get out of there, Baynard hadn't seen Atticus jump onto the back of the trawler. The first indication he had of anyone's presence was when the blinding flash of light came bursting through the early morning haze directly at him. Mistaking it for the Coast Guard, Baynard spun the wheel hard. The trawler heaved hard to port as she came abruptly about and headed in the opposite direction.

Atticus fought hard to hang on as the big boat heaved to port; he too was confused as to what was happening. It didn't dawn on him that Baynard was crazy enough to try and shoot the channel, at least not until one of the big surges rose up and dropped the aft of the trawler right down on one of the boulders lying just beneath the surface. As it hit, a loud grinding crunch filled the air; it was then that Atticus realized Baynard was panicky enough to do anything, even take on the Boils.

A hundred yards ahead was the end of the channel. The huge waves out beyond rose up over the big reef and then crashed through the Peppers, thundering with the roar of a hundred surfs; water and spray shot fifty feet straight up into the air as the bombardment smashed repeatedly into the huge granite pylons.

As they headed down the center of the channel toward the waiting gates of hell, Atticus tore off his heavy flak vest, slipped out of his shoes, pulled himself up over the stern rail, and rolled onto the deck. He jumped to his feet and started for the wheelhouse. As he reached the open door, Baynard glanced back.

With one hand still on the wheel and the other trying to negotiate his AK47, Baynard doubled over as Atticus plowed into his midsection. The impact sent them both sprawling down the companionway steps and onto the floor of the quarters below. Baynard's weapon flew from his hands and skidded under one of the bunks. He managed to free his handgun from its holster, but Atticus grabbed his wrist and slammed it back against the bulkhead; the handgun too went crashing to the floor. Swinging Baynard's arm up over his head and around his back, Atticus twisted it up between his shoulder blades. Baynard winced in pain. With his free hand, Atticus retrieved the nightstick tethered to Baynard's side and threw him toward the stairs. "We've got to get this thing turned around!" he barked.

Baynard stumbled to his feet and started up the stairs.

Atticus followed.

When Baynard reached the top, instead of stepping into the wheelhouse, he spun around and sent a kick straight back at Atticus. Atticus managed to sidestep the blow, but the glancing impact was enough to throw him off balance. That split second was all Baynard needed; before Atticus could recover, Baynard grabbed him by the forearm and flung him over his shoulder. Atticus went crashing into the bulkhead; the nightstick flew from his hand.

Suddenly, there was a loud screeching sound beneath the hull; the boat shuddered and heaved hard to starboard. Both Atticus and Baynard were thrown across the wheelhouse. The stern rose, the propellers lost their bite, and the big diesels whined loudly as they revved up. Then as another surge rose beneath the boat, the trawler righted itself, wallowed in the boiling rampage, and continued on.

Atticus pulled himself to his feet. They were just yards from the end of the channel now. Ignoring Baynard, he rushed forward to the wheel and began flinging it hard to port. Baynard tackled him from the side. Again the impact knocked Atticus off his feet and sent both of them crashing to the floor. "What's the matter, Gunner?" Baynard screamed as he scrambled back to his feet, nightstick in hand. "You afraid to die?"

Atticus got up.

"You've screwed up everything, you meddling son of a bitch!" he screamed. "But at least I'm going to have the pleasure of seeing you die! Just like the Raptor got rid of that old man and those kids! You should have seen it, Gunner; the old man cried like a baby trying to keep those boys from drowning as they went under unable to free themselves from the anchor rope!"

Atticus started for the wheel again. Baynard stepped in front of him; Atticus paused. "Come on," Baynard said with a sick calmness in his voice. "Let's see what you're really made of."

Atticus faked a step forward and then pulled back quickly. As Baynard stepped into a thrust with his stick, Atticus fended the blow off to his left, and at the same time jabbed the point of his open hand directly into Baynard's chest with all his might. The impact sent a shock through Baynard, paralyzing him in his tracks. Turning to his left, Atticus wrenched the nightstick from Baynard's hand. He rammed the end of the nightstick straight into Baynard's throat. Spinning around, Atticus came around once more; this time with every bit of strength he could muster, he smashed Baynard across the face with the broadside of the club. Baynard staggered back, blood gushing from his mouth. The whole left side of his face was caved in; his left eye was pushed from its socket and hung precariously off the side of his face. He stumbled into the open door and then fell out onto the deck.

Without hesitation, Atticus turned and grabbed the wheel again, but it was too late. Coming up off the port bow was a huge wave; it looked like a mountain. He spun the wheel desperately to starboard, but a deluge of water came careening down over the top of the boat. Smashing through the windows, it filled the wheelhouse with a torrent of green water. Then as the bow emerged, climbing diagonally up the face of the wave, a torrent of water swept Atticus off his feet and sent him crashing back into the aft of the wheelhouse. He grabbed hold of the open door frame. As though in slow motion, the big trawler, standing almost vertical on its stem, fell off. As it dropped its bow, it slid broadside up and over the crest of the wave, and then it yawed hard to port and slid down the back side into the trough of the next wave. The stern rose again, and all Atticus could see was the glistening black face of a solid wall of granite coming straight at the boat. The bow plowed into the waiting pylon, crumpling it like tinfoil. The stern rose high; there was a loud sound of twisting steel. The impact wrenched his grip from the door jamb, and Atticus was thrown into the boiling rampage of water. Shocked by the numbing cold, he tumbled helplessly. Totally disoriented, his shoulder struck something hard with a glancing blow as he broke the surface.

Shaking the water from his face and taking a deep breath, Atticus looked around. Another huge wave lifted him up over the crest. The trawler, still pinned to the granite pylon, was just slipping beneath the surface. As each wave swept beneath him, Atticus looked for some sign of Baynard, but there was nothing—only the roar of the turbulent seas.

Fighting desperately to ward off panic, Atticus swam to the left as the next great swell rose up from behind. The big wave catapulted him forward. Like a leaf going down a drain spout, Atticus was swept through an opening between two large boulders. For a moment, he spotted Baynard twenty yards off to his left but lost sight of him as the water threw him forward.

Bobbing back to the surface once more, he looked around. As he rose up on the crest of the next wave, he spotted Baynard again; he was down in the trough, pinned between two pylons. Atticus tried swimming toward him but again the water rose, and with it Baynard disappeared for the second time; this time would be the last; Atticus would never see the Nazi worshiper again.

The next pylon came up so fast Atticus had little time to think about Baynard. Again he swam as hard as he could to get himself into position, and again he was swept between the rocks. After the second encounter, the big rocks were more staggered and farther apart, so Atticus had little trouble avoiding them. But his relief was short-lived; even though he was less than twenty-five yards from shore, he was being swept away from shore much faster than he could swim. The real question now was, in these heavy seas, would he be able to make it to shore before being swept out to sea? If not, he would have little chance of survival, for no matter how capable a swimmer he might be, he would soon be overcome with hypothermia.

Unable to close in on shore, Atticus kept his head up in order to maintain his bearings and tried to maintain strong steady strokes, but it was hopeless; his arms and legs were already growing numb with cold. Soon maintaining headway was no longer of concern; now simply keeping his head above water was a major chore. At first Atticus was frightened, and then he became angry. A thousand scenarios tumbled through his head. He thought about the kids and Laura. His mind began to drift; thoughts became jumbled; reality became mixed with fantasy; he began to hallucinate. The emerald-green water seemed like a translucent sky; an endless world through which he was floating like a butterfly. He thought he saw a shark swimming on the surface next to him; then it was a whale—no, a boat. His mind played tricks as it drifted in and out of reality. He knew he was hallucinating, but suddenly, there it was again. This time it closed in on him and grabbed him; he wanted to fight but had no strength left.

When Atticus opened his eyes, he was lying on the pitching floor of a boat—too weak and numb to move. The deck was wet and slippery as the water slurped continuously up over the side. It all seemed so vague, so nebulous; he had trouble sorting things out. Someone grabbed him under the arms and propped him up under the protection of the cuddy cabin; it was Butch. Atticus tried to smile but could not.

Butch propped his lethargic friend up against the bulkhead and started rubbing Atticus's arms, legs, and neck vigorously. "Come on, old buddy," he said as he massaged, "don't give up on me now." He slapped Atticus. "Come on, Atticus!"

—•◆•—

Atticus knew Butch was there; he could hear him talking, he could even see him, but he couldn't feel anything; everything seemed so far away. Then he began to tremble. It started first in his chest and stomach, finally it expanded down his legs and arms; his whole body began to shake violently. He shook so hard his teeth rattled uncontrollably.

Butch began to grin. "That's more like it," he said as he reached back into the cuddy cabin to retrieve an old sleeping bag. He wrapped it around Atticus. "When you begin to feel the cold, it's a good thing," Butch went on. "That means you're returning from a close encounter with Davy Jones's locker."

Shaking so hard he could hardly control his movements, Atticus tried to respond but still could not.

"For a minute there, I was beginning to think you were going to check out on me," Butch said. "If I'd gotten here five minutes later, you would have."

Butch stood up and looked around. He limped back over to the helm, triggered the engines, and began crawling southwest over the rolling swells back toward the lee of Little Winter Island. He looked back down at Atticus. "Any sign of Baynard?" he asked.

Still unable to talk, Atticus shook his head.

"I didn't think so," Butch replied. "When that crazy bastard headed down the channel right smack dab into the waiting arms of the Boils, I thought I'd never see either of you again. When you plowed into the first pylon, I took off around Little Winter, hoping to work my way up into the lee of the Boils just in case. I still can't believe it; it was like I ran right up on top of you. Do you realize what the odds are of that happening in all this water? No doubt about it, my friend; you're one lucky son of a bitch. You're one of the very few people who have gone through the Boils in a storm and lived to tell about it." Butch grinned down at Atticus. "And you did a good share of it without a boat. Jesus Christ, if Quint were still alive, he'd be envious as hell; you know that Gunner? Envious as hell!"

Atticus tried to smile as he pulled the sleeping bag up tight around his shoulders. Everything was beginning to come back into focus now. "What about the others?" he mumbled through chattering teeth.

Butch shrugged. "I don't know," he replied. "That's where I'm headed now. Baynard is likely dead; that's all I know."

"Butch," Atticus said, "he may have already been dead before the Boils got him."

"What do you mean?"

"I mean I tried to kill him, and I may have succeeded."

"That's called self-defense, Gunner."

Still shivering, Atticus shook his head. "No, it was more than that," he said. "Baynard confirmed that Quint and the boys were murdered;

he gloated about it. He was there. I saw red; I wanted him dead, and I did my best to kill him."

"But you don't know for sure that it was you that killed him."

"No, not for sure."

"Did he say he killed Quint and the boys?"

"No; someone called Raptor did, but he was there. You ever heard of anyone called Raptor?"

Butch shook his head. "Raptor; that's a bird of prey."

Atticus nodded. "I'm going to find that son of a bitch, Butch, if it's the last thing I do, I'm going to find him, and I'm going to kill him."

"You're in no condition to think about that right now," Butch replied, "but let the Boils take credit for killing Baynard."

Atticus didn't say anything more for the next few minutes. Finally he spoke again, "Why me?" he asked. "Why didn't the Boils take me? It's like it just spit me out and then directed you right to me. How do you explain that?"

Butch shook his head again. "I don't know," he replied. "Like I said, maybe you're just one lucky son of a bitch."

"Yeah," Atticus replied, "maybe."

—•◆•—

By the time they reached the harbor on Big Winter Island, the sun was well above the horizon, and although there was still a heavy swell running, the wind subsided to a mild breeze out of the west; it was going to be a warm day. Atticus had recovered substantially, but every muscle in his body ached.

Barker was waiting on the dock as they approached. "I had to go after Gunner!" Butch said as they came up alongside the dock; he threw a rope up to Matt.

"Yes, I know," Matt replied as he tied the boat off. "I saw most of it from the top of the cliff. Did you call the Coast Guard?"

"Yes," Butch replied. "They should be here anytime now."

Shunning the warmth of the sleeping bag, Atticus climbed up and out of the boat; Matt helped him. "I can't believe you're still alive," he said as Atticus stepped onto the dock.

"How did it go on this end?" Atticus asked.

Barker shook his head. "The chief is dead," he replied.

Just then, a Coast Guard helicopter came roaring in over Little Winter Island. Unable to land, it hovered overhead.

"Get them on the horn and tell them everything is secure!" Matt shouted to Butch. "Tell them to send a landing party in as soon as the cutter arrives!"

Butch did as he was told, and after the captain of the chopper informed him the cutter would arrive in about forty-five minutes, it veered off and disappeared over the trees again. As the sound of the chopper faded, neither Atticus nor Butch made any comments about Inspector Dampit.

"And Baynard?" Matt went on. "I assume he's dead."

Atticus nodded; Matt started back up the path. "I'm coming with," Atticus said. He looked back at Butch.

Butch pointed at his ankle.

"I'll give you a hand," Atticus said.

"No, you go ahead; I'll be fine right here."

Atticus paused for a second and then nodded. "I'll be back shortly," he said. "Don't leave without me." He turned to follow Matt.

"Here!" Butch barked, throwing Atticus an old pair of boots from the boat. "You'll need these!"

Atticus smiled and put them on.

———————◆◆◆◆———————

Matt was quiet most of the way up the cliff. Finally, he spoke. "We had to kill four of them," he said. "They're all up in the shed with Will and Pontiff."

When they reached the old barn, Will was sitting on the ground by the open door, weapon across his lap and arms draped over his knees; he looked exhausted. Pontiff was sitting on a chair just inside the door, facing the prisoners; his weapon was also resting on his lap. The woman was over by the table, sitting on the floor. She was tied to a post with her head dropped forward; she was the one Pontiff had subdued. The other two captives were sitting in the middle of the room, hands tied behind their backs and bound together; their shirts were tied around their heads as a blindfold. Laid out in a row at the far end, in front of the cots, were five draped bodies.

Pontiff looked up at Atticus as they entered. "Well, look who's here," he said.

"Ease up on it, Pope," Matt replied.

Atticus ignored Pontiff and walked over to the chief's body. Matt followed and knelt down next to Atticus; the chief's body was draped with his own coat. Atticus lifted it from the chief's face and looked at what was left of him. "He got it in the neck," Matt said softly. Atticus lowered the coat and stood up again. He then walked over to the woman and knelt down in front of her.

She looked up at Atticus.

Atticus reached out and tilted her head back and to the right; her neck was sliced, but not deep enough to be fatal. "Help will be here soon," he said.

"Is Baynard dead?" she asked.

Atticus nodded.

"Did you kill him?"

Again Atticus nodded.

She studied Atticus for a moment or two and then spoke again. "I knew you'd be trouble the minute I saw you at Baynard's place," she went on. "They call you the Moonhawker, but you're no match for the Raptor."

"And who is this Raptor?" Atticus asked.

She looked down at the floor again.

Atticus took her by the chin and turned her face back toward him. "Why did they kill an old man and three kids?"

"Because they saw too much," she replied.

Suddenly a hand grabbed Atticus's shoulder. "We'll do our own interrogating if you don't mind," Pontiff said, standing over Atticus.

As Atticus rose to his feet, he noticed the indelible German prison markings on Pontiff's right wrist. Atticus looked at Pontiff and then down at his wrist again. "Auschwitz?" he asked.

Pontiff gave him a nod but did not smile.

"You're a Nazi hunter, then."

Again Pontiff nodded. "I am a Jew, Gunner; I hunt Nazis because they butchered my entire family. You are a German; why do you hunt them?" he asked.

"I'm of German descent," Atticus replied, "but I am an American."

"That still doesn't answer the question."

Seeing the tension, Matt walked over between the two men. "That's enough!" he said. "We've all had a hard night; it's time to stand down."

"Do you need me anymore?" Atticus asked Barker.

"No," Matt replied, "but if you and Butch want to wait until the Coast Guard cutter gets here, they'll take Butch's boat home for him, and you and Butch can ride back to the island on the cutter."

"Thanks, but Butch would never leave his boat, and I'm with him, so I think we'll head back on our own."

"Suit yourself," Barker replied.

"Gunner!" Pontiff said as Atticus started to walk away. "Just remember, it's not over yet! What happened here tonight stays here!"

Atticus continued to walk without responding.

"You say anything to anyone and you'll answer to me!" Pontiff barked; his words echoed through the empty barn.

CHAPTER 16

Wind, Sleet, and Fire

By early Sunday morning, the state crime lab, an FAA crash investigation team, some Coast Guard brass, and every media source from miles around had all converged on Washington Island.

Ironically, in spite of all the activity that morning, Atticus and Butch managed to arrive back home unaware of the media frenzy. It wasn't until Atticus walked into the house and saw the television blaring away that he realized the extent of all the publicity. Pictures of the crash site were being shown, and a spokesman from the FBI was reading a prepared statement. Atticus, of course, was immediately pressed by Laura and the girls to fill in all the details, which he did as minimally as possible, intentionally leaving out all the gory facts. The rest of that day was gone almost before it began. It seemed as though Laura and the girls had just arrived when Atticus found himself standing on the dock, waving good-bye. By that time, however, he was so dead on his feet he had trouble thinking of anything other than sleep.

Ten minutes after he returned home, he was in bed and fast asleep; so much so, he never heard the phone ring four different times or the pounding on the front door at about seven o'clock that evening. It was

6:30 the next morning when he awoke; even then, he had all he could do to crawl out of bed and stagger into the shower.

On his way to school, Atticus met Butch's car coming from the opposite direction. Butch flashed his lights; Atticus stopped. "You look bright eyed and bushy tailed this morning," Atticus said as he rolled down his window and looked over at Butch's tired but grinning face.

"I'm headed down to the ferry dock to pick up some parts for the co-op; I was hoping to catch you," he said. "How ya feeling?"

"I could use another ten hours of sleep," Atticus replied, "but other than that, I guess I'll survive; how about yourself?"

"Well, with all the TV people at my house all day long yesterday, I didn't get to bed until after ten."

"TV people?"

"Yeah, didn't they talk to you?"

"I saw a TV crew getting on the boat when Laura and the girls left, but I haven't talked to anyone."

"I'm afraid I wasn't that lucky. That's what happens when you live right on the main road."

"What did you tell them?" Atticus asked.

"They kept pressing, but I didn't tell them much of anything; I figure if the FBI wanted them to know something, they'd have to do the talking. I'm surprised they didn't hunt you down."

"I wonder how they found out we were there."

"Oh, there were enough people around the crash site; I'm sure the word spread fast. I still can't believe you managed to avoid them. By God, Gunner, I am convinced, in some ways you do lead a charmed life."

"I tried to tell you that before, but you just don't listen," Atticus replied with a grin.

"Yeah, right," Butch said, shaking his head. "I wonder what the hell Mrs. Doebuck and her uppity-ups are going to think of their old buddy Baynard now?"

Atticus shrugged.

"By the way," Butch went on, "I forgot to tell you, I talked to the Kitchems. He's an airline pilot, and his wife, June, is an accountant with school finance experience. He's retiring, and they are moving to the island in a couple months; she might be interested in Vivian's job. She's going to be calling you to talk about it."

"Sounds good," Atticus replied. "What about a replacement for Nordien?"

"Yeah, there's that too; I talked to Billy Stock; he works with me at the co-op. He's a good guy, and he said he'd be willing to serve out the rest of Nordien's term on both boards, but he can't start until the first of the year."

Atticus glanced at his watch. "I got to go," he said. "I'm already late; Greta is probably calling my house right now. I wish she would consider taking the job permanently; she's something else."

Butch laughed. "By the way," he said, "did Jody Kerfam ever find you?"

"No; why?"

"She was looking for you yesterday evening. She stopped by, said she had been down to the Hersoff place but you weren't around. She seemed pretty determined."

Atticus shook his head. "No, I haven't seen her, and I was home all evening. I'll see her this morning though; she's working at school today. I'll see you later." Atticus stepped on the accelerator.

———•◆•———

When Atticus arrived at school, there was a van parked in his spot; it had "Channel 14" written in bold letters diagonally down the back quarter panel. At the side entrance of the school, surrounded by eight or nine high school kids, was a woman reporter and her cameraman. Atticus found a different parking place and pulled in. When he got out of the car, some of the kids spotted him and immediately drifted inside, but three of the boys stayed behind and continued to talk to the reporter.

"Okay guys," Atticus said as he approached. "Come on, it's time to get inside." The kids broke off the conversation and went inside without protest.

The woman looked over at Atticus. "Mr. Gunner?" she said into her foam-covered mike. "You are Mr. Gunner, aren't you?" The cameraman zeroed in on Atticus.

"That's right," Atticus replied.

"Do you mind answering a few questions, sir? Is it true you were with the FBI when they made the drug bust Saturday night?"

Atticus sidestepped around her as she poked the microphone in his face; he continued toward the door without responding.

"Did you see it happen?" she went on, following him inside.

Atticus turned around. "Hold it," he said, raising his hands. "We're trying to run a school here; I'm going to have to ask you to leave."

"You didn't answer my questions, sir," she went on.

"No, and I don't intend to," Atticus replied.

"Why? Is there something you're trying to hide?"

"Yeah, lady, you hit it right on the head," Atticus replied sarcastically as he eased her and her companion back out the door and pulled it shut.

Frank and a group of students were standing in the hall, observing the encounter. They began to shuffle into the science room as Atticus turned toward them; Frank lagged behind. "Seems you're a real celebrity this morning," he said to Atticus. "And here I thought the Halloween party was going to be the big event of the weekend."

"Now don't you start in on me," Atticus whispered.

"Well, you've got to admit, people are a little curious."

"Yes, I know."

"You were there, weren't you?"

"Yes."

"Well then, tell me about it."

"No," Atticus replied. "I've been told to keep my mouth shut with everyone, and unfortunately that includes you."

"Hey, Mr. Gunner!" Allen Greshion piped up from his desk over in the opposite corner of the room. "When you going to fill us in on all the gory details?"

"Never!" Atticus came back. "You're going to have to wait until it comes out in a movie!"

"That good, huh?" Allen replied.

Atticus grinned and shook his head, and then he winked at Frank as he continued across the room toward his open office door.

"You're here," Greta said, looking up from behind her desk as Atticus entered. "I didn't think I'd see you this morning."

"Well, my total being may not be here, but I'm here physically." He took off his coat and hung it on the coat rack.

"You must have really been in a hurry; you forgot your beloved hat."

"No, I lost it."

"Well, at least you're here," she went on.

"I'm afraid to ask," he replied as he sorted through the messages on his desk, "but what is that comment supposed to mean?"

"Sylvia was just down here; Jody never showed up this morning."

"She probably overslept again; did you try calling her?"

"Yes; several times, and all I get is a busy signal."

Atticus glanced down his list of island phone numbers; picked up the receiver and dialed her number. There was a click, and then he too got a busy signal. He hung up the receiver. "What is she scheduled to do this morning?" he asked.

"She was supposed to help with the special reading group and then supervise the study hall. This afternoon she was to supervise the woodworking class so you could meet with Brian. When she called me at home yesterday, I knew she wouldn't show this morning."

"Yesterday? What did she say?"

"It isn't so much what she said as it was the way she said it. She was looking for you. She said it was very important, and if I saw you, you should call her right away. I told her it wasn't likely that I would see you, but I could try to call you at home; I did, and you didn't answer. I knew if you didn't call her, she wouldn't show up this morning out of spite, and I was right. You didn't call her, did you?"

"No."

"I didn't think so. She's been like that for years, even before she lost her son."

Atticus got up out of his chair. "Go ask Frank to send up one of the high school kids to help Sylvia. I'll run out to Jody's place and see if I can find out what's going on." He slipped into his coat, exited out the front door, and hurried over to the Bronco, hoping to avoid the TV people, but they had already left.

———————•◆•———————

When Atticus arrived at the Kerfam farm and pulled into the poorly maintained drive, Jody's truck was parked over in front of the old barn. He drove up to the sheet of plywood laid out on the ground for a walkway and stopped. The house, which was once white with green shutters, was now graying and in serious need of paint. He got out of the Bronco and went up to the front door. When he knocked, the door unlatched and creaked slightly open. Atticus poked his head inside. "Jody? It's Atticus Gunner!"

No one responded.

"Jody?" he hollered even louder. There was still no response, so he stepped inside. "Jody! It's Atticus Gunner!" he barked again.

Atticus walked across the front room and into the kitchen. The burner on the electric stove was red hot, and the bottom of the metal teakettle sitting on top of it glowed with equal intensity. He grabbed the towel hanging on the oven door and removed the empty kettle from the burner, set it in the sink, and then turned the burner off. There was a cup sitting on the table with an unused tea bag in it. He noticed a double-barreled shotgun leaning against the chair on the other side of the table. He picked up the old gun and broke it open; two fully loaded shells popped out and tumbled to the floor. Atticus picked them up and put them on the table. He closed the weapon and placed it back where he'd found it.

Noticing the wall phone over by the window was hanging off the hook, Atticus walked over and hung it back on the receiver.

Something was amiss; an uneasy feeling flushed over him. He pushed the lace curtains aside, looked out the window toward the barn, and then released them and walked back into the front room. He went over to the staircase that led up to the second floor and called her name again. Still getting no response, he went upstairs and looked in both bedrooms; they were a mess, but she wasn't there. Certain that something had happened to her, he hurried back down, out the front door, and over to the barn. He went up to the open loft door and stepped inside; it smelled of stale hay. "Jody!" he hollered again. His words echoed through the barn and caused a flutter of wings as a covey of pigeons flew out the open haymow doors. After looking around, he went back outside and around to the empty cattle stays below; again he found nothing.

On his way back to the house, he glanced inside her truck as he passed by. Then he noticed a light shining from the basement window; he broke into a run. As he reached the bottom of the basement steps, he stopped dead in his tracks. Shining on the wall from behind the furnace was an unmistakable shadow. He walked around the furnace; there, hanging from a rope tied to a rafter, was Jody Kerfam. She was facing the opposite direction with her head cocked unnaturally to the side and her feet dangling helplessly two feet above the floor. In front of her, tipped on its back, was a wooden chair. His first inclination was to release the pressure from the rope in hopes she might still be alive, but the minute he touched her, he knew it was far too late; she was cold and stiff. Atticus stepped back. The body swung slowly around; her mouth was open, tongue swollen and protruding; she gazed with lifeless eyes off into space. Atticus closed his eyes for a moment and took a deep breath.

He went back upstairs, picked up the phone, and dialed the school. On the third ring, Greta answered. "Greta," he said calmly, "I'm at the Kerfam place. Call Doc Burnett and have him come over here right away; Jody's dead."

———◦———

Atticus was standing on the front porch when the old ambulance/hearse arrived; Bill Ditch, Orvis Oldbuddy, and Butch were in it. As they pulled up into the yard, Doc Burnett came driving up over the hill and joined them.

Atticus just stood there as Butch and the others removed the stretcher from the ambulance and hurried up toward the house.

The doctor hurried past them. "Where is she?" he asked.

"In the basement," Atticus replied.

The three men followed the doctor with the stretcher and headed for the basement. Butch glanced at Atticus but said nothing. Atticus followed but waited at the top of the steps.

In about fifteen minutes, the doctor reappeared, black satchel in hand. He came up the stairs without saying a word. The other three men, with Jody's body draped and strapped to the gurney, began negotiating their way up the stairs.

"How is it you found her?" the doctor asked Atticus.

"She didn't show up for work," Atticus replied.

The doctor shook his head. "Well, you won't have to worry about that anymore."

"How long has she been dead?" Atticus asked.

"My guess is about eight hours."

"Broken neck?"

"No," the doctor replied, "she didn't do a very efficient job of it; she choked to death. Did you find a note or anything?"

Atticus shook his head. "I haven't really looked," he replied.

The three men made it up the stairs, rolled the gurney out the front door, and then loaded it into the ambulance.

"Well, after this last weekend, I'm not about to call the county coroner back up here," the doctor went on as he drifted toward the door. "I'll send the body down to Sturgeon Bay; they can do an autopsy if they want, but as far as I'm concerned, it was suicide."

Atticus didn't respond.

"Mr. Gunner, I'll make out the official report and contact Reverend Watson so he can notify the family."

Atticus followed the doctor out the front door and onto the porch. Butch was just coming back up to the house. "Maybe you should look around a little bit to see if there is a note or something," the doctor said, "but be careful; don't disturb things too much. The county may want to send someone up here to investigate."

"I'm afraid that someone is already here," Atticus said.

"Oh that's right, you're the law up here now, aren't you?" the doctor replied. "Well, then I guess it's your problem." He continued down the steps and out to his car. Then both he and the ambulance left.

Butch looked up at Atticus. "You okay?" he asked.

"Yes, I'm fine," Atticus replied as he turned and walked back into the house.

Butch followed. "You seem a little taken back."

"That's because I need a new hat."

Butch didn't respond.

"Butch, how long have I been the part-time cop on this rock?"

"I don't know; three or four months. Why?"

"Do you realize that in that short time, I've encountered, if my count is correct, the death of thirteen people by unnatural causes; that's if you include old Bert Federman. I'd be willing to bet a cop just about anywhere doesn't have that much fun in such a short time."

Again Butch didn't respond.

"The bedrooms upstairs look like they might have been ransacked."

"That doesn't surprise me," Butch replied as he looked around. "She wasn't much of a housekeeper."

"She had a loaded shotgun next to her at the kitchen table, Butch."

"Maybe she was going to use it, but at the last minute changed her mind and hung herself instead."

"A person who is contemplating suicide doesn't start a cup of tea, then right in the middle of it, decide to go and hang herself."

"Are you an expert on suicide now?"

"Why was she so hell-bent on finding me yesterday? Maybe she just wanted to say good-bye; you think maybe that was it?"

"Look Atticus, we've been through hell in the last forty-eight hours—you more than me, but I think you're making too much of this. Jody Kerfam has lived on this island for the last fifteen years. Her and her kid moved up here after she dumped her drunken old man; she's had a tough life. I mean, look around you; the woman didn't have a pot to piss in, and now she doesn't even have her kid. The glory years ended when her parents died. She lived on the small amount of income she generated from that stupid little paper she published, along with what little money she could pick up working at the school. What the hell has she got that anybody would murder her for? And that is what you're implying, isn't it?"

"I don't know what I'm implying."

Butch put his hand on his forehead; he rubbed it slowly and then looked at Atticus again. "Okay, what are you thinking?"

"You know yourself that she was desperate to find me. She told Greta she had something important to talk to me about."

"That still doesn't connect her to anything."

"No, but try this; you told me a long time ago that there were rumors of a connection between the island and the underworld."

"First of all, Atticus, the drug thing blows my mind as much as it does yours, but all that other shit I told you is just folklore; no one who lives here really believes that stuff, and besides, what has that got to do with this?"

"Suppose it's true. Inspector Dampit said Baynard and his crew were selling drugs to a syndicate. I think that's rather obvious, but Baynard wasn't smart enough to run anything on his own. Then there's the Pope."

"The Pope?"

"Yes; Pontiff; he's a Nazi hunter, and he's not here just because of Baynard. I think Baynard, and his crew, were the risk takers, only things went afoul last Saturday night. With the plane crash, the money got confiscated, and with the Winter Island raid, so did the drugs. That left someone with a serious problem, and not just Baynard. And who was the guy in the shadows when we went over to Baynard's? He was clearly calling the shots. He wasn't part of the crash and wasn't encountered during the raid. And who is this Raptor character? Maybe they're one and the same. What if he heard about the crash and came to investigate?"

"Okay, just for the sake of argument," Butch went on, "let's say your assumptions are all correct. First of all, that's a problem for the FBI, not you. And second, what does that have to do with Jody Kerfam?"

"The night of the crash, I heard Jody's old truck pull in up on the road; I'd bet a million dollars she ended up nosing around the crash site; what if she found something and this person got wind of it somehow? And while she was trying to get the information to me, they got to her first. Maybe they just staged it to look like a suicide; maybe it's more work by this creep they call the Raptor."

"Atticus, that's all speculation."

"Butch, I've tried every scenario I can think of, but no matter how I play it, the tune always seems to come out the same. There is definitely something going on here on this island that's more than speculation."

Butch shook his head. "You do realize if there's any validity at all to what you say, you're dealing with something that's a hell of a lot bigger than us. And if these people, whoever they are, get wind of your thinking, they're going to zero in on you."

"Maybe they already have; I've been told I'm now a target for the Raptor."

"Atticus, you need to take all of this to the FBI."

"I know. I'm going to try to get hold of Barker."

"What about Pontiff?"

"I've thought of that; he doesn't particularly like me, but he knows a hell of a lot more about all this than I gave him credit for. But before I take it to the FBI, I need a favor."

"Like what?"

"The Cline boys don't much like me either, so I don't think my talking to them would yield much of anything, but they might talk to you."

"About what?"

"They were watching the road the night of the crash; see if you can find out if they encountered anybody interesting, including Jody."

"Hell, Atticus, they might be involved themselves; what makes you think they'd divulge anything to me? Or anyone, for that matter."

"Yes, I know, but they're also stupid. It might make them feel important to throw a few names around; you can handle them. They might be involved, but I doubt their knowledge goes very deep. I doubt they have the slightest idea who's calling the shots, except for maybe Hepper."

"Hepper?"

"Just a thought."

Butch shook his head and took another deep breath. "Okay, I'll try," he said.

"Well, I better get back to school."

"What are you going to tell the kids at school?"

"I don't know. Come on, you need a ride."

"That's right, I do."

"And don't tell anyone we've talked about this," Atticus went on, "not even your wife; I want you to stay as clear of all this as possible; let me be the bad guy if there has to be one."

"I agree, but I also think you need to get out of it too; it's a job for the FBI, not the island cop."

"And by the way," Atticus went on as he walked around to the driver's side of the Bronco, "I really do need a new hat."

"You afraid your brain will get cold?"

"No, I just look better with a hat."

Butch shook his head again.

Atticus stood with his hands folded as they lowered the casket into the ground. There weren't many people at the gravesite. Jody's ex-husband didn't show, so with the exception of the Shernies, who had developed a kinship with her after the loss of their boys, there were very few people to mourn the passing of Jody Kerfam.

"Feels like snow," Frank said to Atticus after it was over and they were walking back to Frank's car.

"Certainly does," Atticus replied as the cold wind swept around him. "I'm hoping it holds off for a little while yet though, at least until I get my boat out of the water."

"Haven't you got that thing out of the water yet?"

"No."

"I thought Pickle was taking care of that for you."

"He is," Atticus replied, "but it takes time to build a crib; besides, like everything else on this island, it just seems to take longer. He's got the mast down and the rigging off, and he plans to lift her out of the water tomorrow, if the weather cooperates. So I'm hoping for the best."

Atticus had come to the funeral with Frank, so when they approached Frank's car, he opened the passenger door and got in. Frank went around and got behind the wheel. "Kind of sad when the only people at your funeral are those asked to be there," Frank said as he put the key in the ignition.

Atticus looked back at the gravesite; the grave crew was already shoveling dirt back into the hole. "Sure is," he replied solemnly.

"Evidently the death of her boy finally got to her."

"Evidently," Atticus replied.

"You sure couldn't tell it by the way she behaved at school," Frank continued. "She always seemed so upbeat." Frank backed out onto the road and headed back toward school. "I guess that just goes to show you," he said, "you can't always tell when a person is contemplating suicide, especially if they're really serious about it."

"I guess not," Atticus replied as other thoughts tumbled through his head. Things had gone just as Atticus expected: there was no autopsy; her body wasn't even sent off the island. Oh, there was a minimal inquiry; the county coroner did talk with the doctor, but that was it; he'd never even bothered to call Atticus.

———————

By the time Atticus left school, it was sleeting hard, with a bitter wind blowing out of the southeast. After arriving home, the first thing he did was build a roaring fire. As he watched it consume the kindling with a loud snapping noise, he unzipped his coat and squatted down in front of the fireplace. He threw a couple of logs on it and then went over to the window facing the lake. Hands in his coat pockets, he looked out across the yard. Dusk was beginning to settle in and the light from the fire flickered warmly in the dark room. The sleet tattered at the glass like hundreds of tiny fingers rapping at the window to come in. Atticus was glad it was only Wednesday; if this were Friday, there would be no boat, and he would not be heading for Madison as planned.

He walked back over to the fireplace and replaced the fire screen. He then went upstairs to shed his work clothes. When that was finished, he went back down into the kitchen and got something to eat. Finally, he lounged back into the softness of the big sofa to soak up the warmth from the fire and listen to the storm rage outside. Relaxed but tired from the day's events, Atticus drifted off.

Startled by the ringing of the phone, he got up, threw another log on the dying fire, and hurried over to answer it. "Mr. Gunner," came the voice from the other end. "This is Pickle. Do you think you could come down here and give me a hand? This storm has stirred up a good chop out on the channel, and I'm afraid it's going to give your boat a pounding if we don't move 'er. Matter of fact, I think you better find someone to come with you; it'll take more than the two of us to handle her."

"Absolutely," Atticus replied. "I'll be down there as soon as I can."

"Yeah, I think you better."

Atticus hung up the receiver for a second and then picked it up and dialed. It rang. "Hello?" came a woman's voice.

"Karen, this is Atticus. Is Butch home?"

"Sure, Atticus; just a minute." She turned away from the receiver. "Butch! Telephone!" she shouted. "He's in the bathroom," she said, turning her attention back to Atticus. "Boy, isn't this some weather?"

"Yes ma'am, it sure is," Atticus replied. Finally, he heard Butch's voice approach in the background. Karen announced it was Atticus and handed the phone to her husband.

"Gunner?" came his voice in his usual rough manner. "If you're about to tell me you're without power, I really don't give a shit, especially tonight!"

"The power's fine," Atticus replied, "but I do need your help."

"Of course you do; why else would you call me on a night like this?"

"Because I miss your sweet voice," Atticus replied jokingly.

"Yeah, right."

"No, Pickle just called; I've got to go down and help move my boat. We need one more person, and you're the only one I can think of that's dumb enough to go out on a night like this; how about it?"

"He hasn't got her out of the water yet?"

"No."

"Well, if she's still sitting where she was, I'd say we better get moving. I'll meet you down at his dock."

"Thanks," Atticus replied, and then he hung up the receiver.

When Atticus arrived, Butch and Pickle were already down by the boat. He pulled into the yard behind Butch's wagon. The big yard light hanging overhead flooded the area with a dull whiteness as it swung wildly in the wind. Atticus hurried toward the dock. The sleet hissed like sand as it pelted everything in its path. The *Moonhawk* was dancing like a restless stallion in the rough chop as Atticus approached. Every once in a while, she'd yank at her moorings and then prance sideways, slamming into the wooden enclosures of her concrete stall.

"Atticus!" Butch hollered. "Climb on board and keep her away from the dock! Pickle and I will take the lines and try to guide her around to the lee side!"

Without hesitation, Atticus jumped on board. The deck was slippery and wet. Hanging onto an icy stanchion, he managed to kneel down and fend off the dock with his left foot. The sleet burned as it bit into his hands and face. With the mast and rigging gone, not only was there little to hang onto, but the sloop looked naked and helpless in its chaotic surroundings. With Pickle holding the stern line and Butch at the bow, they managed to guide the boat back out of the slip. Once free, the *Moonhawk* swept past the end of the dock quickly. Ducking under the passing stern line, Atticus managed to undo the line from the ice-covered portside cleat and transfer it to the starboard before it became taught again. Finally, the two men, pulling as hard as they could, managed to slowly walk her back in along the lee side of the dock. Once there, they restored the lines. The *Moonhawk* was still being battered by spray and sleet, but she was rested in a more gracious manner. Frozen to the bone, Atticus breathed a deep sigh of relief.

"Well," Pickle barked, turning his back to the wind, "that should do her, boys; the weather willing, I'll lift her out tomorrow! But for now, I'm headed for the house! If you wish to come in and set a spell, you're welcome!"

Atticus put his hands inside his coat pockets in a feeble attempt to warm them. "Thanks for the invite," he said, "but if you don't mind, I'd like to check things out below deck to make sure she's ready for winter, then I'm heading for home; it's been a long day!"

"Suit yourself," Pickle replied. "Butch?"

"I'm going to do the same; thanks anyway!"

Atticus fumbled with the lock as Pickle headed for the house. "Come below and get out of the wind!" Atticus barked to Butch as he slid open the hatch.

Butch climbed on board and followed Atticus below, closing the hatch behind them. The wind hissed as the frozen rain pelted the exterior of the cabin. "Man, she's a bitter one out there," Butch said, stepping down off the companionway ladder. He started rubbing his hands together. "My fingers are completely numb."

Atticus took out his flashlight and began shining it around. Butch stood looking out the cabin window and listening to the hail tatter on the deck above. "I'd sure as hell hate to be out on the lake tonight," he said, still rubbing his hands.

Atticus didn't reply; instead, he stuck his head inside the cabinet under the sink.

"Ya know," Butch went on, still staring out the window, "it was a night just like this exactly one year ago that the *Edmund Fitzgerald* went down; one year exactly. You wouldn't think any kind of a storm could put down a boat damn near a thousand feet long, would ya? How does that song go? 'One wonders where the love of God goes when the witch of November comes stealing'?"

Satisfied the water tank had been properly drained, Atticus backed out of the cabinet.

"I remember talking to Quint that night," Butch continued softly. "He told me there would be trouble on the lakes that night." Atticus looked up at Butch as he talked. "Quint had a way of knowing things like that," Butch went on. "It was in his blood." Then Butch turned away from the window and sat down on the quarter berth. "That's all in the past now."

"I'm afraid so," Atticus replied. Then after pausing for a long moment, he spoke again. "You haven't had a chance to talk to either of the Cline boys yet, have you?"

Butch looked back at Atticus. "Yes, I talked to Tom just before I went home for supper."

"And what did he have to say?"

"Well, he and his brother didn't see a single stranger that night, but they did see Jody Kerfam. They also saw Doebuck's big black Cadillac; they couldn't see who was in the car, but they're sure it was his car."

"Really?"

"That was my reaction. Atticus, you haven't contacted Agent Barker yet, have you?"

"No, not yet," Atticus replied, "I intend to call him tomorrow. I thought maybe I'd try to arrange a meeting while I was in Madison this weekend." Atticus paused for a moment and then went on. "Butch, isn't it a little unusual for Doebuck to be up here this time of year?"

"You just can't leave it alone, can you?"

"Just curious."

"Well, his wife never comes up this time of year, but the old man does quite often. He uses his place to entertain business clients; as a matter of fact, he's up here right now with some gray flannel suit types. But I thought we talked about that before."

Suddenly, their conversation was interrupted by the sound of Pickle's voice. "Butch!" he was shouting from the yard. "Butch!"

"What?" Butch yelled back as he stuck his head out of the hatch.

"I just received a fire call; you have to go!"

"Shit!" Butch replied. "Leave it to someone to overload their stove on the first cold miserable night."

"Don't tell me you're on the fire department too?" Atticus asked.

"I'm on everything," Butch said as he went up the steps and out into the cockpit. "Where is it?" he shouted to Pickle.

"Over at the old Kerfam place! Sounds like the house is full ablaze!"

Butch looked back at Atticus; they both stared at one another for a moment, then without saying a word, Butch took off toward his car. Atticus locked up the boat and hurried over to the Bronco to follow.

———•◆•———

The road was dark and deserted as Atticus drove across the island. The glow from the fire was visible in the dark sky well before he was halfway to the site. He pulled off to the side of the road in front of the old farm and turned on his flashing lights. The island's only fire truck was up in the yard, pumping streams of water from two separate hoses into the house. It was totally engulfed in flames, which were fiercely fanned by the heavy wind. There was little left that was recognizable; it was a roaring inferno.

Atticus got out of the Bronco, pulled his collar up, and walked up into the yard. In spite of the wind, the heat from the fire felt hot against his face. There were two men at the end of each hose and one at the truck; six or seven others were just standing around, watching. There was little they could do; there was little anyone could do.

Butch spotted Atticus; he left the others and walked over to him. "How's that for a fire?" he asked as he approached.

"You sure won't have to worry about water damage," Atticus replied.

"No, there won't be much left but a hole in the ground by the time it's over."

"Any idea how it started?"

Butch shook his head. "I suppose it could have been an electrical short," he replied. "The power to the house hadn't been shut off yet. But by the time it's out, there won't be enough left to tell for sure, so I doubt we'll ever know."

"No surprise about that."

"Atticus, I know what the hell you're thinking; damn, you're suspicious about everything. There isn't one thing here to indicate that someone started this on purpose; it's just a coincidence."

"Right."

"She's already dead! Why in the hell would anyone burn her house down now? That doesn't make sense."

"Unless they didn't find what they were after and wanted to make sure no one else did either."

Butch shook his head. "I better get back over there," he said. "You going to stick around?"

"It doesn't look as though there is much I can do here; I think I'll head for home. Let me know if you find anything, okay?"

"Sure—I'll see you later." Butch started back toward the fire truck.

"Hey!"

Butch stopped and looked back at Atticus.

"Thanks for the help tonight."

Butch shrugged. "That's what friends are for."

Atticus smiled, gave him a thumbs-up, and then started toward the Bronco. As he came to the end of the drive and was walking along the edge of the blacktop, he pulled the car keys from his pocket and accidentally dropped them to the ground. When he bent down to pick them up, in the brightness of the flashing lights from the Bronco, he noticed a matchbook lying along the edge of the blacktop. He glanced at it for only a second and then picked it up; it was wet and soggy. The cover was blank. There was just one match missing, and on the inside of the cover, a WATS number written in pencil. There was nothing about it that really jumped out at Atticus until he looked back up at the fire. Maybe it was just his desperation bubbling to the surface; after all, finding something of significance, the way he'd just found this matchbook, was more than a little unbelievable, but nonetheless, just like one has that feeling of déjà vu once in a rare while, a strong sense of discovery flooded over Atticus and would not let go; he stuffed the matchbook into his coat pocket.

CHAPTER 17

The Order of Raptors

It was a frosty Friday morning as Atticus leaned back in the seat with both hands on the steering wheel. He was glad to be taking the morning boat; he needed desperately to get away for a while, not just because of all that had happened, or because he had arranged a meeting with Agent Barker, or even because he was headed for Madison to see Laura and the girls, but because the isolation that came with winter habitation on the island was getting to him.

He glanced at his watch; it was 10:15. It would be 12:30 by the time he reached Green Bay, and that would put him in good shape for his one o'clock meeting with the inspector. Good shape, that is, with everything except the meeting itself; Atticus still had no idea of how to proceed. Somehow the idea of simply turning information over to Barker didn't wash very well, especially after the way he was treated the last time they'd met. He felt compelled to take part in the continuing investigation. Beyond the fact that he had signed a secret contract to do just that, he had now become intellectually entangled, and the fire that once burned deep within him had been rekindled.

Atticus was a small boy when the Second World War took place, but during his stretch in the military, he couldn't escape the horrible crimes against humanity that were committed because of it. And even though many people seem to accept what had happened, Atticus did not. Not only does the world continually repeat the atrocities of the past, but there is a strong tendency to do it with the same greed and ignorance of those who went before us.

Excluding the horrible roles played by Mussolini, Stalin, and others, it was Hitler by most accounts who was considered a true megalomaniac. It is frightening to realize that in a period of twelve short years (1933 to 1945), such an individual could rise to a state of total power whereby he managed to destroy his entire nation, to say nothing of the horrors he brought down upon the rest of the world.

It is equally frightening to know that only three out of every ten people in Germany survived Hitler's wrath. There's no question that the preexisting conditions that followed the First World War did much to precipitate what happened in Germany prior to the Second World War. But nonetheless, what started out as the National Socialist German Workers' Party rapidly evolved into the totalitarian state of the Third Reich under the control of Adolf Hitler; a government that not only took over absolute control of all aspects of their society, but brought into existence a social order that promoted persecution, torture, and death of anyone considered unacceptable by the self-proclaimed elite. One could say that such a condition was brought about by the existence of an untethered evil state, but it was the people by the thousands who enthusiastically pledged total obedience to the Führer; it was the people who blindly relinquished all their rights one by one until they had no rights; and it was the people who did it in a frenzy of self-righteous greed and enthusiastic participation.

It disturbed Atticus deeply to discover that after the war, literally thousands of Nazi activists escaped Germany without answering for their crimes, and many did it with the support and cooperation of the Odessa, a secret organization run by the very people who supposedly stood up against such atrocities; the Catholic church being one of them. It was in this light that Atticus had participated as a Nazi hunter. He helped to research and find disappeared Nazis, only to learn that not only had most been secretly dispersed throughout the world, including into the United States, but many of those who were helped not only felt absolutely no remorse for what they had done, but still proclaimed Nazism as their true calling.

———⟡———

When Atticus opened the door to the inner office and stepped in, Agent Barker stood up. "Atticus," he said, stepping forward and extending his hand. "How are you?"

"Just fine," Atticus replied.

"You're right on time."

"I'm always on time."

"Yes—well, you remember Damon Pontiff, I'm sure," he continued, gesturing toward Pontiff, who was leaning on the far windowsill, his back toward Atticus.

"Yes, I remember Pontiff," Atticus replied. "It's only been a week."

"So it has. With the death of Inspector Dampit and everything, I guess it just seems longer. Sit down."

"Yes, I'm sure it does," Atticus said as he pulled out a chair and sat down. "I also know we're all busy, so I'll get right to the point."

"Please do," Matt replied, sitting back down across the table from him.

"Mr. Pontiff and I are here for the same reasons. Oh, there may be a different twist in our approach to the issues, but the bottom line is the same, and we both know what that is."

Pontiff turned around and looked at Atticus, but he still said nothing.

"We're both Nazi hunters," Atticus went on. "I may not have the same deep personal convictions for the hunt that you have, Mr. Pontiff. And I certainly don't have the wealth of experience you have, but I do have some valuable assets to bring to the table; assets without which neither of us are likely to reach our goals."

"Well, I'll give you one thing, Gunner," Pontiff said, "you sure as hell got guts. But you never did answer my question, Gunner; why do you hunt Nazis?"

"I signed a contract."

"In other words, a bounty hunter."

"Let's just say they made me an offer I couldn't refuse."

"Who you working for?"

"I can't tell you that," Atticus replied.

"Why would I want to work with you?"

"Because I have information you don't, and I know you have information I don't. If we put our heads together, we might just be able to make some real progress. On top of that, I'm on the inside; you're not."

Pontiff walked over to the table and sat down. He looked at Atticus for the longest time, and then he spoke. "What kind of information?"

"For starters, I've been targeted by a Raptor."

Again Pontiff looked at Atticus for some time. "You know what a Raptor is?" he asked.

"I have an idea," Atticus said.

472

"A Raptor is a specially trained Nazi assassin. As far as we know, there are only six or seven of them in the world." Pontiff paused. "What else do you know?"

Atticus shook his head. "This isn't tit for tat, Pope. We either work together, or we don't work at all."

"I call the shots," Pontiff said. "And what I say is nonnegotiable."

"No," Atticus replied. "There are extenuating circumstances; I will not implement anything that will jeopardize the school or my family. You feed me information and I'll call the shots. In return, I'll see that you're kept abreast of everything as well as be in on the kill."

"Not a chance."

"All right," Atticus said. "Suit yourself." He rose to his feet.

"Wait a minute," Pontiff said. "Sit down."

Atticus sat back down.

"Who told you that you were the target of a Raptor?"

"Baynard; just before he died. He also told me a Raptor was responsible for the death of Quint Jebson and the three boys with him."

Again Pontiff sat quietly for a minute or two, and then he spoke again. "Like I said, a Raptor is a highly trained secret assassin, but he is more than that; he is a male of German heritage, well educated, a lawyer or engineer, speaks at least two languages, highly trained in the Gestapo-styled art of killing, and above all, a true believer in the reaffirmation of the Nazi party. In short, Gunner, if a Raptor is after you, you're probably a dead man walking."

Atticus made no response.

"They work alone," Pontiff went on, "but they are not self-directed; they work under the direct orders of an organization called the Order, sometimes referred to as the Order of Raptors. The organization is headed by a former Nazi SS colonel who escaped from Germany in

1945. I've been tracking him for thirty-one years. His name is Munster Engullia, also known as the Scorpion. He made it to Colombia, changed his name, and disappeared. Rumor is he's in the United States now."

"If he was a colonel in 1945, that would put him well into his sixties by now," Atticus replied. "What makes you think he's still active?"

"We know he is," Pontiff replied. "About a year ago, we managed to infiltrate the Swiss banking system. A large sum of money came in from Afghanistan. Some of that money was deposited into a known Raptor's family account. The rest went to Panama, so we tracked it. It bounced around the world through several corporations to launder it, and although we lost track of the specific cash, we did manage to establish the related corporate fund transfer channels, and some of it ended up right here in the Midwest. Where the Order's money was skimmed off, we don't know, but we do think we're getting close to the source."

"That doesn't mean it's the same person," Barker added.

"Like I said, I've been tracking this man for over thirty years; I know how he operates; I know how he thinks; it's the same man."

"Do you have a name?" Atticus asked.

"No, not yet," Pontiff replied, "but after the island bust, I think he's close; maybe even on Washington Island."

Atticus thought of Munster Doebuck immediately but said nothing. "Let's go back to the Raptor thing," he continued. "If I'm being targeted, why hasn't he hit me? Or better yet, my family? That would certainly get rid of me as a threat."

"That's an excellent question, Gunner," Pontiff replied. "As a matter of fact, I've asked myself that same question. If our boy is indeed on the island, I'm sure you're a thorn in his side. I'm thinking you're too close to home base, and the Scorpion is afraid of the attention taking you out might bring. After all, keeping his identity from being discovered would be of paramount importance to him, even above getting rid of you; especially now."

"Why especially now?" Barker asked.

"The Order is probably a go-between," Atticus replied as though the question was directed toward him, "and they've just blown it on both ends; that puts them in a precarious position. Am I correct, Pope?"

"Very good, Gunner."

"But that kind of danger hasn't seemed to bother the Raptor before now," Atticus continued. "He risked everything taking out Quint Jebson and three boys. Why would he care now?"

"An active Raptor works under the direction of a taskmaster. He never comes into direct contact with the Scorpion; he doesn't even know who the Scorpion is. In other words, the taskmaster probably wasn't present at the onset, and as a result, the Raptor had no way of knowing he was making a miscalculation."

"Is there a code name for the taskmaster?" Barker asked.

"He's called the Broker," Pontiff replied.

"Do you know who he is?" Atticus asked.

"We're getting close," Pontiff said.

"What do you think is going to happen now?" Atticus asked.

Pontiff leaned back in his chair. "Oh, they're going to do their best to get rid of you, Gunner. First, they'll do everything they can to get you fired; if that doesn't work, the Scorpion will eventually turn the Raptor loose to finish the job."

"I want my family and my lady protected around the clock," Atticus said, looking straight at Barker, "and not with the same half-assed approach your people pulled with that Emil character."

"It's already been done," Matt replied. "But what about the school?"

"Hurting more kids in that school would really bring the wrath of God down on them. That would really be stupid, and stupid is one thing they're not," Pontiff replied.

"One more thing, Pope," Atticus continued. "I can tell by the way you talk you've got somebody other than me feeding you information from the island; who is it?"

"Just like you, there are some things I can't tell you," he replied. "But I can tell you this; they have a code name for you out there; you're called the Moonhawker."

"Yes, I know," Atticus replied.

"You sure you don't want me calling the shots?" Pontiff said. "You're like a sitting duck, you know."

Atticus stood up. "No," he replied. "Not this time."

"Mind if I ask what your plan is?" Pontiff asked.

"For now, I simply intend to keep the pressure on until something breaks. If I were to make an educated guess, I would agree with you, Pope; they're going to come at me with a full-on political press, and everything else will be kept at low profile, at least for now."

"I'd also suggest you do a real good job at watching your back, Gunner," Pontiff replied.

"I always do," Atticus said as he walked toward the door. But just before he stepped out, he stopped and looked at Barker. "Now that Dampit is gone, who's going to be the new top dog here?"

Barker shrugged. "I'm sure you'll hear as soon as I do."

Atticus walked out without any further comment.

It was early evening by the time Atticus drove into the parking lot at Laura's place. The air was cold, and it was spitting snow. He got out of his car and hurried up the walk toward her building with his overnight bag in hand. He went straight up to her apartment. When he arrived, there was a note taped to the door: "Atticus, let yourself in. Love, Laura."

He unlocked the door, went inside, and threw his bag over on the couch. On the table was a second note: "Sorry," it said, "I had to work tonight. Big project and the deadline is Monday. I couldn't get out of it; should be home by 8:30. Hope you're not too upset. Food is in fridge, help yourself. See you in a bit. I love you, Laura."

As he was walking over to the refrigerator, the phone rang; he went over and picked it up. "Hello?"

"Atticus?" came Laura's voice from the other end of the line. "I'm sorry," she said. "I really couldn't get out of work tonight. You going to be all right?"

"I'll survive," he replied. "How long before you can leave?"

"It might be as late as nine o'clock. Why don't you give the kids a call?"

"They won't be around until tomorrow."

"I guess you'll have to watch TV then."

"Thanks," Atticus replied, "but I think I'll save that for the island. Maybe I'll go find a fast-food joint and fill up on some good ol' greasy hamburgers and fries."

Laura laughed.

"I've also got some friends I might call. I haven't seen them since I took the job on the island."

"Good; then I won't feel so bad. I'll see you around nine, okay?"

Atticus smiled. "I'll be fine."

"Oops, I got to go," she said. "I love you. I'll see you; bye."

Atticus hung up the receiver.

As he started for the door, he felt something in his coat pocket. He reached in and pulled it out; it was the matchbook he'd found at the Kerfam farm. With everything else going on, he'd almost forgotten about it. He looked at it a second and then walked back over to Laura's phone and dialed the WATS number. The receiver clicked; there was a long pause, and then it rang. "Wholesale Import/Export," came a woman's voice. "My name is Cathy; may I help you?"

"Ah—yes," Atticus replied. "My name is Bill Green, and I represent the Minnesota Glass Company. Our firm is interested in setting up an international outlet for our products, and a friend gave me this number to call."

"Mr. Green, this is just an answering service. You'll have to talk to one of their consultants, and I'm afraid there is no one available at this time of night."

"I see," Atticus replied. "I guess I'm really operating in the dark. I wonder, could you tell me where the firm is located?"

"The main office is here in Chicago, but they have six other branch offices. Where are you calling from?"

"Milwaukee."

"In that case, the Chicago office is certainly the closest; would you like for me to arrange for one of the consultants to contact you?"

"Thank you, I'll just call back another time."

"I'd be happy to arrange that appointment."

"No, that's okay; I'll call back later. Thank you." Atticus hung up the receiver.

Atticus wrote the name of the company under the WATS number and stuffed the matchbook back in his pocket.

A little before nine, Atticus arrived back at Laura's apartment building; she was just pulling into her parking place. He tapped on the horn and pulled into the vacant space next to her. They both got out; Laura hurried to him, and they kissed.

"Let me look at you," she said, beaming up at him. "Yep; you're just as handsome as I remember."

"I should stay away more often," he replied, smiling.

Laura grinned and then gave him another peck on the lips. "Tell me," she said, "what did you do without me tonight?"

"Well, I had two hamburgers and some fries, and went over to Bob and Grace Thrison's for a visit."

"Isn't he the principal at West High?"

"That's right."

"Were they glad to see you?"

"Yes; as a matter of fact, they're throwing a party tomorrow night, and insisted I come."

"Well, I hope you told them you had other plans."

"They also insisted I bring you along; do you mind?"

"Atticus, do we have to? We have so little time together as it is."

"I'm sorry," he said. "They wouldn't take no for an answer." He tapped her on the nose with his finger. "We'll just stay for a short time."

At noon Saturday, they picked up the girls, spent the afternoon at the mall shopping, had supper out, and took in an early movie. At about nine o'clock, they dropped Stacie off at a friend's house where she was spending the night, and then proceeded to take Inger home.

Inger, who was sitting in the front seat between Laura and her father, looked up at her dad as he pulled up in front of her house. "I don't suppose Mom would let me stay out any later, huh?"

Atticus looked down at her and shook his head. "No, I don't suppose," he replied.

Inger nodded. "Well . . ."

"Kind of a short visit, wasn't it?" Atticus said.

Inger nodded again. "When will you be going up to the island?" she asked Laura.

Laura glanced at Atticus and then back down at Inger. "I'm hoping for Christmas," she said, "and if your dad can work it out with your mother, maybe you and Stacie can come up for part of that time."

Inger looked down. "That's a long time away," she replied.

"I know," Atticus said, "but with school and everything, the time will go by quickly. Besides, I'll be down a couple more times before then."

"I know," Inger replied. "It's just that it's so boring here; nothing ever seems to happen here like it does up there."

"What in the world do you mean by that?" Atticus asked.

"I mean like finding dead people."

"Doing what?" Laura replied.

Inger realized she had inadvertently raised a topic that had not yet been discussed. "Oops," she mumbled, glancing first up at Laura and then at her dad.

"Is there something going on that I don't know about?" Laura continued, looking at Atticus.

"Just a minute," Atticus said. "Inger, where did you hear that?"

"Stacie said I wasn't supposed to tell."

"Tell what?" Atticus asked.

"Tell about the letter she got from Joni."

"I see, and what exactly did Joni say?"

"She said you found Nathan Kerfam's mother hanging in her basement."

"Is that true?" Laura asked Atticus.

"Yes, it's true," Atticus replied, glancing over at Laura. He then turned his attention back to Inger. "Did she also write that it was a suicide?"

Inger nodded.

Laura continued to look at Atticus.

"I was going to tell you," he said, "but I haven't had a chance."

Inspite of the awkwardness of the moment, Inger simply couldn't contain her curiosity. "What did she look like?" she asked, looking up at her dad again.

"Never mind what she looked like," Atticus replied. "I hardly think that's an appropriate topic for discussion. Come on, I'll walk you to the door." Atticus opened the door and got out.

Inger scooted out behind him. "I just wanted to know," she said, looking back at Laura.

Laura couldn't help but smile. She winked. "I'll see you," she said.

"Yeah," Inger replied, "maybe in a couple of weeks." Then she scurried off. "You mad at me?" she asked her father as they walked toward the house.

"No, I'm not mad," he replied.

"I didn't know you hadn't told Laura."

"Well, I certainly won't have to worry about that now, will I?"

"Do you suppose she was so sad about Nathan," Inger went on as they approached the front steps, "that she decided to end her own life?"

Atticus looked down at her and shook his head, and then he smiled. "That's possible," he replied. "We'll talk more about it when I call this week, okay?"

Inger went up the steps; when she was level with her dad, she turned toward him again. "Okay," she replied, "but I don't know why we can't talk about it now."

"You have to go; that's why. Now give me a hug."

Inger complied. When she was done, she looked her dad in the eye. "I'm sorry," she said.

Atticus smiled. "Ya know something," he said, "some day I hope you have a little girl just like yourself, and I hope I'm still around to witness it."

Inger frowned.

"You'll know what I mean then," he went on. "Good-bye; I'll call Friday." He winked, and then he turned and walked away.

Inger stood there and watched her father walk toward the car; finally she turned and scurried inside.

———— ·•◆•· ————

As Atticus drove north on University Avenue, Laura continued to pursue the issue of Jody Kerfam's death. He filled in all the official details, but said nothing about his real thoughts on the matter, or the meeting with Barker.

When they finally reached the Thrisons', there was a large number of cars parked along the street in front of the house. Atticus pulled into the first empty spot. When they got to the front door, Atticus rang the bell; the door opened. "Hello Grace," Atticus said.

"Atticus Gunner, come in," she said. "I told Bob you would come—and this must be Laura."

"Yes, it is," Atticus replied. "Laura, this is Grace Thrison."

Laura smiled at her and said, "How do you do?"

Grace stepped aside and motioned them in. "Bob's in the other room," she said. "He'll be happy to see both of you, I'm sure."

Grace was taking their coats just as Bob came from the living room on his way to the kitchen. Spotting Atticus in the entranceway, he stopped immediately. "Well, I'll be damned," he said, approaching them. "I was wrong, Gunner; I told Grace you'd never show tonight. Come on in."

"I told you I would," Atticus replied.

"Yeah, but you've told me lots of things." Then he looked at Laura. "He's so damned independent—I've learned not to take him too seriously about anything."

"Tell me about it," Laura replied.

Bob smiled. "So you're Laura."

"I'm afraid so," she answered.

"Well, it appears as though he at least has good taste in women. Come on; let me introduce you to some real people." He put his arm around her shoulder and started leading her toward the living room.

Laura glanced back at Atticus. Atticus just grinned and shrugged.

"Bob, now behave yourself," Grace said. "If he embarrasses you, Laura, just tell him to buzz off."

"Don't pay any attention to her," Bob countered. "She always sticks up for Atticus—come on," he said, coaxing her along.

Grace took Atticus by the arm. "She's very pretty," she said to Atticus as they walked into the living room behind them. "You watch out for her, and don't let him embarrass her."

Atticus smiled. "Don't worry," he replied, "she's very capable of holding her own."

"I hope so," Grace said. "I'll put your coats in the bedroom." Then she walked away.

The room was practically wall-to-wall with people; some sitting, some standing, but most were people Atticus had never seen before. They were all busy talking and laughing. As Bob took Laura through the crowd, it was obvious by the passing comments that many of them were teachers from Bob's school.

Bob introduced Laura to four men standing over by the fireplace. Then he turned partially toward Atticus as he approached. "And if you can believe it," he said, motioning toward Atticus, "this beautiful creature is with that character." The men laughed; Laura smiled but glanced at Atticus to let him know she was a bit uncomfortable.

"Come over here, Gunner," Bob continued. "I've got some people I want you to meet. This is Randy Pulmer," he said, motioning toward a big man standing in front of the fireplace. "He's the guy that took your job." Then he went on to introduce the others. Finally, he came back to Atticus. "Atticus here is quite a celebrity; he's the guy I was telling you about. He's the full-time school administrator and full-time constable out on Washington Island. And as Randy mentioned a short time ago, he's the one who told the press to buzz off when they tried to interview him."

In the meantime, Grace returned and politely nudged Laura. "Come on," she whispered, "they're going to be chewing on that for at least an hour." She grabbed Laura by the arm and withdrew her from the group.

Atticus immediately found himself answering questions about the drug bust and what it was like to live on an island. His responses were very brief, because not only did he not care to talk about it with these people, but he was beginning to wish they hadn't come at all.

As the conversation dragged on, Bob glanced behind Atticus, smiled, and gave a mischievous nod. Atticus turned to see what he was up to. Standing directly behind him was a tall, lanky man in his midfifties; he had horn-rimmed glasses and was wearing a grin from ear to ear.

"I'll be darned!" Atticus exclaimed, ignoring the others who were still blabbing on. "How are you, Professor?" he asked, taking the man's hand and shaking it warmly.

"I'm still hanging in there," he replied. "We miss you on the courts though."

The tall man was Cliff Danti, an economics professor at the university. His specialty was the military/industrial complex and its impact on the rise of terrorism throughout the world. He'd written several books on the topic, including a recent one that analyzed the self-published *Turner Diaries*, which is a how-to book based on a formulated six-step program to bring about the rise of a new Nazism in America.

Atticus not only had had him as a professor in graduate school, he also knew him personally through his handball exploits with Bob Thrison. He and Atticus had gotten into a heavy discussion about the Vietnam War one day after a doubles match. Ever since then, the professor had taken a special liking to Atticus and often went out of his way to engage him in conversation.

"It's good to see you," Atticus replied.

"I see you're managing to stay involved in world affairs," the professor went on. "I was following the news about Washington Island, and darned if your name didn't pop up."

"That's because the island is a small place," Atticus replied.

"Maybe it's not as small as you think," the professor said. "The author of *The Turner Diaries,* William Pierce, is holed up on an island just off the coast of Seattle. There are drug issues there too, and believe it or not, he's also in conflict with the FBI. The interesting twist is that he's also a Nazi and committed to the reaffirmation of the Nazi party in this country. Care to tell me what's going on up there on that island of yours?"

Atticus smiled but didn't respond.

"I know you well enough, Atticus Gunner, to know you didn't go up to Washington Island just to feed the seagulls. Damon Pontiff got hold of me today, and I have a very strong suspicion you know who he is. At any rate he's very interested in you Atticus. And just so you know, I also know he's a Nazi hunter and wouldn't be interested if it didn't have something to do with Nazis. We need to talk." He nodded for Atticus to follow as he worked his way back into the empty dining room. He sat down at the table and motioned for Atticus to sit. Atticus sat down at the table across from him. "All right, my friend," the professor continued. "Talk to me; what's going on?"

Atticus smiled at the man again. "All right," he said, "for starters, have you ever heard of a company called Wholesale Import/Export?"

"No, I haven't," he replied, "why?"

"I'm looking for some answers, and they might be able to provide them."

"You're looking to make some connections between Washington Island and what?"

"Nazism; the drug trade; illegal arms trade; all of the above."

"Who are you working for, Atticus?"

"I'm the local cop."

"Ya right. Who else you working for?"

"I can't tell you that, sir."

"And you want to know if there is a connection between this company and the answers you're seeking?"

"Yes," Atticus replied. "You know there were drugs involved in the Washington Island bust; that was publicly revealed by the FBI, but what you don't know is there was also some sort of a weapons trade that took place recently; I know there's a connection, but I don't know how to make it, and if I'm going to solve this thing, I need to know."

"Where did you hear about the weapons thing?"

"I can't tell you that either," Atticus replied. "I don't want Pontiff to know that yet."

"You mean you don't trust him?"

"It isn't that I don't trust him; it's just that we don't share the same priorities."

"You mean like the school, your kids, and that young lady you brought with you tonight."

Atticus nodded.

"I understand," the professor responded. "And I would concur; it's important that you keep them as far removed from this as possible. I don't suppose you can tell me where you got the name of this company either."

"For now, let's just say I came on it by accident."

The professor leaned back in his chair. He looked at Atticus again. "I've never heard of the Wholesale Import/Export Company," he said after a long pause, "but that doesn't mean anything. Front shops, by design, have a way of coming and going rather rapidly in the business of the underworld."

"Is there any way you can dig into it, to see if there's anything, even a suspicion?"

"Where is this company located?"

"Chicago."

"You seem to be putting a lot of emphasis on that company for just coming on it by accident."

"Yes, I know," Atticus replied.

The professor continued to look at Atticus for what seemed an eternity. Finally he took a deep breath. "All right," he said, "I'll do some digging. You'll have to give me a week or so."

"That's not a problem."

"I suspect you'll be easy enough to find; I'll give you a call when I have something."

"Thank you," Atticus said as he stood up. He started to walk away.

"Atticus!" the professor called out.

Atticus stopped and turned around.

"What should I tell Pontiff about you?"

Atticus smiled. "The truth."

"And what is the truth?"

"Whatever you believe it to be," Atticus replied. He smiled at the professor again and then walked away.

CHAPTER 18

The Professor and the Pope

It was only 5:10 in the afternoon but it was already getting dark. Atticus leaned back in his desk chair and stretched his arms. The island was experiencing its first real snowfall of the season. He gazed silently out the office window and watched the snow as it blew off the roof and swirled down past the window. The school was quiet; the kids and teachers were gone. Turning his attention back to the array of papers on his desk, he tilted his chair forward and returned to his work.

"Hey Atticus," Frank said, popping his head in the open hall door, "you going to stay here all night?"

Atticus looked up at Frank, standing in the doorway with his coat and boots on. "No, I'm about ready to wrap it up," he replied. "What are you doing here? I thought you left with the others a long time ago."

"I had some papers to finish correcting, and I thought I'd take advantage of the quiet to get them done."

"Same here," Atticus replied. "These damn state reports are about two weeks overdue; if I don't get them done soon, they'll be sending the state auditor up after me."

"You headed for Madison this weekend?"

"No, I'm afraid I'm going to have to work on these; how about yourself?"

"Well, if the weather cooperates, which seems very unlikely right now, I thought I'd head down to Green Bay for the weekend. I doubt I'll be able to scam a Packers ticket, but I can always sit in some bar and watch the game on one of those new big-screen TVs. Why don't you forget those damn reports and come with me?"

"Thanks, but no thanks," Atticus said.

Frank smiled. "That's okay, I'm sure if you were going off-island, you'd be headed for Madison anyway. Well, at any rate," he went on, "I don't think I'd stay here much longer if I were you. I was just outside and swept off my car; we got about a foot of snow out there already. If the wind picks up and she starts drifting, you might not get home, even with the Bronco."

"I'll keep that in mind," Atticus replied. Just then the phone rang; Atticus picked it up. "School; Mr. Gunner speaking."

"I'll see ya later," Frank whispered loudly.

Atticus waved him off as the voice on the other end spoke. "Atticus? This is Professor Danti."

"Well, how are you doing, sir?" Atticus replied.

"Just fine—I got your information."

"Excellent," Atticus said. "I really didn't expect to hear from you until next week. What did you find?"

"Well, it seems your hunch may have been worth something."

Atticus leaned forward in his chair a bit.

"For starters, Wholesale Import/Export isn't listed in the D&B. For a business with four branch offices, that's very unusual. From what I could track down, they seem to be connected to a group of unrelated retail stores: import novelty shops, things like that, and a couple of larger US firms. So there really wasn't anything substantial there, but when we started looking overseas, it got interesting. Now I want you to understand, this is not cast in concrete, but they do a substantial amount of business with a South Africa–based firm called Blue Water Inc., a registered arms broker."

"Registered? What do you mean?"

"That means legitimate. But what's interesting is Blue Water almost lost its South African home about a year ago when an unrelated investigation turned up their name as a black market arms trader. Nothing ever came of it, however; speculation is that they bought their way out of their predicament. But looking at the investigation records, it seems they were accused of selling black market arms to a young radical organization in Afghanistan called Al Qaeda."

"Any documented US connections?"

"Only the ones I mentioned. We didn't have time to check out all of them, Atticus, but those we did seem to be legitimate."

"So where does that leave us?"

"With two things: one, this company you gave me is too big not to be listed in the D&B, and second, the fact that they're connected to Blue Water leads me to speculate something is fishy."

"Who were the two American firms?"

"The Z&B International Shipping conglomerate and Up Star Corp."

"Bull's-eye!" Atticus replied.

"What do you mean?"

"You just made the connection. Tell me, Professor, did you give this information to Pontiff?"

"Yes, this afternoon."

"And what did he say when you told him about my inquiry?"

"Nothing."

"Did you give him the same information you just gave to me?"

"Pretty much, yes."

"And was a Munster Doebuck on that list of 'persons of interest' that Pontiff gave you? You know, the one that had my name on it?"

"Yes, it was."

"Professor, I want to thank you. You can't imagine how much you've helped me. I owe you."

"You don't owe me anything, Atticus; just be careful. If you indeed are on to something, you could very definitely be in harm's way."

"Yes sir, I'm well aware of that."

"Take care."

"I will," Atticus said as the phone clicked on the other end. He hung up the receiver, but as he did a loud *clunk* came from the darkened classroom next to the office. Atticus got up and walked over to the door, reached in, and flicked on the light; Brian was going out the other exit. "Brian!" Atticus barked.

Brian stopped and turned around. "Yeah?" he replied.

"Can I help you with something?"

"Ah, no—I just came in to close a window I left open in the shop, and I saw the light on in your office; I was going to turn it off, but then I heard you in there, so I was just going to leave when I accidentally bumped into a chair."

"Why didn't you turn the lights on instead of stumbling around in the dark?"

"I guess I forgot. I'm sorry if I startled you."

"I'm sure you are. Tell me, isn't that Doc Burnett's old pickup I see sitting outside there?"

"Yes, he's letting me use it until I get my car running again."

"Really? I didn't know you were having car troubles."

"Well, you know how it is with old vehicles."

"Yes, I do, and it's good to have a close friend like that to depend on."

"Yes, it is, especially when I don't have a four-wheel-drive vehicle provided to me like you do."

"That's true, but then you don't have the responsibilities I do either."

"No, you're right there; I wouldn't want your job for anything."

"Well, good night, Brian. Drive carefully out there; I'm sure the roads are a mess, and I wouldn't want to see anything happen to Doc Burnett's pickup."

"Yes sir; good night." Brian exited through the far door, headed down the hall toward the main doors, and out to the parking lot.

———•◆•———

The snow was deep and the roads unplowed, but because it was light and fluffy, Atticus had little problem negotiating his way with the Bronco. Coming to the drive, he turned off the main road and headed down through the woods toward the Hersoff place. Dressed in winter splendor, the trees sparkled like glitter in the reflection of the headlights. Even the sound of the engine was muffled to near silence as Atticus drove through the soft blanket of white. His thoughts turned to Laura and the girls; he wished they were waiting for him here instead of a cold empty house. The only solace was the thought of a warm fire and some food.

Once inside the porch, Atticus stamped off the snow and opened the door. He'd no more than hung his coat up when the phone rang. He picked up the receiver. "Hello?"

"Mr. Gunner?" came the voice from the other end.

"Agent Barker," Atticus replied.

"How did you know it was me?" he asked.

"I recognized your voice," Atticus replied. "Besides, I was expecting you to call."

"Then you've heard."

"From the professor? Yes."

"I've heard Pope called a lot of things, but never Professor," the inspector said.

"What are you talking about?" Atticus asked.

"I'm talking about Pontiff; did he call you?"

"No; why?"

"We've got a new boss and Pontiff just up and walked out."

"What do you mean?"

"I mean the entire case has been turned over to Chief Inspector Willow out of Washington, and Pontiff didn't like it, so he up and walked out; he refuses to work with the man."

"Wait a minute; you're moving way too fast," Atticus replied. "Didn't you talk to Professor Danti?"

"Pope talked to him, but how did you know that?"

Ignoring the inspector's question, Atticus continued, "Then you have no idea what the professor told Pope?"

"That's right, but I still want to know how you know about Professor Danti?"

"That's a long story," Atticus replied.

"That's a long story we want to hear, Atticus. How about if we come up there?"

"Who's we?"

"Paula, the chief inspector, and me."

"No," Atticus replied. "I don't think that's a good idea." He paused for a moment and then continued, "I'll tell you what—if you really have something worth talking about, I could meet the three of you at North Point on Saturday morning."

"We do have something worth talking about; that sounds good."

"If everything is on schedule, the boat will leave here around nine o'clock," Atticus said. "I'll be on that boat; I don't intend to stay overnight, but it usually takes them an hour or so to get their business finished on the other side, so we'll have an hour. Is that agreeable?"

"Agreed. We'll see you on Saturday."

"Saturday morning," Atticus replied, and he hung up the receiver.

That night, the Arctic front that had caused the previous day's snow tracked unexpectedly south out of Canada. The wind switched to the northeast, and by six o'clock Friday morning, not only had the temperature fallen to five degrees below zero, but it began to snow again—hard. This time, along with the snow came the wind: a full winter gale. Visibility dropped to zero and both school and the boat had to be cancelled. By Friday night, the entire island was socked in under deep drifts and an additional eighteen inches of snow.

Atticus's plans to meet with Barker on Saturday had to be cancelled. However, even though Sunday was bitter cold, the boat was able to run and the meeting was rescheduled. It was a dark gray day; cold air drifted in from over the open water, blanketing everything with a heavy freezing fog that clung to the skin with a bone-biting chill and left the island covered with a thick translucent coating of milk ice.

With the defroster running full blast, Atticus drove slowly toward the ferry dock. The snow banks were high, and in spots where the wind had roared through an opening in the trees, the drifts were over five feet high; in these areas, there was little more than a single lane opened by the big island plow. When he arrived at the dock, Atticus parked the Bronco out of the way as much as possible and went on board the waiting ferry. There were no cars, but the mail van and the grocery truck were being loaded. Soon the boarding ramp was lifted, the boat horn blasted through the cold morning air, and the ferry slowly pulled away from the dock.

Atticus stood topside in the back of the boat and out of the cold as much as possible. Standing at the rail, he pulled his collar up and tucked his hands deep into his coat pockets. The dock faded into the mist as the boat churned its way down the channel toward the open lake.

The winter boat was a modified V-bottom, double-deck, sixty-nine-footer. She only carried eight to nine cars on a partially enclosed main deck that loaded off the port side, but because of her large diesel engine, big prop, heavy steel bottom, enclosed car deck, and hull design, she not only was a hefty weather boat for her size, but an excellent icebreaker as well. The *Otterman* was the lifeline to the mainland in the winter. She ran daily whenever possible.

Holding true to early December, the big lake seethed with columns of fog rising from her surface like steam from a cauldron. Atticus went inside the warm passenger cabin. Besides himself and the two-man crew up in the wheelhouse, there was no one on board. He sat quietly by himself staring out the window into the shapeless haze.

When they finally docked at North Point, the outline of the mail truck sitting dockside was all that could be seen under the heavy veil of fog. Then a car came out of the mist and parked up next to the woods; its lights went off.

Zipping up his jacket, Atticus left the cabin and went down to the main deck. The captain and his mate were securing the boarding ramp. Atticus jumped off the boat. "Don't forget, Mr. Gunner," the captain barked. "We'll blow the horn when we're ready to go!" Atticus waved his acknowledgment as he trudged through the snow up toward the waiting car.

As he approached, both Barker and Smith got out to greet him. They opened the rear door and motioned Atticus into the back seat. As Atticus crawled in, a black man in his midfifties, sitting on the opposite side of the rear seat, smiled at him. Atticus smiled back but said nothing. Barker got back in behind the steering wheel, and Paula returned to the front passenger side; once secure, they both turned partially toward Atticus. "How was the trip over?" Barker asked.

"Cold," Atticus replied.

"Atticus," Barker went on, "this is Chief Inspector Willow from Washington; he's the new case manager for the Washington Island investigation."

Atticus gave him another nod and smiled.

"How long do we have?" the chief inspector asked Atticus calmly.

"About one hour," Atticus replied.

Barker unbuttoned his coat. "Well then, we'd better get at it," he said.

"I'm listening," Atticus replied.

"For starters," Barker went on, "Inspector Willow is very concerned for your safety."

"Really?" Atticus responded, looking at the inspector. "And why would that be?"

"Tell me, Mr. Gunner," the chief inspector said, "how did you get involved in all this anyway?"

"Just lucky, I guess," Atticus replied.

"What do you mean by that?" the inspector asked.

"Agent Barker knows what I mean, as I'm sure you do too."

"But I'd like to hear it from you."

Atticus leaned back in his seat and unzipped his jacket. "Sir," he said, "you might be a master at this game; I don't know and I don't care, but I'll tell you what: I'll try not to insult your intelligence if you'll give me the same consideration."

The inspector didn't respond immediately. "All right," he replied. "I'll lay it out. There are two major organizations involved in the drug trafficking business in this country: the Colombian Cartel, and the Sicilian Mafia. The Mafia is by far the oldest; they are well organized and disciplined. Discipline for them means order and stability; with it they have managed to buy substantial political influence throughout the Western world. Their primary drug business has been the trafficking of heroin by way of the so-called Golden Triangle of Southeast Asia. For some time now, they have enjoyed a very lucrative, exclusive market in this country.

"The Colombian Cartel, on the other hand, is a very young organization. And where the Mafia may be the epitome of order and discipline, the cartel has a reputation for unpredictability and ruthlessness. What they lack in political influence, they gain through intimidation and violence. They kill one another and anyone else who gets in their way. They're also becoming well entrenched in the United States and are rapidly growing. What I'm getting at is this: the drug bust on Big Winter Island confiscated a little over six hundred pounds of heroin, all of which came from Colombia. What that means is that either the cartel is attempting to move in on the Mafia, or the Mafia has found a new partner. Either way, neither of them would hesitate one second to give you the deep six if they thought you were a threat to their operation. Am I coming through, Mr. Gunner?"

"If the Mafia or the cartel wanted to kill me, why haven't they?" Atticus replied. "They've certainly had plenty of opportunity."

"I doubt they care much about your existence at this point, but that could change rapidly, particularly if you continue to keep your nose in it."

"You people sure do have an interest in where my nose is, but setting that aside, why should I assume your theory to be correct?"

"Mr. Gunner, I hardly think you're in a position to challenge my thinking."

"It must be nice to be so confident," Atticus replied. "Tell me, does Pope buy your theory?"

"What Pope does or doesn't buy is irrelevant, and it has nothing to do with our discussion here."

"Oh really?"

"Yes, really," the inspector replied. "Mr. Pontiff tends to chase shadows; I deal with facts."

"Then perhaps you should deal with these facts, Inspector," Atticus responded. "My kids came onto a small arms stash over on South Manitou last summer; while there, they also had an encounter with a man later discovered to have connections with Baynard, the leader of the drug-running pack who died during the bust on Winter Island. Baynard was the leader of a small radical Nazi organization on Washington Island. He may have been a true believer, even a member of the neo-Nazi movement, but I doubt seriously he was a member in good standing of the cartel or the Mafia.

"Second, I obtained a WATS number, and with the help of a friend at the university, we managed to establish a connection between a black-market arms dealer in South Africa to a prominent island summer resident by the name of Munster Doebuck, who, I might add, also has a close connection to the Baynard clan."

"How did you make these connections?" the inspector asked.

"The night of the plane crash on Washington Island, a woman by the name of Jody Kerfam was at the crash site," Atticus went on. "Two days later, I found her hanging in her basement. It was ruled a suicide, but it wasn't. I'm certain she found something at the crash site that she wasn't supposed to, and because of that, she was murdered."

"That's nothing but speculation, Mr. Gunner."

"Perhaps, but that's where I got the WATS number, so what I'm trying to point out here is, your gang rivalry concept doesn't cover all the bases; I believe there's strong evidence to suggest there's a third entity involved."

Paula cleared her throat. "Sir," she said to the inspector in an almost apologetic manner, "I think we should hear Gunner out."

The inspector sat quietly, looking at Atticus for a few moments, and then he spoke. "All right, Gunner, so what is your theory?" he asked.

Atticus shook his head. "That's where I fall short; I'm not sure I have one yet. Where's Pontiff now?"

"In Chicago," Inspector Willow replied.

"Doing what?"

"Seeing how far back he can trace the roots of your Munster Doebuck."

"Sounds to me like he's on the right track," Atticus replied.

"I didn't think you cared much for Pontiff, but forget that; enlighten me."

"Where are Baynard's men now?" Atticus asked.

"In jail," the inspector replied.

"I assume they're being held over for trial?"

"That's correct."

"Have they turned state's evidence?"

The inspector paused; he glanced over at Paula. "Paula is our trial attorney," he said, looking back at Atticus. "She'll have to answer that for you."

"No," Paula said to Atticus without delay. "Baynard's companions have not turned state's evidence."

"Have they shed any light on the term Raptor?"

"No," she replied again, shaking her head. "Nothing."

"Have you gotten anything at all from them?"

"Again I'm going to have to reply with a negative," she said.

Atticus continued to press. "Do you think there's a possibility they really don't know much?"

"That's an interesting point," she replied to Atticus. "What makes you ask?"

"I'm thinking Baynard's group really doesn't know a whole lot."

"To be honest with you, that's the same conclusion I've come to," she replied.

"So what happens to them now?" Atticus asked.

"We intend to proceed with the prosecution," she replied. "We've got more than enough to indict them for murder, so they're bound over for trial in federal court."

"That's enough information, Mr. Gunner," the inspector said, "if you've got something credible, let's hear it."

"All right," Atticus replied. "I think your theory about the Mafia and the cartel is probably true; partially, that is. As I said before, I also think Pope is a hell of a lot closer to the truth than you think. I think there's a third party involved; I think it's Pope's Order of Raptors, and I also think there's a strong possibility that Munster Doebuck could be the Scorpion that Pope refers to."

"I'm listening," the inspector interjected.

"I don't pretend to have all the answers," Atticus said, "but let's suppose that the Scorpion, in his quest for money, somehow convinced both the Mafia and the cartel that the best road to economic success in the US was to form a joint venture, rather than a range war. Suppose he somehow talked himself into being the intermediary for this joint venture; for a piece of the action, of course. If you think about it, it's really very logical. The Order of Raptors is a secret organization with an underground reputation for efficiency and confidentiality, well-informed, with contacts all over the world; it's a perfect match for the job."

"All right, assuming this Order of Raptors does exist," the inspector replied, "and assuming they are involved, why would they connect with Baynard and his outfit? What value did Baynard bring to the table?"

"Good point," Barker interjected. "According to Pontiff, the Scorpion keeps himself totally removed from all operations. So if Doebuck is the Scorpion, why would he expose himself to someone as obvious as Baynard?"

"Being close to Baynard didn't necessarily mean he exposed himself," Atticus replied.

"That still doesn't explain why," the inspector added.

"Well," Atticus went on, thinking out loud, "the Order of Raptors by definition is not a big organization; besides, from what Pope said, it doesn't seem likely they would get directly involved. I suspect they needed an operative; someone they could buy for the sake of the cause; true believers; someone like Baynard and his group. Maybe even someone they could buy with cheap but hard-to-get goods, like military small arms."

"I'm following you," Paula said, "the weapons stash at South Manitou."

"Precisely," Atticus replied. "At least payment in part, and for that, Baynard and company did the handling of the drug shipment, or shipments."

"If that's the case, the Scorpion didn't deliver," Paula said. "Not only did we get Baynard, but we got both the drug shipment and the money."

"And Doebuck is in very deep shit," Barker concluded.

"Maybe," Atticus replied.

"What do you mean?" the inspector asked.

"I mean there's a very good likelihood that his employers, just like Baynard, don't really know his identity. He probably made all the arrangements through his subordinate, a man called the Broker."

Barker leaned back in his seat again. "Do you really believe the Mafia or the cartel would turn over that kind of money to someone they don't even know?"

"They may not know who the Scorpion is," Paula interjected, "but they may well know the reputation of the Order of Raptors."

"I'm also starting to think Doebuck made three significant miscalculations, from which he is frantically trying to recover," Atticus interjected. "First of all, he didn't anticipate the murder of Quint Jebson and those boys. Second, he didn't take into consideration the advent of bad weather when he arranged for a drug transaction on Halloween night. And third, although it may sound a bit arrogant, I don't think he anticipated the likes of me."

"What makes you think you're a threat to him?" the inspector asked.

"Because I'm closing in on him, and he knows that. But I'm not the real threat; what he's really worried about is, after his major screwup on Halloween night, what his employers might do if I manage to ID him."

"Gunner, I hope you realize just how vulnerable you are," the inspector said. "He could take you out in a hundred different ways before you even knew what was happening. For example, a well-placed shot from someplace in the woods while you're walking from your car to your house would do the job."

"No, for now, like Pope said, he's going to try to play it safe by simply getting me fired," Atticus replied. "He'll only go the Raptor route if he has to. And if that happens, it'll be a whole new game; that guy's an assassin. Worse than that, he enjoys killing. He's got a reputation to keep. His taking me out will be far more elaborate than simply shooting me from the cover of the woods."

"I don't like it," the inspector replied.

"I don't either," Atticus said. "But there is something inside me that won't let me stand down; I'm going to have to face this animal at some time, I'm sure. And when I do, I'm going to do everything I can to take him out, and I think he knows that, and I also think that's an unacceptable challenge to his ego; so when he comes to take me on, it'll be with arrogance and a sick sense of honor."

"Where is the Broker in all this?" Barker asked.

"I don't know," Atticus replied. "That's why I need all the input from Pontiff I can get. For all I know, this Raptor and the Broker are one and the same. The only physical information I have about the

Raptor is he either smokes Turkish cigarettes or wears fancy shoes, or maybe both."

Paula looked at the inspector. "What do you think, sir?" she said. "It all makes sense."

"Yes, I'm afraid I have to agree," the inspector replied. "Is there anything else we need to discuss, Mr. Gunner?"

"Well, there are other people I find suspicious; people like Hepper Greshion, even Tom Cline, but I haven't figured them out yet. And there are situations, like my landlady, that have me totally befuddled. But as to prime topics, I think we've pretty much covered it."

"You realize," Paula continued, "even if everything Mr. Gunner has told us is true, we're still a long way from any kind of indictment."

"I realize that," the inspector replied. "As much as I despise him, step one is to have a heart-to-heart talk with Pontiff; we need his input."

Just then the ferry whistle sounded. "I've got to go," Atticus said, zipping up his coat.

The inspector glanced out the window at the boat and then looked back at Atticus. "All right," he replied, "we'll keep in touch." The inspector extended Atticus his hand. "You're either very smart or very wrong," he said to Atticus. "But I guess you already know that. Let's hope you're smart enough to stay alive until we can work our way through all this."

Atticus remained stone sober as he shook the inspector's hand, but he made no comment. He opened the car door and got out. He nodded at both Smith and Barker, slammed the door shut, and hurried off down the hill toward the boat.

CHAPTER 19

Staying Behind

As the elementary kids bundled up and headed outside for recess, the upstairs hall became a noisy place. Atticus, who had been standing in the hall talking with Sylvia about the Christmas program, started down the steps on his way back to the office. Halfway down, he came upon a little first grader sitting on the steps struggling with his boots.

Atticus paused. "Need a little help there, Jesse?" he asked, sitting down on the step next to the boy.

Jesse looked up at Atticus. "Thith boot don't fit tho good," he replied through his missing teeth.

"Well, why don't you let me take a look at it?" Atticus said, noticing the boy had the left boot on his right foot.

The boy handed Atticus the other boot.

Atticus looked it over very carefully. "You know," he said after a moment or two, "I'll bet this boot would fit better on that foot, and that boot on this foot; should we try it?"

The boy nodded, so Atticus made the switch and helped him pull them on. "There," he said when he was finished. "What do you think?"

Jesse grinned his approval. "Thankth, Mithter Gunner."

"You're welcome," Atticus said as the boy hurried down the stairs to join the others outside.

Just as Jesse headed out the door, he met Butch on the way in. Butch let the youngster pass and then entered; he spotted Atticus on the steps just getting back to his feet. "You have to sit down and rest already?" he said with a straight face.

"You got that right," Atticus replied. "Overworked and underpaid; that's me. What are you doing here all bright eyed and bushy tailed on this cold winter morning?"

Butch hesitated. "Atticus, I need to talk to you," he said seriously.

"Well, fire away."

"Not here; someplace private."

"Well, you're in luck; I've got playground duty this morning. So as soon as I get my coat, we can talk outside if that's okay."

Butch didn't respond; it was obvious to Atticus he was in a very serious mood. Atticus stepped past him, grabbed his coat from the rack, and headed out the door. Butch followed right behind.

Outside, they walked along the sidewalk until they were in full view of the playground. Atticus pulled up his collar. "What's up?" he asked, looking out at the kids playing.

"We got problems," Butch replied. "Serious problems."

Atticus looked at him. "Why doesn't that surprise me?"

Butch shook his head. "I don't even know where to begin."

"How about at the beginning?"

"I just got off the phone with Adrian Fruger. He wants to meet with me at one o'clock today in the ferry office."

"Aren't you working today?"

"Yes, of course I am. But when I reported in this morning, I was told Adrian made arrangements for me to have the afternoon off, so I called him."

"Wow, I didn't know he ran the electric co-op too."

"Atticus, they're out to get you, and I don't mean in a small way."

"Who's they?"

"Just about everyone; at least everyone with clout. You've pissed off a lot of people, Atticus."

"Well, that's my specialty; tell me, how is it they intend to get me?"

"You name it."

"Slow down, Butch; now, who's involved, and what exactly is it I've supposedly done?"

"For starters, they're coming after you with a morals charge. Not only are they accusing you of inappropriate behavior with a woman much younger than yourself, but they're also claiming you've made inappropriate advances toward some of the high school girls. They're saying you're unfit to serve this community as either the schoolmaster or the constable."

"And who is they?"

"I don't know for sure who all is involved; Adrian is, for one. He mentioned a group of concerned citizens: Brian Karmel, Doc Burnett, Reverend Watson, Hepper Greshion—there were others."

"Anything else?"

"They're also accusing you of dereliction of your duties. They say you're never around when you should be; as the school administrator, you're always gone when you shouldn't be. As a police officer, you're not patrolling the roads at night like you should; you're not checking on the security of properties like you should; and when you do encounter a problem, you overreact with excessive force. They claim you're spending all your time on matters that aren't even related to the island, and that's not what we're paying you for."

"Do they have names behind each of these charges?"

"I don't know; the way Adrian talked, it's all of them. Atticus, they're organized."

"Adrian Fruger told you all this on the phone?"

"Yes."

"So why is he meeting with you?"

"He's not just meeting with me. He's running a special boat to bring Sheriff Dawson up here, and he's also asked Greta to be there. Why he's bringing the sheriff here, I don't know."

Atticus pushed his hands deep into his pockets and stared off at the playground.

"This is the worst damn news I've ever had to deliver to anyone Atticus, but you surely can't be surprised; I told you something like this was going to happen a long time ago."

"No, I'm not surprised, I expected it; I'm just disappointed."

"Disappointed?"

"Yes; disappointed that I so grossly underestimated them. That was stupid."

"That point is a bit moot right now, don't you think?"

"Yes, it is; fool me once, shame on you; fool me twice, shame on me."

"I'm afraid I'm not following."

"It's not important, Butch, but what is important is for you to show up at that meeting."

"Oh, I don't have much choice; I was told to be there, but what are you going to do?"

"Right now I'm going to go upstairs and take over Sylvia's class so she can participate in an investigation with you. There are a total of nine girls in the high school. I want you and Sylvia to interview each one of them privately in my office. I also want you to talk to every staff member, with the exception of Brian Karmel, of course. I want you and Sylvia to look for any hint of validity to the charge. I'm certain there isn't any, but I want it confirmed before they have time to manipulate anyone."

"Wouldn't it be better to do this with Greta instead of Sylvia?"

"No, Greta can take over my supervisory duties this morning. I don't want her in that office with you and Sylvia; that would constitute a quorum, and you'd be guilty of holding a board meeting without proper public notice. Sylvia's not only honest, she'll carry a lot of credibility for what you find."

"What about the charge of improper behavior with your girlfriend and dereliction of your duties as a police officer?"

"Don't worry about those; I'll take care of them on my own. The real concern right now is to clear up this thing about the high school kids."

"If Greta comes to Adrian's meeting, that will be a quorum too." Butch said.

"Yes, it will, but I'll deal with that at the meeting; you just keep your mouth shut about it, okay?"

"That damned Karmel. You should never have hired that son of a bitch."

"I didn't hire him," Atticus replied. "You did."

Butch shook his head as though he hadn't heard Atticus and continued to talk. "Atticus, that's just the tip of the iceberg. I know there is nothing to the charge, but as board president, I'm forced to investigate. You and I both know it's Karmel. He's managed to suck up to the Burnetts, and in doing so, he's gained access to the ears of the island's power structure; they're the ones who believe him. Adrian's first comment was how he's concerned about the sex maniac down at that school. They think your relationship with this Bock girl is immoral, especially considering you work with young people. And now, with this thing about you and the high school girls, they're certain there must be some truth to it; after all, Karmel is right down there at the school, and he certainly ought to know what's going on. He's not alone either; Vivian and Nordien are out there working just as hard to discredit you."

Suddenly, the cold air was shattered by the piercing clang of the school bell.

"He also wonders," Butch went on, "if you're not too busy playing out some kind of lover/detective fantasy to be running the school. He thinks you're a very sick person, Atticus. He even said Doebuck heard you were in trouble with the Department of Public Instruction, and that the state superintendent was considering having you removed."

There was little doubt what was going on even before Atticus heard Doebuck's name, but still the thought of it all made his guts boil.

"Atticus, they're going to move on you, and I'm not going to be able to stop them."

Atticus started walking back toward the school.

"Look," Butch said, catching up to him, "I tried to tell you this was going to blow up in your face. You've alienated the doctor and the Doebucks, just to mention a few; Vivian and Nordien are certainly not friends of yours; Karmel must hate your guts for some reason, and now you've got Adrian on your ass. As far as this drug thing goes, everyone on the damned island knows you met with the FBI last

Sunday morning—what the hell is going on there? Oh, and I thought we had things straightened out with the DPI; is there any truth to them removing you?"

"I'm sure Doebuck has some of his influential friends putting pressure on, but they're not going to remove me, Butch. Damn, how I hate politics," Atticus said as he opened the school doors to go inside.

"Oh, that's good," Butch replied, following him through the doors. "I can stand up before the people and tell them to please excuse my friend here; he just doesn't like politics. That ought to straighten things out."

Atticus stopped at the foot of the stairs. "Butch, slow down; have you had any complaints about how I'm running the school, other than from Brian?"

"No."

"How about my performance as constable?"

"Yes."

"Well, that goes with the territory. And as to the FBI, yes, I did meet with the FBI last Sunday, but it was related to island business. As constable, that's my job. Butch, I haven't shortchanged the school, but I don't intend to turn my back on murder. Five, maybe six island people have been murdered on this island Butch; you damn right that's important to me; my kids could have easily been number seven and eight. Quint and the boys were very special people, and I intend, regardless of what it takes, to see that their deaths are avenged."

Butch looked down at the floor, shaking his head again; he took a deep breath and looked back up at Atticus. "You're right," he said, "and I'll stand with you."

"Thank you. Now, conduct your investigation; I'll see you in Fruger's office this afternoon."

Atticus continued up the stairs, leaving Butch standing by the office door.

At two o'clock, Atticus pulled up to the ferry office. There were several cars in the lot, most of them ferry employees, but he saw Butch's old wagon, Greta's Chevy, Adrian's Buick, and Sheriff Dawson's unmarked squad car. He drove the Bronco into the empty stall next to Butch's wagon and parked.

As he walked into the terminal, he met two ferry employees dressed in cold-weather work clothes coming out; they greeted Atticus warmly, and he smiled and greeted them back. Inside, he walked up to the counter. Adrian's daughter, who was sitting behind the counter reading a magazine, looked up with a startled expression. "Mr. Gunner!" she exclaimed. "What are you doing here?"

"I'm here to attend the meeting," he said as he walked around the end of the counter and toward the closed office door.

"Sir, you can't go in there; that's a private meeting."

Atticus walked past her and opened the door. Adrian, the sheriff, Greta, and Butch all looked up as Atticus walked in. Adrian stood up. "What in the hell do you think you're doing?" he barked at Atticus. "This is private property, and this is a private meeting!"

"No, I'm afraid you're wrong, Mr. Fruger," Atticus replied. "Butch and Greta are both elected officials of the school board and the police committee, and their being here together constitutes a quorum of each, thereby making this an official public meeting of both organizations. Further, because the meeting was called without proper notice, I'm going to shut it down and ask one of them to leave—Greta, do you mind?"

Greta got up immediately. "No," she replied, "I was very uneasy about this anyway." She excused herself and walked out.

Adrian looked at the sheriff. "Can he do that?" he asked.

"I'm afraid so," Sheriff Dawson replied. "If what he said is true, you had no business inviting them here."

"Well, it's not a public meeting now!" Adrian barked. "So get out, Gunner!"

"Not until it's revealed what, if anything, was presented to the school board and the police committee," Atticus said. "That's the business of the public, and I'm here to see that the public is served."

"We were asked to call a special meeting to terminate your employment as school administrator and as constable," Butch replied.

"Were the charges presented to you in writing?"

"Yes."

"As the executive advisor to both boards, I'd like to see them."

Butch handed Atticus the two pieces of paper; he looked them over. "The charges seem to be clear enough," Atticus said, "but there are no names attached to clarify who is making these charges. Before they can be officially accepted by either board, the names of those making the charges will have to be attached. Is that understood, Mr. Fruger?"

Adrian mumbled an affirmative along with a couple of choice swear words.

"Well, gentlemen," Atticus said. "Sheriff, it's good to see you again. Butch, I'll be talking with you later." He turned and started to walk out.

"Just a minute, Atticus," Sheriff Dawson blurted out as he rose from his chair and started to put his coat on. "I'll leave with you if you don't mind; I don't think there's much purpose in me staying here. Adrian, I'm assuming you've made arrangements for the boat to take me back to the mainland?"

"Yes, of course," Adrian mumbled.

"Ah, I'll come too," Butch said, rising from his chair. "Mr. Fruger, you can get me those papers as soon as they're complete." Butch smiled at Adrian and turned to follow the others out.

⬥

"Atticus," Sheriff Dawson said as the three men walked out to the cars, "I got to hand it to you, you do have a way with words; you managed to stop that witch hunt right in its tracks."

"Oh, it's anything but over," Atticus replied as he walked around the Bronco. "That was just the beginning."

"So I've heard; I had a brief conversation with Paula Smith; she was looking to clarify the official relationship between your island position and the county. In the process of that conversation, she gave me a brief synopsis of what's going on. I'd suggest you be very careful, constable."

"Careful is my middle name," Atticus replied. He looked over at Butch, who was opening the door of his car. "Butch, how did your investigation go?"

"Excellent," he said. "There's absolutely nothing to substantiate the school charges. As a matter of fact, quite the opposite was expressed, but we didn't talk to Brian."

"I'll take care of that myself," Atticus said as he opened the door of the Bronco.

Butch paused. "No rough stuff, Atticus."

"Now you know I would never manhandle our friendly industrial arts teacher."

"Atticus, I'm serious," Butch said, looking over his car at him.

"And Sheriff," Atticus said without looking back, as he got into the Bronco, "I lost my hat, and everyone knows you can't be a good cop without a proper hat; I can't seem to get my boss here to get me a new one, so can you get me a new hat?" He pulled the door shut without waiting for a response, started the engine, and drove out of the lot.

Sheriff Dawson glanced over at Butch as though he were looking for some kind of explanation; Butch simply shrugged and shook his head as he got into his wagon.

———●◦●———

After school that night, Atticus waited for Brian to walk past the open office door on his way out of the building. When he finally went hurrying past, Atticus grabbed his coat and followed. As they approached the parking lot, Brian looked back and spotted Atticus closing the distance between them. "Mr. Gunner, I didn't see you back there," he said.

"I need to talk to you," Atticus replied as he approached.

"Well, I'm in kind of a hurry," Brian said as he opened his car door. "Do you think it could wait until tomorrow?"

"No, I don't think so," Atticus replied, reaching out in front of Brian and closing his car door for him. "I think we'll talk now."

"About what?"

"I understand you're concerned about my inappropriate behavior."

"I don't know what you're talking about."

"I'm talking about the charge that I've been making inappropriate advances toward high school girls."

"I never said anything like that."

"The charges had your name on them."

"I might have said I thought you appeared to be a little too friendly with the girls, but I never said anything like that."

"Then perhaps you better straighten Adrian Fruger out; he thinks you did."

"I'm sorry if he misunderstood; I'll certainly talk with him."

"I think that would be a very good idea," Atticus went on. "Ya know, I used to know a guy who loved to charm snakes."

Brian got a puzzled look on his face. "Do what?"

"I said, charm snakes; you know, someone who likes to confuse and mislead snakes into striking at the wrong target. Well, one day this guy got careless; ended up getting bit by the very snakes he was charming; ended up dying a horrible death."

"I have no idea what you're talking about, but I'll be sure to keep that in mind if I ever come in contact with any snakes, Mr. Gunner."

"You do that, Mr. Karmel," Atticus said as he opened the door of the Bronco. "Because I'd sure hate to see that happen to you; going the deep six by way of a snakebite is a real bad way to go. Good night."

On Saturday, December 22, Atticus was standing at the rail of the *Otterman*. His ex-wife had called, and due to some scheduling issues at the hospital, she had to work both Christmas Eve and Christmas Day. Atticus felt bad for her, but on the upside, that meant the girls would be able to spend Christmas with their father, and he was absolutely elated over that prospect. In addition, not only was Laura bringing the girls up to the island with her today, but she had invited her parents and sisters to come up later to spend part of the holidays with them.

Atticus pulled his collar up tight around his neck; he looked off into the distance. As endless as the cold wind blowing incisively out of the north was, so too was the ever-moving snow that swept silently across the featureless landscape. The whole of Green Bay, as far as the eye could see, including the passages between the islands, and especially the one the Indians used to call Death's Door, was now covered with a solid sheet of snow-covered ice. Cold, clear, and dissolute, the bright midday sun reflected off the panorama with an austere beauty. To the south, at a distance of about five miles, was North Point Bluff, the location of the winter dock; it rose up out of the distant haze like a mirage. It was there that Laura and the girls would be waiting.

This was the first real winter crossing for Atticus, and in spite of the captain's reassurance at the onset, every time the boat ground to a halt with a loud trembling shudder, and black diesel smoke bellowed from the stack as they attempted to back off the thick ice for another run at it; Atticus wondered if they would make it or have to turn around and go back, thereby spoiling his Christmas plans.

Brought back from his thoughts by the chill of the wind, Atticus retreated to the warmth of the passenger cabin. He sat down on one of the side benches along the wall. Unlike the last trip, this time there were several other men on board, all islanders. A number of them were sitting around the bench tables in the middle of the cabin, playing cards and drinking beer. There was an ordinance against open intoxicants on the boat, but Atticus said nothing. One of the men looked up at Atticus. "Would you like to join the game, Mr. Gunner?" he asked.

"No thanks," Atticus replied.

"School administrators don't play cards?" another man asked, grinning at Atticus.

Atticus smiled. "I don't want to take your money," he said.

They all laughed and went back to their card game. Finally one of them looked back up at Atticus again. "Don't worry Mister Gunner, we'll make it across," he said reassuringly.

———— ••◆•• ————

Following the trail of broken pack ice from the previous day's run, the *Otterman* turned slowly to the west in order to avoid one of the huge ice shoves. As long as the captain could stay within the boat's previous path, she made good headway. It was only where the ice had shifted, closing in on the open water, that the going slowed to a snail's pace.

Finally, after three long hours, Atticus was once again standing at the rail as they approached the dock. A number of vehicles were waiting; among them was Laura's car, and sure enough, there was Inger standing out at the end of the dock, waving exuberantly. Atticus waved back. Laura and Stacie emerged from the car to join Inger; they all waved.

———— ••◆•• ————

From the very moment Atticus stepped off the boat and held each of them close, he knew this would be a Christmas to remember. The girls were beaming with excitement, and Laura's warm smile melted the cold as though it were the middle of July. The welcomes gave way to laughter, the laughter to questions, and soon Atticus was once again surrounded by the warmth and exhilaration of feminine companionship.

The rest of that day was spent watching both Laura and the girls acclimate themselves to a world very different from when they had last seen it. The slow bumpy ride back through the ice, an island shrouded beneath a heavy blanket of powdery snow, heavily frosted windows, and a tightly closed house warmed by a crackling fire in the big fireplace was to each of them a fantasy come true; a true winter wonderland, nestled in the excitement of Christmas.

———•◆•———

The next day and a half was a busy time at the Hersoff place. Even though Atticus felt he had already prepared appropriately prior to their arrival, the house was once again given a thorough cleaning. There was grocery shopping and baking; the big recreation room was cleaned and organized; they wrapped presents and searched through Cynthia's stuff until they found boxes of Christmas decorations.

Even for Inger, who usually counted every hour as it approached Christmas, the time flew until the morning of Christmas Eve finally arrived. Excited, everyone rose at the crack of dawn to an early breakfast. Then, while Laura stayed behind to make final preparations for her family's arrival, Atticus and the girls ventured out into a gently falling snow to cut a Christmas tree.

When at last they were finished decorating the tree, Laura and the girls all stood back as Atticus plugged in the lights. He went over and stood behind the girls. It was indeed beautiful, the most beautiful tree Atticus could ever remember. The warm glow of the lights reflecting off the walls, the frost-covered windows, the smell of pine, and the delicious essence of pumpkin pie all combined with the flicker of the fire to give the room a perfect feeling.

After carefully placing all the gaily wrapped gifts under the tree, everyone bundled up for the trip to the ferry dock to meet the boat. Although the arrival of Laura's family made Atticus a little uneasy at first, it soon passed. Her parents were warm and friendly, and Atticus was absolutely astonished how rapidly the girls became reacquainted with Laura's sisters, especially Rita, who was very close to Stacie's age.

Christmas Eve blossomed with equal exuberance. The gentle snowfall that continued throughout the day laid a light fluffy cover over the already thick blanket of white. When nighttime finally arrived and a full moon made its appearance, the newly fallen snow sparkled with an iridescent glow. Inside the house, two roaring fires were kept ablaze—one in the living room, and the other up in the big stone fireplace in the recreation room. An early sit-down supper was served with all the trimmings. Later, the girls spent the early part of the evening playing games up in the recreation room, while the adults washed dishes. At midnight they all attended mass at the small Catholic church up on Jackson Harbor Road, after which presents were exchanged along with the singing of Christmas carols in front of the roaring fireplace in the living room; it was a grand night.

———————•◦•◦•———————

Later the next afternoon, everyone went on a rented sleigh ride. Afterward, they sat around the fire in the recreation room, drinking hot chocolate and kidding one another about the afternoon's events. When the phone rang, Stacie ran down to the dining room to answer it. "Dad, it's for you!" she shouted up the stairs.

Atticus left the group and headed downstairs. "Who is it?" he asked as he passed Stacie coming back up the steps.

"I think it's Cynthia," she replied, wrinkling up her nose.

Atticus walked over to the phone and picked it up. "Hello," he said calmly.

"Mr. Gunner," came the voice, "this is Cynthia."

"Hi, Cynthia, Merry Christmas," he said. "What can I do for you?"

"I'm sorry to call you like this," she said, "especially on Christmas Day and all, but something has come up." There was a long pause. "You're going to have to move," she said.

Atticus was so stunned he didn't know how to respond. "When?" he asked.

"Right away," came the reply.

"Right away? I just sent you two months' rent not more than a couple weeks ago; I even have the cancelled check back."

"Yes, well—I'll return your money."

"I don't know what to say," Atticus replied. "Moving would be extremely difficult for me right now. Is there something I've done to cause such harsh action?"

"No—no; it's nothing like that," she said apologetically. "I'm afraid you're just going to have to get out."

"Cynthia, I don't know where I could possibly move to right now."

"I'm terribly sorry," she said, "but I guess you'll have to work that out for yourself. I've notified Hepper to check on you in a couple days; if you're not out by then, he's instructed to do whatever is necessary to see that you do get out."

"Look, Cynthia, that's not . . ." The phone clicked and then went dead. Atticus stood there for a moment and then hung up the receiver.

As Atticus walked slowly back up the stairs, he felt overwhelmed. He had been completely blindsided; there was no doubt that this was another ploy to make his stay on the island impossible, and that Doebuck was somehow behind it. But to come from Cynthia blew his mind; it simply did not fit her profile.

Profound as all this was, the order to move didn't emerge as his most pressing issue. Not only did this latest twist present a number of problems for which he had no ready answers, but it also meant that instead of returning to Madison for New Year's Eve with Laura and the girls, as they planned, he would have to stay behind. And he had absolutely no idea how he was going to break that kind of news to them. Equally troubling was, he couldn't tell them the truth; not only did he not want them involved in any way, but he didn't even want them to know what was going on. Atticus was finally under siege, and the girls had to be removed as far out of harm's way as possible.

Atticus knew something like this was going to happen; the writing was on the wall. He should have seen it coming; the fact that he didn't made him question his abilities. Doebuck and company were finally implementing a full political attack; the battle was on. And for Atticus to assume that it wouldn't happen until after the holidays was really a tactical blunder. He should have assumed that the attack would come at the most inopportune time and from a most unexpected direction.

With his mind racing for possible answers, he walked back into the recreation room; the only immediate conclusion he could come to was that for now he would say nothing.

——◆——

Laura and Atticus drove back home in the Bronco after seeing her family off. Stacie and Inger were over at Joni's for the afternoon. Atticus was very quiet. The signs were subtle, but Laura detected the change in his behavior. At first she dismissed it, but as it hung on, she began to grow concerned. Unfortunately, the right opportunity to bring it up never seemed to present itself; perhaps now was the time. She looked over at him. "Well," she said, "tomorrow morning we'll all be on our way to Madison. Then perhaps we can manage some time for ourselves."

Atticus nodded but made no other response.

After a couple of minutes, Laura looked back over at him. "Do you want to talk about it?" she asked.

Atticus didn't respond.

"I know something is bothering you," she said.

Atticus turned left on Westside Road and continued toward the Hersoff place. Finally, he just blurted it out. "I won't be going back with you and the kids tomorrow," he said.

Laura looked at him. "What?"

"I said I won't be leaving with you and the girls tomorrow."

"What do you mean?" she asked. "The girls are planning on it, and so am I."

"I know," Atticus replied, "but I can't."

Stunned, Laura stared at him. "And what about our plans for New Year's Eve?"

Again Atticus didn't respond.

Laura looked forward again without saying a word; she stared out the windshield. She thought she understood Atticus by now, but this time, for whatever his reasons, she was having a great deal of trouble dealing with it. She sat quietly the rest of the way home. After they drove into the yard and stopped, she spoke again, but this time without looking at Atticus. "When did you decide not to come home with us?" she asked.

"A couple of days ago," Atticus replied.

"I see, and what were you going to do, wait until we got on the ferry to tell us?"

Atticus took a deep breath and let it out slowly. "I'm sorry," he said. "I didn't know how to tell you."

"Oh well, that makes it all right then," she replied sarcastically.

"I've got some reports that I absolutely have to get done," he said apologetically.

"Atticus, don't lie to me!"

Atticus started to speak but she interrupted. "Don't bother," she said. Then she opened the door and got out. She paused and looked back at him once more. "The girls and I will leave without you tomorrow."

She slammed the door and walked into the house without looking back.

———————◆•◉•◆———————

When the girls arrived at home, they knew immediately something was wrong. Atticus was sitting in the living room, staring at a blank television screen, and Laura was up in her bedroom, packing.

At supper, Laura told the girls that their father would not be coming back to Madison with them; neither of them asked why, nor did Atticus attempt to explain. Whether this was reminiscent of a time both Stacie and Inger wished to forget, or they simply felt it was best not to pursue, it was never discussed, not even with each other.

The next morning brought no change; the house was uncomfortably quiet as the girls packed. The ride to the ferry dock was equally silent.

Joni was waiting at the dock when they arrived. Although Stacie had forgotten they made plans for Joni to ride across with them, she made light of it and attempted to behave as though everything was perfectly normal. Taking charge, she quickly organized who would carry what;

she and Joni helped Laura with her bags, Atticus carried Stacie's, and Inger carried her own. No one complained, not even Inger.

———◆———

Atticus walked on board behind the others. By the time he placed the bags up in the bow with the others, Laura was already headed up the stairs to the passenger deck. Atticus said nothing.

"Good-bye, Dad," Stacie said, putting her arms up around her father's neck and giving him a quick kiss on the lips. "We'll call next weekend."

Atticus nodded. "Good-bye, honey," he said.

"Aren't you coming over with us, Mr. Gunner?" Joni asked.

"Ah—no, I'm afraid not," Atticus replied.

Stacie grabbed Joni by the arm and hurried her off up the stairs.

Atticus watched as they left and then turned his attention to Inger, who was standing there quietly waiting. "Well, old timer," he said, kneeling down, "how about a kiss?"

Inger gave him a kiss and then hugged him tight. Finally, she let loose. "You gonna be all right?" she asked as she stepped back.

Atticus looked into her big blue eyes; he nodded. "Yes—I'll be all right," he said. "Make sure Laura and Stacie are too, okay?"

Inger nodded.

He pulled her close and hugged her one more time. "Well, I guess you better catch up with the others," he said, releasing her.

Inger took a few steps toward the stairs and then stopped and turned toward her dad again. "It was a good Christmas," she said, "the best ever."

Atticus smiled and nodded; he had all he could do to keep the tears from coming.

Inger turned and went up the stairs.

Atticus stepped off the boat just before they pulled up the boarding ramp. Laura and the three girls were standing by the railing, watching him. Atticus waved; Joni and Stacie waved; Laura raised her arm and then lowered it again; Inger waved, but ever so slowly.

CHAPTER 20

In the Presence of Evil

The cold snow crunched beneath his feet as Atticus trudged along the path out to the woodpile. Alone and depressed, it had been twenty-four hours since Laura and the girls left. He had hoped Laura would call last night after she got home, but she didn't. He even thought seriously about calling her, or the girls, but for some reason he couldn't do either. Everything seemed to be closing in; still, there was a determination deep down inside that just wouldn't let go.

Loading his arms with wood, Atticus started back for the house. As he did, the sound of a vehicle coming down the drive broke the silence. Hepper Greshion pulled into the yard with his old pickup and stopped. Atticus wasn't surprised; he'd been waiting for him to show.

Hepper greeted Atticus with a quick "Hello" as he opened the door and got out.

Without saying a word, Atticus continued past the front of Hepper's truck and toward the house. He went up inside the porch and slowly stacked the wood on the floor next to the front door. When he was finished, he came back outside.

"Here," Hepper said as he pulled an envelope from his breast pocket and handed it to Atticus. "This is for you." Atticus took the envelope. "It's your refund," Hepper went on.

Atticus opened the envelope and looked at its contents; it was a check signed by Hepper.

"That's the correct amount, isn't it?" Hepper asked.

"This check is from your account—signed by you," Atticus said.

"That's right; I take care of Cynthia's business on the island; you know that."

"I tried calling her twice," Atticus said, "there was no answer either time. Perhaps you can tell me why she wants me out."

"No, I'm afraid not," Hepper replied. "What she does, or why she does it, is none of my business. As far as that goes, it's none of yours either. She plain and simple wants you out, so out you go."

"And where would you suggest I go?"

"I don't really give a damn where you go. You could always leave the island. From what I hear, there are quite a few folks that would look favorably on that, myself included."

Atticus looked at Hepper once again and then back down at the envelope. "Hepper," he said, "I'm afraid I can't accept this." He put the check back into the envelope and held it out for him to take back.

"I don't think you understand," Hepper said. "You don't have a choice!"

Atticus took in a deep breath and let it out slowly. "Well, my stupid friend," he said, "I'm afraid that's where you're wrong. My business is with Cynthia, and as such, she's required to give me proper notice, and your check doesn't quite do that. Besides, I have a cancelled check that states I've paid her two months in advance. So as far as I'm concerned, I'm going to be right here for at least two more months."

Hepper stepped forward. "Perhaps you didn't hear me," he said. "We want you out!"

Atticus tore the envelope in half and dropped it on the ground.

"You'll pay for that, asshole!" Hepper snorted as he started toward his truck.

Atticus stepped in front of him. "Let's get something straight," Atticus said, holding his hand out so Hepper couldn't get the truck door open. "I don't think you want to piss me off, and right now I'm very close to being just that. I want you to go back over there and pick up that check, and then I want you and your fat ass out of here! Do I make myself clear?"

Hepper walked back over and picked up the torn envelope pieces. He then went back to his truck.

Atticus stepped aside.

"You're going to be sorry you did that, Gunner," he said as he opened the truck door.

"Greshion, I don't know much about you right now, but you can bet I'm going to do some digging, and God help you if your name turns up as having anything to do with the unsolved issues on this island, and that goes for your friends too."

Hepper got into his truck without another word and drove off up the driveway.

<hr />

As Atticus finished breakfast, the phone rang. He walked into the dining room to answer it. "Gunner," came Butch's voice on the other end of the line, "so you are here."

"Afraid so," Atticus replied.

"I thought you were going down to Madison with the girls until after New Year's."

"I decided to stay behind."

"How come?"

"I have some things I need to take care of. I'm glad you called though; tell me, do you still look after the Doebucks' place?"

"Yeah, why?"

"He's not up here, is he?"

"No, he's probably someplace warm; why?"

"When's the last time you checked on his place?"

"What are you getting at?"

"How about taking me over there again; I'd like to look around once more."

"What's going on, Atticus? Are you working for the FBI now?"

Atticus paused for a second. "I work for the island, remember?"

"Bullshit; why don't you tell the FBI to do their own digging? They'll never thank you for any of the help you give them."

"I wish I could," Atticus replied.

Butch paused. "Damn you, Atticus," he said after a few moments. "What happens if we get caught?"

"Then you'll take me over there?" Atticus asked, ignoring Butch's question.

"What the hell choice do I have?"

"When?"

"We're waiting on parts at work, so I guess I could do it this morning. I'll pick you up in a half hour, but this is the last time, Atticus; the very last time." The phone clicked as Butch hung up.

Atticus stood there with the receiver still up to his ear for a few moments, and then he reached over to the wall mount and hook flashed. As he waited for the dial tone, he heard a double click on the line, sort of like an answering machine turning off and on. When the tone came, he dialed Cynthia's number. The connections went through, and it started to ring. But just like before, it rang and rang with no answer; finally he hung up. As he did, he thought again about the clicking sound. He reached for the receiver and picked it up again to listen; the dial tone came on in the normal manner. Dismissing it, Atticus returned the receiver to its hanger.

———•◦•———

As they pulled into the Doebucks', it was obvious that a substantial effort to keep the place open through the winter was being maintained; the drive was plowed, with huge banks of snow everywhere. Butch pulled up in front of the house and stopped. They both walked up to the house; Butch put his key into the lock and tripped the latch; they went inside.

Walking in ahead of Butch, Atticus looked around. Everything was just as he remembered it, but this time it didn't seem quite as inspiring; the animal trophies hanging on the walls were overwhelming and, to some degree, grotesque. "Butch, tell me about Hepper Greshion," Atticus blurted out as he walked over to the other side of the room and opened a desk drawer.

"Now don't mess things up," Butch said before answering. "Hepper Greshion? Why?"

"Is he connected to Doebuck in any way?" Atticus asked as he pulled out the drawer and looked inside.

"For Christ's sake, no! Where in the hell did you come up with that?"

"I'm just asking," Atticus replied.

"Well, obviously he knows the Doebucks, just like everyone else on the island," Butch went on. "Ya know, Atticus, the Doebucks have touched a lot of people up here; and I mean in a positive way; they're hardly looked on as criminals."

"I know," Atticus replied.

"What are you looking for, anyway?"

"I really don't know. I'm just looking."

"This is against the law, you know."

"Right now, I am the law."

Butch shook his head.

"Tell me more about Hepper," Atticus went on as he walked into the hall and down toward the bedrooms. "I know he's Joni's uncle, and I know he owns the Sunset Harbor Hotel, but what else is he?"

"To be honest with you, I don't really know," Butch replied as he followed Atticus. "He's kind of a loner. He runs the hotel, does a little scuba diving, runs a food stand during the carnival, does a little ice fishing in the winter—I don't know. Why the interest in Hepper Greshion all of a sudden?"

"Cynthia called me Christmas Day and ordered me out of the house."

"You mean the Hersoff place?"

"That's right, and she sent Hepper over to do the dirty work."

"When did that happen?"

"This morning."

"Christ, he sure as hell didn't waste any time; I just saw him and Tom come in from off-island this morning. What are you going to do?"

"I've already paid her in advance, so I don't intend to do anything, but that didn't seem to slow Hepper down."

"Well, Hepper looks after the Hersoff place for Cynthia; ya know that. And Tom Cline is his close buddy, and Tom doesn't like you for obvious reasons, so it's not surprising if Hepper feels the same way. But going back to Cynthia, why does she want you out of the house? She's not in tune with the rest of the island's elite in any way, so where in the hell is she coming from?"

"That's the part that doesn't figure," Atticus replied, walking into the main bedroom. "Cynthia is one of the few summer people that seems to like me; she looks on me as a mystical warrior of some sort; I don't think she'd move me out of her own volition."

After looking around the room, Atticus bent down and looked under the bed. He paused and then looked back again. "For God's sake, look at this," he said. "The man's got a safe built into the floor under his bed; it's even encased in concrete."

Butch bent down and looked. "So what's so unusual about that? I would imagine a lot of rich people have a safe built into their house someplace."

"Just seems like a strange place to have it," Atticus replied. "The contents must be real important if he feels he needs to be right on top of it, even when he's sleeping."

"You've been trying to implicate Doebuck ever since the night of the plane crash," Butch said, standing up again. "Why? I mean, what am I missing?"

"There are connections, Butch," Atticus replied, knowing Butch wasn't privy to all the latest developments, and he did not want to get him involved any more than necessary.

"Do you still think Jody Kerfam's death is connected?"

"Yes," Atticus replied as he opened a dresser drawer.

"Atticus, the island is a small place," Butch said. "There are all kinds of crossover connections with everybody and everything. That doesn't necessarily mean there's an implication to a crime. If Quint was murdered, I want to see his murderer brought to justice too, but that's a job for the FBI, not you."

Atticus made no response.

"If you were making some kind of headway instead of just pissing people off, it would be different, but you're no closer to solving anything now than you were two months ago."

"Perhaps you're right," Atticus said as he closed the last dresser drawer. "At least as far as this place is concerned. Let's get out of here."

Butch watched Atticus as he walked past him, and then he shook his head again as he followed him back into the living room.

When they arrived back at the Hersoff place, Butch drove into the yard and stopped. Not a whole lot had been said on the way home. Butch watched as Atticus opened the door to get out. "By the way," Butch said, "I saw Brian at the store yesterday. I thought I'd pump him a little to see if I could get a rise out of him, but he had nothing negative to say about you. Apparently, you must have had an effective heart-to-heart talk with him."

"Either that, or he knew you'd bring it back to me," Atticus said as he got out of the car.

"Either way, you must have had an impact."

"Well, you know me," Atticus said with a deadpan expression, "I'm a very influential person."

"Perhaps more than you think. What did you do about the state superintendent thing?"

"I told him if he didn't back off, I wouldn't vote for him next time."

Butch smiled but didn't really find the remark funny. "What are you up to this afternoon?" he went on.

"I'm going out to the old Kerfam farm to look around."

"There's not much out there but a hole in the ground, and that will be full of snow."

"I know," Atticus replied, "but I still want to go out there."

"I'd go with you, but there is no way I could get the whole day off again."

"Perhaps you should give Adrian a call."

"Very funny," Butch replied. "I think you should be taking things a whole lot more serious than you are, Gunner; I mean it."

"I'll keep that in mind," Atticus said as he slammed the car door shut and started for the house.

⸺⬩◆⬩⸺

After having a bite to eat, and dressing in his warmest clothes, Atticus was just about to go out the door when the phone rang. It was Butch. "Atticus, I got to thinking as I was eating lunch—there was something between Hepper and Old Man Doebuck a few years ago. I'm not sure it's of any value, but . . ."

"I'm listening," Atticus replied.

"Well, about seven years ago, Hepper just about went belly-up. Rumor was that he was going to lose everything. It was also rumored that Doebuck stepped in and gave him the money to get back on his feet. No one knows for sure what happened, but one day he didn't have a pot to piss in, and the next day he was back up and running, and with the addition of a freight business. Like I said, I don't know what value that is, but it is a possible connection."

"That's what I mean, Butch; there are always these little innuendoes. In and of themselves, they don't say much, but there's so many that after a while one just can't dismiss them anymore. I think you've just made another connection; I just don't know what it means yet."

"Yeah, well, I hope you know what the hell you're doing. Are you still going out to Kerfam's?"

"Yes."

"Why don't you wait until I can go with you?"

"I'll be fine. I'll talk to you later." Atticus hung up the receiver.

———•◆•———

When Atticus got to the Kerfam place, he pulled over to the side of the road and stopped. On the big tree just off to the side of the unplowed driveway was a makeshift wooden sign with the words "KEEP OUT" scrawled in big black letters. He turned off the engine, put on his wool hat and gloves, and then got out.

Except for the sound of the wind blowing through the trees in the front yard, the place was silent. Trudging through the deep snow, Atticus made his way up to the edge of the basement and looked down inside; everything was so covered with snow; it seemed pointless to be there. The only sign of life was a set of rabbit tracks along what was once the back of the house.

Jody's old pickup sat off to the side of the barn, just as she had left it, and the door to the haymow was still open; he stepped inside. The wind made a low whistling sound as it rushed through the openings in the walls, and up in the rafters the occasional coo of a pigeon filtered down through the interior. Atticus took a deep breath; again there was nothing of interest.

Finally, he went back outside. Walking over to the truck, he wiped the snow off around the door and yanked it open; it gave a rusty creak. Kneeling down in the snow, he felt under the seats; he checked the glove box; finally he pulled the back of the seat forward and crawled inside in order to see behind it.

"Hey! What the hell do you think you're doing here?" came a booming voice from behind.

Startled, Atticus turned his head. Rifle in hand, wearing a pair of snowshoes and a nasty scowl, was Tom Cline. Atticus crawled back out of the truck to face him.

"What—you too God damned dumb to read the sign out front, Gunner?"

Atticus didn't respond.

"That truck is private property, so get the hell out of here!"

Atticus slammed the truck door shut. "I didn't realize you were the official caretaker, Tom; when did that happen?"

"That's none of your business."

"I just made it my business."

"Well, I don't see you sporting your stick, and I'm holding the gun, so that doesn't really mean jack shit now, does it asshole? I'd just as soon blow you away as look at you. So if I were you, cop or no cop, I'd get the hell out of here while you still can!"

"Boy, you and Hepper move fast; didn't the both of you just get back from off-island?"

"So what's your point, dipshit?"

Fearful of misjudging Tom's stupidity, Atticus simply turned and started to walk away without further comment.

"You're nothing but a God damned troublemaker, Gunner; so if I shot you, I'd be doing the island a favor!" Tom barked as Atticus approached the road where the Bronco was parked.

Atticus stamped the snow off his feet and glanced back up toward the old truck. To his amazement, Tom was leaning on the roof of the pickup, aiming his rifle directly at him. Before Atticus could do anything, the antenna on the Bronco whipped with a loud *zing*, followed immediately by the crack of Tom's rifle. Atticus ducked; Tom laughed.

"Tom, what are you trying to prove?" Atticus shouted as he raised his head slightly above the fender.

"Just want you to know I'm a damn good shot!" Tom replied with a chuckle. "By the way, where's your girlfriend, Gunner?"

Keeping a low profile, Atticus opened his truck door and crawled inside. He started the engine, put it in reverse, and backed up along the road. Once over the top of the hill and out of sight, he turned the Bronco around and proceeded back toward home. He took a couple of deep breaths to calm himself. There would be a time to deal with Tom Cline, but for now Atticus would simply put it on hold.

Coming back to the present, Butch's wagon was coming up behind Atticus with the lights flashing on and off; Atticus pulled over to the side of the road and stopped.

Butch got out of his car. "I was hoping I'd catch you," he said as Atticus rolled his window down. "Agent Barker has been trying to get ahold of you. He finally gave up and called my place and talked to Karen."

"What did he want?" Atticus asked.

"You're supposed to pack enough clothes for a couple days and be at the school parking lot by three o'clock. A Coast Guard helicopter is going to pick you up."

"What's up?" Atticus asked.

Butch shrugged. "All I know is he said it's very important—be there!"

Atticus glanced at his watch; it was 2:20. "Do me a favor," he said. "Keep an eye on my place while I'm gone. I don't want to come back and find all my stuff out on a snow bank or something."

"I'll take care of it," Butch replied.

Atticus stepped on the accelerator.

———————•◦•———————

It was exactly three o'clock when Atticus pulled into the school parking lot. While he was getting ready, he wondered what could possibly be so important. He parked the car and glanced at his watch again. Suddenly, the sound of a big chopper coming in over the trees broke the silence. Atticus grabbed his overnight bag and got out of the Bronco. In a flurry of blowing snow, the big machine settled down in the middle of the parking lot. Immediately, the door slid open and a young Coast Guardsman jumped out and hurried toward Atticus. "You Mr. Gunner?" he shouted above the roar of the engine. Atticus gave a nod, and the young man motioned him toward the chopper. Bending down as he hurried, Atticus approached the machine and got in; the young man was right on his heels. The airman slid the door shut behind them.

"Where's Agent Barker?" Atticus asked the young navigator.

"I don't know anything about an Agent Barker," he said. "All I know, sir, is we've got orders to deliver you to the Green Bay airport. So sit down and make yourself comfortable; it's about a forty-five-minute trip."

Atticus sat down and placed his bag between his feet. The engine revved and they lifted off, climbing up over the trees. The island fell behind as they headed out over the ice-covered lake.

Cloudy and gray, dusk was just settling in as they approached the city of Green Bay. Ahead, Atticus could see the airport, its blue lights glowing in the gloom of early evening. Coming in well away from the commercial landing field, next to the corporate charter hangars, they settled down in front of one of the big hangars. About fifty yards away was a red and white twin-engine Bonanza with the engines running and the boarding door open. Barker was standing just off from where they were landing, his dark dress coat blowing in the turbulence caused by the chopper's big blades.

The chopper's engine died down as the young man came back into the cargo area again; at first, the silence was almost deafening. He opened the door; Atticus grabbed his bag and got out. Barker came forward immediately to meet him. "What's going on?" Atticus asked.

"Come on," Matt said, taking him by the arm and motioning toward the waiting plane, "we're headed for Madison."

"What for?"

"I'll tell you on board," he replied over his shoulder.

They both climbed on board. Atticus sat down while Matt closed the door and motioned for the pilot to proceed. The engines started to whine as they cranked up. Finally, Matt sat down in the seat across from Atticus. He didn't say anything at first, and then it hit him. "Are my kids all right?" he asked.

Matt nodded. "Yes," he said, "your kids are fine; we've got both of them and your ex-wife in protective custody right now."

"Matt, what the hell is going on?" Atticus asked, his anxiety jumping a thousand percent. "It's Laura, isn't it?"

Again Barker nodded. "Yes; she's been hurt, Atticus."

Atticus felt his stomach wrench into a knot. "What do you mean?" he asked. "How bad?"

"I don't know," Matt replied. "She's in University Hospital. When I talked to Willow, they didn't know the extent of her injuries."

Atticus put his face in his hands; his body trembled. Finally, he leaned back in his seat and stared out the window. He sat silently for the longest time. Matt looked on but made no attempt to explain further. The plane finished taxiing out to the end of the runway, paused, and then took off into the early night sky.

After about twenty minutes, Atticus spoke again, but without turning toward Matt. "What happened?" he asked.

"We don't know the details," Matt replied. "But apparently she was grabbed as she left work at noon yesterday. Then on Old Knob Hill Road, she somehow managed to escape by jumping from the vehicle."

"How did you find out about it?" Atticus asked.

"She kept asking for you, and one of the paramedics on the scene recognized your name from all the TV coverage; he mentioned it to the police; they finally made the connection and called us."

"Where in the hell were your people?" Atticus asked, still looking out the window. "I thought they were supposed to be keeping her safe."

"We're checking into that," Matt answered. "Inspector Willow wants to talk to you as soon as we arrive."

"To hell with Willow," Atticus replied. "I want to go directly to the hospital."

"That's where we are headed."

———— •◆• ————

By the time they arrived at the hospital, it was dark. Atticus hurried up to the front entrance; Matt had to run to keep up. Heading straight to the information window, he asked for Laura's room number.

"She's in room 402," Matt said as he caught up.

Before the receptionist could respond, Atticus was headed up the stairwell on a run; again Matt had all he could do to keep up.

Bursting onto the fourth floor, Atticus looked up and down the hall. Then he spotted Laura's mother and two of her sisters walking toward him. Inspector Willow and a uniformed officer were standing further down the hall in front of an intensive care room.

"Oh Atticus!" Laura's mother exclaimed, giving him a quick embrace. "We've been waiting for you to get here."

"How is she?" Atticus asked.

"She's pretty banged up," Rondel replied, "but she's going to be okay."

"I knew something like this would happen when she moved to the city," her mother went on.

"Mom, she's going to be all right," Robin said, putting her arm around her mother's shoulder.

Without further comment, Atticus stepped around them and continued down the hall. He hurried past Willow without saying a word. Matt, who had finally caught up, attempted to stop him, but Willow motioned to Barker to let him pass.

The police officer standing in front of the door attempted to stop Atticus. Atticus paused and looked back at Willow; Willow gave the officer a nod, and he too stepped aside for Atticus to pass.

Atticus pushed the door open slowly and stepped inside. Except for a small night lamp, the room was dark and quiet. Laura was lying quietly on her back, covered with a green sheet; she was wearing a blue hospital gown. A nurse was changing the plasma bag on the stand next to her bed. On the other side, a doctor was standing quietly, looking at the clipboard in his hand. In front of him, a heart monitor beeped softly.

Atticus stepped forward. Laura's face was white; her eyes were closed. Both sides of the bridge of her nose were blackened, and there was a large bandage over her right forehead. Two tubes were coming from her nose, and her right arm was in a cast clear to the elbow.

The doctor looked up. "Are you Atticus Gunner?" he asked softly. Atticus nodded.

"She's been asking for you," the doctor said.

"How is she?" Atticus asked.

"Well, she won't be jogging for a while," the doctor replied, "but she's a very lucky woman. We just about lost her. If the paramedics hadn't arrived when they did, she would have bled to death."

"What's the extent of her injuries?"

"She has a three-inch laceration on her forehead, a slight concussion, a broken arm, and another three-inch laceration on her upper left thigh; other than a substantial loss of blood at the scene, she's doing fine now."

Atticus closed his eyes for a moment; he blamed himself for this. Then he approached the bed; he took her left hand in his gently. She opened her eyes slightly, gave Atticus a vague smile, and closed them again.

"She's been sedated," the doctor said.

Atticus nodded.

"She needs her rest, Mr. Gunner."

"Yes, I know," Atticus said. "I'll leave in a minute or two."

"All right," the doctor said, "just a couple minutes though." He held up two fingers to the nurse and walked out of the room.

The nurse slid a chair up for Atticus; he sat down. Holding Laura's hand in both of his, he looked at her. She lay very still; her breathing was slow and even. The color was gone from her cheeks. He stroked her hand. Laura opened her eyes again and looked at Atticus; she tried to speak.

Atticus reached out and touched her on the lips. "You're going to be okay," he whispered. "Right now you need to rest."

"It was Tom Cline," she mumbled softly.

"Are you sure?"

She nodded. "I'm sure," she whispered and closed her eyes again.

Atticus sat quietly, holding her hand. The seconds turned to minutes, and the minutes to five. Finally, the nurse came over and touched Atticus on the shoulder. "You're going to have to leave," she whispered.

Atticus nodded, stood up slowly, and slid his hand gently from hers. Laura never moved.

Willow and Barker were still standing in the hall when Atticus emerged. Atticus walked directly over to them. "I want to see my kids," he said.

"Paula's bringing them here right now," Matt answered.

"While we're waiting, we need to talk," Willow said. "We can use the office down by the nurse's station."

When they got to the office, Atticus followed the two men inside. "We found Miss Bock's car over on the east side," Willow said as he sat down on the corner of the desk facing Atticus. "The crime lab is going through it now, but we don't have a whole lot to go on."

Just then Pontiff came into the office and closed the door behind him. He and Atticus glanced at one another, but neither said a word.

"Did Miss Bock say anything to you while you were in the room?" the inspector asked.

Atticus got up out of his chair, walked over to the glass wall, and pulled the curtain back slightly; he looked out for a second or two and then turned toward Willow. "No," he said calmly.

"We have a strong suspicion, Atticus, but that's all we've got."

Atticus sat down again; he looked over at Pontiff. "And what are you doing here, Pope?"

"I'm making contact with you," Pope replied.

"Contact with me?"

"You and I both know you're like a shark that's picked up the scent of blood in the water, and now you have every intention of following it until you can move in for the kill."

Atticus didn't respond.

"I've got a whole lot of years behind me tracking these animals," he went on. "They're testing your resolve, Gunner. They'd like to see you cut and run. Right now, they're not sure what you are or what you're really capable of. You can bet they've looked into your background, just like we have. They know you've got special training; they know you're intelligent and well educated; they know you're a loner; hell, they even know you dislike politicians, corporate power, big money, and big government. But what they don't know is what you're going to do next. But you do, don't you, Gunner? And so do I."

Pontiff walked around the table and sat down facing Atticus. "You're closing in on the queen bee, or should I say king bee, but if Doebuck is our man, and I'm sure he is, he's worried. But there is something I know that you don't know, Gunner; he's called on the services of the most elite Raptor he's got. And that, my friend, is where I come in." Pontiff paused momentarily. He reached inside his coat and pulled out a photograph. He handed it to Atticus. "Have you ever seen this man before?"

Atticus looked at the picture; it was of a tall, dark, thin, athletic, good-looking man in his midforties. He could have been of any number of nationalities; his hair was black with flecks of gray, and he sported a black but graying mustache. Atticus didn't recognize him, and he shook his head.

"His name is Diablo," Pontiff said. "Claims to be Mexican, but we find no record of that, so his origin is uncertain. What we do know is he works exclusively for Doebuck, travels all over the world for him; he has a large villa in the South of France. We have pretty good reason to believe he might be the Broker."

"Does he smoke?" Atticus asked.

"Yes, as a matter of fact he does; why?"

"Just curious," Atticus replied.

"He was educated at Oxford and has a degree in international law," Pontiff continued. "He's coolheaded, very shrewd, self-confident, and cocky. He also speaks a number of languages, including Pashto, a Persian dialect. He's no one's fool, Atticus."

Atticus looked at the picture again.

"We don't know if he's ever been on the island, but we suspect he has; Doebuck doesn't venture very far without him these days. There's one more thing," Pontiff said. "Since Doebuck's name came into the picture, we've been doing a great deal of digging. Six days ago, one of our operatives in Colombia picked up something from a phone message that you may find relevant. The call was from Doebuck's corporate headquarters to Diablo, in Bogota. The message was for Diablo to return stateside to address the final resolution of the 'Moonhawker account.'"

Atticus looked at the picture again.

"It might be a coincidence, Gunner," Pope said, "but I don't think so, and I doubt you do either."

Atticus continued to stare at the picture. "No," he said softly, "it's no coincidence."

This time, Inspector Willow stood up. "If we move to pick him up, he'd walk in less than forty-eight hours, and we would blow our chances to take this organization down. We're looking for a grand jury indictment, Atticus. We need your help to accomplish that."

"What about Laura and my kids?"

"We're going to put them in protective custody until it's over; they'll be in hiding and guarded around the clock by the best people we've got."

"Either way," Pontiff said, "as I see it, you really don't have much choice, but you already know that too."

"You're our means of keeping the pressure on," the inspector said.

"You mean bait."

The inspector said nothing.

"Gunner," Pontiff said, "we have an operative on the island that may be able to help."

"You mean Frank Seamy," Atticus replied.

Pontiff nodded his head in disbelief but said nothing.

"For the longest time, I thought it was Brian Karmel, but his behavior is so stupid I gave up on him. After putting all the pieces together, I knew it had to be Frank."

At that moment, Paula opened the office door and stuck her head in. "They're here," she said.

"After I see my kids, I want Pontiff to drive me to Chicago," Atticus said.

"Chicago!" Willow exclaimed. "Tonight?"

"I want to talk to my landlady."

"Why not just call her?" the inspector asked.

"She doesn't answer."

"I'll send Matt down to talk to her in the morning."

"No," Atticus replied, "tonight. And I want Pontiff to drive."

Pontiff looked up at Atticus. "You think Doebuck's pulling her strings?" he asked.

"Yes," Atticus replied.

The inspector paused for a moment. "That would make for a very long night."

"We'll survive," Atticus replied.

"Okay; done," the inspector said. "Can you live with that, Pope?"

"If Gunner can make it, I can," he replied.

"Good; then it's settled. After Chicago, you both report back here." The inspector turned abruptly and walked out with Matt on his heels.

Pontiff looked up at Atticus again. "My picture?" he asked.

Atticus handed it to him and walked out of the room.

———— ◆ ————

Atticus was directed across the hall to a room where his family was waiting. He paused for a moment and then went inside. Inger was sitting on the bed next to her mother, and Stacie was over by the window. When Atticus entered, they all looked up. "Dad!" Inger barked as she hopped off the bed and ran to meet him. Atticus knelt down to give her a hug. Then he looked up at Stacie, who had come forward a few steps but paused. Atticus smiled at her, and then she too came to her father and received a big hug.

"They won't let us see Laura," Inger said to her father.

Atticus nodded. "I know."

"How bad is she?" Stacie asked.

"She's going to be as good as new," Atticus replied.

"What's wrong with her?" Inger asked.

"She's got a broken arm and a couple of cuts."

"Did those men do it?" Inger asked. "And is that why these people are guarding us?"

"Yes," Atticus replied. "That's why these folks are looking after you; they're FBI agents."

"What's that?" Inger asked.

"Oh Inger," Stacie said, "don't ask so many stupid questions."

"I can if I want to!" she snapped back.

"Hold it," Atticus interjected. "They're special police, okay? And you guys are going to have to do everything they say for the next few days."

"Dad, I can't even see my friends," Stacie replied.

"I know," Atticus said with a nod. "They have to keep you completely hidden for a few days."

"Do you think those guys will try and find us?" Inger asked.

"No, it's just a precaution," Atticus replied.

Stacie said nothing.

"Are you going to be hiding with us?" Inger asked.

"No honey, I'm not," Atticus replied. There was a long pause, and then he spoke again. "Look, I'm going to have to leave in a few minutes, and I want to talk to your mother before I do, so I want you guys to go out in the hall and talk to Paula for a minute, okay?"

Paula, who had been standing quietly by the door, piped up. "Come on, girls," she said. "I'll take you down to peek in on Laura for a second or two."

Inger followed Paula, and so did Stacie, but just before Stacie went out the door, she stopped and looked back.

"It's going to be okay," Atticus said reassuringly. "I'll see both you guys in just a few days."

Stacie nodded and then continued on her way.

Atticus turned his attention back to his former wife, who had been completely silent since he came in. She got up off the bed from where she was sitting. "I know I owe you an explanation for all this," he said, "but to tell you the truth, I really don't have one."

"The girls told me pretty much what was going on," she replied.

Atticus nodded.

"Does Laura really only have a broken arm and some cuts?"

"Yes," Atticus replied.

"And how long is this charade going to go on, Atticus?" she asked.

"I don't know. Hopefully, not for more than a few days."

She looked at Atticus for a few more seconds and then turned and walked out without saying another word. Atticus didn't try to stop her, nor did he attempt to say anything further.

It was close to eleven o'clock by the time they reached downtown Chicago; Pontiff was driving. He had called ahead to the South

Horndale Police Department and made arrangements to pick up a black and tan escort when they got there.

They met their escort on State and Sixteenth, and then followed them to Twenty-Seventh Street. There they turned right and went down about two blocks. The street was narrow, with rundown buildings on both sides. The snow, blackened by the filth of the inner city, lay like mud on the streets and sidewalks. Pulling over to the curb, they stopped across the street from an old dilapidated hotel that looked more like a flophouse than an apartment building. Atticus had expected something quite different.

Pontiff got out of the car; Atticus followed. They were joined by two uniformed policemen. "That's it," one of the officers said, nodding toward the hotel. "You want us to go in with you?"

"Yes," Pontiff replied.

"Pope, she's not going to talk with me if we go in there with an army," Atticus said.

"Sorry, Atticus; we'll stay out in the hall while you talk to her, but we're all going in."

Atticus made no further protest.

Inside the lobby, behind a rickety counter, shrouded in a steel cage, was a grubby-looking character sitting at a table eating a submarine sandwich. Atticus walked up to the barred window. "I'm looking for Cynthia Hersoff," he said. "Can you tell me what apartment she is in?"

The man kept eating; finally, he wiped his mouth with a dirty napkin and looked up at Atticus. "Never heard of her," he said.

Pontiff walked around the counter to the open mesh door and stepped in behind the counter.

"Hey shithead, you can't come in here!" the man said as Pontiff walked up to the table where he was sitting. "Get the hell out of here!" he barked as he wiped his greasy hands on his dirty T-shirt.

Leaning on the table with both hands, Pontiff looked the grubby little man in the eye. "The name is Hersoff," he said softly. "Perhaps you've forgotten."

"Eat shit, cop!" he replied.

With that, Pontiff grabbed the table and threw it off to the side; it slammed hard into the back of the counter, and both the plate and the sandwich went splattering across the floor. The man jumped from the chair and attempted to reach for a button under the counter, but Pontiff grabbed him by the wrist, twisted it behind him, and threw him up against the back wall. With his other hand, he grabbed the clerk by the back of the neck and squeezed just beneath his ears. With his neck stretched and his face pushed forward against the wall, his beady little eyes wide open, the clerk mumbled without further hesitation, "she lives on the second floor."

Pontiff released his grip. "Apartment number?"

"Two forty-eight," the clerk said, rubbing his wrist, "but I don't think they're home; at least Fit hasn't picked up their mail for four days."

"Fit?" Pontiff asked.

"That's the guy she lives with; he's an epileptic. We call him Fit. Ya know, you damn near broke my wrist."

"You press that button, and I'll break more than your wrist," Pontiff replied. "Grab the key; you're coming with."

"You got a search warrant?" the clerk asked.

"No," Pontiff replied, "but if you make these poor officers go get one, they're going to bring the fire marshal back with them to shut you down. And if that happens, you won't have the money to pay your hospital bill."

"What hospital bill?"

"The one you're going to have after your boss finds out what you cost him."

Still rubbing his wrist, the clerk took the key from the board and led the way up the stairs, mumbling under his breath the entire way.

When they reached the apartment, Pontiff motioned for the clerk to step aside. Everyone moved off to the side of the door. Pontiff reached out and knocked on the door; nothing. He knocked again. The sound of a radio playing drifted through the door. Atticus sniffed the air; there was a faint but definite smell, like a rotting animal of some kind. At first, Atticus thought it was coming from the hall, but as he stepped closer, he realized it was coming from inside the apartment. Atticus and Pontiff looked at one another; nothing more needed to be said.

"Give me that key," Pontiff said to the clerk.

Pontiff inserted the key, turned it, and pushed the door open; the gagging smell of death poured into the hall. "Jesus Christ!" Pontiff said, pulling out his handkerchief and putting it over his nose. He went in; one of the officers followed. Atticus paused; a sick feeling swelled in the pit of his stomach.

In a matter of seconds, the officer who went inside reappeared with his hand over his mouth and nose. "Get on the horn," he said to his partner. "Get Homicide up here!"

The second officer hurried down the hall. The clerk just stood there as though he were in a stupor. Atticus pulled his coat up over his nose and went inside. The place was in a shambles: lamps were tipped over, one of them still on; a kitchen chair was thrown clear across the room; and the radio was playing. Then Atticus saw it: in the center of the living room, sprawled out on her back, nightgown torn wide open, saturated with blood long since crusted and turned black, and grossly bloated, was Cynthia; her neck sliced from ear to ear. Atticus turned away.

"Gunner, come in here!" Pontiff barked from down the hall.

Pontiff was standing in the doorway to the bathroom as Atticus approached. "Is that the guy she lived with?" he asked, pointing into the bathroom.

Atticus stepped past him. There in the tub, still partially filled with dark bloodstained water, was the naked corpse of the man who had been with Cynthia up on the island. He too was lying on his back, head tilted back beneath the water, stomach cut wide open, with his intestines pulled out and floating in the water. Atticus nodded and turned away for a second time.

"That poor bastard was tortured," Pontiff said.

Again Atticus nodded.

"I'll have to call Willow and get an investigative team down here to work with the locals; we'll head back to Madison."

Atticus walked back out into the hall. He stood there in silence.

"What in the God damned hell is going on here, anyway?" the clerk blurted out. "I don't give a shit if someone decided to kill the old bitch, but at least they could have done it someplace else. Now I'll be the one who has to clean the damn mess up."

With that, Atticus reached over, grabbing the little fat man by the arm and back of the shirt, and threw him down the hall. The clerk stumbled and fell as he crashed into the railing at the top of the stairwell. Atticus followed him and threw him again, this time down the stairs. Within seconds, Atticus was down the stairs and on top of him.

By the time Pontiff and the police officer got down the stairs and grabbed Atticus in an attempt to restrain him, Atticus had the obnoxious little man backed up against the counter cage with his feet up off the ground. "Gunner! Gunner!" Pontiff screamed in his ear. "Back off, man; he may be a miserable son of a bitch, but he didn't kill those people!"

Slowly, Atticus released his grip. The clerk slid down the cage to the floor; he was shaking with fear but said nothing. With the encouragement of Pontiff and the officer, Atticus stepped back.

———————•◦•———————

It was 4:15 in the morning when Pontiff pulled into an all-night diner on the outskirts of Madison. Atticus hadn't said a word since leaving Chicago. "I need some coffee," Pontiff said as he pulled into a parking place.

Pontiff got out of the car; Atticus followed. They went inside and slid into an empty booth; the waitress brought them coffee. "Want something to eat?" Pontiff asked.

"No; just black coffee," Atticus replied.

Both men sat there, quietly drinking their coffee; finally Pontiff looked up at Atticus again. "I know this is a hell of time to ask, but what's your plan from here, Gunner?"

Atticus shook his head. "I'm not sure," he replied, "as soon as I'm certain Laura and my kids are safe, I'll be heading back to the island. I haven't thought beyond that."

"You could take a couple of days off, you know; no one would complain about that."

"I'm the cop there, remember? But you already knew the answer to that question, Pope, so where are you going with this?"

"Easy, big fella," Pontiff went on. "I'm not trying to agitate you; I'd just like to talk without Willow and the Feds breathing down our necks."

"I'm listening," Atticus replied.

"I know you have every intention of going back to that island. For the benefit of a successful return, however, I'd like to make sure we're on the same page. We—and by we, I mean the CIA—know that taking out the Order of Raptors is extremely important. My superiors want it done clean and without CIA involvement or implication. But just so you understand, while we need your help, with or without you, we have to take them out."

"And you want my help?"

"In two ways; first, we know you're Doebuck's primary focus, and he has to take you out one way or another, but you already know all that. Second, right now you're not only the best shot we've got at getting them without direct involvement, we also know you have every intention of tripping his trigger, and that makes you a force to be reckoned with."

"You seem pretty certain in your thinking."

Pontiff paused but didn't respond to Atticus; instead, he continued on. "Like I said before, Doebuck is going to try and get rid of you through political channels first; that's the cleanest way for him, but if that doesn't work, he's got Diablo."

"Let's go back to the trigger tripping thing. How is it you think I'm going to trip his trigger?"

"You don't push easy, Gunner; you'll trip his trigger, all right."

"And Diablo?"

"If you're asking me if I think you can take him, I don't know. You tell me."

"And where is Willow in all of this?"

"Willow is a cautious man; I don't think he knows what to do. I know he doesn't think he can stop you from going back without force, but I also know he thinks working with you is his only way to a successful conclusion of this case."

"He's right on all accounts, and frankly, so are you. And just for the record, I have every intention of taking them out," Atticus replied.

"Yes, I know."

———✦———

At five o'clock, Atticus and Pontiff stepped off the elevator on the fourth floor of the hospital. Willow and Matt were standing in the hall, talking to the doctor.

"How is she?" Atticus asked as they approached.

"Well, she's stiff and sore," the doctor replied, "but she's going to be just fine. We've taken her down to run some more X-rays and an ultrasound, just to be sure there's nothing else. She should be back in about a half hour."

"When will she be able to leave the hospital?" Atticus asked.

"That's between you and the inspector here," the doctor replied.

Willow motioned to Pontiff to lead the way to the office where they'd met the night before; Atticus followed.

"I showed her the photo of Diablo," Willow said. "She didn't recognize him at all. She said the man was careful to make sure she never saw his face; he was wearing a ski mask."

Atticus knew that Laura had intentionally misled Willow, but said nothing.

"Was her assailant alone?" Pontiff asked.

"Yes; she also told us it was just a fluke that she escaped. She was thrown against the passenger door latch when they went around a corner, and it simply came open; she rolled out onto the street. Her abductor slammed on the brakes, but when he saw all the people who witnessed it, he took off."

"Do you think it was Diablo?" Matt asked Pontiff.

"No," Pontiff replied, shaking his head. "That was way too sloppy for someone of his caliber; he may have been in on the planning, but it wasn't Diablo. Who was it, Gunner?" Pontiff asked as though he knew Atticus was hiding something.

Atticus sat down in a chair but said nothing.

"Last night, Mr. Gorpon called the Green Bay FBI office trying to locate you," Willow said, looking at Atticus. "Because you were unavailable, I took the liberty of calling him back. It seems a group of islanders has called for a special joint meeting of the board of education and police committee to demand your resignation. Gorpon said they want to meet before you get back; the meeting has been called for tomorrow night at 8:30. He also told me Doebuck was leading the pack, and that he was going to be there."

Again Atticus made no response.

Pontiff looked at Atticus.

Atticus got up out of his chair. "I need a ride to the ferry," he said. "Barker, are you up for a morning drive to the north woods?"

"Wait a minute," Willow said.

"There's no time to wait," Pontiff replied. "Gunner is doing exactly what he has to."

"I don't like it; there's no substance; no backup; there's no plan, and if Gunner gets in over his head, what then, Pope?"

"We'll put a SWAT team and chopper on standby in Sturgeon Bay. Our contact can be through the Coast Guard; Gunner's got a ship-to-shore in his Bronco. We can be on that island in forty-five minutes."

The inspector took a deep breath. "A hell of a lot can happen in that much time."

"Have you got a better plan?" Pontiff asked.

"Gentleman, I've got to go," Atticus broke in. "Do I get that ride?"

The inspector took another deep breath and nodded his head. "Go ahead," he said.

Atticus and Matt started for the door.

"Atticus," the inspector said, "we've got a team investigating your landlady's homicide. I'll keep you posted."

Atticus nodded.

"They'll be shadowing every move you make; they probably have your house wired," Willow went on, "so be careful."

Atticus nodded again. Just before he went out, he stopped and looked back at Willow. "Will you talk to Laura and my kids? Make sure they understand I'm okay."

Willow nodded.

"Wait a minute; I'm coming with," Pontiff said as he got out of his chair.

"Not this time," Atticus replied.

"Just to make sure you get there all right," Pontiff said as he followed Atticus and Barker out into the hall.

"Suit yourself," Atticus replied over his shoulder, "but I'm afraid I'm not going to be much company; I intend to sleep most of the way; you should be doing the same."

"Don't worry about me."

"Worrying about you is the least of my concerns."

"Will you two shut up?" Matt barked. "I'm not going to listen to the two of you wrangle all the way up to North Point Ferry Dock."

CHAPTER 21

A Welcome to Hell

Agent Barker turned right as they were coming into Gills Rock and headed down through the woods toward North Point Ferry Dock. He glanced at his watch; it was 11:20 a.m.; they had made good time coming up from Madison. The sun was shining, but it was cold. Atticus was in the front seat next to Barker with his head back against the seat; he'd been asleep since they left Madison. Stirring, Atticus opened his eyes. "We're just about there," Matt said. Atticus lifted his head and looked around. Pontiff, who was in the back seat, opened his eyes and sat up.

As they emerged out of the woods and drove into the parking area, Barker swung off to the side of the lot up next to the big pine trees at the edge of the woods. The *Otterman* was tied off at the end of the pier with the loading ramp down. The ferry crew was unloading mail from the mail truck to the boat, and the island grocery truck was parked and waiting to be loaded; there was no one in either truck.

Atticus reached over the back of the seat to retrieve his overnight bag.

"Don't forget, your home phone is likely to be tapped," Barker said.

"I won't," Atticus replied.

"Oh, and remember, 'Big Bird' is the code word for calling in the chopper."

"Yes Matt, I remember everything," Atticus replied again.

Just then, a long black Cadillac came rolling slowly into the lot down by the dock. Atticus watched as it continued toward the loading ramp. "Well, what do you know?" he said as though he were talking to himself. "Look who is here, and a day early."

The three men watched as the shiny black limo came to a stop behind the grocery truck. The driver's door opened, and out stepped Doebuck's bodyguard. After a second or two, both the front and rear passenger doors opened; Old Man Doebuck emerged from the front seat, and two other men stepped out from the back. One of them was Diablo; Atticus couldn't ID the second one. The driver stretched and got back in; Doebuck and his two companions walked down to the boat and boarded.

"Would you look at that?" Pontiff said softly. "Can you believe the arrogance?"

"Who is the other man?" Atticus asked.

"I don't know," Pontiff replied.

"My guess is he's Doebuck's lawyer," Barker replied.

"I don't like this, Gunner," Pontiff said. "Maybe I should come with you."

"Not this time, Pope. This is on my watch, and I think I'm going to make the ride a little extra interesting for our friends."

"What's your plan?" Pontiff asked.

"Can you and Matt take out Doebuck's bodyguard and drive the car up into the woods without being seen? I don't want either him or that car to make it on board the boat."

"I think we can make that happen," Pontiff replied. "But I still don't know what your intentions are."

"I'm going to test the waters by putting a little pressure on Doebuck and his buddies." Atticus got out of the car.

"Gunner," Pontiff said, leaning forward in his seat, "don't underestimate these bastards. To them it's still 1945, and those arrogant assholes think they're legitimate Gestapo."

"I'll keep that in mind," Atticus replied.

"What do you want us to do with the bodyguard?" Barker asked.

"I don't care what you do with him; just keep him out of circulation. Doebuck and company will be up in the passenger cabin," Atticus went on. "They won't be looking out at their car. Besides, the grocery truck is completely blocking their view. The ferry crew is busy, so they won't be a problem. We've got a good shot at pulling this off, but there's no room for error."

"What if the ferry workers finish what they're doing before we get the job done?" Barker asked.

"If they move in the direction of Doebuck's car, I'll distract them. Just remember, we've got no time to waste." With that, Atticus closed the door and started toward the dock.

———◆———

As Atticus was about to step on board, he glanced back and saw Pope open the door of the black Cadillac. There was a sudden but silent scuffle that was over just a quickly as it started; Pontiff pushed the driver over in the seat, got in, backed up the car, and drove off toward the woods.

Captain Joel glanced up as Atticus approached. "Mr. Gunner," he said in a whisper, "Doebuck and his cronies are on board."

"I know," Atticus replied.

"They got a meeting called for tomorrow night; you know that too, right?"

"Yes, I know that too."

"You're welcome to ride up in the wheelhouse with us if you like."

"Thanks," Atticus replied, "I'll come up after we get underway."

Atticus went straight up to the wheelhouse, put his overnight bag inside, and then went to the passenger cabin. As he opened the door, Doebuck and his two friends were standing along the far wall, looking out at the ice-covered lake. He stepped inside, pulled the door shut, and sat down on one of the side benches. The man with Doebuck who Atticus didn't recognize glanced in his direction. Atticus may not have known who he was, but from the expression on the man's face, it was obvious he knew who Atticus was. He turned back to Doebuck and whispered something in his ear; Doebuck turned immediately and glanced over toward Atticus. The look on Doebuck's face was one of complete amazement. Atticus gave him a slow but deliberate nod. Doebuck turned away. Shortly after, Diablo glanced over and gave Atticus a warm but arrogant smile; Atticus smiled back.

Even though the lake ice around the boat was broken into large chunks, it had closed back in around the boat while they were docked. Finally, the horn blew and the *Otterman* began backing away from the dock; each time a block of float ice slid under the stern and hit the big propeller, the boat would shudder. Atticus got up and walked outside to the stern rail; he leaned on his elbows and looked down at the churning mayhem behind the boat.

It wasn't long before Diablo came out of the cabin and approached the railing next to Atticus. He reached inside his long black leather coat and retrieved a silver engraved cigarette case. Pressing a button, the case flipped open; he took out a cigarette, stuffed it between his narrow lips, and held the case out to Atticus. "Cigarette?" he asked.

Atticus looked down at the neatly aligned row of Turkish cigarettes in the open case, and then he looked up at the man he had so long wondered about.

"I work for Doebuck," the man said in a distinct British brogue while lighting his cigarette. "The name is Diablo."

"I know who you are," Atticus replied.

"And you are?"

"Your worst nightmare," Atticus replied without looking at him.

Diablo also leaned against the railing and took a deep drag off his cigarette. "So you're the infamous Mr. Gunner," he said. "They even have a code name for you, can you believe that? But I must say, old boy, I'm a bit taken aback; somehow, I thought you would be more impressive."

Atticus didn't respond.

Just then, the stranger in their party came up on the other side of Diablo. "Where is Gunta?" he asked Diablo softly. "He's not on the boat."

Atticus thought he recognized that voice but couldn't place it.

Diablo stood up and looked at the stranger. "What do you mean?" he asked.

"I mean he's not on the boat, and neither is the car!"

Diablo looked back at Atticus. "Okay, funny boy, I hope you're not trying to play some kind of game; that would be a very stupid maneuver."

Atticus just smiled at him, and then he stood up and started back toward the cabin door.

The stranger stepped out from the rail in front of Atticus; Atticus paused and looked at him. After a quick glance, Atticus recognized the shoes; now he knew who he was; he was the man in the shadows at Baynard's. His thoughts went back to the island deaths. He had all he could do to contain the hatred that flooded through him; he knew this was the man he was looking for; this was the Raptor, but he said nothing.

Atticus looked back at Diablo. "We're not going to have a clash here," he said to Diablo. "That is, unless you plan on falling on your own sword, and I don't think you're ready for that just yet."

The muscles in Diablo's face twitched as he glared at Atticus. "You may be right this time, Gunner, but you can bet we'll meet again, old boy." He motioned for the Raptor to step aside.

Atticus gave the Raptor a cold hard stare as he stepped aside. Then he looked back at Diablo once more and smiled. "By the way," he said, "how are things back at the villa?" He took a couple of steps, stopped, and looked back at Diablo again. "Oh, and I almost forgot; I've got a message for you and your boss; we put the word out letting everyone know just who you are, and who your old buddy Doebuck really is. I'm sure your business associates are most anxious to talk with both of you as soon as they get the word. You may carry on now—old boy."

It was clear to Atticus as he walked away, he had struck a chord with Diablo, but as to his companion, there wasn't even a hint of being rattled.

Atticus opened the door to the wheelhouse.

"Come right in," Captain Joel replied.

Atticus stepped in and closed the door. The two deckhands were sitting on the bench shelf that stretched across the back of the wheelhouse. Atticus pushed his bag off to the side and slid up on the bench next to them. "If anyone comes up here," Atticus said. "I'll do the talking, okay?"

"Is that to say I'm to expect company?" Joel asked.

"Yes, I'd say that's a possibility," Atticus replied.

Joel smiled. "Whatever you say goes; I guess tonight you're going to be the man."

"Yes, tonight I'm the man," Atticus replied.

It wasn't long before the door opened, and standing there on the step was the Raptor. "Captain," he said, "Mr. Doebuck would like for you to call the terminal and have the receptionist arrange a ride for us. And we'd also like to know where our car and driver are."

Atticus leaned forward so he could be seen. "And you are?" he asked.

The Raptor looked at Atticus with a cold stare. "The name is Vonpuk," he replied.

"Well, Mr. Vonpukie, or whatever it is, I've commandeered this boat and I'm afraid we can't do that."

"I beg your pardon?"

"It's against the rules," Atticus said.

"There are no such rules."

"Oh yes, I'm afraid there are; they're called my rules."

"The terminal will be closed by the time we reach the island, so how do you suggest we get a ride?"

"Well, there's a pay phone just outside the ferry office; it usually works. You can try that."

"Mr. Gunner, I've been very accommodating to you thus far, but for your sake, you better hope that phone works." Vonpuk gave Atticus another very cold look and closed the door.

Captain Joel shook his head. "Mr. Gunner, you sure got guts," he said.

"Yeah, but what about us?" the deckhand sitting on the bench next to Atticus said. "I have to go back there and collect the ticket money."

"Not this time, son," Atticus replied, "this is a free ride for everyone."

"And if Mr. Fruger doesn't see it that way?" Captain Joel asked.

"You just tell him that I made the decision."

Again Joel smiled and shook his head.

"Joel, when you get back, you're done for the day, right?" Atticus asked.

"That I am," Joel replied.

"As the island cop, I'm afraid I'm going to have to ask you for another favor; could you give me a ride to the school so I can pick up the Bronco?"

"Not a problem, but it'll take me a little time to unload, shut everything down, and secure the boat for the night."

"That's okay. I want to stick around to see how Doebuck and his friends solve their little dilemma anyway."

"I hope they don't solve it by calling your bluff," the other young man sitting on the far side of the wheelhouse said.

"What makes you think I'm bluffing?" Atticus asked.

No one responded.

<hr />

After docking back on the island, Atticus went down on the car deck and watched as the crew began to unload the mail into the ferry line pickup parked on the dock. Soon Vonpuk came down the steps and left the boat without as much as a glance in Atticus's direction; he trudged off through the blowing snow up toward the darkened ferry terminal. It was of small consolation, but watching him step gingerly through the deep snow in his fancy shoes made Atticus feel good.

Atticus went back up on the passenger deck and peeked through a cabin window to see how the other two were faring; they were sitting back in the corner, side by side; Diablo was puffing on a cigarette, and Doebuck was sitting quietly with his hands folded on his lap. For a moment, until he remembered what Doebuck stood for, he looked like a pathetic old man. Atticus wondered if the years of running, and the horrors he was guilty of, might finally be coming home to roost.

In about thirty minutes, along came Hepper Greshion in his old pickup. He drove right up to the boat; Vonpuk was with him. Vonpuk got out and came up the stairs to the passenger cabin. Soon, all three men went down and crammed into Hepper's truck. Their choice of a ride didn't really surprise Atticus. He stepped out to the rail, where he was sure they would see him. He stood there as Hepper turned around and drove away in the blowing snow—four people crammed into Hepper's dumpy old pickup. Atticus smiled and then spoke softly to himself: "You may be a long way from Auschwitz, you godless bastards, but you're running out of room to run now."

———◆———

After thanking Joel, Atticus stepped out from the captain's car into the school parking lot. The Bronco was right where he'd left it. The school, still closed up for Christmas break, was dark. Atticus's first inclination was to get into the Bronco and hunt down Tom Cline, but after he thought about it, he decided to wait; Tom wouldn't be going anyplace. Instead, Atticus trudged over to the school, unlocked the doors, and went into his office. He picked up the phone and dialed Butch's number.

"Hello," came Butch's voice from the other end.

"Butch; this is Atticus. I'm back."

"Where are you?"

"In my office. Is everything okay at the Hersoff place?"

"Yes, everything is fine. I was just down there and hauled some wood in for you, but there is something I need to tell you."

"Go ahead, this phone should be secure."

"Atticus, when I was hauling wood, I went around to the back of the pile because there was less snow on that side, and as I was loading my arms, I uncovered something."

"You uncovered something?"

"Yes, a leather pouch. I opened it, and it was full of papers written in some foreign language. I don't know what they say, but they were all water stained and stuff; I'm sure they're from that plane crash. I think Jody Kerfam stashed them there."

"Still think her death was an accident?"

"No."

"What did you do with the pouch?" Atticus asked.

"I put it right back where I found it."

"Did anyone see you, Butch?"

"No."

"Okay, I'll talk to you in the morning. Meet me at the restaurant at seven-thirty."

"What are you going to do now?"

"Go home and try to catch up on some sleep."

"Will you be safe there?"

"Oh yes, they won't be on the hunt tonight."

"Okay; I'll see you in the morning then." The phone clicked.

———•◆•———

The next morning, Atticus was in the restaurant eating breakfast when he noticed Hepper drive up to the mercantile across the street and go inside. In less than twenty minutes, he came out toting four bags full of groceries. He put them in the back of his pickup, crawled in behind the wheel, and took off in a hurry. Although the connection between Hepper, the Clines, and Doebuck had now been confirmed for Atticus, he still didn't understand the full nature of it. The death of Cynthia and her companion were also brought front and center, not that Hepper had anything to do with the killing, but the involvement of the Order seemed a sure fit.

Atticus also thought about the leather pouch Butch found. He had retrieved it from the woodpile and brought it inside last night to study its contents, and while he couldn't decipher the writing on the papers either, he knew enough to suspect the writing to be in Arabic of some form. Judging from the number of signatures at the bottom, he concluded it to be a contract of sorts. Atticus was certain it would be of value to Pontiff, so he stashed it back behind the woodpile until he could turn it over to him.

Shortly thereafter, Butch came wheeling in and parked next to the Bronco. Atticus got up, put his money on the table, and hurried out. As he came out, he motioned for Butch to get in the Bronco. After they were in, Atticus looked over at him. "Are you working today?" he asked as he started the engine.

"Yes, I am, but I did get a call from Adrian early this morning. Just what in the hell was that ordeal on the boat all about last night?"

"We'll talk about it later."

"Later? Atticus, this is later. We have a witch hunt tonight, and you're the witch they're hunting. So how much later would you like to make it?"

"Sorry," Atticus said. "Doebuck and a couple of his lap boys were on the boat, and I decided to apply a little pressure."

"Oh, well, you sure did that. The unfortunate thing is you also managed to throw more wood on the fire."

"Butch, the meeting tonight is the final push to get rid of me, but it will only turn into a witch hunt if you let it. All you have to do tonight is run the meeting and make sure that doesn't happen; I'll fend off the rest of the fireworks."

"Your smooth talking may not be enough to get you out of trouble this time."

"That's when voting your own judgment comes into play."

"Atticus, you're a good friend, but I have to live here; I am an islander."

"I realize that; but don't let these people push you into doing something you don't agree with; that's not in your best interest, and it's certainly not who you are."

"You forget, I'm only one vote."

"Butch, I'm willing to take it as it comes; you need to be ready to do the same. Now, have you informed all the staff members as to what is going on tonight?"

"Yes; did you talk to the state?"

"I've talked with Kozuszek; DPI has no intention of stepping in on this."

"That's a relief, and everyone on the staff intends to be there. Everyone except for Frank, that is; I don't know where in the hell he is."

"You mean he's off-island?"

"No, he's been back since the day you left. I just can't seem to catch him at home, that's all."

"Have you been out there?"

"Yes, I went over there just before coming here; his car is there, but he isn't."

Atticus thought of the Kerfam ordeal. "How long has he been missing?" he asked.

"I don't know. Like I said, I was just out there this morning. His snowshoes were gone, with tracks leading into the woods, so he's probably out hiking around like he always does."

"This early in the morning?"

Butch shook his head. "I don't know," he said. "He could have gone out there yesterday for all I know."

"Have you seen Tom Cline lately?"

"No. I just saw Hepper though, headed for the east side like a bat out of hell. Which reminds me—ya know, Atticus, there probably won't be many people at the meeting tonight."

"Why do you say that?"

"We're supposed to have a big blow tonight, and it's supposed to get colder than hell. Some of our best allies are probably out on the ice right now, jerking their nets."

"I'm afraid I'm not following you."

"A heavy wind means a big ice shove. If you don't get your nets in before it hits, they're gone forever. I've seen ice shoves push ice up on the shore twenty feet high; takes out trees like they weren't even there. It takes a real wind to do that, and as a result, people won't be venturing outside much; meeting or no meeting."

"Right now, that seems the least of my worries. What about Adrian; think he'll be there?"

"Well, if you'd asked me that question yesterday, I'd probably say no, but after your performance on the boat last night, I don't know. Either way, his mouthpiece will be there, I'm sure of that. And his little confidant Brian will be right by his side."

"You better get to work; I'll see you tonight."

"Did you look at the contents in that pouch?" Butch asked.

"Yes, I did, and I agree with you."

"So what are you going to do with it?"

"For now, it's in a safe place. I'll see that it gets into the right hands."

"Where are you headed now?"

"I'm going to see if I can find Frank, get some groceries, go home, and get ready for tonight."

Butch shook his head. "You're either one cool son of a bitch or you're crazy as hell."

"Right now, crazy is probably closer to the truth."

Butch got out of the Bronco and slammed the door shut. He waved Atticus off as he headed back toward his old wagon.

It was close to three by the time Atticus made it home. He built a fire, made himself something to eat, and sat down on the couch to plan his strategies for the night. He had five hours before the meeting.

After about twenty minutes, he got up and went over to the phone. He had gone out to Frank's after leaving Butch but couldn't find him, so he picked up the receiver and dialed his number again for the third time. The phone rang several times, but there was no answer. He thought he'd try the school on the chance he might be there. Atticus hook flashed for the dial tone; that's when it happened again: there was a triple click on the line. He hung up, thought about what Willow said concerning his phone, and then went back into the living room.

He pushed the couch aside, threw back the rug, exposing the trap door that led to the basement, and opened it. Grabbing his flashlight from the cabinet, he made his way down the rickety steps into the musty-smelling darkness. He shined the light around. A couple of mice scurried across the floor; cobwebs and junk were everywhere. He made his way over to the outside wall under the dining room. Shining his light up along the floor joist, he looked for the phone line. After finding it, he followed the line with the light beam along the base of the joist.

On the back of the house, under the bathroom, it disappeared up the wall behind the fiberglass insulation and then reappeared again going into the crawl space under the furnace room. The insulation had obviously been torn away and pushed back in place, so Atticus walked over there. Lifting the spun glass away, he shined his light up into the location; there was a junction box. The original line went through the wall to the outside; the other went out through the furnace room. Atticus hurried back upstairs.

Throwing on his warmest clothes, he went outside. The setting sun was now casting long shadows across the snow, and it was getting cold; strong gusts of wind were already beginning to blow. He trudged through the deep snow around to the back of the house. He could see where the regular phone line came out and went up the side of the building to the connecting box. The second line came out from under the furnace room, went along the base of the garage, and disappeared under the snow. Holding the line loosely, he followed it, yanking it up as he proceeded. The line went across the yard and into the woods, down into the drainage ditch and through the culvert under the driveway. On the other side of the drive, he kicked away the snow until he found it again. He picked it up and continued on. The line went through the woods and came out behind Hepper's old hotel.

Atticus relocated the line along the foundation of the hotel. From there, it went along the base of the building and finally inside through the corner of one of the basement windows. He knelt down in the snow. Rubbing the frost away from the window, Atticus peered inside. There was a card table and a folding chair set up just below the window. On it was an automatic tape recorder connected to the line. Seeing no one around, he continued to work his way along the foundation, wiping the snow away from each of the basement windows, looking inside as he went.

It was at the last window when everything went sour; just as he looked in the window, he felt a sensation of danger; he looked up, but it was too late; Hepper was coming straight at him with a steel post. Hepper swung the post with all his might; it hit Atticus in the back with a glancing blow; the impact sent him sprawling into the snow face-first. With a sharp pain shooting across his upper back, Atticus struggled to get back to his feet. Hepper came at him for a second try; Atticus rolled to the right. This time, Hepper missed. Slipping in the snow, Hepper fell to his knees, and before he could regain his balance, Atticus was able to tackle him. The powdery snow swirled in bellows as they tumbled over and over down the hill back toward the woods.

Managing to regain his stance first, Atticus grabbed Hepper by the collar and yanked him to his feet, but just as he was about to put

Hepper out of commission, he was knocked off his feet. He felt like he had been kicked from behind by a mule; the pain was excruciating. Gasping for breath, Atticus struggled desperately to get up. Somewhere in a world out of focus, he could see Tom Cline towering over him. He shook his head in an attempt to clear it. Tom swung his club. Atticus managed to throw up an arm in a feeble attempt to ward off the blow, but the impact struck him across the shoulder and along the side of the head. He saw a flash, and then the world went completely topsy turvy. Tom stepped forward and kicked Atticus hard in the stomach. Atticus doubled up as the world went blank.

"That's enough!" Hepper grunted as he staggered back to his feet. "You'll kill him!"

"So what?" Tom replied, kicking Atticus again in the ribs. "The son of a bitch deserves to die!"

"Not here," Hepper said. "Not without Mr. Doebuck's permission."

"What the hell is the difference?"

"You want to tell him that?"

Tom mumbled to himself but backed off.

"Come on," Hepper said, "let's get him in the hotel before someone sees us."

———◆———

The two men grabbed Atticus under the arms and dragged him around to the front of the hotel, up the steps, and inside. They dragged him into the parlor off Hepper's living quarters and dumped him on the floor. Hepper got some rope. Then with Tom kneeling beside Atticus's head, Hepper tied his arms behind, bound his ankles, and finally gagged him.

When they finished, Hepper got up and sat on the corner of the couch; he took a couple of deep breaths to regain his composure. "I'm going to call Doebuck," he said. "While I do that, you go down by the lake and get the snowmobile."

Tom rose to his feet, gave Atticus another kick in the shoulder blades for good measure, and then walked out.

Hepper dialed the phone and waited. "Hello," came a voice on the other end.

"Is Mr. Doebuck there?" Hepper asked nervously.

"Who's calling?" came the voice.

"This is Hepper Greshion; it's an emergency."

The line went silent for a few moments, and then came a response: "This is Munster Doebuck."

"Mr. Doebuck, this is Hepper Greshion. I'm sorry to bother you sir, but . . ."

"Hepper, I told you to never call me here; what is it?"

"Tom Cline and I caught Atticus Gunner snooping around the hotel; he found the phone line. I've got him tied up here in my living quarters."

"You've got Gunner tied up?"

"Yes sir; I figured you'd want to know right away."

"Did anyone see you?"

"No sir."

"Stay there; I'll have someone over there right away. Do nothing; do you understand?"

"Yes sir."

The phone went dead; Hepper hung up the receiver.

———•◆•———

Edna Doebuck's island car, a 1948 baby blue Cadillac, came around the corner and stopped at the end of the driveway in front of the hotel. There were two people in it: Diablo, who was driving, and Vonpuk, who was sitting next to him. Vonpuk got out and walked up to the hotel; Diablo drove off.

As Vonpuk walked up the steps, Tom arrived with the snowmobile. Hepper opened the door and Vonpuk went inside. Tom ran up the steps and followed them in.

"He's in here," Hepper said.

The stranger proceeded into the parlor without saying a word.

"And what did you say your name was?" Tom asked as he stepped around the man.

"I didn't," the stranger replied, looking past him.

"Wait; I know who you are," Tom came back. "You're the guy Baynard called Raptor."

Vonpuk looked at him but made no comment. Instead, he looked down at Atticus lying on the floor and then back up at Hepper. "Are you sure no one saw you?" he asked.

"Positive," Hepper replied.

"No one followed him either," Tom chimed in.

Hepper nodded. "Tom came up behind him through the woods; if anyone had been there, he woulda seen them. Right, Tom?"

"There was nobody there," Tom replied. "You gonna kill him?"

The stranger looked briefly at Tom and then back over at Hepper again. "That's your pickup out front, isn't it?" he asked Hepper.

Hepper nodded.

"We'll put Gunner in the back with me; you drive us over to Doebucks'." He then looked at Tom again. "I want you to go through the woods to Gunner's place; take the same trail he made, cut the phone line off at his house, gather it up, and bring it back here. When you're finished with that, get a big branch and sweep over the trail to hide the tracks from his place to the hotel; the wind will take care of the rest. Can you handle that?"

Tom gave a nod. "But I still want to know if we're going to kill the son of a bitch."

Without warning, the stranger turned on Tom; in a flash, he had him face-down on the floor with the sharp end of a knife pressed firmly up under his chin. "One more stupid comment from you, and I'll cut your head clean off," he said. "From this point on, you'll do what you're told, when you're told, and you'll keep your mouth shut unless asked to speak. Do you understand?"

"Okay, okay," Tom muttered.

The stranger released his grip and allowed Tom to get back to his feet. "After you're finished, bring that snowmobile and sled over to Doebucks'. Make sure no one sees where you're going."

"Sir," Tom said with a tremble in his voice. "Please, just one question."

Vonpuk glared at him. "What?"

"We've got all our fishing gear in the sled; should I unload that stuff first?"

"No," the stranger replied. "If someone does see you, you'll be far less conspicuous if you leave things just as they are. Now get moving."

Tom left without further comment.

———•◦•———

Dusk was settling in as Hepper drove into the Doebucks' yard. Other than Mrs. Doebuck's car up under the trees in front of the house, there was no sign of life. Vonpuk tapped on the rear window of the truck, motioning for Hepper to drive over to the big carriage barn. Hepper did as he was told, and then the two men got out and dragged Atticus from the back of the truck.

Carrying him inside, they dumped Atticus on the floor like a sack of flour. "You stay outside by the truck until I return," Vonpuk said to Hepper. He then walked away toward the house. Hepper followed him out of the barn as far as the truck, and stopped and stood there.

As a gust of wind swung the barn door partially closed with a loud creaking sound, Atticus began to regain consciousness. He saw Doebuck's house, and he knew he was tied up, but not a whole lot else seemed to register. When he finally realized just how serious his situation was, he had all he could do from going into a complete panic. He looked around. Hepper was outside; he could see him through the crack in the door. At that very same moment, highlighted by the light that came through the crack in the door, he saw the white pearl handle of a jackknife stuck in the wall just below a roll of twine. Without hesitation, he turned over on his stomach, pulled his knees up under himself, and then using the wall as added support, lifted himself up to a kneeling position. The knife was now at eye level. Atticus batted at it with his head. The first try only knocked the blade to the side and cut him slightly on the forehead. But on the second try, it fell to the floor and landed in the loose hay in front of him. Flopping back down to a prone position, he worked his way around to where the knife was behind him. With cold fingers, he finally touched the blade. Working the knife around carefully, he palmed the blade in his glove and slid it partially up his sleeve.

As he scooted around, Atticus bumped into something hard in the hay behind his head. He twisted around to see what it was; lying there, gazing out at him from inside a large plastic bag, was Frank's body. He was very cold, very hard, and very dead. Atticus cringed.

Suddenly, the sound of footsteps crunching in the cold snow outside shattered the silence; Atticus froze. The footsteps stopped and a man started to talk to Hepper; it was Doebuck. "Hepper, things aren't going at all as we had hoped," Doebuck said in a low but calm voice. "I'm afraid we're going to have to make some adjustments, and do it quickly. You and Mr. Cline are going to have to help; there will be a substantial reward in it for both of you if you do well. Can I depend on you?"

"Yes sir, as always," Hepper replied.

"When Mr. Cline gets here, I've got a job for the both of you out on the lake."

Atticus drew the knife from his sleeve and started to cut desperately at the ropes that bound his wrist.

"Mr. Doebuck, I'm not questioning your judgment," Hepper said, "but this is no night to be out on the ice."

"I realize that, but we don't have much choice. That's why I've decided to ask you and Cline to do the job; you boys know your way around out there."

"Well, let's not wait too long then," Hepper replied. "That ice is going to be on the move later, and I sure as hell don't want to be out there when that happens. What is it you want us to do? Get rid of Gunner?"

"We'll talk about that as soon as your partner gets here. In the meantime, I want you to go up to the house, get a cup of coffee, and warm up; my associate here will go with you. Diablo and I have some things to talk over."

That was the first Atticus realized that Diablo and Vonpuk were also outside with Doebuck.

"Yes sir," Hepper replied. Then there were footsteps walking away.

"Sir," Diablo said after the sound of footsteps faded, "you're not really going to follow through with those buffoons, are you? That dumb bastard Cline couldn't even take care of Gunner's girlfriend without screwing it up."

"For the job of getting rid of Gunner and his frozen buddy, yes. They won't be returning from the ice, however—our Raptor will see to that."

"What about Vonpuk? Does he know your real identity?"

"No," Doebuck answered. "All he knows is he's been assigned to work with us—just like last summer. Diablo, I'm going to keep this man with me until I get things straightened away here. In the meantime, I've made arrangements for a plane to fly in here tonight at eight to pick you up; you're booked on a midnight flight out of Chicago for Geneva. I've removed the organizational files from my safe; you'll be taking them with you; they're no longer secure here. You know what to do when you get to Switzerland."

"And what about you, sir?"

"They're very close to us; if we panic, we could end up in deep trouble. I intend to go to the meeting tonight as though nothing happened. I'll contact you in about six weeks."

"And when Gunner and his friend don't show at the meeting?"

"That's part of why I'm going to stay here and ride out the storm."

"They're going to know something has happened to them."

"Knowing it and proving it are two very different things. That's a very big lake out there, and they won't have a chance of finding anything until the ice is gone next spring. By then, we'll be long gone."

"What about your bodyguard?" asked Diablo.

"He's a devoted Nazi; he'll do what he has to for the cause. One way or the other, he'll turn up in due time."

"We're into the cartels for a great deal of money, and their influence is pretty much worldwide now. So if, as Gunner said, they've put the word out, and they learn our identity, we'll have to go deep into hiding, maybe even as deep as into the mountains of Afghanistan. Are you prepared for that, sir?"

"One thing at a time," Doebuck replied. "As soon as Cline gets here, I want you to get the boys on their way. As I said before, Vonpuk has been instructed to see that they do not return, so the loose ends here will be taken care of. After they're off to the lake, I want you to pick up the briefcase at the house, and then take Hepper's truck to the airport to catch your ride. Oh, and don't leave any prints on Hepper's truck. Nor do I want any blood traces in that garage; there are to be no traces of violence in this residence. Do you understand?"

"Yes sir. What are they to use to weigh the bodies down?"

"There are two lengths of logging chain in the garage; they should do nicely."

Just then, Tom Cline pulled into the yard on Hepper's snowmobile. The pull sled behind the snowmobile rumbled as it dragged across the blacktop. Tom pulled up to Hepper's truck and stopped.

"I'll see you in the house after they're on their way," Doebuck said to Diablo. He then walked away without as much as acknowledging Cline.

"Where's Hepper?" Tom asked Diablo after the old man left.

"He's up at the house; go get him," Diablo replied.

The last few strands of rope around Atticus's wrist severed, and his left hand broke free. He shoved the knife into his pocket, put his arms behind himself again, wrapped the loose end of the rope around his wrist a couple of times, and held it tight to appear as though he was still tied up. Diablo walked in the door and flicked on the light just as Atticus finished.

"Well, Gunner, we meet again," Diablo said as he walked over to Atticus and knelt down next to him.

Atticus pretended as though he was just coming around.

"This time I'm afraid will be our last time old man," he said as he smiled a greasy smile and stood up again to light a cigarette. "You've caused us a great deal of trouble, my stupid friend," he said. "If I had the time, I'd see that you paid for it like your friend Seamy there." He walked over to Frank's body and kicked away the hay, exposing the entire frozen corpse; his body was badly mutilated.

Atticus closed his eyes.

"That's right," Diablo went on. "You didn't know that, did you? The Raptor said he begged like a baby and sung like a bird. He was CIA, you know; I'll bet you didn't know that either." He walked back over to Atticus. "And here, all along, we thought you were." He shook his head. "If we'd known the truth, we would have gotten rid of you a long time ago."

Just then, Hepper and Tom walked in. The Raptor was directly behind but hung back and stood by the door.

Diablo glanced over at them as they entered. "Well, what do you know?" he said to Atticus. "Here's your ride to eternity."

Atticus glanced at them.

"Come here," Diablo said, motioning to the Raptor. Vonpuk took a couple of steps forward. "You've met this fellow," Diablo went on, "but I don't think you've been properly introduced; this is the man they call the Raptor. He's the one who killed your old friend and those kids last summer." Diablo chuckled as though he got great joy thinking about it. "He removed the anchor chain from the old man's boat, tied it to everyone on board, including the old man, then made the kids walk the plank, so to speak. The old man struggled to stop it, but couldn't. Damnedest thing I ever heard. After it was over, the Raptor here sunk the old man's boat out in the deep water past the Boils. You don't like that?" he said, watching Atticus squirm. "Well, they spotted Baynard and his boys unloading goods from a Hungarian freighter, the same goods we lost to the Feds because of you, you son of a bitch! That stupid old bastard ran right up alongside and asked what in the hell they were doing; can you believe that?"

Atticus glared at Diablo. He tried to swear at him through the gag, but it simply came out as a mumble.

Diablo smiled and walked back over to Atticus. He reached down with his cigarette; Atticus tried to pull away, but Diablo managed to crush it out on Atticus's forehead anyway. Atticus writhed in pain. "Oh, that's okay, old boy," Diablo went on, chuckling, "that deep water out there is cold; it will soothe that burn."

Apparently unable to contain himself, Hepper spoke up. "You guys killed those kids?"

The Raptor moved over behind the two islanders.

Atticus watched.

"You didn't seem to have any pangs of guilt about murdering the Kerfam woman," Diablo replied. "Why should you care now?"

"That's different," Hepper said.

"Really? How so, cowboy?"

"He's right; it makes no difference," Tom interjected.

"You better listen to your friend," Diablo said.

Hepper said nothing more.

Atticus just grunted.

"What's that you say?" Diablo asked Atticus. "Why did we kill the Kerfam woman? Is that what you want to know? She had some very important papers of ours. You know something else, old man? That old hag proved something to me; you can't tell a book by its cover. She was the toughest old bird I've ever come across; she wouldn't talk no matter how we threatened her. Hell, it was Hepper here who finally kicked the chair out from under her; right, Hepper?"

Hepper stood motionless as Atticus stared at him.

Diablo glanced at his watch. "Well, let's get on with it," he said. "Tom, you and Hepper take those two pieces of chain lying over there and throw them in your sled. Then load Gunner and his buddy on top. Take them out to the deep water and put them through the ice."

"Aren't you going to kill Gunner first?" Tom asked.

"No," Diablo replied. "Mr. Doebuck was very adamant about no blood being shed here. What you do with him after you get him out there is up to you. Just make sure he dies and goes on a one-way trip to the bottom of the lake. Is that clear?"

"Yes sir," Tom replied as he grabbed the chains and took them out. "It'll be a pleasure."

When Tom returned, both he and Hepper picked up Frank's frozen body, carried it out to the sled, and threw it on board. Finally, they came back to get Atticus. Atticus held tight to the rope, making sure his hands didn't come loose as they manhandled him into the sled next to Frank.

"When you get out there, make sure those chains are real secure," Diablo said to the two men while at the same time winking at Atticus. "We don't want old Gunner here floating up to the surface next spring, now, do we?" With that, he reached down and removed the gag from

Atticus. "You got any last words, old man?" he asked Atticus with a big grin. "After all, we're not barbarians," he laughed.

"I'll see you in hell," Atticus said. Then he spit on him.

Diablo's face sobered as he looked down at his coat. He took his hanky out and wiped the spit carefully from the lapel; he looked at Atticus. "Gunner," he said in a sadistic tone, "if your woman manages to survive, I'm going to rape and butcher her; then I'm going to do the same to your kids; think about that on your way to your grave." He turned abruptly and motioned for Hepper and Tom to proceed.

"Maybe I should take that other snowmobile over there," Tom said to Diablo. "That way I can ride behind and make sure Gunner doesn't try anything funny while our backs are turned."

The Raptor stepped forward. "Sorry," he said calmly, "that machine's got a bad headlight; it's not going anywhere."

"Maybe I can fix it," Tom replied as he walked over toward the snowmobile.

The Raptor stepped in front of him. "I said it's broken; now just get on the back of that machine and get moving!"

Tom gave a shrug, went back to Hepper's snowmobile, and climbed on behind. Hepper gave the machine some gas and took off with the sled in tow; Diablo and the Raptor watched silently as they pulled out of the yard.

———·•·•·———

The minute the sled went down the bank and out onto the open ice, the north wind made its presence fully known; it was bitter cold. The night was clear; above, the full moon shined cold and white. To the south, dark and hazy against the moonlit sky, lay Bondin's Rock. As they moved away from shore, Atticus tried to snuggle as deep into his coat as possible. Frank's hard frozen body, head raised precariously up off the sled, bounced and jiggled as the sled's steel runners thumped across the ice.

The eastside lake ice was different than anyplace else around the island; it was exposed and unprotected from the open lake. Evidence of numerous fractures left the surface rough and scarred, with upended pieces of slab ice of every size and configuration scattered throughout the entire area. Then there was the snow; steadily on the move, it swept across the endless expanse, hiding the true surface features beneath its powdery veil. Except for the huge slabs, translucent in the moonlight, standing like sentinels against a naked horizon, it was as though they were traveling across a mystical wasteland, cold and colorless; like death itself.

Atticus glanced back; the silhouette of a single rider on an unlit snowmobile came down off the bank and started to follow about two miles behind.

Every little while, Tom would look back at Atticus, but between glances, Atticus retrieved the knife and continued to cut the rope around his ankles. It took several tries, but the rope finally severed.

Making sure it appeared as though he was still bound hand and foot, Atticus attempted awkwardly to find something in the sled beneath him that could serve as a weapon. Frank's unyielding presence made the effort most difficult. Finally he touched something very hard and very cold; it was the steel head of a double-bladed ax. As Atticus felt the blade a second time, a cold calculating sense of purpose flooded over him.

Approaching a huge ice shove, Hepper slowed down. "There's open water!" he shouted back over his shoulder to Tom. Along the outer edge of the rift was a ten-by-hundred-foot slice of open water.

Hepper drove slowly around a number of big pieces of upended slab ice and through a small opening in the shove. Finally he stopped along the open water. He killed the engine; only the forlorn moan of the howling wind was left to break the empty silence. The two men dismounted. Hepper made his way carefully over to the edge of the open water, where he looked down into the ink-black liquid. "This is perfect!" he shouted back to Tom.

Tom turned toward Atticus. "Now," he said to Atticus as he approached, "the moment I've been waiting for." Atticus drew his legs up. "What's the matter, asshole; afraid to die?" Tom said with a big grin as he reached for Atticus.

Without warning, Atticus struck; kicking out with all his might, he caught Tom smack in the middle of his face with both feet. The impact sent Tom stumbling back; he fell onto the snowmobile and tumbled down to the ice. Hepper turned, but it was too late. As Tom struggled back to his feet, Atticus sprang from the sled and swung the ax over his head with all his might. Tom never made a sound as the full impact of the blade slammed deep into the top of his skull. He staggered back with the ax buried deep in his head. Blood spurted from the grisly wound. A gurgling sound came from his open mouth; Tom turned toward Hepper as though he were dismayed by the experience of his own death. He dropped to his knees and tipped backward, landing on the ice with a thud; he was dead.

For a moment, Hepper stood staring at his fallen companion. By the time he came to his senses, it was too late; he turned to run, but before he took two steps, Atticus plowed into him from behind; Hepper catapulted head first down onto the snow-covered ice. Before he could recover, Atticus came up under his arms and around the back of his head and locked his hands; he had Hepper in a full nelson. Hepper tried desperately to struggle free, but Atticus bore down with all his might. Hepper's arms extended helplessly outward; there was a choking grunt of pain and a muffled thud. As the trachea crushed and his neck snapped, Hepper shuddered violently. Then just as quickly as it started, it was over; his body went limp; he too was a dead man. Once again the sound of the howling wind reclaimed the gruesome sight.

With his fingers frozen almost beyond feeling, Atticus reached down and took Hepper's fur hat and put it on, and then he retrieved Hepper's ice fishing mittens from the snowmobile and slipped them on over his frozen fingers.

Knowing he had little time to spare, Atticus searched for signs of the approaching Raptor. His wait was short-lived; about two hundred yards down the landward side of the rift, he saw the snowmobile; it was stopped; a lone figure had just dismounted. He was headed into the rift with a rifle in hand.

Crouched down, Atticus worked his way over to Tom's body; he yanked the ax from his skull and hurried into the rift. When he'd covered half the distance between himself and his adversary, he crawled to a position of surveillance and raised his head. He could see Hepper's snowmobile off to his left. Frank's frozen remains lay precariously across the sled's box like a log with twisted branches protruding awkwardly. Hepper's body lay silently on the open ice, Cline's was partially hidden behind the sled, but there was no sign of the Raptor. Lowering himself, Atticus moved under an icy overhang to hide until he could figure out what to do next.

Protected from the wind, the snow scurried off the top of the overhang and swirled down on Atticus as he waited; he was trembling. Off in the distance from the north, a low rumbling sound rose up above the sound of the wind. It continued for a few seconds and then subsided; it sounded like distant thunder. Atticus listened intently for it to reoccur, but there was nothing.

Forgetting the sound, he watched as a dark silhouette walked out onto the open ice in front of him; he was about forty yards away. Rifle held in a ready position, the figure made his way slowly toward Hepper's sled. Atticus squeezed the handle of the ax in nervous anticipation.

The Raptor came around the far side of the sled next to the open water, and even though he moved cautiously, once he realized that Hepper had been taken out of the picture, he instinctively squatted down and looked around. When he spotted Cline's grisly remains, his suspicions were confirmed, and his mission instantly changed. Instead of simply taking out the two dum-dums he had been assigned to eliminate, he was now facing a very different adversary, and one who was obviously far more dangerous than what he had been psychologically prepared to confront. He looked cautiously around once more and then silently moved off into the rift again. Atticus knew from the very moment of discovery, although surprised, the Raptor welcomed this new challenge, and the hunt for Atticus was on.

For some reason, Atticus's mind flashed back to the first day at the Hersoff place; he and the girls were sitting on Cynthia's couch; he could still hear her words. How strange it was that the events of his life so closely paralleled what she said. Could it be that in her strange, demented way, she really had a premonition of what was to come? And although he still wondered what her real involvement was, he was overwhelmed by the strangest feeling of all—he felt absolutely no empathy for his victims, no remorse, nothing; and for the very first time, he felt no fear. It was almost as though his being here was meant to be. He put his head down and took a deep breath. As he let it out, it turned to steam and swirled off into the crisp night wind. Then without further hesitation, Atticus too grabbed his primitive weapon and moved off into the rift toward his dangerous and hated enemy.

◆◦◆◦◆

As Atticus moved cautiously forward, he listened and watched intently for any noise beyond the incisive howl of the wind. Just as he was about to move again, he heard a cracking sound; it was far off to the north, but moved rapidly to the south; the entire rift reverberated with its passing. The hair on the back of his neck bristled; he now realized that the "thunder" he heard before was the ice beginning to break up. Struggling to maintain his cool, Atticus hurried over to the shoreward edge of the rift. Once there, he slid down a huge piece of shove ice and stepped silently out onto the open ice. There it was; a huge crack running down from the north along the rift past Atticus, it then arched out in the general direction of Bondin's Rock. Another crack veered off to the left about sixty yards away and disappeared back in the rift. It all became very logical now; given the water currents and the prevailing winds around the island, the rift was like a fault line in the ice field. This was the location where other shoves had occurred and would likely be the location of the next; given the ferocity of the wind, Atticus was sure it was about to happen again.

Overcome with a sense of being watched, Atticus turned his head to look behind. Standing between two jagged twenty-foot-high pylons of ice, looking straight at him, was the Raptor. Atticus dove for cover, but as he did, something ripped through his arm like a kick from a mule and splattered the ice behind him. He never heard the report of the rifle, but the sensation of a hot poker being rammed through his upper right arm left little doubt as to what just happened. Landing on the jagged ice, Atticus winced with pain. He rolled over, grabbing the wound; the blood oozed out around his mitten, saturating his coat sleeve. Gritting his teeth, he scrambled to his feet, grabbed the ax, and stumbled off back into the rift again.

Atticus crawled in behind an upended slab of ice. Backing up tight against his crystal enclosure, he braced himself. His heart was pounding. He reached quickly into his pocket and retrieved the knife. With his left hand, he sliced his coat sleeve from the cuff up to just past the wound. Peeling the loose end of his sleeve away from his blood-soaked arm, he wrapped it tightly around the wound. Finally, with his good hand and his teeth, he tied off the wrapping with a remnant of cloth.

Once again, the silence was broken by distant rumbling, but this time it continued. Another loud cracking sound shattered the night not more than twenty yards away. Atticus felt the ice shiver. Soon, the shivering turned to a tremble. Then with snapping and growling, the upended twenty-foot-high sentinels of ice around him began to slowly change their posture.

Slipping and stumbling on the moving ice, in spite of the pain in his right arm, Atticus clawed his way to the top of the rift. The whole ice field north and east of the island, clear up to the Boils, had given in to the relentless pressure of the strong north wind. The overwhelming strain caused the field to fracture along the rift and begin its slow but relentless march to the south. Bondin's Rock, rounded by eons of such torture, gave the moving field its only real resistance. There, like the pinnacle of some great wheel, the ice thundered in a loud report as it piled itself high up on the rock during the slow and grueling process of swinging off to the south. Atticus looked around; it was as though the terror of the night had given way to the eruption of hell; the world around him was beginning to disintegrate. He glanced back just in time to see Hepper's snowmobile and sled swallowed up by the ice. Frank's body tipped from the sled, only to be caught and raised up by the edge of a large piece of ice as it rolled over in the boiling mayhem; then Frank, along with everything else, was gone.

Jumping from slab to slab, Atticus worked desperately to get clear. Sidestepping a hole that opened directly beneath him, he caught the edge of an upended slab with his ax and pulled himself up. Sliding down the other side, he landed on the open ice. Just as he got to his feet, the ice under him separated as a fissure darted out diagonally in front of him. Running, he jumped to the adjoining piece. Sliding as he landed, he fell to his knees.

As Atticus rose to his feet, he was startled by the sudden reappearance of the Raptor not more than twenty feet away; he too had escaped the rift. Their eyes met; the two men stared at one another. For Atticus it was as if time stood still; even the wind seemed to go silent. The Raptor raised his weapon, but before he could pull the trigger, Atticus raised the ax over his head and threw it with all his might. The Raptor was forced to sidestep in order to avoid the twirling blade, but in the process he slipped and fell to one knee. At the same time, the ice the Raptor was standing on broke free and started to burrow down under the pressure of the oncoming field. He began to slide; unable to check his descent, he went crashing into the water.

He bobbed back to the surface, gasping for breath from the shock of the freezing water; the Raptor groped for the edge of the ice. As he did, a huge, crystal-clear slab of three-foot-thick ice rose up out of the depths behind him. Glistening in the moon as the slab rose to an almost vertical position, the gaunt figure of a man appeared from within. Colorless and decayed, arms stretched wide, frozen deep within the bowels of his icy host, the remains of old Quint gazed down on the Raptor with a ghostly stare. Stunned with awe, Atticus watched in dismay. Like Captain Ahab, rising from the depths on the back of the great white whale, his lumbering host fell slowly back toward the surface. With a deep muffled rumble, the huge slab closed over the Raptor like the jaws of some great serpent. There was a scream, and then all went silent. The man whose evil deeds were responsible for the death of so many, the man whom Atticus had sought for so long, the man he had come to hate, was finally gone. Once again, the moan of the wind and the trembling thunder of the disintegrating ice field recaptured the sounds of the night.

After what seemed an eternity, a great sheet of ice broke free and started to twist under the imposing pressure. Stepping gingerly, Atticus jumped across an open fissure; he hurried toward the Raptor's snowmobile, still out on the open ice.

He yanked on the starter cord; the machine came to life. As Atticus threw his leg over to mount, another fissure opened directly in front of the snowmobile. Atticus clamped down hard on the throttle; the machine lunged forward crossing the fissure. Hanging on with all his might, and the throttle full on, the machine screamed across the open ice toward shore.

Whether or not Quint had truly risen from his icy grave to call for justice, Atticus would never know for sure, but it didn't seem to matter now. He couldn't help but think that at last justice had been served, and Quint's spirit was finally free from the anguish he must have endured.

At the sight of open water ahead, Atticus's thoughts were brought back to the present. He stopped. He glanced first to the north and then to the south; as far as he could see in both directions, there was open water. Looking across the sixty-foot-wide expanse of water, it became apparent that the entire field under him had separated from shore and was now on the move. He looked off in the direction of Bondin's Rock; he knew it was there that the focal point of the opening rift would be. He also knew it was his only chance to make shore. He squeezed hard on the accelerator again.

Coming to a stop about a quarter mile out from Bondin's Rock, he watched as huge sections of field ice slid up slowly onto the rock, broke under the pressure, and then slithered into a huge jagged pile along the rocky enclave in front of the old house. Moving in closer, Atticus watched intently. He knew he would only have a moment to make his decision. By now, he was so cold he was beginning to lose feeling in his extremities, especially in his right arm. He waited.

A huge slab of ice moved slowly up the rocky shore and into the cedar trees. Slanted at about a thirty-degree angle, the upper end was about ten feet in the air; this was it. Without hesitation, Atticus squeezed the accelerator full on; he hit the base of the ramp at full tilt. The next thing he knew, he was crashing head over heels into the cedars. Everything was a blur until he landed with a muffled thud in the deep snow among the cedars.

Moving slowly at first, Atticus finally managed to get to his feet. His right arm was oozing blood again, and his shoulder was extremely sore, but other than a few scratches from the cedar bows, he seemed okay. The snowmobile had not fared so well; smashing into one of the big boulders, it was now nothing more than a piece of twisted steel and broken fiberglass. Grabbing hold of the cedar bows to help his ascent,

Atticus clawed his way up the steep bank. The snow was deep, making progress very difficult. Behind him, the ice thundered endlessly as it piled up over what remained of the snowmobile.

In spite of the numbing cold, being up in the trees and out of the bitter wind was in itself a relief. When Atticus reached the top of the bank, he trudged on toward the main road. Knowing that time was running out, he pushed forward with all the strength he could manage.

He spotted a summer home nestled back in the trees off to the right. The house was dark, but the automatic yard light glowed through the snow-covered trees. Stumbling up the steps and onto the front porch, Atticus tried the door; it was locked. Using his elbow, he smashed one of the panes of glass, reached inside, and opened it. Groping for the light switch, he turned them on and stepped inside; the warmth was like heaven. He stumbled over to one of several pieces of lawn furniture pushed into the living room for the winter and flopped down. Taking off Hepper's mittens and hat, he unzipped his coat and lay his head back in total exhaustion.

After sitting quietly for only a moment, he raised his head and looked at his watch; it was 7:20. He got up and went over to the phone. He picked up the receiver; the dial tone came on. With numb fingers, he dialed Butch's number.

"Hello," came the voice on the other end.

"Butch, this is Atticus."

"Where in the hell have you been?" Butch barked. "I've been calling you for the last hour and a half! The meeting is in little more than an hour!"

"I know," Atticus replied. "Look, I don't have time to explain, but I need your help right away. Grab your shotgun and pick me up on the main road just past the sand dunes. I'm at the Newtons' summer place now, but I'll meet you out on the road."

"Atticus, what in the hell are you talking about?"

"I'll explain later; just hurry; time is of the essence. And Butch, keep this to yourself." Atticus hung up the receiver.

Finding his way into the bathroom, he opened the linen closet and grabbed a clean towel. He folded it and then undid the binding around his arm; he peeled the frozen, blood-soaked remnants of his coat sleeve away from the wound. To his surprise, the wrapping looked much worse than the wound itself; a neat hole went in one side of his upper arm and out the other. Amazingly, it missed the bone. His arm was a mess with clotted blood, but Atticus wrapped the towel around the wound anyway. He then proceeded to rebind it with the coat sleeve. When he finished, he went back out to the main room, picked up his hat and mittens, put them on, zipped up his coat, and left.

Butch was driving fast as he came around the bend just past the sand dunes. Spotting Atticus in the sweep of the headlights, he slammed on the brakes. Butch reached over and opened the passenger door as Atticus came around the front of the vehicle. Atticus crawled in and pulled the door shut; Butch looked at him. "Holy shit!" he said. "I better get you to the Doc."

"It looks much worse than it is," Atticus replied. "Did you bring the gun?"

"It's in the back seat. Are you sure you're okay?"

"I'm fine," Atticus reiterated. "Head for the airport." He reached over the seat and retrieved the shotgun and the box of shells next to it.

"Atticus, you're all bloody."

"I know; I'm fine," Atticus said again.

"What the hell is going on?" Butch asked as he wheeled the car around.

"I'm going to close the lid on the Order of Raptors once and for all," Atticus replied as he opened the box of shells and proceeded to load the weapon.

"Atticus, what in the hell are you talking about?"

Atticus looked at his watch. "It's 7:45," he said, totally oblivious to Butch's question. "I want you to drop me off by the airport and then go home and call the Coast Guard in Sturgeon Bay. Tell them to come to the school right away. They'll ask for a password; it's Big Bird; can you remember that?"

"Yes, but what are you going to do now?"

"I'm going to settle some unfinished business. Now it's very important, Butch; have you got everything straight?"

"Yes, but . . ."

"After you make the call, I want you to go to the meeting. If the FBI gets there before I do, have them arrest Doebuck. If I get to the school before they do, I'll come into the meeting through my office. When Doebuck turns his attention to me, watch him. I don't think he has a weapon, but if he makes the slightest move, and he most certainly will, take him down; understand? Don't let him get away!"

"What the hell am I supposed to do before you get there?"

"Run the meeting."

Turning left on Range Road, Butch floored it as they shot up over the hill.

"When you get within sight of the airport, slow down to normal speed," Atticus went on. "I don't want anyone there to expect anything, and don't turn into the drive; just go by. At the stand of pines down behind the hangar barns, let me out, and then proceed as normal."

As they came down Airport Road and past the entrance to the small airport, Atticus spotted the pickup sitting next to the main hangar barn. "Isn't that Hepper's truck?" Butch asked.

"Yes, it is," Atticus replied, "but it's not Hepper. Keep going."

Once behind the pines and out of sight, Butch pulled to a stop. As Atticus opened the door, Butch looked over at him. "Are you sure you know what you're doing?" he asked.

"Yes, this is one time I'm very sure," Atticus replied as he got out of the car with the shotgun in hand.

"Perhaps I should come with."

"No," Atticus replied, "you've got a phone call to make, remember?" He closed the car door quietly; Butch took off.

As the sound of the car faded down the road, Atticus crawled up the snow bank and headed into the big pines along the edge of the road. When he reached the other side of the trees, he squatted down and listened. The back of the barn was about twenty feet away now. With the moon much higher in the sky, things were even brighter than before. Other than the wind banging a piece of loose tin on the back of the barn, and the wind moaning as it went through the big pines, all was relatively quiet. Keeping low, Atticus hurried across the clearing. He worked his way along the back of the building until he came to the loose tin. Carefully he pried it open enough to squeeze through and ducked inside.

Directly in front of him was an old biplane; further down was a single-engine Cessna used for island medical emergencies. In front of the Cessna, the hangar door stood wide open. Just outside, standing with his back to the door and smoking a cigarette, was Diablo. A large briefcase was sitting on the ground next to him.

Atticus released the safety on the shotgun. Cautiously, he moved past the tail section of the Cessna, up along the fuselage, and then he ducked down under the wing and into the shadows of the dark building. Diablo wasn't more than twenty feet away now. Holding the weapon at his hip, Atticus raised the muzzle and pointed it at Diablo. The drone of a plane sounded overhead; it was Diablo's ride.

"Going someplace, Broker?" Atticus asked calmly.

Startled, Diablo jumped at the sound of a voice.

"You move, and I'll blow you in half," Atticus went on.

Diablo froze.

"I want that briefcase," Atticus said, "and I really don't much give a shit how I get it."

Diablo seemed completely dumbfounded.

Atticus remained in the shadows but moved over to the opposite side of the door. "What's the matter, Broker, don't you recognize my voice?" he asked.

"Vonpuk, this isn't funny," Diablo said nervously.

"No, I'm not your Raptor, but does the word 'Moonhawker' ring a bell?"

"That's not possible," he said. "Gunner's dead."

Atticus stepped from the shadows. In a single motion, Diablo pulled his handgun as he spun around; his weapon flashed in the general direction of Atticus, but at the same moment there was a loud thundering blast from the muzzle of the shotgun; Diablo flew back as though he had been rammed in the chest by a locomotive. As he landed flat on his back, his hat flew off and his handgun went skidding across the blacktop.

Atticus approached and stood over him. Diablo shuddered as he looked up at Atticus; a ragged, six-inch hole had been torn through his leather coat and penetrated deep into his chest; the blood began to spread out in a large pool on the tarmac under him. "No, I'm not dead, Diablo," Atticus said with a calmness in his voice, "but you soon will be, and I want to be the first to welcome you to hell."

Diablo made an indistinguishable gurgling sound, and then his eyes glazed over as he stared aimlessly up at the star-filled sky; a gust of wind tumbled his hat down the runway. Atticus stood there for a few moments watching the hat roll away, and then without as much as another glance downward, he stepped over Diablo's body, picked up the briefcase, and started to walk toward Hepper's pickup.

Just as Atticus was about to open the door to the truck, a twin-engine plane came in right over the top of the barn, it shot over Atticus and settled down on the runway. Atticus watched as the plane came to a stop at the far end, its flashing lights blinking in the bright moonlight. It turned around and then began taxiing back toward the barn. With his shotgun still in one hand, and the briefcase in the other, he walked out slowly to meet it.

The plane came within yards of Atticus before whoever was on board realized he wasn't Diablo. The engines revved and the left brake went on. Atticus had to duck in order to avoid being hit by the right wing as it spun around. Setting the briefcase on the ground, he pumped another shell into the chamber and aimed the shotgun; he paused. The plane started to move away as it picked up speed. Finally, it lifted off into the night. Atticus lowered the weapon and watched until the blinking lights disappeared into the silvery night haze.

———•◆•———

It was 8:40 as Atticus wheeled Hepper's old truck into the parking lot at school. The meeting was well under way, but no FBI. Atticus parked and grabbed the briefcase; he went into the school through the front door. There was no one in his office, but both doors were wide open and the lights were all on. He walked through the office and stepped into the back of the meeting room. Ironically, Doebuck was standing with his back to Atticus, addressing the board. "I realize I have no children in school," he was saying, "but as a taxpayer and citizen of the island, I think it is extremely important that our children be exposed to school people and law enforcement personnel of indisputable character. For that reason, I agree with Adrian; Mr. Gunner has got to go."

Sylvia and Spence, who were sitting just off to the left, were the first to notice Atticus. Sylvia gasped out loud. "Good Lord!" she exclaimed; Atticus looked a sight. Spencer stood up. By then other people were turning around; there were gasps of dismay. Doebuck looked back, and his mouth dropped open.

"What's the matter?" Atticus said calmly as he walked toward the front of the room. "Surprised to see me, Mr. Doebuck? Or would you rather be called Scorpion?"

Doebuck said nothing.

"As long as you're addressing the board," Atticus went on, "perhaps we should give the folks here a little of your real background. Perhaps we should tell how you deal with the devil, trade arms and drugs, to say nothing of orchestrating assassinations. Or to really give them the flavor of your character, Mr. Doebuck, tell them how you had Quint Jebson and three island boys murdered."

A semi hush fell over the room.

"Tell them how you were the real boss behind Baynard and his group, and how Hepper Greshion and Tom Cline worked for you. Tell them how Hepper and one of your thugs hung Jody Kerfam in her basement; or how you murdered old Bert Federman; tell them how you were personally involved in the murder of Frank Seamy."

Stunned, the crowd became deathly silent.

"Or how about Cynthia Hersoff and her companion," Atticus went on. "Tell them how you had their throats cut, and how you authorized the torture of her disabled companion."

Still there was no response from the room full of people.

Doebuck looked around nervously. "I have no idea what he's talking about," he said. "He's crazy!"

"Mr. Doebuck, I have the briefcase." Atticus held it up for all to see.

The windows began to rattle as a chopper settled down out in the parking lot. Knocking over a couple of chairs as he went, Doebuck shoved Adrian aside and started for the door in a panic. Butch scrambled up over the board table and wrestled Doebuck to the floor before he made it halfway across the room. Dumbfounded, everyone simply watched as Butch rendered the old man helpless. At that moment, Inspector Willow and his entourage barged in. The inspector directed Barker to handcuff Doebuck and looked around for Atticus. Spotting him in one of the chairs where he had collapsed, Willow hurried over to him. "Is there a doctor in the house?" he barked at the small crowd.

"Right here," Doc Burnett replied as he pushed his way through the crowd toward the inspector.

Inspector Willow and Spencer helped Atticus to his feet. "Pontiff," the inspector said over his shoulder as they helped Atticus toward the office, "send all these people home!"

"Butch stays," Atticus mumbled as he staggered along. "He's with me."

"Right, he's with you," the inspector replied.

They shoved everything off Atticus's desk and set him down on it. The doctor sent Butch to his car to get his medical bag and began unraveling the wrapping around Atticus's arm. Two troopers escorted Doebuck out to the chopper while Barker and Pontiff dispersed the confused crowd; even Adrian, who insisted he had a right to remain, was forced to leave. In the meantime, the doctor sent Sylvia to round up a pan of warm water and some soap; she did, and then she and Spence also departed.

Atticus sat on the corner of his desk through it all. He felt as though he had been relieved of a terrible burden.

Butch returned, and so did Pontiff and Barker. Atticus managed to regain his composure, and while the doctor worked on his arm, he slowly revealed the night's events. He told everything except the part about Quint; he said nothing about that. When he reached the part about the airport incident, the inspector stopped him momentarily, instructed Barker to get two troopers out there to secure the site, and then allowed Atticus to continue. Pontiff stood in the doorway, listening.

When Atticus finished telling his tale of horror, the inspector stood up and looked at the doctor. "Doctor, I know this is a very connected community, and there will be pressure on you to divulge what you just heard, but I want to make it very clear, you are not to disclose anything to anyone; if you do, there will be serious consequences; do you understand?"

The doctor nodded.

"Now that the air is clear in that regard, how is he?"

"Well, it's a clean wound, no bone damage that I can see, but he's lost a fair amount of blood, and he's pretty banged up," the doctor said as he secured Atticus's arm in a sling. "I would suggest, however, you take him off to a hospital to be checked over."

"Not tonight," Atticus said.

"Look, Mr. Gunner, I'm not a surgeon, and this is not an operating room."

"I know," Atticus replied.

The doctor looked at the inspector, but getting no response, he finally started packing his medical tools back into his case. "You're a very bullheaded man, Mr. Gunner," he said. "I'll want to see you in the morning then," he continued as he washed his hands. "And I'll be leaving if you don't need me anymore," the doctor said to the inspector.

The inspector gave him a nod.

At the door, the doctor stopped and looked back at the inspector. "Like I said, it appears he's lost a substantial amount of blood; I don't think he should be left alone tonight."

"I'll stay with him," Butch replied.

The doctor left.

Pontiff went over to the table and sat down; he opened the briefcase. After a few moments, he looked up at the inspector. "I think you'd better look at this," he said.

The inspector walked over to the table; Pontiff got up out of his way; the inspector sat down and started going through the contents of the briefcase. After a few minutes, he looked up at Pontiff and then over at Atticus. "Do you have any idea what's in this briefcase, Gunner?" he asked.

"Yes," Atticus replied, "not specifically, but in general."

"Inspector, some of that stuff can't get out; probably ever," Pontiff said.

"Yes, I realize that," the inspector replied. "Atticus, I'm afraid I'm going to have to put another gag order on you and your friend here, but this time for an indefinite period."

"I don't care what you do," Atticus replied as he stood up, "just as long as we're not involved."

"Inspector, come morning, the island folks will have lots of questions, and so will the press," Barker interjected. "We're going to have to say something."

"I'll prepare a statement," the inspector replied, "but the contents of that briefcase will not be revealed. Are we all clear on that?"

"Let's go home," Atticus said to Butch.

"Gunner, I asked if we are clear on that point."

Atticus nodded as Butch got up to follow. "Yes, Inspector," he replied, "we understand." He started for the door but paused. "What about Laura and my kids?" he asked without turning to face the inspector.

"They are safe, and I'll see that they're allowed to get in touch with you in the morning," Barker replied.

Atticus nodded. He glanced over at Pope but said nothing.

"Gunner, there's one more thing," the inspector said as Atticus started for the door again. "Apparently your landlady thought a great deal of you."

Atticus stopped and turned around.

"She left a will. Seems you're now the proud owner of the house you live in, along with her entire fortune I might add. Oh, there will be a waiting period to see if anyone steps forward to contest it, and there will be probate, of course, but all things considered, I'd say you're about to become a very wealthy man, Mr. Gunner."

Atticus made no comment.

Butch looked over at Atticus as he started up his old wagon. "What about the leather pouch Jody Kerfam found? You didn't say anything about that."

"I know," Atticus replied with a nod. "There will be plenty of time for that; I'll see that it gets into the right hands."

For the rest of the drive to the Hersoff place, Atticus said nothing.

Butch drove down into the yard and stopped. "Well," he said after a moment or two, "it appears this place is yours now."

Atticus looked out the window at the big old house, shining quietly in the moonlight, but said nothing.

"I'll go in and start a fire for you," Butch said.

"No, that's all right," Atticus replied.

"The doc said someone needs to be with you, Atticus."

"Thanks, but not tonight."

Butch was going to protest but didn't.

Atticus opened the door and got out.

"I'll see you at school in the morning then," Butch said.

Atticus nodded. "Yeah, in the morning," he said as he slammed the door and walked away, "but not too early in the morning."

CHAPTER 22

By Decree, and an Owl in a Tree

It was noon when Atticus pulled into school. It was a bright sunny day. He pulled up next to Butch's old wagon and parked. Greta's Chevy was parked next to Butch, and Hepper's pickup was still where he'd left it the night before, but now there was a yellow crime scene tape strung around it. The chopper was gone; even Doebuck's island car was gone. Pulling his coat up over his shoulder and around his sling, Atticus got out and started walking toward the front entrance.

Butch came out and waved as Atticus approached. "How ya feeling?" he asked.

Atticus grinned. "Ever try taking a shower with one arm?"

Butch laughed.

"I see they've impounded Hepper's truck."

Butch nodded. "The Milwaukee crime lab was flown in late last night; they're out at the airport right now. They've also got two small planes flying out over the ice looking for bodies; after the wind last night, they won't find much."

"I imagine they impounded your shotgun."

Again Butch nodded.

"Sorry about that."

Butch shrugged. "Don't worry about it," he said. "You can afford to buy me a new one now."

Atticus smiled. "Who's here besides you and Greta?"

"Pope is waiting for you."

"And where is he?"

"Last I looked, he was in the boardroom lying on one of the tables."

"What about Willow?"

"He left on the big chopper last night."

"And Barker?"

"Barker's got Mrs. Doebuck's car; I think he went out to the airport."

"You ready to bring in the New Year tonight?"

Butch shrugged. "Well, it's been a tough one, but for those not involved, I guess you'd have to say it turned out to be an all-around good year."

"Well, the island will certainly have a New Year's weekend to remember, that's for sure." Atticus walked up the steps and entered through the front doors; Butch followed.

As he walked into the office, he was amazed to see everything was picked up and rearranged neatly on his desk. He looked over at Greta and smiled. "Good morning, Greta," he said. She smiled at him as he threw his jacket on the coat rack.

"Want me to go get Pontiff for you?" Butch asked.

"No thanks; I think I'll talk to him alone if you don't mind."

"No problem," Butch replied as he sat down at the table where he had his coffee mug sitting.

"So—what are the two of you doing here today anyway? Especially you, Greta; you don't really have to be here."

"Well, for one thing," Butch replied, "I'm here to make sure you're okay, remember? But both Greta and I thought it was a good idea to hang around until all the unpleasant activity subsides."

"That might take awhile," Atticus said as he proceeded through the open door and into the meeting room. Pontiff was standing with his back to him, looking out the window. "I was told you were lying on one of the board tables," Atticus said as he approached.

"I was," Pontiff replied without turning around.

"I was also told you wanted to see me."

"Right again."

"Well, here I am."

Pontiff turned around. "How's the arm?" he asked.

"I'll survive."

"So where are you headed from here, Gunner?"

"Maybe to the Dawn for a bite to eat; other than that, home. Why?"

"No, I mean where to from this place?"

"I haven't really given that much thought."

"From everything I hear, you're a rich man now."

"So I've been told."

"Your landlady may not have flaunted it, but through her inheritance, she apparently had substantial holdings in both England and Australia; you, my friend, are about to receive a very large fortune."

Atticus didn't respond.

"So, are you thinking to spend the rest of your life here on this rock?"

"I can think of a lot worse places to spend my days," Atticus replied. "Then there is school; it starts up again in a few days, and I'm most definitely going to finish out my contract. After that, I don't know."

"I don't think you realize it yet, but you're not the same person you were when you came here."

"None of us are," Atticus replied.

"There's been a transformation, Gunner. Without a whole lot of effort, you could become a legend."

Atticus sat down on the corner of one of the desks. "You're something else," he said, shaking his head. "So you think the forces of evil now see me as the caped crusader?" Atticus chuckled. "I find it hard to believe that you actually expect me to respond to something that stupid."

"That's what I like about you, Gunner; you question everything."

"What are you really here for, Pope?" Atticus went on. "Is this a recruitment visit?"

Pontiff smiled. "You ever heard of the OSI?" he asked.

"No."

"We hunt Nazis; past, present, and future."

"You've already blown that horn, only I thought you said you were CIA."

"I am."

"Well, if my knowledge of the Second World War serves me right, the CIA was as responsible for the escape of high-ranking Nazis into this country as was anyone. Seems to me you people can't make up your mind as to who the bad guys really are; I suppose it depends on what they've got to offer."

Pontiff ignored the comment and continued on. "We could use a man like you, Gunner; you're smart and resilient, but I'm not telling you anything you don't already know. I am trying to emphasize a point: the Nazi movement is anything but dead, and to think that something as evil as Nazi Germany will never happen again someplace else in the world is about as unrealistic as the caped crusader thing."

"Well, if I ever have the urge to save the world, I'll let you know, but don't hold your breath."

"Oh, I'd never do that, Gunner, but if you change your mind, get in touch with me."

Just then, Barker pulled into the lot with the Doebuck's blue Cadillac. "Well," Pontiff said, "my ride is here to take me to the airport."

"Good luck," Atticus replied. "By the way, there's a leather pouch out in the Bronco; it's from last fall's plane crash. I suspect there's some good stuff in it; you might want to take that with when you leave."

Pontiff looked at Atticus. "From the Kerfam woman?"

Atticus nodded.

Pontiff turned and started for the door.

"Pope," Atticus said. "Whatever happened to Doebuck's bodyguard?"

Pontiff paused and looked back at Atticus. "Poor Nazi bastard shot himself right through the head."

"What about Old Man Doebuck?"

"They whisked him off to Washington; my guess is they'll expedite him to The Hague."

"And what about Mrs. Doebuck?"

"She's from old money, you know; the shipping conglomerate was started by her father. How much of it got commingled into old man Doebuck's escapades, no one really knows, but I suspect she'll come out of it smelling like a rose. I'm sure she'll never show her face on this island again; her attorneys will dissolve all her assets here, but she'll probably turn up as part of the aristocracy in Europe someplace. Money makes the world go around, you know. Oh, I forgot, you're part of that now; who would have thought?" Pontiff winked at Atticus and walked out of the room.

Atticus stood there in the window and watched as Pontiff reached inside the Bronco and retrieved the pouch; he held it up for Atticus to see, gave him a thumbs-up, got into the Cadillac with Barker, and left.

There was an abruptness about the Pope's departure; Atticus knew he'd never see him again. Yet he also knew there would always be people like him; oh, the players would change, the organizations would change, the locations would change, the tactics and the technologies would change, even the rhetoric would change, but the game would always be the same. There's an old proverb that is as true in the world today as it was a hundred years ago: "The more things change, the more they stay the same."

"Mr. Gunner?"

Atticus turned to see Greta standing in the doorway. "You're wanted on the phone," she said.

Atticus walked back into the office.

"It's the ferry office," Greta said, handing him the phone.

Atticus took the phone. "Mr. Gunner here," he said.

"Mr. Gunner, this is Adrian Fruger. I just received a call from the boat; because of all the ice today, they're still about two hours out, but Captain Joel informed me that there are three young women on board coming over to see you, and one of them has her arm in a cast. Perhaps you might want to come down to meet the boat when it comes in."

Atticus smiled. "I'll do that."

"The captain also told me the youngest one is up in the wheelhouse talking his ear off."

Atticus smiled again. "Yes, I suspect she is."

"No harm done," came the response. "Oh, and by the way, welcome to Washington Island."

The phone clicked dead. Atticus took the receiver away from his ear and slowly hung it up.

"Greta, you and Butch are going to have to hold down the fort," Atticus said after a short pause. "I've got a boat to meet."

"Oh, speaking of boats," Greta interjected. "Sheriff Dawson sent a package up for you a few days ago, but with all the commotion, I completely forgot about it." She reached under her desk and pulled out a shoebox with a gold ribbon tied around it; she handed it to Atticus.

Atticus undid the bow and opened the box; inside was a brand-new baseball cap with "WI PD" embroidered in bold letters across the crown. Atticus carefully took the hat out of the box, adjusted the band, and put it on his head. "You can't be a good cop unless you got a good hat," he said as he took his coat off the rack and walked out of the office. They could still hear him talking to himself as he went through the outside doors. "To be good, you gotta look good."

Greta smiled at Butch and winked; Butch simply shook his head as usual.

⊷◆⊶

Driving through the woods, an owl flew across the road and landed in an old oak tree just ahead of the Bronco; the powdery snow fell from the branch as the big bird settled down on it. Atticus momentarily brought the Bronco to a stop. Turning its head toward Atticus, the owl blinked and looked at him. For some reason, Atticus thought back to the time Jody Kerfam picked him up on this very road. It seemed a long time ago now, but her words still rang clear: "You either love this place or hate it," she'd said, "but either way, it gets into your blood." Then just as silently as it had appeared, the owl left his perch and flew off into the woods. Atticus smiled as he stepped on the accelerator again.

As the Bronco disappeared around the bend and the sound of the wheels crunching through the snow faded into the distance, a gust of snow swirled across the road and dissipated up in the trees. All that was left in this moment of time was the silence of a winter woods—that is, until the distant sound of the ferry horn came echoing softly through the cold crisp air on that last day of December 1976.

Author Biography

George Fox completed his graduate work at the University of Wisconsin and spent thirty years of his professional life as a public school teacher, principal, and finally school superintendent. Fox spent the first two years of his school management experience working for a small island community school in northern Lake Michigan; a school district of one hundred kids, K through twelve. It was during these two years, isolated on this small island, he first scratched out the rough draft of his island adventure. Now, fifteen years after his retirement, thirty plus years after the experiences, with encouragement from his wife and daughters, he picked up the remnants of that old manuscript, restructured it, and embellished it into *The Moonhawker.*

Although his remaining career was spent elsewhere, he maintained a summer residence on Washington Island until he retired. To this day, he still lives along the shore of Lake Michigan, just sixty miles from his beloved island; a place that forever became deeply etched into both his and his family's memory.